MAIN

The Restoration of Leather Bindings

D1548694

DATE DUE

MAY 01 1992	
MAI NOV 09 1992	
MAI JAN 1 2 1993	
MAI APR 1 0 1993	
MAR 2 8 1994	
7/18/95	

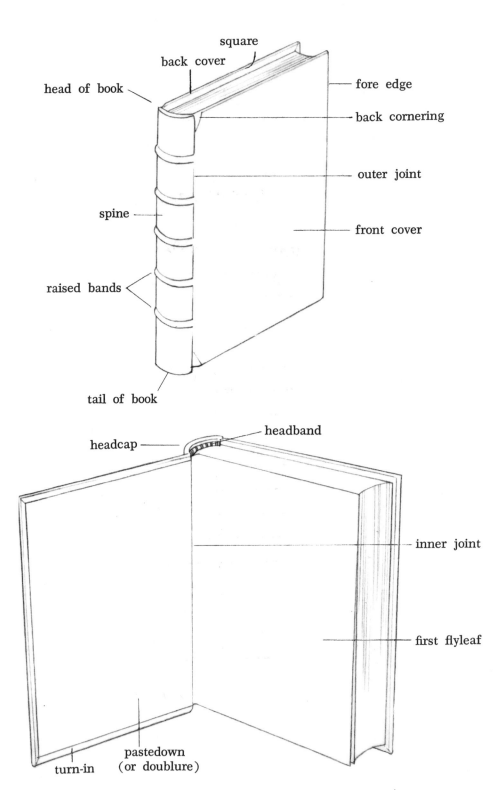

Parts of a hand-bound book with full leather covers and raised bands.

LTP Publication No. 20

The Restoration of Leather Bindings

Revised Edition

Bernard C. Middleton

Drawings by Aldren A. Watson and Seymour Fleishman

American Library Association • Chicago • 1984

Composed by FM Typesetting in Linotype
Primer and Century Schoolbook

Printed on 60-pound Glatfelter,
a pH-neutral stock, and bound
in 80-pound Warren's Lustro Dull
by Malloy Lithographing, Inc.

Published simultaneously in the United Kingdom
by Adamantine Press, Ltd.

Library of Congress Cataloging in Publication Data

Middleton, Bernard C., 1924–
    The restoration of leather bindings.

    Bibliography: p.
    Includes index.
    1. Bookbinding—Repairing. 2. Books—Conservation
and restoration.   3. Leather work—Conservation and
restoration.   I. Title.
Z271.M53   1983   025.7   83-15371
ISBN 0-8389-0391-6

Printed in the United States of America.
91 90 89   6 5 4 3

Contents

Illustrations

Author's Note
to the Revised Edition

Much has changed in the field of binding restoration since this book first appeared in 1972. Substances have been introduced which aid the lifting of deteriorated leather from tight backs, changes in the tanning and treatment of leather are proposed, new suppliers of materials have emerged and others have changed address, and new books and periodicals have appeared, so the text has been brought up to date to the best of the author's ability. Many restoration techniques are now dealt with in greater detail and a new chapter on the rebinding of antiquarian books, with information on the fitting of clasps, has been added, together with a section on the treatment of vellum bindings, in the hope of increasing the usefulness of the book. Details of very recent advances in the manufacture of longer-lasting leather and in the treatment of deteriorating leather have also been summarized.

For bringing to my notice various errors and omissions in the first edition I am greatly indebted to Paul Banks, Sydney M. Cockerell, Edgar Mansfield, and Roger Powell. My thanks are due to Marianne Tidcombe for compiling the index, also for reading the typescript of the new chapter in the present edition and for making constructive suggestions for its improvement. My thanks go to Nicolas Barker, Roy Russell, and Mirjam M. Foot of the British Library, and to Betty M. Haines of the British Leather Manufacturers' Research Association for their cheerful co-operation, and to Vanessa Marshall for drawing my attention to the use of Lewiscraft Leather Cement. I am grateful to the British Library Board for permission to reproduce the photograph of the bindings of the *Codex Sinaiticus*, and to The Board of Trinity College, Dublin, for allowing me to reproduce the photograph of one of the bindings of the *Book of Kells*. The photographs were kindly supplied by Sydney M. Cockerell and Roger Powell, respectively. Finally, I would like to thank my editor, Mary Huchting, for her ever-courteous vigilance and helpfulness.

Preface to First Edition

The restoration of old and worn bindings has not been, until fairly recently, the subject of systematic study nor has it been taken seriously enough by librarians, binders, or even conservators. Since the beginning of the nineteenth century and the introduction of mass-production methods in the binding of books, there can be no doubt that the general level of hand craftsmanship in the field of restoration has been very low. Most European countries have had a small number of specialists, some of whom have been, and are, brilliant, both technically and artistically; but for the most part, restoration work has been done by craftsmen who have no special knowledge of the techniques and styles of earlier periods, have no particular interest in the subject, and are fortuitously put on to the work or taken off it as day-to-day circumstances in craft binderies demand. The idea has been commonly held that if a man is a competent binder he is competent to "patch up" old bindings at odd moments. This is, unfortunately, not so. Even of those who are engaged regularly in this highly specialized and difficult field of craftsmanship, very few have taken the trouble to study early binding techniques and methods systematically and objectively so that bindings can be accurately and sympathetically restored. We see tragic proof of this on all sides; we see, for example, crude mutilations and ludicrously inappropriate ornamentation on too many fine old books that could have been restored very nearly to their original condition by properly trained craftsmen.

The purpose of the book restorer, as I understand it, is to make worn or damaged books usable again, and to restore them as nearly as he can to their original condition, while at the same time prolonging their life as much as possible. He must attempt to make the repairs as unobtrusive as is compatible with reasonable strength, but he should stop short of deliberate falsification with the intent to deceive a future owner of the book into believing that the book is in its original, pristine state. In my view, however, complete and unthinking adherence to this latter principle in every detail is not vital. For example, it seems to me that if a sliver of new leather is let into one end of a slightly cracked joint and this is done more for the sake of appearance than for structural gain, no harm has been done if the repair is undetectable. On the other hand, one should hesitate to add a tooled and artificially aged lettering piece to a binding if the binding had not been lettered in the first place; apart from any other consideration, such an addition might confuse collectors, bibliographers, and other historians of bookbinding.

Between these two extremes there is much that calls for the application of common sense and discretion. Temptations are numerous because a great many owners of books want them "doctored" undetectably for one reason and another. The craftsman's pride is another hazard because he may well be regarded as incompetent if he does not comply with the owner's instructions, and in any case, the achievement of a perfect or near-perfect piece of restoration can be a challenge which sweeps aside all other considerations. Whether one places greater emphasis on strength or on appearance must depend to some extent on the importance of the book, the taste of its owner, the use to which it is to be put, and the strain to which it is likely to be subjected. Maximum strength and period fidelity are two sometimes conflicting factors which the conscientious restorer must constantly endeavor to balance and which frequently call for extremely difficult decisions.

Book restoration is a demanding craft which calls for training, experience, and a considerable amount of skill. It also calls for discipline, patience, and steady nerves when things appear to be going badly—for example, when a spine is being removed from an important book for later replacement and begins to disintegrate into many fragments. In a situation like this the spine can usually be saved if one keeps calm, but it may very easily be lost if one panics and becomes unnerved.

The information and advice which follow are the result of my own experience and are the best known to me. There are, however, few absolutes and necessarily many "ifs" and "buts" in restoration work. One can only outline various alternatives and give timely warnings so that a choice can be made in light of the reader's previous experience, if any, and in light of the conflicting factors with which he may be faced when dealing with a particular book. Seemingly bad methods can sometimes be effective when employed intelligently by a conscientious craftsman, and seemingly good methods can be ineffective or even destructive when used by a poor worker. Experience, intelligence, and imagination must be combined if the work of the restorer is to be successful. Finally, the book restorer should be interested in the past, especially in the crafts of earlier periods, and feel that what he is doing is important; otherwise he will not have the spirit to carry on and do fine work.

This volume would have been much less informative but for the generous efforts of a number of people who have its subject very much at heart. My thanks are due in particular to Harold W. Tribolet, manager of the Graphic Conservation Department, R. R. Donnelley & Sons Company, The Lakeside Press, Chicago, for giving me the benefit of his long experience of craft binding, and to Herbert L. Hanna of the Library Technology Program of the American Library Association for his perceptive criticisms. I am also grateful to H. Richard Archer, curator of the Chapin Collection at Williams College; to Paul N. Banks, hand binder and conservator of the Newberry Library, Chicago; to Margaret C. Brown, chief of the Processing Division of the Free Library, Philadelphia; to Verner W. Clapp of the Council on Library Resources, Incorporated; to Richard W. Luce, Assistant Librarian, Montana State University; to Stewart P. Smith, head of the Serials Department at the University of Missouri; and to Nancy and Colton Storm, hand binders of Sedona, Arizona, all of whom have given generously of their time in reviewing and criticizing the manuscript, particularly in its early stages. I wish to thank the Council on Library Resources, Incorporated, for providing the funds which made its publication possible. I am also indebted to W. H. Langwell, F.R.I.C., for his advice on certain chemical matters; to Sydney M. Cockerell for permission to base figures 3, 22, and 23 on illustrations in his *The Repairing of Books* (London: Sheppard Press, 1958); to my bindery assistant, Eric Horne, for help with the preparation of the photographs; and to R. B. Fleming & Co. Ltd., of London, for their expertise in producing the photographs. Finally, I want to thank my father, who is himself a bookbinder, for reading the manuscript, and my wife, Dora, for her help with proofreading.

BERNARD C. MIDDLETON

The Restoration of Leather Bindings

1 Introduction

There were many predecessors of the book as we know it today. The most common immediate ancestor of the modern book was the Roman *volumen*, which was derived from the Egyptian papyrus roll and the Greek *biblion*, and consisted simply of a roll of parchment or papyrus. Also in use in Roman times were the *diptych* and *triptych*, in which two and three leaves, respectively, of a rigid material such as wood or ivory were laced together at one edge to produce something not dissimilar to the modern book (see fig. 1). In fact, it was probably the *polyptych* (multi-leaved) which suggested to someone the idea of the *codex*. The latter consisted of a number of sheets of paper, parchment, or vellum fastened together at one edge and is the basic form of the modern book. One advantage of the codex is that it provides easier access to the information contained in it than does the roll, which was often quite long and required a great deal of cumbersome unrolling and re-rolling to reach a particular place in the text. In addition, the codex permits the use of both sides of the leaves, whereas in the roll form of the book, only one side could be used.

The codex began to evolve sometime around the second century A.D. and soon supplanted the roll. Since that time most books have consisted of a number of sheets of vellum, parchment, or paper, with the sheets gathered into sections fastened together at one edge by some sort of sewing or stitching through the back folds, although many books have been and are formed of single leaves which are also fastened together at one edge in one fashion or another.

The leaves or sections of a book in the form of a codex may be held together in a number of different ways.

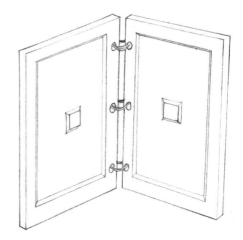

Fig. 1. Diptych (*above*) and triptych (*below*).

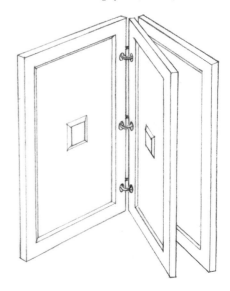

1

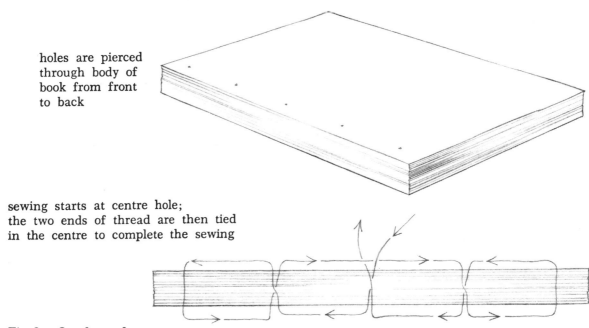

holes are pierced
through body of
book from front
to back

sewing starts at centre hole;
the two ends of thread are then tied
in the centre to complete the sewing

Fig. 2. One form of
stab sewing.

FASTENING THE LEAVES

Stab-sewing, in which the thread or other material passes through the entire body of the book from front to back (see fig. 2), is the simplest form of sewing and was widely used on papyrus codices in the Mediterranean area during the first few centuries of the Christian era. It has always been a popular method in the Orient and was much used in England and America from the fifteenth to the eighteenth centuries for books, usually thin ones, which were sold in wrappers (temporary paper covers). Book papers with low tearing strength, such as art papers, are often more strongly secured by stab-sewing than by sewing through the folds. In modern times many periodicals and booklets have been stab-sewn with metal staples. Stab-sewing often makes it difficult to open a book, although this may not be a serious drawback if the margins are sufficiently wide and the paper is sufficiently flexible. In general, stab-sewing is satisfactory only for those books which were designed for it from the beginning.

Coptic sewing, practised in Egypt and the surrounding areas about thirteen hundred years ago, consists of holding the sections to each other, and sometimes securing them to the boards, solely by means of thread which passes through the folds and then from section to section, usually knotted between each section. There are no supplementary thongs, cords, or tapes. This method spread from the Mediterranean to northern Europe (including Britain), but fell into disuse in thc latter area when raised-thong sewing was adopted in about the eighth century.

Paradoxically, modern machine sewing is very similar in its basic techniques to Coptic sewing. Although earlier in the era of machine sewing, tapes and even cords were often used, nearly all publishers' hard bindings today are machine-sewn in a manner very similar to Coptic sewing.

Raised-thong (or cord) sewing. By about the eighth century the more substantial method of sewing the sections to raised leather thongs had come into use in northern Europe and seems to have been widely adopted almost immediately. It was almost the only method employed until about 1600 (in the sixteenth century a comparatively small number of books were sewn on strips of vellum), and has been in use for at least certain kinds of binding ever since. Late in the sixteenth century hemp, jute, or flax cord began to be used in place of thongs, the latter having the unfortunate tendency to become brittle and break unless made of alum-tawed leather. Earlier books were usually sewn to double thongs or cords, with the thread carried around them in a figure-8 or herringbone pattern. Later, single cords became more common, with the cords completely encircled by the thread.

One of the main advantages of sewing on raised cords or thongs is that the cords or thongs can be much thicker (and therefore stronger) than would be possible if the book were sewn on *recessed cords* (see below). In addition, raised cords or thongs, in a binding in which all the elements are properly balanced, provide a gentle spring-like force, distributing the stress of opening the book over a relatively wide area. This aids substantially in retention of the shape of the book with use. In books sewn on raised cords or thongs, the spine of the cover is stuck down to the backbone of the book (with or without intermediate linings) to form what is called a tight-backed book, though when this type of sewing was first used there was no adhesion of the leather.

Recessed-cord sewing. The making of sawcuts in backbones so that the cords are sunken flush with or slightly below the surface of the backbone, rather than raised above it, was started in Europe at the end of the sixteenth century, mainly in cheap retail bindings. In this case the thread is simply passed across the cords rather than around them, thus making the sewing process easier and faster and consequently cheaper. The great majority of modern leather bindings are constructed with a combination of recessed cords and a *hollow back* (see below).

Books printed on stiff paper generally open more easily with this type of construction than with raised cords or thongs and a tight back. However, there is almost certainly a loss in durability because thinner cords must be used and also because the making of the sawcuts inevitably results in at least some weakening of the backbone, although the importance of this latter factor is sometimes overemphasized.

Books sewn on recessed cords often have fake raised bands glued across the backbone to give the appearance of books sewn on genuine raised cords or thongs.

Tape sewing. Tape was first employed during the second half of the nineteenth century in publishers' case bindings. This construction is very strong, and books thus sewn have the advantage of opening easily. The sewing process usually involves passing the thread across the tapes, but sometimes the tapes are encircled by the thread. Few books bound in leather are originally sewn on tapes, however, and this type of sewing will not be discussed in this volume.

Overcasting. One of the two basic ways of fastening single leaves is by passing thread through and around the back edges of a group of leaves to form made-up "sections," which are then sewn all-along or two-sections-on. Large books of plates have been overcast since the sixteenth century, and hand overcasting has been used since that time in various situations where single leaves are involved. Alternatively, this kind of sewing can be done so that the needle and thread also pass through two or three previously sewn sections and at the same time attach the sections to the cords or tapes. This method, which saves time and obviates the possibility of gaps appearing between the sections, is called *oversewing.*

In 1920 the oversewing machine was invented. This device, which is almost universally used in American library binderies and some European ones, sends thread diagonally through the back edges of groups of leaves in such a way that sections are formed and at the same time are firmly anchored to each other. Books which were originally made up of conventionally folded sections are normally reduced to single leaves by trimming off their back edges prior to machine oversewing. This form of sewing is practically indestructible, but it produces a book which does not open freely unless the paper is quite thin and from which it is virtually impossible to remove the thread. If the book ever has to be rebound, it is almost always necessary to again trim off the back edges of the leaves.

Adhesive binding. The second basic method of holding single leaves together depends solely on some form of adhesive. This method (or group of methods) is also called perfect binding, unsewn binding, threadless binding, or flex binding. It was first introduced in the 1830s, with natural rubber (caoutchouc) as the adhesive. This material had a tendency to deteriorate fairly rapidly, ultimately reducing the volume to a collection of loose leaves. With the introduction of improved adhesives in this century, adhesive binding has become very widely used, especially for paper covered books.

ROUNDING AND BACKING

The purpose of rounding is to prevent the backbone of a book from becoming concave. This can happen when a book is stood upright on the shelf, or even in the case of books which are stored flat when they are heavily used. It is also a method of accommodating the swelling of the backbone caused by the added thickness of the sewing thread. The shoulders created by the backing operation have, at least in tight-jointed books, the double function of helping to preserve the shape of the spine and providing support for the back edges of the boards while the book stands on the shelf.

Virtually all books which were produced until the end of the fifteenth century had flat or almost flat backs, giving them a brick-like appearance, especially as they did not normally have squares, that is, the covers did not project beyond the edges of the leaves of the book. There seems to have been no attempt to form shoulders until the early years of the sixteenth century, and even then they were rudimentary. As books were normally shelved flat on their sides in mediaeval times, it is clear that rounding and backing, which are so important for modern books, were not then quite so vital.

ATTACHMENT OF BOARDS

Three principal methods have been used for attaching a book to its covers.

1. The ends of cords (either raised or recessed) are frayed out and pasted down on the *outer* surface of the boards. In some early bindings, leather thongs were nailed into recesses cut into the outer surfaces of the boards. Usually, however, instead of being pasted or nailed, the cords or thongs are laced in, that is, passed through holes in the boards. In Coptic or Coptic-style sewing, the thread used to sew the backbone was often laced through holes in the boards.

2. Books sewn on wide strips of vellum or on tapes were often attached by splitting the boards horizontally along the joint edge, inserting the slips, and gluing the split portions of the board back together (see fig. 3). The earliest examples of this technique date back several hundred years, but for all practical purposes the history of split boards can be said to date from the beginning of the nineteenth century, when they were used in England in spring-back ledger bindings, and since the 1880s they have been used in English-style library bindings. Modifications of this style have occasionally been employed in some expensive fine bindings during the last thirty years or more. French joints (see below) are almost invariably used with split boards.

3. As early as the beginning of the eighteenth century (in some Dutch quarter-leather bindings, for example), boards were attached to books sewn on vellum strips by gluing the ends of these strips to the *inner* surfaces of the cover boards. Vellum strips were also laced through the joints of vellum-covered bindings and of limp-paper or vellum covers. Similarly, adhesion to the inner surfaces of cover boards was used in some eighteenth-century English almanacs. However, in most of these almanacs, which were sewn on recessed cords, there were no slips, the cords having been trimmed off at the joints, and the boards were simply held on by the endpapers. When cloth case bindings were introduced early in the nineteenth century, the boards were attached to the book by the frayed-out slips of recessed cords glued to the inner surfaces of the book boards and covered over by the paste-downs, though many early cased books were sewn in the French style (without cords or tapes). In the latter style, the attachment of case to book depended on the adhesion of the endpapers and a reinforcing slip of paper glued to the spine and to the boards under the endpapers. This type of binding was the forerunner of the modern case binding, in which no cords are used and in which the boards are attached by a cloth lining (the "mull," "crash," or

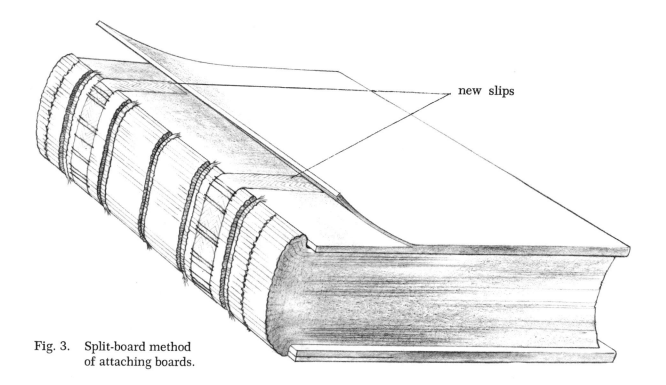

new slips

Fig. 3. Split-board method
of attaching boards.

"super") across the backbone, the ends of the lining being glued down on the inside of the boards and covered by the pastedowns.

There are not many hard-and-fast rules here, and many of the techniques mentioned above can be and have been used in different combinations, such as tapes being laced into boards, or cords being glued into split boards.

BACK LININGS

The Coptic type of book structure seems to have involved a loose hollow back; that is, while the sides of the cover were pasted to the outsides of the boards, the spine of the cover was not pasted down to the backbone. Soon after the advent of raised cord or thong construction it became the usual practice to paste the leather spine directly to the backbone to form what is called a tight back, so that the backbone and spine moved together as a unit when the book was opened.

The hollow back comes in two basic forms: the hollow tube and the loose hollow. In the hollow tube construction, a piece of stiff paper is folded and glued in such a way as to provide a flattened tube between the spine of the cover and the backbone of the book, with one or more of the layers of the tube attached to the spine and the others to the backbone (see fig. 47). The hollow tube is almost invariably an accompaniment of recessed-cord sewing. Nearly all fine trade bindings of the past century or so have been constructed with recessed cords and a hollow tube—often with fake raised bands pasted down over the tube.

Case bindings almost invariably have a loose hollow back. That is, the inside of the spine is usually lined with a strip of paper, while the backbone itself may also have one or more linings of various types; but there is no paper tube connecting the two.

The type and number of linings attached directly to the backbone have varied widely. In sixteenth-century and earlier tight-backed bindings and in some modern tight-backed bindings there arc ordinarily no linings at all. In some cases, however, linings are used with a tight back to ensure a smooth spine or to give extra support to the backbone. Modern French fine binders tend to use many layers of paper to make the spine smooth and also to make it rigid, so that any tooling on the spine will not be disturbed by the backbone "throwing up," or arching, heavily when the book is opened.

COVERINGS

Many kinds of materials have been used to cover the outside of books, including paper, wood, ivory, canvas, cloth, velvet, tortoise shell, metal, vellum, and various kinds of leather. In the case of leather it has been the usual practice in all periods to cover the boards completely with leather, but in mediaeval times the leather sometimes covered only the backbone and about half the width of the boards, leaving the remainder of the boards exposed. Early in the eighteenth century a new style, consisting of a strip of leather across the backbone and on to the sides a short distance, with small leather corners and with the remainder of the board covered with various kinds of paper, began to emerge and to gain popularity as a cheap binding. Towards the middle of the nineteenth century the amount of leather on the sides had increased so that it covered about a quarter of the width of the boards, and the size of the leather corners had increased proportionately. Later in the century the so-called three-quarter binding arrived in which the leather (usually goatskin) on the sides and at the corners almost met, but fortunately this not-very-attractive style did not last long.

As the reader will realize from the above brief summary, there are many ways in which books have been bound during the course of history. It would be quite impossible in a volume of this kind to deal with the restoration of all of these types of bindings. Not only will our discussion be limited to books bound, or at least partially bound, in leather, but almost entirely to that type of binding which, due to its prevalence in most modern "rare book" library collections, is today the principal concern of the librarian-conservator, namely the sixteenth-through-nineteenth-century book printed on paper, with folded sections sewn by hand on raised or recessed cords or thongs, with either a tight or hollow tube back and with tight joints. Tight joints are those in which the boards are brought up flush to the shoulder of the book, as opposed to the book with French joints. French joints, in which the boards are positioned a short distance away from the shoulders of the book, are mostly found in case bindings, although they are occasionally found in other types of bindings as well.

There will, however, be a short discussion of the restoration of the caoutchouc binding, which is not only case-bound, but consists of loose, single leaves bound with adhesive instead of being sewn. This type of binding is included because it is very often a leather-bound book, and because of the frequency with which surviving examples require repair or restoration.

It will, however, be found that many of the techniques discussed in the volume are equally applicable to bindings other than those described above.

2 Definition of Terms

Each craft has its own special terminology. The ancient craft of hand bookbinding has, over the centuries, developed its own highly specialized language to describe its techniques, tools, and materials. Because those who practise this craft today are relatively few in number and widely scattered, and because of the long history of the craft, during which terms have been freely borrowed from a number of languages and from other related crafts, there are differences in the terminology used in various parts of the English-speaking world. The following is a list of terms as they are used in this volume. Whenever possible, the alternative terms are also given.

Adhesive Bindings. Bindings in which the back edges of a book made up of single leaves are secured together solely with some kind of adhesive. Sometimes referred to as "perfect," "threadless," "unsewn," or "flex" bindings. See also *Caoutchouc Bindings.*

All-along. A method of hand sewing a book in which the thread passes in and out and around or over the cords, thongs, or tapes along the whole length of the inside fold of each section from kettle-stitch to kettle-stitch (see fig. 35). In some early examples, up to about the twelfth century, the headbands were included and were not sewn separately. Sometimes referred to as *all on.* See also *Oversewing; Two-sections-on.*

All On. See *All along.*

Alum-tawed Leather. Leather (usually pigskin, but occasionally goat or other types of skin) treated with alum instead of tanbark or other tanning agents. The surface of early tawed leather sometimes resembles vellum in its hardness after use on early books, but unlike vellum, which usually has a smooth surface, tawed leather typically retains the hair follicles or grain of the skin. Alum-tawed skins are often found on books bound from the Middle Ages on and have demonstrated great durability and permanence. An example of tawed pigskin is shown in figure 12.

Aniline Dyes. See *Stains.*

Art Paper. Paper with a smooth, often glossy, clay coating. Used for printing finely detailed illustrations. Usually called *coated paper* in the United States.

Backbone. The edge of a book along which the leaves or sections are fastened together in binding. The term "backbone" is often used to describe the portion of the outer cover which covers the back of the book, and which is usually lettered with the title of the book, the author's name, etc. In order to avoid confusion, this portion of the cover will be referred to in this volume as the *Spine*, and the term "backbone" will be restricted to mean the back edge of the body of the book.

Back Cornering. The removal of board from the four corners of

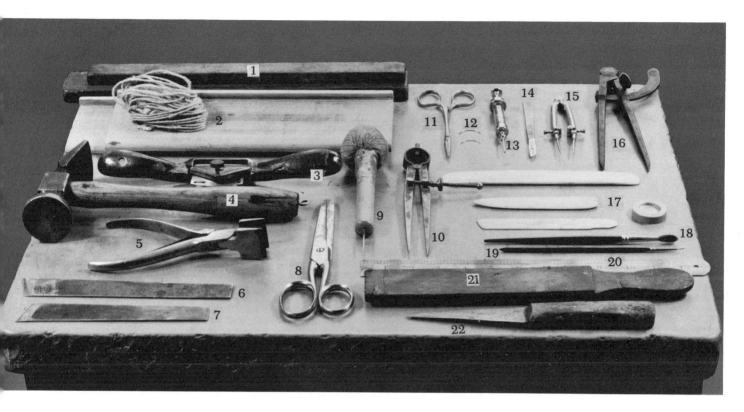

On the left
(back to front)

1. bandsticks
2. tying-up boards with cord
3. spokeshave
4. backing hammer
5. band nippers
6. lifting knife
7. paring knife

In the centre
(left to right)

8. shears
9. piercer for overcast cloth joints
10. spring dividers

On the right
(left to right)

11. Spencer Wells forceps
12. curved needles
13. hypodermic needle and syringe
14. scalpel
15. dividers for lettering
16. compass

(back to front)

17. 3 folders and circular container for shell gold
18. brush for local staining of leather
19. fine brush for shell gold
20. steel straight-edge
21. strop
22. general purpose knife

Fig. 4.   Paring stone with most frequently used tools.

the boards at the joints. Back cornering of the type shown in figure 43A was employed from the sixteenth century to the last quarter of the eighteenth, the purpose being to make a space for thick turn-in leather. From the last decades of the eighteenth century back cornering has involved the cutting away of a small triangular piece of the outer surface of the head and tail ends of the boards. The cut is made so that the inner corners of the boards remain intact (see fig. 43). The purpose is to relieve strain on the joints of the book when the boards are opened, and also to facilitate the setting and shaping of the headcaps before they are tied with thread (see fig. 62). Some leading British binders now back corner on the inside instead of the outside as a means of structural improvement.

Back Folds. The folds through which the sections are sewn, stapled, or otherwise fastened to each other. Sometimes, in context, they are referred to merely as the *folds.*

Backing. The splaying over and hammering of the backs of the leaves or sections of a book to form shoulders to accommodate the thickness of the cover boards (see fig. 42). This is normally done after rounding, in an operation commonly referred to as rounding-and-backing. See also *Rounding.*

Backing Boards. Bevelled, wedge-shaped boards of wood (sometimes faced with metal) placed on either side of books when they are being backed in the lying press (see fig. 42).

Backing Hammer. A hammer with a solid claw and a face with a slightly rounded surface, somewhat resembling a shoemaker's hammer, used for both backing and rounding. (A backing hammer is shown in fig. 4, and one may be seen in use in fig. 42.)

Back Linings. Various layers of cloth, paper, or leather used for reinforcing or stiffening the backbone of a book. The operation of placing these materials on the backbone is usually referred to as *lining up.* See also *Mull.*

Backsaw. See *Tenon Saw.*

Backstrip. See *Spine.*

Band Nippers. A hand-held device, made much like a pair of pliers, with straight, flat jaws, usually fitted with a spring to separate the jaws (see fig. 4). Used for moulding leather over raised bands.

Bands. 1. The cords or thongs on which the sections of a book are sewn. Often, particularly in hollow-backed books, grooves are sewn into the backbone of a book and the cords are laid into the grooves so that they lie flush with or slightly below the surface of the backbone, in which case they are referred to as *recessed cords.* If the cords or thongs are not recessed, they form ridges across the backbone of the book and are referred to as *raised bands.* In raised-band sewing, the sewing thread encircles the cords, whereas in sewing on recessed cords, the thread merely passes across the outside of the cords (see figs. 34 and 35). Raised bands are sometimes not sewn into the book, but are merely pasted or glued across the backbone, particularly in a hollow-backed book sewn on recessed cords, to give the appearance, when covered with leather, of genuine raised bands. In this case, they are called *fake* or *false bands.* The loose ends (called the *Slips*) of genuine raised bands are used to attach the boards to the body of the book, whereas fake or false bands almost invariably terminate at the shoulders of the book, and therefore are not used to attach the boards. 2. In a more restricted sense, "bands" are the ridges across the spine of a book, under which the raised cords or thongs (whether genuine or fake) lie. The terms "bands" and "cords" are often used interchangeably.

Bandsticks. Lengths of smooth wood of various widths used for pressing leather down on either side of raised bands (see fig. 4). Sometimes they are made with a groove along the length of one side which fits down over the band and to some extent serves the same purpose as band nippers.

Bath Brick. Made from mingled sand and clay deposits in a river near Bridgewater, England. It comes in either block or powdered form and is used in England for, among other things, scouring and cleaning the leather surfaces of gold cushions.

Binder's Board. See *Millboard.*

Blind Tooling. See *Tooling.*

Blocking. See *Tooling.*

Boarding. For an explanation of this process, see page 60.

Board Paper. See *Pastedown.*

Boards. A general term used for *Pasteboard, Millboard, Straw-board,* etc., all of which are used to form the foundation for book covers. They are made of various pulped or laminated fibrous materials pressed into large, flat sheets, which are then cut to size and covered with cloth, or leather, or other materials, to form the book covers. Called "boards" because in early bindings they were usually made of wood. (Wooden boards are occasionally still used in the restoration or repair of certain types of old bindings.) The earliest "boards" were probably made of *papyrus.* Also called *cover boards,* or *book boards.*

Book Boards. See *Boards.*

Bristol Board. See *Card.*

Cambridge Style. A style of decoration usually employed on calf bindings, and to a lesser extent on those covered with sheep. It originated in England during the second half of the seventeenth century and was popular until about 1730. The style was revived during the second half of the nineteenth century for the rebinding of antiquarian books and is still employed for that purpose. A rectangular frame is left plain while the borders and central area are sprinkled. The characteristic blind tooling consists of two-line fillets, a roll around the central rectangle and corner tools (see fig. 100).

Cancel. A printed leaf which has been inserted in a book in place of the original printed leaf because of printing errors or change of mind by the author. Usually, the cancel is attached to the stub which was left when the original leaf was cut off.

Caoutchouc Bindings. Nineteenth-century books consisting of single leaves held together by means of a rubber solution (caoutchouc) applied to their back edges. This type of binding was a predecessor of the modern *Adhesive Bindings*. Other types of adhesives are now used, mostly various kinds of PVA. (Note: the word caoutchouc is pronounced approximately as "cow-chook.")

Caps. See *Headcaps*.

Card. A thin paperboard, often with smooth surface suitable for writing or printing. Also called *cardboard* or *bristol board*.

Cardboard. See *Card*.

Carragheen (or *Carrageen*) *Moss*. A seaweed which yields a gelatinous extract (called carrageenan, or carrageenin) used to make a size for the marbling of paper. See also *Marbled Paper; Sizing*.

Cartridge Paper. A strong, hard, rough-surfaced paper, heavily sized, used for a number of purposes in bookbinding, particularly for lining backbones. Called "cartridge paper" because it was originally used for the making of gun cartridges.

Case Binding. In a case-bound book, the cover is made separately from the rest of the book and put on in one piece, as distinguished from the type of binding in which the cover is assembled on the book.

Casing-in. The process of attaching the cover to the body of a book in case binding.

Catch Stitch. See *Kettle-stitch*.

Catchword. A word under the last line on the page of a book, used to indicate the first word which will appear at the top of the following page. This was used in earlier times as an aid to the printer in imposing the press forms, and to the bookbinder in gathering and assembling the sections of a book.

C-clamp. See *G-clamp*.

Chain Stitch. See *Kettle-stitch*.

Chipboard. See *Thames Board.*

Cleaning Off. The removal of glue from backbones after rounding and backing. This is effected by soaking the backbone with paste for a few minutes, scraping it with a blunt edge to remove the glue and paste and then wiping clean with a damp rag.

Coated Paper. See *Art Paper.*

Codex. The flat, hinged form of a book consisting of single leaves, or of sections made up of folded leaves, fastened together on one side. The codex began to supersede the roll form of the book at least as early as the second century A.D.

Collating. The process of assembling a book in proper order, and of checking the completeness of the book and the correct sequence of the leaves.

Common Calf or *Sheep Binding.* A leather binding of the simplest kind (often not headbanded or backed, and without either a pastedown or lettering on the spine), executed for the inexpensive retail trade, principally during the seventeenth and eighteenth centuries.

Conjugate Leaf. Leaves which are joined together as one continuous piece of paper are said to be conjugate. For example, in a sewn or stitched book, either half of a four-page sheet is conjugate with the other half when they are joined together at the back fold.

Copperas. A green hydrated ferrous sulphate, sometimes called iron sulphate or iron vitriol. Has many industrial uses including the production of writing inks and pigments, and in engraving and lithography. It has been, and sometimes still is, used for sprinkling leather to achieve a decorative effect. See also *Sprinkling.*

Coptic Bindings. Leather bindings, produced in Egypt from the third to the eleventh century, in which the sections are held together by thread with a series of kettle-stitches. Many of the earliest boards consisted of layers of papyrus, and were attached to the book by loops of thread as an integral part of the sewing.

Copying Press. See *Nipping Press.*

Cords. See *Bands.*

Cores. See *Headband.*

Cottage (Cottage-roof) Style. In this style, which was popular in England during the last four decades of the seventeenth century for the decoration of *turkey* bindings, the central rectangular panel has a broken pediment at the top and bottom and the covers are usually elaborately gold tooled.

Cotton Wool. Raw cotton wadding. Called "absorbent cotton" in the United States. Much used as an applicator for stains, dyes, etc., and also for wiping, blotting, and many other bindery operations.

Cover Boards. See *Boards.*

Crash. See *Mull.*

Crêpeline. See *Silk Gauze.*

Cross Direction. See *Machine Direction.*

Cutting Press. See *Lying Press.*

Doublure. See *Pastedown.*

Drawing On. The act of moulding leather on to the binding.

Duodecimo. See *Folio.*

Edging Knife. See *Paring Knife.*

Endbands. See *Headband.*

End Leaves. See *Endpapers (plural).*

End Lining. See *Pastedown.*

Endpaper (singular). See *Pastedown.*

Endpapers (plural). The papers, coloured or white, printed or decorated in some way or plain, at the beginning and end of a book. They are not generally included in the pagination of the book. In the simplest and most common form, the endpapers consist of a single folded sheet of paper, one leaf of which is pasted down to the inside of the cover board to form the pastedown. The other leaf forms a flyleaf, and the fold connecting the two leaves usually forms part of the inner joint of the book. (A variety of endpapers is shown in fig. 39.) Endpapers are also sometimes called *end leaves* or *end sheets (plural)*. See also *Flyleaf; Pastedown*.

End Sheet (singular). See *Pastedown*.

End Sheets (plural). See *Endpapers*.

Fake or False Bands. See *Bands*.

Fanfare. A French style of decorating book covers, c. 1560–1640, comprised of allover geometrically formed compartments filled with small ornamentation, such as flowers, foliage, arabesques, and so forth.

Feathering. Used here as the process of paring the edges of leather so that a slight raggedness results, especially in grainy skins. This is done to improve the adhesion of the edges when they are stuck down, and also so that they will not form an unsightly ridge where they lie over or under another layer of material.

Fillet. A brass wheel attached to a shank and handle, with one or more raised designs on a narrow working surface. (Strictly speaking, the designs on the working surface of a fillet consist only of straight lines, but similar tools with other narrow designs are also commonly called fillets.) Used for decorating a book cover. (The large wheeled tool lying on the finishing stove in fig. 94 is a fillet. See also fig. 6.) The term is also used to mean the impressions made with this tool. See also *Pallet; Roll*.

Finishing Press. A small, horizontal, adjustable press (somewhat similar to the *Lying Press*, but smaller) used for holding a book while it is being lettered or tooled on the spine (see fig. 94). Usually made of hardwood, it consists of two parallel beams (or "cheeks") connected by screws, which are situated near each end and are used to tighten or loosen the press.

Finishing Stove. A small stove used for heating the finishing tools used in decorating the cover of a book (see figs. 5 and 94).

Finishing Tools. A general term used to refer to the various hand tools used to decorate the cover of a book, such as *Fillets, Pallets, Gouges,* and *Rolls.* (A few simple finishing tools may be seen in fig. 6.)

Flat Back. A book the backbone of which has not been rounded (see *Rounding*) is said to have a flat back.

Flesh Side. See *Hair (Grain) Side.*

Flyleaf. The leaf (or leaves) forming that part of the *Endpapers* not pasted down to the inside of the cover board (see Frontispiece). See also *Made Flyleaves.*

Folder. A small, hand-held tool (formerly made of bone, but now more often of plastic), more or less knife-shaped, used in folding sheets to form a smooth crease in the folded edge, and for many other binding processes. (A folder is shown in fig. 4, and one is shown in use in fig. 58.)

Folds. See *Back Folds.*

Foliating. The numbering of leaves (not pages). This system of numbering preceded the modern system of paginating. See also *Paginating.*

Fig. 5. Gas finishing stove.

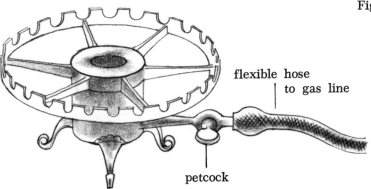

flexible hose
to gas line

petcock

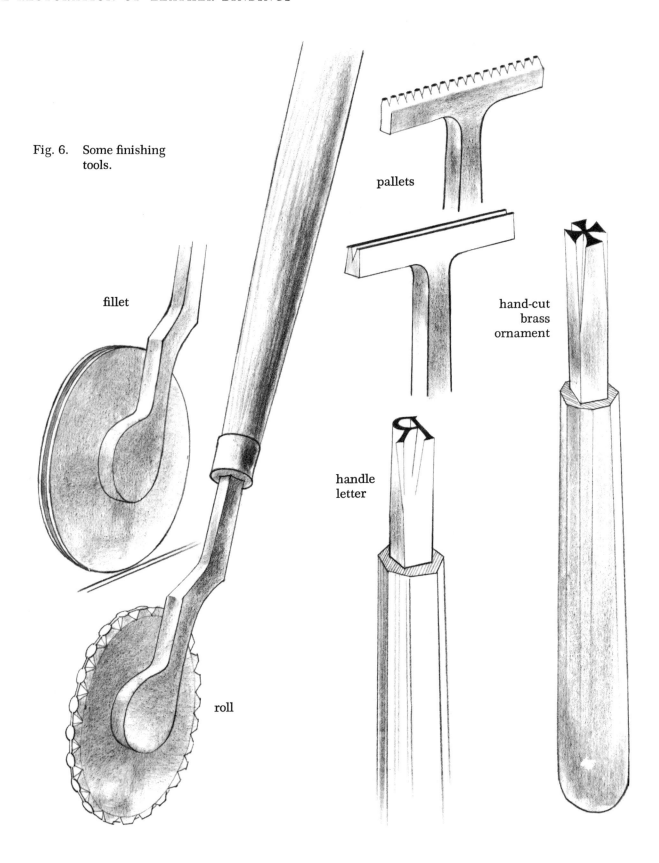

Fig. 6. Some finishing tools.

fillet

roll

pallets

hand-cut brass ornament

handle letter

Folio. Originally, this term and related terms such as *quarto, octavo,* and *duodecimo,* signified the number of leaves formed by folding a single sheet of book paper. Thus *folio* designated a sheet folded into two leaves of four pages; *quarto* a sheet folded into four leaves or eight pages; and *duodecimo* a sheet folded into twelve leaves or twenty-four pages by cutting four leaves from a 12mo imposition and inserting them into the 8vo. These folded sheets generally formed a section of a book, except in the case of folios, where occasionally a number of folded sheets were inserted one into the other to make up a section. As an indication of book or page size, these terms have largely fallen into disuse, except perhaps in antiquarian book circles, because of the confusion arising from the fact that the page size resulting from these various folds depends on the size of the original sheet of paper used on the press to print the book; and whereas press sheets came in relatively few sizes through about the seventeenth century, since that time, with the advent of many new kinds of printing presses, press sheets in a great variety of sizes have been used. The term "folio" is sometimes loosely used by librarians today to mean any book which is too large (more than approximately 12 inches high) to be stored upright in the standard bookstack shelving. Such books are often stored flat in a separate section of the bookstack.

Foot. See *Tail.*

Forceps. See *Spencer Wells Forceps.*

Fore Edge. The front edge of a book; the edge opposite the back-bone or spine (see Frontispiece).

Fore Edge Painting. A painted decoration on the fore edges of the leaves of a book, usually done with water colours. The painting is usually done with the edges slightly fanned out. The edges are then squared up and gilded or marbled. The painting is thus invisible until the edges of the leaves are again fanned out. An English innovation of the mid-seventeenth century.

French Grooves. See *French Joints.*

French Joints. These are the grooves in the cover which result when the boards are positioned a short distance from the shoulders of a book, leaving a gap between the shoulders and the boards. This kind of a joint is usual in case-bound books, and is often used when other kinds of books are covered with vellum or very thick materials, so that the covers can hinge more freely. French joints are also called *grooved joints, French grooves,* or *sunk joints.* See also *Tight Joints.*

French Paring Knife. See *Paring Knife.*

French Sewing. A method of sewing sections together through the folds by kettle-stitches without the use of cords, thongs, etc.

Full Bindings. Bindings in which the entire cover (back and sides) is formed of the same kind of material (leather, cloth, paper, or whatever). See also *Half, Quarter,* and *Three-quarter Bindings.*

Furbishing. This term generally refers to non-structural improvements of the binding, such as cleaning, sticking down loose leather, colouring rubbed areas, and applying leather dressing.

Gathering. See *Section.*

Gauffered. This term refers to book edges, almost invariably gilt, which have been decorated with hot finishing tools which indent small patterns into the paper. Also spelled as *goffered.*

G-clamp. A small, general-purpose clamp, operated by means of a flat-ended screw. So called because of its shape. In the United States, usually called a *c-clamp* (presumably for the same reason).

Gilded, Gilding. See *Gilt Edges.*

Gilt Edges. The edges of the leaves of a book which have been covered with gold leaf. The edges of a book treated in this way are said to be *gilded,* and the operation of applying the gold leaf is called *gilding.*

Glaire (Glair). An adhesive mixture containing egg white or a solution of shellac. Used as a sizing in preparation for gold tooling, it causes the gold to adhere to the surface of the cover when a hot tool is pressed on it. Egg glaire is also used as an adhesive in gilding the edges of the leaves of a book by hand.

Glass Paper. A strong paper faced with powdered glass and used in abrading or smoothing surfaces such as wood and leather. Sometimes called sandpaper although, strictly speaking, sandpaper is faced with sand or natural flint instead of powdered glass.

Gluing Up. The rubbing of glue or other adhesives on and between the back folds of the sections prior to rounding and backing the backbone of a book (see fig. 40).

Goffered. See *Gauffered.*

Gold. The gold used by bookbinders and restorers comes in three forms. 1. *Leaf gold.* This is genuine gold, at least 23-carat, alloyed with a small amount of silver and copper. It is supplied in books containing 25 leaves, each 3¼ inches square. The leaves are extremely thin (about 1/250,000 of an inch). 2. *Real gold foil.* Consists of genuine gold atomized on to a prepared carrier film in vacuum chambers, or gold leaf attached to the film with an adhesive. This is subsequently treated with heat-sensitive size that acts as a form of glaire so that the impression of a hot tool will transfer the gold to material which has not been previously prepared for tooling by the application of egg or shellac glaire. 3. *Shell gold.* So called because it used to be supplied in small mussell shells. Similarly shaped plastic containers are now used. It can also be bought in small blocks. It consists of genuine gold powder held together with a size. It is transferred to the object being treated by means of a wet paint brush and can be used for filling in small areas of tooling when the original gold is missing. (A container for shell gold can be seen in fig. 4.)

Gold Cushion. A pad consisting of a wooden board with a layer of cotton wool covered with rough leather, flesh-side uppermost. Used as a working surface when cutting gold leaf to size.

Gold Foil. See *Gold.*

Gold Knife. A flat-bladed knife with a wooden handle. The blade is usually about 6 inches long and ¾ inch wide, and has a smooth, moderately sharp cutting edge on one or both sides. It is used to manipulate gold leaf and to cut it into the requisite sizes and shapes.

Gold Rubber. A piece of tacky rubber used to remove and collect surplus gold after tooling.

Gold Sizing. See *Glaire*.

Gouge. A finishing tool the working surface of which forms a segment of a circle. Used to impress curved lines on book covers.

Grain. In paper also called *Machine Direction*. In leather, the markings, or texture, of the outer, or *Hair (Grain) Side*.

Grain Direction. See *Machine Direction*.

Gravy Browning. A water-soluble colouring material useful for achieving a certain effect when the margins and edges of leaves are being stained and aged. See also page 54.

Grooved Joints. See *French Joints*.

Guards. Strips of cloth or strong paper used to strengthen or reattach conjugate leaves before the book is resewn. Also used to provide a hinge for inserted pictures, maps, or plates.

Gum Tragacanth. A gummy substance which exudes from a plant found in eastern Europe and Asia Minor. It was much used in former times, and to a lesser extent today, as a size for paper marbling. See also *Marbled Paper*.

Hair (Grain) Side. In the processing of an animal skin to make leather, the thin outer layer, or epidermis, of the skin is removed together with the hair, wool, or fur. The innermost, or subcutaneous, layer of fatty flesh is also removed. The thick, dense layer of skin that lies between these two layers, called the derma (or corium) is the part used to make the leather. The surface of the derma which lies immediately beneath the epidermis, and which is exposed by its removal, is called the hair (or grain) side. This is the side of the leather that is usually stained, polished, or otherwise treated to give it its final finished appearance. The underside of the derma, that is, the side exposed by the removal of the sub-cutaneous layer, is called the *flesh side*.

Half Bindings. Bindings in which the spine, a portion of the sides, and the corners of the cover are formed of one kind of material (usually leather) and the rest of the sides of another (such as cloth or paper). See also *Full, Quarter,* and *Three-quarter Bindings*.

Handle Letters. Single brass letters with long metal shanks for mounting in wood or asbestos handles. Used for the hand lettering of book covers. (Several handle letters are shown lying on a finishing stove in fig. 94. See also fig. 6.) Also called *hand letters,* or *letter tools*.

Hand Letters. See *Handle Letters*.

Hard Grain (Morocco). Goatskin with a deep pin-head grain produced by hand-boarding (for a description of boarding, see page 60). An example of hard grain goatskin is shown in figure 12. See also *Morocco Leather; Straight Grain (Morocco)*.

Harleian Style. This refers to a decorative scheme commonly found on the bindings made for Robert Harley, Earl of Oxford (1661–1724) and his son Edward. Typically, this consists of an elaborate border built up with one or more rolls, and a central ornament in the shape of an elongated lozenge built up with small tools, all in gold.

Head. The end of the book at the top of the page (see Frontispiece). See also *Tail*.

Headband. In early bindings or fine bindings, a piece of embroidery sewn on by hand over a strip of leather, stout cord, or other material at the head and tail of the backbone of the book (see Frontispiece, and figs. 46B thru 46F). The strips of leather, cord, etc., on which the headbands are sewn are referred to as the *cores* of the headband. The band at the tail of the book is sometimes called the *tailband*. Headbands and tailbands are sometimes referred to, collectively, as *endbands*. In most modern publishers trade bindings, the headband, if used, consists of a piece of machine-woven material which is glued on the backbone, rather than sewn on. See also *Stuck-on Headbands*.

Headcap. The visible portion of the fold of leather where it turns in at the head and tail of the spine (see Frontispiece). (Strictly speaking, the cap at the tail end of the spine should be referred to as the *tailcap*, but usually the caps at both ends of the spine are called headcaps, or simply *caps*.)

Hinge. See *Inner Joint; Outer Joint.*

Hollow Back. The type of back in which the spine of the cover is not stuck down to the backbone as in a tight-backed book. A tube-like paper lining is sometimes situated between the backbone and the spine (see fig. 47). If there is no tube, the book is said to have a *loose hollow*. When the leaves of a book, or the covering materials, are stiff and thick, a hollow back usually enables the book to open more freely than would be the case with a tight back. See also *One On and One Off; One On and Two Off, etc.; Tight Back.*

Incunabula. Books printed before 1501.

Industrial Methylated Spirit. A type of *methylated spirit* which contains no pyridine. It consists of ethanol with 5 percent methanol.

Inner Joint. The inside hinge of the cover, made of the fold of the endpapers and/or a strip of supplemental cloth or leather (see Frontispiece). Sometimes referred to as the (inner) *hinge*.

Jaconet (Jaconette). Thin white cotton cloth treated with a size which enables it to remain stable for a short time after the application of adhesive. Often used as a reinforcing material in bookbinding because it provides good strength without bulk.

Japanese Tissue. A soft, strong, fairly transparent, long-fibred, and absorbent paper made from the fibres of a variety of Japanese plants, especially the mulberry. It is available in a variety of thicknesses and colours. It is a very versatile paper, and according to the thickness used, it can be employed for patching leaves, for the overall lining of leaves as a reinforcement, for mending tears, for reinforcing the back folds of sections, or for mending inner joints.

Jogging. See *Knocking Up.*

Join. A bookbinding term used to indicate the point at which two pieces of material come together or overlap.

Joint. See *French Joints; Inner Joint; Outer Joint; Tight Joints.*

Kettle-stitch. This term is most likely derived from the German "kettel-stich"—a stitch that forms a little chain—but it is thought by some to be a corruption of "catch-up-stitch." It is the knotted thread which joins the sections together at the head and tail of the book (see fig. 34). It is sometimes called a *chain stitch,* or *catch stitch.*

Klucel G. Supplied by the Hercules Powder Company. It is hydroxypropylcellulose and can be dissolved in ethanol, isopropanol industrial methylated spirit, or water for use as a sizing and reinforcing medium for paper and as a consolidant (in IMS) for leather.

Knocking-down Iron. A heavy, T-shaped piece of iron (see fig. 7). When clamped in a press, the knocking-down iron forms a solid base for hammering down the cords or tapes used to fasten the book to the boards, or for other similar types of binding operations.

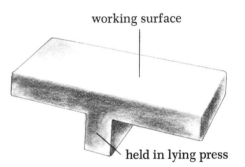

Fig. 7. Knocking-down iron.

Knocking Up. The process of squaring up the edges of a book (or a pile of sheets of paper). This usually involves dropping and knocking the backbone and then the top edge of a loosely held book on to a flat surface until the leaves or sections are well aligned. This process is often referred to, particularly in the United States, as *jogging.*

Kraft Paper. A strong brown machine-made paper widely used for wrapping purposes, and in bookbinding for lining the backbone of the book. It can be obtained glazed or unglazed, ribbed or plain.

Label. A piece of paper or other material bearing the title of the book, the name of the author, etc., which is fixed either to the spine or the side of the cover of a book. (A label is shown being tooled in fig. 94.) In a leather binding it is usually made of leather of a contrasting colour. It is also known as a *lettering piece.*

Laced-in. See *Slips.*

Laid Paper. Paper hand made on a screen-like mould of closely set parallel horizontal wires which are crossed at right angles by vertical wires spaced somewhat farther apart. The wires produce more or less prominent ribbed lines in the finished paper. In machine-made paper a similar effect is achieved by the use of a specially prepared roll, known as a "dandy roll." See also *Wove Paper.*

Laying Press. See *Lying Press.*

Leaf. A single sheet of paper, parchment, or vellum, each side of which forms a page of a book. See also *Conjugate Leaf; Page.*

Leaf Gold. See *Gold.*

Leather. The skins of a wide variety of animals, preserved and prepared by chemical and mechanical treatments. The most commonly used skins for the binding of books are goat, calf, sheep, and pig, but many other types of skin have been used at one time or another (including human skin). The grain and texture of a variety of bookbinding leathers is shown in figure 12. See also under names of specific types of leather. See also *Hair (Grain) Side.*

Leather Dressing. There are many different formulas for leather dressing, consisting of various mixtures of oils, waxes, solvents, and softeners. The purpose is to lubricate and soften certain kinds of leather. (See page 62 for the recommended formula.)

Lettering Pallet. See *Pallet.*

Lettering Piece. See *Label.*

Letter Press. See *Nipping Press.*

Letterspacing. The insertion of spaces between the letters of the words in a line of type.

Letter Tools. See *Handle Letters.*

Lifting Knife. A knife with a shallow bevel on one side only, and with a short cutting edge running at an angle across the width of the blade (see figs. 4 and 15). Usually shaped by the restorer himself to fit his own individual needs. The steel of the *paring knives* from which lifting knives are usually made is often too soft to withstand the hard wear involved in lifting tough millboard and leather, so it is a good idea to cut down machine hacksaw blades. It is important to ensure that they have been tempered all through and not just along the edges. The knives are used in restoration for lifting pasted-down leather, paper, and so forth.

Lining Paper. See *Pastedown.*

Lining Up. See *Back Linings.*

Loose Hollow. See *Hollow Back.*

Lying Press/Cutting Press. A horizontal press (turned according to need), somewhat larger than a *Finishing Press,* usually consisting of two parallel beams (or "cheeks") connected by a large screw near each end used for tightening and loosening the press. This press is used for clamping or holding a book while backing, trimming the edges of the leaves, and many other binding operations (see fig. 8). Also called a *laying press.*

Machine Direction. This is the direction in which the fibres in a piece of machine-made paper tend to lie, due to the motion of the paper-making machine. When the finished paper is moistened, the fibres swell more across their width than along their length, so that the paper has a greater tendency to expand at right angles to the machine direction. The machine direction of paper should normally run parallel with the joints—or from head to tail—of the book. Also called *grain direction,* or *Grain.* The opposite direction is called the *cross direction.*

Made Flyleaves. Flyleaves, usually of coloured or decorated paper, which have been lined with uncoloured paper (see fig. 38). See also *Flyleaf.*

Marbled Paper. Paper decorated by transferring to its surface intermingled colours which have been floated on a gum solution, or size. As the name implies, many of the traditional patterns resemble

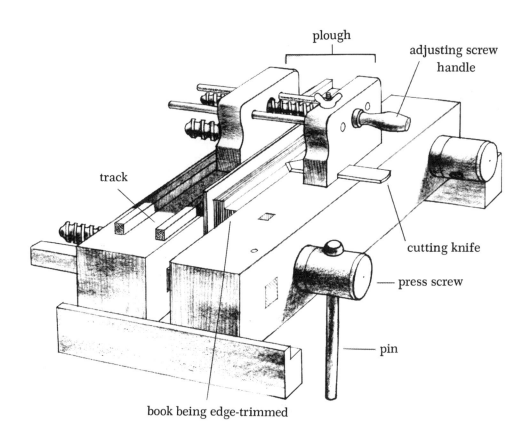

Fig. 8.   Lying press and plough.

marble, though in all periods there has been no pretence at exact imitation. Many of the most marble-like papers were produced at the turn of the eighteenth and nineteenth centuries. The manufacturing process involves preparing a bath of size (usually gum tragacanth in early times, but now more often made from carrageenan, which is derived from carragheen moss) on the surface of which colours are floated and then sometimes combed into patterns. The spreading or contraction of the colours on the size (their surface tension) is controlled by the addition of alum or ox gall and the latter also prevents the blending of the colours. A sheet of paper dampened with alum water is lowered on to the colours which are floating on the surface of the size; when the sheet is lifted off it is found that the colours have transferred to the paper and remain firm while the paper is washed in running water to remove clinging size. In uncombed marbles, blobs of colour are thrown on to the size so that a decorative effect is achieved without the aid of a comb or stylus. Marbled papers are sometimes now reproduced by lithography, but they lack the quality of the originals. See also *Carragheen Moss; Gum Tragacanth.*

Methylated Spirit. This consists, by volume, of 90 percent ethanol, 9.5 percent methanol, 0.5 percent pyridine, with small amounts of petroleum and methyl violet dye. Used for, among other things, the dilution of spirit stains. See *Industrial Methylated Spirit.*

Millboard. A dense, hard-milled, machine-made book board made of pulped waste paper. The better grades of millboard used to be hand-made of rope fibre. Called *binder's board* in the United States. See also *Boards.*

Morocco Leather. This term was formerly used to indicate the North African origin of goatskin leather, but is now used generically to cover goatskin from all parts of the world. Some examples of morocco leathers are shown in figure 12. See also *Hard Grain (Morocco); Straight Grain (Morocco).*

Mull. An open-weave variety of coarse, sized muslin used for reinforcing or stiffening the backbone and joints of books. In the United States, similar cloths are usually called *crash* or *super.* See also *Back Linings.*

Muslin. A plain-woven cotton fabric, made in various qualities from coarse to sheer. For bookbinding purposes, it is usually sized, starched, or glued to avert stretching or shrinking.

Nipping. Pressure of very short duration applied in a press or clamp.

Nipping Press. A small press consisting essentially of a fixed, horizontal iron or steel plate, and a movable iron or steel platen that can be raised and lowered by means of a long, vertical screw (see fig. 9). Used for applying quick and even pressure during a variety of binding operations. Also called a *letter press* or *copying press*, as these presses were used in offices for copying letters before the invention of carbon paper and photocopying machines.

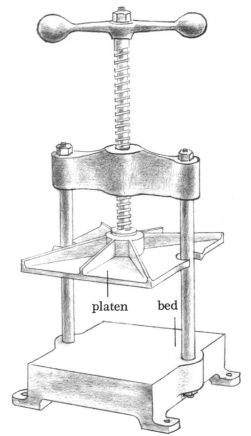

platen   bed

Fig. 9.   Nipping press.

Nylon Gossamer. A very thin, fibrous and transparent non-woven material much used for the lamination of paper, usually after the material has been impregnated with heat-set resin. Neutral pH.

Nylon Size. Soluble nylon dissolved in industrial methylated spirit. A 3 percent solution is used as a paper size for very weak paper, and as a fixative for water colours and manuscript inks when paper is being bleached or subjected to other wet treatments. See also *Sizing; Resizing.*

Octavo. See *Folio.*

One On and One Off, One On and Two Off, etc. These terms are used to refer to the construction of the tube in a hollow-backed book. If each side of the tube consists of a single thickness of paper, one side being stuck down to the backbone of the book and the other to the spine of the cover, the construction is referred to as *one on and one off* (see fig. 48). If the tube is made so that one side is made of a double thickness of paper and the other side of a single thickness, with the single thickness stuck to the backbone and the double thickness stuck to the spine, the construction is referred to as *one on and two off* (see fig. 47); while if the same tube is put down with the double thickness stuck to the backbone and the single thickness stuck to the spine, it is referred to as *two on and one off*. Where both sides of the tube consist of a double thickness of paper, the construction is referred to as *two on and two off*, and so on.

Outer Joint. The flexible part of the covering material (leather, cloth, or paper) on which the board opens (see Frontispiece). Also called (outer) *hinge*. The term "joint" is sometimes used to indicate the ridge or abutment formed by the *Backing* operation to accommodate the cover board. This ridge is, however, more often referred to as the *shoulder* of the book. See also *French Joints; Inner Joint.*

Overcast Cloth Joint. A reinforcement for the attachment of the cover to the book which involves sewing one edge of a strip of cloth on to a shoulder of the book and then sticking the other side down on the inside of the cover board (see figs. 25 and 26).

Overcasting. See *Oversewing.*

Oversewing. In hand binding, a method of sewing books made up of single leaves or single folds, or containing sections with badly damaged folds, to cords or tapes on the sewing frame, which at the same time catches up previously sewn leaves or sections, as distinct from *overcasting* (sometimes called *whipstitching*) in which sections are sewn separately and then sewn *All-along.* In mass-production library binding, especially in the United States, a form of oversewing produced on a special sewing machine is widely used. (A book is shown being oversewn by hand on the sewing frame in fig. 32.)

Ox Gall. Bile obtained from the gallbladder of an ox. Used in the preparation of the colours for marbled paper.

Page. A single side of a leaf of a book. See also *Leaf.*

Paginating. The numbering of pages, as distinct from the numbering of leaves. See also *Foliating.*

Pallet. 1. A finishing tool with a long, narrow face bearing lines or a design, used for decorating the covers of books (see figs. 6, 92, and 94). 2. A tool used for holding and heating type for titling book covers. The latter is also called a *lettering pallet* or *typeholder.* See also *Fillet; Roll.*

Papyrus. A writing material made from the pith of a giant sedge found in the region of the Nile and used by the ancient Egyptians, Greeks and Romans. It was made by placing strips of pith (the nearer the centre the higher the quality) in a row and then overlaying them with another row placed at right angles to the first. These were moistened and beaten or pressed, a process which released natural gum and provided adhesion. The earliest extant specimen was found in a tomb of c. 3000 B.C.

Parchment. See *Vellum.*

Paring Knife. A variety of knives is used for paring leather, depending on the preferences of the individual binder. See *Lifting*

Knife for the best readily available kind of steel. For paring and bevelling the edges of leather, the paring knife (sometimes called an *edging knife*) shown in figure 15 is often used, although some binders prefer the *French paring knife*, which has a handle and a broader blade. For the overall paring of leather, many binders today use the *Spokeshave*.

Paring Stone. Used by the binder for shaping and paring leather, or for any other operations which require a smooth, hard surface. It must be sufficiently heavy so as not to move about when leaned against while one is working. The tools shown in figure 4 are lying on the surface of a typical paring stone.

Pasteboard. In popular use, a term often applied to any stiff board or cardboard of medium thickness. It originally meant boards formed by laminating or pasting together a number of sheets of waste paper. See also *Boards*.

Pastedown. That part of the *Endpapers* pasted down on to the inside of the cover board (see Frontispiece). It is sometimes referred to as the *board paper*, or the *endpaper (singular)*. If it is laid down independently of, and is separate from, the *Flyleaf*, it is called a *doublure* (doublures are often made of materials other than paper, such as leather, vellum, or silk). The pastedown is also called the *end lining, end sheet (singular)*, or *lining paper*.

Paste-grain. Usually *Skiver* leather with a distinctive grain made possible by pasting and drying the surface to form a kind of glaze. The grain and texture of paste-grain leather are shown in figure 12.

Paste Papers. Papers on which the decorative designs have been made with paste to which colouring matter has been added.

Paste Wash. Paste thinned with water. The consolidation of a powdery or rough leather surface can be obtained by means of a wash-over with a paste wash. Great care needs to be exercised in the selection of bindings for this treatment, however, as it may blacken some leathers. It also tends to harden the leather and prevent the penetration of dressing, so this treatment is more suitable for leather on the sides than for the spine and joints.

P.I.R.A. (Printing Industries Research Association) Test. This is an accelerated age test for vegetable-tanned leather which involves treating a specimen of leather with large amounts of sulphuric acid and hydrogen peroxide. If the test piece emerges from this treatment blackened and gelatinized, the skin from which it came is likely to deteriorate in a polluted atmosphere containing sulphur dioxide. However, a long-term storage programme has raised doubts as to the validity of the test.

Platen. The moving plate in a press, such as a standing or nipping press.

Plough (Plow). A device for the trimming of books and boards. It consists of two parallel blocks of wood connected by one large screw with a handle. The left-hand part of the plough fits into a runner on the left cheek of the *Cutting Press* and the other side of the plough carries an adjustable knife which is gradually moved inward by the turn of a screw and slices into the book or board as the plough is moved back and forth (see fig. 8). The plough has been in use since the early years of the sixteenth century, during which time there have been few improvements. However, during the last two years the design of ploughs has been considerably advanced to make it a much more precise tool. In this, only the knife and not the whole right-hand side of the plough moves as the book is trimmed.

Potassium Lactate. Used here to mean an aqueous solution of potassium lactate and a fungicide. It acts as a protective salt for leather to prevent acid damage and fungus attack. (See page 67 for the recommended formula.) It is likely to decline, shortly, in favour of other treatments, for details of which see pages 58–60.

Pressing Boards. Flat boards made of wood (either solid or laminated) or fibreboard used to ensure even pressure when books are placed in a press. (Pressing boards may be seen in use in fig. 66.)

Pressing Tins. Thin metal plates used during pressing, mainly to exert local pressure at those places which would not otherwise receive it; for example, when a book is pressed after the turn-ins have been stuck down, tins are placed between the boards and the book. Another use for pressing tins may be seen in figure 66.

Pulling. Reducing a sewn book to loose sections (or in the case of adhesive bindings, to loose leaves) by removing the entire cover, the endpapers, the headbands, the lining on the backbone, the cords or thongs, and the thread (or adhesive). Pulling is sometimes referred to as *taking down*.

PVA. Used here to mean polyvinyl acetate emulsion adhesive.

Quarter Bindings. Bindings in which the backbone and a small portion of the sides are covered with one kind of material, and the rest of the sides, including the corners, with another (in very early bindings, the rest of the boards were left uncovered). See also *Full, Half,* and *Three-quarter Bindings.*

Quarto. See *Folio.*

Quire. One twentieth of a ream of paper; 25 sheets in the case of a 500-sheet ream, or 24 sheets of a 480-sheet ream. The term is also synonymous with *Section.*

Raised Bands. See *Bands.*

Rebacking. Renewal or replacement of the leather or other covering material on the spine and joints of a book.

Recessed Bands. See *Bands.*

Re-covering. A book is said to be re-covered when it is provided with a new cover without being resewn, or when new covering material is put on the old boards.

Red Decay (Red Rot). Deterioration of leather in the form of red powdering, found particularly in East India leathers prepared with tanning of the catechol group.

Resizing. The process of passing paper which has become too soft and absorbent through a bath of sizing—usually gelatine or vellum size (the latter is made by boiling scraps of vellum). When advisable, the size may be brushed on or sprayed instead of immersing the leaf in it. The use of these sizes restores strength, abrasion resistance, and "rattle" to the paper, and the water in the size also often removes water stains. A soft size is provided by

Carboxy Methyl Cellulose (CMC). Nylon size is sometimes used for resizing, particularly for very weak paper which cannot be immersed in water, or which would become brittle when resized with gelatine. *Klucel G* is also coming into use for this purpose. See also *Nylon Size; Sizing*.

Roll. A revolving wheel-type tool similar to the *Fillet*, but the working surface is broader. It has raised designs on it and is used to impress repetitive patterns on book covers (see fig. 6). Sometimes (incorrectly) the terms "fillet" and "roll" are used synonymously.

Rough Calf. Calfskin used with the flesh side outwards.

Rounding. The hammering or manipulation of the backbone of a book into a convex shape preparatory to backing (see fig. 41). Rounding accommodates the swelling caused by the thickness of the sewing threads, and also helps to prevent the backbone from falling into a concave shape after years of use or of standing upright on a shelf. See also *Backing*.

Russia Leather. Originally made from calfskin, and later from cowhide, it has a reddish-brown colour, a fairly smooth surface, and a characteristic odour resulting from its impregnation with oil of birch-bark. Almost invariably it is "diced," that is, it has a light latticework of crisscrossing diagonal lines impressed into its surface. This leather was much used in England during the second half of the eighteenth century and the early decades of the nineteenth, but is now seldom used. The early genuine russia leather was a durable material, but later imitations have proved to be very inferior in this respect. The grain and texture of diced russia leather are shown in figure 12.

Scalpel. A small, straight knife sometimes made with thin, changeable blades of various shapes. Used primarily in surgery, it is also a useful cutting tool for delicate bindery work. (A scalpel is shown in fig. 4.)

Section. A number of leaves gathered together, folded (usually), and treated as a single binding unit. Bibliographers often call this a *gathering* or *quire*. See also *Signature*.

Sewing Frame. A piece of wooden equipment used to hold the cords or tapes taut while the leaves or sections of a book are sewn to them. It consists of a flat horizontal platform with an upright at each end connected by a movable crossbar. The cords or tapes are stretched between the crossbar and the platform. It may be of a simple, rigid, box-like construction, but those which have threaded uprights to enable the height of the crossbar to be adjusted are more convenient to use. (A sewing frame is shown in fig. 10, and one is shown in use in fig. 32.)

Shelfback. See *Spine.*

Shellac Varnish. Shellac dissolved in denatured alcohol. Commonly referred to simply as "shellac" in the United States.

Shell Gold. See *Gold.*

Shoulder. See *Outer Joint.*

Side-sewing, Side-stitching. See *Stab-sewing.*

Signature. Sometimes used as a synonym for *Section,* but more accurately refers to the letter or figure often placed at the bottom of the first leaf, or early leaves (e.g., Ci, Cii, Ciii, Civ), of each section as an aid to the binder in assembling these leaves and sections into correct sequence.

Silicon Release Paper. Paper siliconized on both sides. It withstands the application of heat and is more effective than wax paper as a non-sticking material.

Silk Chiffon. See *Silk Gauze.*

Silk Gauze. A very thin, transparent, finely meshed silk cloth, quite strong; often used in bookbinding for the reinforcement of paper and other materials. Also called *crêpeline* or *silk chiffon.*

Sizing. The addition of materials, either to the paper pulp or to impregnate the paper after it is made, to strengthen it and to impart certain other desired characteristics, such as resistance

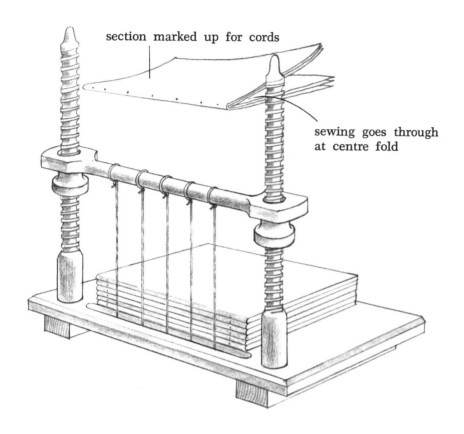

section marked up for cords

sewing goes through
at centre fold

Fig. 10. Sewing frame.

to the penetration or surface-spreading of inks, and resistance to abrasion. See also *Nylon Size; Resizing.*

Skiver. Leather made from the outer, or hair, side of a split skin —usually sheepskin.

Slips. The loose ends of the cords, thongs, or tapes upon which the book has been sewn. These ends are used to attach the boards to the body of the book. They may be pasted down to the boards, or they may be carried through holes in the board, in which case they are said to be *laced-in* (see fig. 54). Occasionally, they are glued into boards which have been split horizontally (see fig. 3).

Solander Case. An elaborate book-form protective container for loose plates, maps, books, pamphlets, etc., with a hinged lid and hinged back or fore edge.

Spencer Wells Forceps. A surgical instrument somewhat similar to stork-nosed pliers. Useful for getting a grip on curved needles. (Spencer Wells forceps are shown in fig. 4, and may be seen in use in fig. 21.)

Spine. The portion of the cover which covers the backbone of a book (see Frontispiece). Sometimes also referred to as the *backstrip* or *shelfback*. See also *Backbone*.

Spirit Stain. See *Stains*.

Spokeshave. A small plane with end handles, originally used by wheelwrights for shaping the spokes of wheels, but used in bookbinding for paring leather. (A spokeshave is shown in fig. 4, and one is shown in use in fig. 55.)

Spring Dividers. A two-legged, compass-like measuring device the setting of which is controlled by a spring and a set-screw (see fig. 4).

Sprinkling. This term is used to indicate the sprinkling or spattering of irregularly shaped spots or splotches of colouring matter on leather covers (usually calf or sheep), or on the edges of the leaves, to achieve a decorative effect. (A method of sprinkling is shown in fig. 93.)

Squares. The portions of the covers of a book which project beyond the edges of the leaves (see Frontispiece).

Stab-sewing. A form of sewing (or stitching) in which the thread, or wire, or other material, passes through the entire body of the book from the front to the back (see fig. 2). Also called *side-sewing*, or *side-stitching*.

Stains. A stain is a suspension or solution of dye or colouring matter in a vehicle. The major difference between stains and other colouring agents is that stains have little or no opacifying power. Thus, when applied to leather, stains impart colour while permitting the grain or texture of the leather to show through. The two types of stain most frequently used in colouring leather in restoration work are *spirit stains*, which are dyes dissolved in methylated spirit, and *water-soluble stains,* which are dyes dissolved in water. The kind of dyes most often used today for this purpose are the synthetic dyes, such as those made from aniline. Spirit stains tend to have greater penetrating power and are faster drying than water-soluble stains. Both types are available in powdered form or as prepared solutions.

Stamping. See *Tooling.*

Standing Press. A heavy vertical press with a platen raised and lowered by a central iron screw, in which books are piled and pressed (see figs. 13 and 65).

Straight Grain (Morocco). Goatskin with creases in one direction on the hair side. Originally, the creasing was done by moistening the leather and boarding it, but a similar effect is now obtained by plating the skins with a heated, engraved steel plate. (For a description of boarding and plating, see page 60.) The grain and texture of a straight grain goatskin are shown in figure 12. See also *Hard Grain (Morocco); Morocco Leather.*

Strawboard. An inexpensive board which is made mostly from macerated straw and comes from Holland. See also *Boards.*

Stuck-on Headbands. In the sixteenth to eighteenth centuries these were strips of vellum embroidered with thread on the top edge by hand, and were used principally in Germany. The centre part was pasted or glued (not sewn) to the backbone of the book, and the ends, on which there was no embroidery, were stuck either to the inside or the outside of the boards. In later varieties, the ends were cut off flush with the joints and were not stuck to the boards. The early nineteenth-century type of stuck-on headband consisted of cloth folded over string. The present-day stuck-on headband is machine woven to approximate the appearance of the hand-embroidered headband. (See figs. 46E and 46F.) See also *Headband.*

Sunk Joints. See *French Joints.*

Super. See *Mull.*

Swelling. The extra thickness of the body of a book at the backbone caused by the sewing threads (and the guarding paper, or cloth, if any).

Tail. The end of the book at the bottom of the page (see Frontispiece). Sometimes referred to as the *foot.* See also *Head.*

Tailband. See *Headband.*

Tailcap. See *Headcap.*

Taking Down. See *Pulling.*

Tawed Leather. See *Alum-tawed Leather.*

Tenon Saw. A small hand-saw, sometimes called a *backsaw,* characterized by a deep, thin blade with very fine teeth. Used to saw grooves in the backbones of books for the recessing of cords (and also for making small openings in the back folds of the sections for the thread used in making the kettle-stitches).

Thames Board. A soft British cover board made from low-grade mixed waste paper. Also called *chipboard.*

Thongs. Narrow strips of leather on which the sections of most books were sewn between the tenth century and the end of the sixteenth century. See also *Bands.*

Three-quarter Bindings. Bindings in which the backbone, the corners, and a variable but fairly large (more than one-quarter) portion of the sides are covered with one kind of material, and the rest of the sides with another. In a true three-quarter binding, the material on the sides and the corners very nearly meet. See also *Full, Half,* and *Quarter Bindings.*

Thrown-back Boards. Book boards in the open position.

Thymol. A crystalline material derived from thyme oil and other oils, or made synthetically, used as a preservative for paste and as a fungicide for mildewed books. It may be applied as a solution in alcohol or vaporized for use as a fumigant.

Tight Back. A book construction in which the spine of the cover is stuck down to the backbone (with or without intermediate linings), in contrast to the hollow-backed book in which the spine is free of the backbone. The backbone of a tight-backed book may be more or less flexible, that is, it may "throw up" or arch to a greater or lesser degree when the book is opened, depending upon the number of *Back Linings,* if any, the thickness of the paper (or the sections) in the main body of the book (see fig. 20), and the method of sewing used. See also *Hollow Back.*

Tight Joints. Tight-jointed books are those in which the cover boards are placed flush with the shoulders. See also *French Joints.*

Tipping On (or *Tipping In*). The attachment of one leaf to another by means of a narrow strip of adhesive along one edge. This technique is also used to attach maps, loose plates, and so forth.

Tooling. The process of decorating leather or other materials with hand finishing tools, such as *Rolls, Fillets, Pallets, Gouges,* and other small decorative tools, all of which are applied to the surface of the material with hand pressure. When this is done without the use of ink, gold leaf, foil, or other colouring materials, it is called *blind tooling.* The similar impression of designs by means of a machine instead of by hand is called *blocking* (in Great Britain) and *stamping* (in the United States).

Turkey Leather. Goatskin imported from Turkey and used by English binders to a limited extent in the sixteenth century and first half of the seventeenth. It was used on nearly all the finely gold-tooled bindings of the Restoration and until the 1720s when *Morocco Leather,* which has a less distinctive grain, gradually came into use.

Turn-in. That part of the covering material which is turned over the edges of the boards from the outside to the inside at the head, tail, and fore edges of the book (see Frontispiece). Sometimes also called the *turnover.*

Turnover. See *Turn-in.*

Two Along. See *Two-sections-on.*

Two On. See *Two-sections-on.*

Two On and One Off and Two On and Two Off. See *One On and One Off, etc.*

Two-sections-on. A method of sewing a book (except for a few sections at front and back) in which one length of thread secures two sections by passing between them at various points (see fig. 34). This is done to minimize the amount of thread used in sewing, and therefore to reduce the swelling of the backbone where that would be a problem, or sometimes merely to save time and labour. In the eighteenth century some thick folios with thin sections were sewn with as many as seven-sections-on. Two-sections-on is often known as sewing *two-on, two-sheets-on,* or *two-along.* As distinguished from sewing *All-along.*

Tying Down. Hand-sewn headbands are "tied down" when the thread used to form them is passed through the backbone to a point below (or above, in the case of the tailband) the kettle-stitch and then taken back up and wound around the core of the headband once more (see fig. 45). This helps to anchor them firmly to the backbone.

Tying Up. In hand binding, the operation of winding a cord around a new cover on both sides of raised bands to ensure the adhesion of the leather (see figs. 57 and 58).

Tying-up Boards. Thin but sturdy boards with right-angle projections, used for protecting the sides and fore edges of the boards when the tying up operation is being performed. (Tying-up boards are shown in fig. 4 and they are also shown in use in figs. 57 and 58.)

Typeholder. See *Pallet.*

Vellum. An animal skin that has been treated with lime and stretched and scraped rather than tanned. The skins are sometimes split (sliced horizontally into two layers), one layer of which is finished on both sides for use as a writing material. Such split skins, most commonly sheepskins, are called *parchment.*

(The terms "parchment" and "vellum" are sometimes used interchangeably.)

Vulpex. A liquid soap (potassium methylcyclohexyloleate), sold in concentrated form and diluted with water or *White Spirit*. It is a very effective cleanser for gold tooling and leather.

Water-soluble Stains. See *Stains*.

Whipstitching. See *Oversewing*.

White Spirit. A petroleum distillate used as a substitute for turpentine.

Wood Paste. Made from finely ground wood meal mixed with wheat paste. Used for filling in cracks or holes in boards, or for building up the corners of boards.

Wove Paper. Paper having a fairly even pattern, or mesh. It is made on a closely woven mould and lacks the distinctive widely spaced lines, or ribbing, of *Laid Paper*.

Wrapper. 1. Formerly, a temporary paper covering for books designed to protect them until they could be put into a permanent binding. 2. The paper cover of a book such as the modern paper-backed book. 3. A book jacket.

3 Workshop Tools, Equipment, and Materials

Book restoration can be practised in a fairly small area—a well-equipped shop including all essential supplies and equipment can be fitted into a room measuring about 22 by 16 feet—but good lighting and a substantial floor are essential. The restorer should work in front of a window if possible, have an electric light above the bench (preferably with adjustable elevation) and supplement this with an adjustable lamp on a long arm fixed to the wall where it will be out of the way. Long-tube or strip lighting of any kind (such as fluorescent tubing) is best avoided because it tends to eliminate helpful shadows. Some form of heating should be available for making paste, etc., and running water should be situated close by. It is very important, however, that the room itself should be dry (no more than approximately 65 percent relative humidity and not less than 50 percent).

A large selection of tools, equipment, and bits and pieces of material, old and new, needs to be kept in stock for a full range of work, otherwise one is likely to be delayed and frustrated quite frequently. Stocking of the bare essentials only is false economy and encourages the use of inappropriate materials, with consequent detriment to the craftsman's work.

The following is not intended to be a complete list of materials and equipment needed for a hand bindery, but is only for the purpose of listing and commenting on the principal items needed to carry out the kind of work described in this volume.

Adhesives. The following adhesives are those most often used in restoration work.

1. Glaire. White of egg has been used for making glaire for gold tooling for about 500 years, but shellac glaire is becoming increasingly popular because it is more convenient to use.

Egg glaire is prepared by mixing the white of an egg with a few drops of vinegar. This mixture is beaten up and then allowed to stand overnight, after which it is strained through fairly fine muslin into a bottle for use. Alternatively, egg albumen crystals can be soaked in water (one part of crystals to four of water) overnight and then strained off for use. Egg glaire works satisfactorily long after it has putrefied, but admittedly the odour is highly objectionable.

Shellac glaire can be obtained in liquid form ready for use. Although there are a number of products on the market, I like and always use the "B.S. Glaire" developed by W. H. Langwell and sold by Russell Bookcrafts.

2. Paste. Historically, most pastes have been formulated from raw or modified starches or dextrins obtained from various plants, such as wheat, maize (corn), potato, sago, rice, and tapioca. They normally form brittle films if not carefully used, and can cause warping due to the swelling and subsequent contraction of the

material to which they are applied. By compounding with humectants such as glycerine or sorbitol, non-warp pastes can be obtained, but they are never as truly flexible as some other adhesives, and the addition of these materials to paste may sacrifice some of its more desirable bookbinding characteristics. Pastes penetrate into the materials to which they are applied more readily and dry more slowly than most other adhesives. For this reason they are often preferred for many hand-binding operations. Properly made, they have excellent adhesive qualities. Modern pastes of completely synthetic materials are available, but hand bookbinders have traditionally used paste made from plain wheat flour and have found it eminently satisfactory for many purposes, and it has the advantage over some synthetic adhesives that it is easily reversible.

Cold-water wheat paste can be made in a few moments by mixing ready-made paste powder into cold water. This paste is satisfactory for bookbinding purposes, but if one wishes to be absolutely certain of the purity of the adhesive it is better to boil one's own wheat flour or wheat starch paste. I prefer the working qualities of wheat flour paste for most operations. Experience would indicate that paste made in this way can last for many centuries, and the process takes little time.

Many binders make paste in the proportions of 340g (12 ounces) of plain white wheat flour to 2 litres (about 70 ounces) of water, but my own preference is for a thicker paste with about 25 percent more flour (425g) to the same amount of water. Some of this paste can always be removed from the pot and thinned down with water for those binding operations which require a thinner paste.

When boiling one's own paste, the flour should be beaten into cold water in a saucepan and stirred constantly while it is being brought to the boil. If it is not stirred, the bottom layer is certain to burn. 10g of loose thymol crystals mixed into paste made with about 2 litres of water will prevent mould from forming for a period of ten days or so, depending on the temperature and humidity. The thymol should be mixed in only after the paste has cooled to a temperature of not more than 120 degrees Fahrenheit, because thymol vaporizes to some extent at higher temperatures. The thymol will not melt below 110 degrees Fahrenheit. Instead of mixing the thymol directly into the paste, an easier method is to dissolve it first into a small quantity of methylated spirit. If fresh paste is made frequently, the addition of thymol is not necessary. A little cold water poured on to the surface of newly made paste will prevent the formation of a skin.

3. Glue. Although many adhesives are called glue, strictly speaking the term refers only to those adhesives made of protein derived from the collagen in animal hides and bones. These adhesives also eventually form brittle films; therefore they are almost always plasticized with humectants. Being protein materials, they are subject to deterioration, and various forms of bactericides and fungicides are often added during the manufacturing process. Glue is a surface adhesive, that is, it does not penetrate readily into the material to which it is applied. It usually sets fairly rapidly, but retains some degree of flexibility over a relatively long period of time. For this latter reason, it is often used in hand bookbinding for gluing up the backbone, because it facilitates the shaping and moulding of the backbone during the rounding and backing operations.

4. Synthetic resin adhesives. There is an enormous variety of adhesives based on synthetic resins available today. The ones of most interest to bookbinders and restorers are perhaps the polyvinyl acetate (PVA) emulsions.

Polyvinyl acetate is a hard, clear, synthetic resin. It is formed from single vinyl acetate molecules (called monomers) chemically linked together into long, chain-like molecules (called polymers) in a process known as polymerization.

As used here, the term PVA refers to the so-called emulsion form of polyvinyl acetate which consists of a fine dispersion of the vinyl acetate polymers in water. Like many modern water-based house paints, the liquid emulsion can be thinned with water, but once the adhesive has dried it becomes soluble only in organic solvents such as acetone, ethanol, and toluene.

Pure PVA adhesive films are rather brittle by bookbinding standards. They can be given the desired flexibility by adding "plasticizers." These substances often have the property of volatilizing or migrating out of the film, however, eventually leaving it brittle once more. In addition, some plasticizers may be harmful to paper or other bookbinding materials. A better way to give PVA flexibility is to copolymerize it with certain other monomers during the manufacturing process. The resulting copolymer is said to be "internally plasticized" and has the desired flexibility characteristics built into its molecule; these characteristics are therefore highly stable for long periods of time under ordinary conditions. Provided their acidity is sufficiently low, such copolymer PVA emulsions can be expected to be quite durable as well as non-damaging to paper and other bookbinding materials. Properly compounded, they also have excellent bonding qualities on a wide variety of surfaces, and they can be formulated with a wide range of properties to meet the various needs of bookbinders and restorers.

One fairly recent development should perhaps be mentioned. As we said earlier, once dry, PVA is soluble only in certain organic solvents. An adhesive which is closely related to PVA is polyvinyl alcohol (sometimes called PVOH). This adhesive is soluble in water after it has dried, but it does not have some of the other desirable properties that PVA adhesives have. However, PVA can be altered chemically so that its properties fall somewhere between those of true PVA and PVOH. The resulting adhesive is somewhat redispersible in water, although it does not truly dissolve. These adhesives therefore may be of interest to restorers, although it must be pointed out that at this date it is not certain how long they will retain their various desirable properties.

As more of these new synthetic adhesives are developed, they may well begin to supplant some of the more traditional adhesives used by hand bookbinders, and to some extent they already have.

Backing Boards. Three sizes, ranging from the longest which will go into the press down to about 8 inches in length, should be sufficient for most purposes. A smoothing plane needs to be used from time to time to restore the edges of wooden backing boards when they are damaged by the edge of the hammer face. Metal-edged backing boards are available, but these are not entirely satisfactory because inadvertent contact between the hammer and the boards can sever the sewing cords, and conscious efforts to avoid this can result in the inadequate consolidation of the backbone. This difficulty does not arise in the case of tape-sewn books, but even with these books the use of metal-edged boards is not recommended.

Band Nippers. It is best to have nickel-plated nippers or those made of some non-rusting material so that they will not stain the leather.

Bandsticks. A variety of widths should be kept on hand. Their surfaces should be kept smooth, so that they will not roughen the surfaces of new leather.

Bath Brick. This material (described on page 13) is used to degrease the surface of gold cushions. After a period of scarcity it is now in more plentiful supply.

Bench or Table. The larger and more substantial, the better.

Benzine (petroleum benzin). Used to clean off the last traces of surplus gold after gold rubbers have been used. (*Benzine* should not be confused with *benzene.* Both of these substances are inflammable, but benzene is toxic as well, and breathing its vapours could be dangerous.)

Board Cutter. A table model with a 30-inch blade will do for most light work, but a heavy iron cutter standing on its own legs is highly desirable. In the latter case the cutter should have a clamp operated by a foot treadle so that both hands are left free to handle the material and to operate the cutting blade (see fig. 11).

Boards. The principal kinds of board suitable for bookbinders' use are:

1. Millboard. Genuine, hand-made rope-fibre millboards are no longer made. The present product (called binder's board in the United States) is made on a machine with high-grade wastepaper and, when milled, is quite tough and serviceable. Heavy rope-fibre board was not made until just before 1700, so, even if available, this type of millboard should not be used to replace the missing boards of a book of earlier date. Four thicknesses of millboard will be found useful: .063, .092, .116, and .144 inch. (In the United States equivalent thicknesses of binder's board are .060, .088, .120, and .146 inch.) Acid-free millboard is currently available in Britain.

2. Strawboard. This board is lighter in weight and more flexible than millboard. It has the disadvantage of being brittle, but this can be overcome to some extent if the corners are reinforced with

thin vellum. Strawboard is less likely than millboard to be affected by a contaminated atmosphere.

3.   Thames board (chipboard). Thames board is softer and less brittle than strawboard. Its softness and impermanence render it unsuitable for use in bindings, but it is handy for such things as protecting the end leaves of a book when it is being pressed, and for similar bindery operations.

4.   Pasteboard. The old pasteboard, made of laminated sheets or pulped paper, cannot be purchased today but it can be made or it can be acquired from abandoned bindings.

All old boards which are in good condition or which can be cut down should be kept for future use (particularly old pasteboard and rope-fibre millboard), because the weight, flexibility, and surface texture of these boards cannot be found in modern materials.

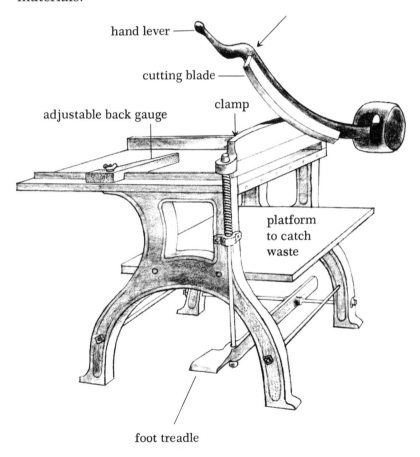

Fig. 11.   Board cutter.

Brushes. For pasting and gluing, round ones, with 1¾- and 2-inch diameters are recommended. Smaller brushes are available, and inexperienced workers may find them easier to use, but the larger brushes save time.

Cabinet. A small table cabinet with many small drawers or trays is useful for the temporary preservation of labels, bookplates, old leather spines, and the like which have to be replaced on the bindings after the repairs have been completed. If ten or twenty books are being worked on concurrently, small items such as these are easily lost. In any case it is a sound plan not to dispose of floor sweepings for some time after a job is finished so that there is a reasonable opportunity to look for missing fragments.

Cloth. A range of colours in high-quality bookbinding cloths should be stocked for the repair of cloth sides. One or two dozen yards of each kind will suffice if the bindery is small. Cloth from the sides of discarded bindings should be preserved. Many of the Victorian embossed grains, for example, cannot now be matched, so material of this kind is useful for the repair of the sides of early nineteenth-century covers.

A good quantity of cloths, such as mull, jaconet, etc., used for repairing, reinforcing, or lining should be kept on hand. As with all materials used in restoration work, only the best quality should be obtained. The use of cheap or unsuitable materials nearly always proves to be false economy in the long run.

Cord. Used for forming the recessed or raised bands on which books are sewn. It is very important that nothing but the best quality be used. Flax cord is preferable because its fibres fray out readily and with minimum loss when making slips, but the range of thicknesses is very limited, at present, so on some occasions they have to be used in combination. The best available cord sems to be Barbour's Flax Seaming Twine, 4/8, 6/8, and 8/8.

Cotton Wool (absorbent cotton). In addition to a variety of other uses, this material is much used for staining leather and for transferring gold leaf from the gold cushion to the prepared leather surface.

Finishing Press. A press with 18 inches between the screws can be used for most of the books one is likely to encounter. Even if the book is too long to go down between the screws it is often possible to grip it in the space above the screws.

Finishing Stove. These stoves can be heated by either gas or electricity. Gas stoves are handier because the heat can be more finely adjusted, and the tools used for decorating, lettering, and so forth, can be held in the centre opening and heated in seconds, but electric ones are cleaner because they are fume-free. A simple hot plate can be adapted, but the expense of buying a standard-model finishing stove is well justified.

Finishing Tools. It is not possible to have too many rolls, fillets, gouges, pallets, and small decorative tools engraved with designs of all periods. Everything except duplicates should be kept because even the most unlikely looking tools are useful sooner or later. Since only part of such a tool may be required, the tool may have to be tipped over slightly on to one end so that only part of the design is impressed into the leather. Tools which are damaged or worn and are of no use to binders producing new work are often acceptable to restorers, who aim at a different standard of finish. New, sharply cut tools often produce the wrong effect in restoration work.

Flour. Plain white wheat flour for making paste.

Folders. A busy craftsman frequently mislays them, so have many at hand. Some hand binders prefer the traditional bone folders, but the better plastic ones are quite serviceable.

G-clamp. Many professional binders and restorers keep their leather in position while they are paring it by applying body pressure against that part of the skin which overlaps the paring stone. If the restorer prefers not to do this, or if the piece of leather is too small, it can be held in position by means of the G-clamp, with a small piece of millboard placed between the surface of the clamp and the leather. A clamp with a 3-inch opening will fit on to virtually all working surfaces.

Glaire. See under *Adhesives.*

Glass Paper. **Various** grades of glass paper and/or sandpaper should be kept on hand. These materials have many uses in bookbinding.

Glue. See under *Adhesives.*

Glue Pot. This should have an inside diameter of about 5½ inches. Various types of glue pots are available, either electrically or gas heated. The cheapest and simplest kind consists of a well for the glue which fits into a water container in a kind of double-boiler arrangement. This stands on a gas ring or electric plate for heating. An iron inner pot should not be used, as the iron may catalyse deteriorative chemical reactions in the glue. Some electric glue heaters are waterless and thermostatically controlled.

Gold. Gold leaf should always be used in preference to foil when one is working on old bindings because foil produces entirely the wrong effect, excellent though the medium is for other purposes, such as lettering or blocking cloth and paper.

Gold Cushion. Sixteen by six inches is a useful size. The cutting of gold leaf can be done more efficiently if the leather surface of the cushion is rubbed occasionally with *Bath Brick,* some other good scouring powder, or a jeweller's abrasive powder (of which there are many grades) to eliminate grease and provide a good cutting surface.

Gold Rubber. This rubber can be bought from bookbinders' suppliers ready for use, but if necessary the binder can prepare his own by soaking pure rubber in a small quantity of paraffin oil (kerosene) to soften it. This should then be allowed to dry out until it is no longer gummy. Too great a quantity of paraffin oil will cause the rubber to liquefy.

The gold can be recovered by a refiner when an appreciable amount has been absorbed into the rubber.

Gravy Browning. The gravy browning referred to here is a proprietary product made in Great Britain (Crosse & Blackwell Ltd.), and consists simply of caramel (sugar colouring, or burnt sugar) with a little salt added. Other types of products are sold for adding colour and flavour to gravies for cooking purposes. Most of these products contain various herbs, spices, and seasonings. The author has not had occasion to use these products and so cannot recommend their use.

Hammers. A broad-faced shoemaker's or cobbler's type will be found useful for many purposes. A small hammer with a ¾-inch face is useful for backing books sewn on raised cords, but if one is careful, a larger hammer can be used for this purpose.

Handle Letters. Some of the modern type-characters look well on modern bindings, but are out of place when used for the relabelling of old bindings. Therefore, care should be taken to stock alphabets which are in sympathy with, or at least do not clash with, bindings of earlier periods. At least four sets are needed for basic requirements, but twenty-four to thirty sets of various sizes and faces are necessary for a full range of work. If handle letters are not available, cast and machine-cut brass or bronze type can be used individually in an electrically heated handle adapted for the purpose, as also can ordinary lead type. Lettering in this manner is necessarily slower than using handle letters, but the range of available alphabets is much greater. As a general rule it is preferable not to use the standard pallet or type-holder, which enables one to tool an entire line of type in one impression, except perhaps on very large sets of books, and they should certainly not be used on bindings dating before the eighteenth century. If type has to be used, it looks better letterspaced and in worn condition so that the impression does not look too flat and sharp.

Headbanding Material. Fairly substantial silk thread in a range of colours should be stocked; very fine thread is not frequently required. Binders' linen sewing thread can be used on most early bindings. Useful thicknesses are No. 25-3 cord for small books, No. 18-3 cord for medium-sized books, and No. 16-3 cord for large books. Some of the linen thread of each grade should be stained in various colours with spirit stain so that, if desirable, headbands with alternating strands of stained and unstained thread can be made.

Thin leather pasted to vellum (off-cuts or waste pieces can be used and then cut into strips as required) makes a good headband foundation for some bindings dating from the early nineteenth century, but firm cord is best for earlier books. Limp cord is difficult and irritating to use because it bends too easily while the headband is being worked, but if nothing better is available it can be stiffened by being rubbed over with thick paste or PVA and dried.

Machine-made stuck-on headbands are available in several widths, and in a variety of patterns.

Hypodermic Needle and Syringe. These are used in restoration for inserting paste or other adhesives into parts of the binding which are inaccessible by other means. Fine needles are useless because only very thin adhesives will pass through them. The largest ones made for medical purposes are suitable and do not make too large a hole in leather. Even larger needles intended for veterinary use can be used for squirting thick adhesives down the backs of tight-backed books to make the leather spine adhere more firmly if it is coming away from the backbone.

Klucel G. Hydroxypropycellulose dissolved in ethanol, isopropanol, industrial methylated spirit or water, used for the impregnation and consolidation of powdery leather. Also useful as a fixative and strengthening size for very weak and brittle paper.

Knives. A good assortment of paring knives, lifting knives, gold knives, and general-purpose knives should be kept on hand. General-purpose knives have many uses, including cutting materials to size and scraping decayed leather off the backs of books. When using a gold knife, one should never touch the blade with the fingers so that oil or grease will not be picked up from the skin.

Knocking-down Irons. In addition to the primary purpose for which they are intended, the restorer will find additional use for them as weights. Half a dozen, each measuring about 8 by 3½ inches (or larger, if available), will be found useful. When used as weights, the base of each one should be lined with card, baize (a coarse woollen fabric with a long nap), or other material to prevent it from staining damp paper or leather.

Leather. Good bookbinding leathers are not easy to obtain, and it is imperative that those engaged in the restoration of leather bindings purchase their leather from established, reputable dealers. Many inferior products are on the market. These leathers are made from poor skins to begin with, and are subsequently tanned or otherwise prepared for use by methods practically guaranteed to produce leathers that do not last well and are virtually useless for fine quality work.

The book restorer has a peculiarly difficult problem in that quite often he is not free to select what he considers to be the most suitable kind of leather for a particular book, but must attempt to match as closely as possible the existing leather on a book which may have been bound centuries ago with leather that is now difficult to find or is simply no longer available. He must keep on hand a good stock of a wide variety of leathers, and must be well acquainted with sources of supply.

A. Alum-tawed Leather

1. Tawed pigskin. This is generally regarded as the most durable leather available for bookbinding. It enjoys the two-fold advantage of high mechanical strength and a built-in ability to withstand the ravages of polluted atmospheres. Tawed skins of various kinds have been made since the days of the ancient Egyptians. The manufacturing process involves soaking the skins in alum and common salt, which makes them snowy white in colour (they gradually turn a creamy colour as they age). This leather is very absorbent and can be coloured with water-soluble dyes without much difficulty, but it is sometimes difficult to pare.

2. Tawed goatskin. This leather is not generally used, but it is available if needed, and is considered by some to be more durable than modern tawed pigskin.

B. Tanned Leather

Most bookbinding leathers are vegetable-tanned, that is, they are tanned with materials derived from natural plants, as opposed to chrome-tanned leathers, which are prepared with chromium salts. Chrome-tanned leathers are extremely durable, physically and chemically, but are difficult to work with, being less supple, and they do not take tooling and decorating nearly as well as vegetable-tanned leathers. They are seldom used for bookbinding purposes, but vegetable-tanned goatskins and calfskins with a small percentage of chrome tannage have come into use in bookbinding in recent years and are thought to have an increased life expectancy. Calfskin so prepared and suitable for the repair and restoration of bindings is made and supplied by G. A. Roberts & Sons Ltd., 2 White's Grounds, Bermondsey, London SE1 3JY.

C. Recent Developments

It has been evident for many years that the use of potassium lactate on new leather, proposed by R. Faraday Innes after his long programme of research in the 1920s and 1930s, does not provide protection against polluted atmospheres to the degree originally anticipated. Some binders, including the present writer, have occasionally found that the leather on their bindings has cracked along the joints and even, in the case of calfskin, become powdery within fifteen or twenty years, which is a depressing state of affairs for a craftsman and an alarming one for those who pay his bills.

When the Conservation Branch in the British Library was formed in 1976 one of the first moves was to instigate a very extensive programme of research into the causes of decay of bookbinding leather, and methods of treating new skins and leather already covering existing bindings. The research was funded by the British Library and conducted by Betty M. Haines of the British Leather Manufacturers' Research Association (BLMRA). The results, published by the Library in 1984, after this book was printed, are far-reaching and of major importance to all who are in any way concerned with bookbinding leather. It would be unwise to quote specified recommendations here because at the time of writing final tests are being conducted at the British Library, but the following is a brief outline of the BLMRA's proposals.

Users of bookbinding leather (for archival purposes) are advised to employ alum-tawed or full chrome-tanned leather, both of which have excellent records for durability. For technical and aesthetic reasons this is not always possible, so the use of vegetable-tanned leather retanned by the manufacturer with aluminium salts is advocated. Exhaustive tests in a gas chamber have indicated that aluminium retannage offers more effective protection against atmospheric pollutants than potassium lactate or citrate.

Although the binder may retan vegetable-tanned leather by immersing the leather in a dilute solution of aluminium triformate or by brushing the solution on the flesh side, it is recommended that the retannage be carried out by the leather manufacturer and that binders purchase aluminium retanned leather. The inadvisability of applying potassium lactate to leather thus retanned with aluminium is emphasized because, as in the case of the semichrome leather now much used by restorers, this can affect the combination of the tannages.

The BLMRA further recommends the use of a wax plasticized polymer, applied as an emulsion to the finished binding as a final polish. This forms a continuous film which, in tests, reduced by 90 percent the absorption of sulphur dioxide into the leather and, as a welcome secondary benefit, prevented change of colour.

In addition to making recommendations for the manufacture of more durable leather, the BLMRA has important advice for the treatment of the vast numbers of books already covered with vegetable-tanned leather, most of which has started to rot. It is claimed that in most cases the treatment will inhibit further deterioration and have a long-lasting effect. The procedure consists of three principal stages:

1.   retannage of vegetable-tanned leather, or of leather which has a vegetable retannage on a mainly chrome tannage, with aluminium triformate;

2.   reinforcement of weakened leather by means of impregnation with a polyurethane; and

3.   coating the surface of the leather with a plasticized polymer.

As a first action it is recommended that the surface of the old leather be cleaned twice with petroleum ether (bp 60–80°C). If the leather also needs to be washed in the normal way there seems to be no reason why this should not be done, provided that it is allowed to dry before proceeding further. Next, aluminium triformate mixed with a certain proportion of methanol is brushed on, the quantity of the solution being carefully related to the area of the leather being treated, rather than to the weight as in the case of unused skins. It is essential to spot-test the binding to check that the alcoholic solution of aluminium triformate does not blacken and embrittle the leather. If it does the retannage stage should be omitted. Some darkening may occur, but this can be minimized if the leather is allowed to dry slowly without the aid of fans or heaters. The retanning with aluminium is said to protect the leather significantly against further deterioration even when this is fairly advanced, a claim which was never made in favour of lactate. Even though, as previously stated, one should not apply lactate to leather which has been retanned with aluminium triformate, tests seem to show that previous use of lactate is unlikely to cause subsequent retanning with aluminium triformate to be ineffective. One is warned that the triformate has a limited shelf-life and should be stored in a refrigerator.

The next stage is reinforcement of the binding's weakened leather with the polyurethane, which is highly penetrative and elastic and which effectively protects the leather against scuffing and absorption of acid. It is diluted with petroleum ether just before use and applied with a small brush. Here, again, the amount applied is calculated in relation to the area of the leather, so two or three applications may be necessary if the prescribed amount is to be absorbed. Excess polyurethane is removed with petroleum ether and then the leather is allowed to "cure" for three days.

Finally, it is recommended that a light coat of plasticized polymer containing wax be brushed over the total area of the binding and then allowed to dry for thirty minutes. When dry, a final rub over with a soft cloth produces a natural patina.

The foregoing, which is only the briefest outline of the important and detailed, but still provisional proposals, is included here merely as an indication of the fundamental changes which are likely to affect all those who manufacture and use bookbinding leather during the next few years.

1. Goatskin. A useful general-purpose leather (often loosely referred to as "Morocco"), with a wide variety of grains. Perhaps the best known are the partly tanned Nigerian skins which are retanned and dyed in England. Native-dyed niger has proved to be a pleasant and durable leather, though in recent years there have been reports of dubious practices in its manufacture by a few tanners. Brick-red is the most common colour of native-dyed niger, and the most useful, but it has an unfortunate tendency to fade.

The surface of straight-grain goatskin is covered with parallel crinkles, produced by the pressure of grained steel plates, in a process called "plating," and the result is very serviceable. The boarded variety of straight-grained leather is produced more naturally by folding the leather over, grain to grain, and then rolling it in one direction with a hand-held board while the leather is wet. This process, known as "boarding," was much used during the closing decades of the eighteenth century and early part of the nineteenth, and in most cases the finish has lasted very well. Boarding in several directions produces a fine pebbly texture known as hard-grain.

The widest possible range of colours and grains of goatskin should be stocked, including hard-grain (with a pin-head or pebbly texture and a hard surface) for the repair of nineteenth-century bindings. Paste-grains (which are sometimes made of other skins than goatskin) are also useful for the repair of some nineteenth-century bindings.

2. Calfskin. The present-day product is much softer and weaker than the leather used three or four hundred years ago, partly because the skins now come from much younger animals. Today, many skins are from animals only two or three days old. The skins usually supplied by tanners are not heavy enough for a great many of the books which need to be repaired, so the tanners must sometimes be asked to provide heavier ones for use on large books.

3. Sheepskin. In its unsophisticated state (when it has not been split, or grained with plates) wool sheepskin has a rather soft surface which tends to be easily abraded, and it can be difficult to prepare for use because of the loose fatty layer which is awkward to pare.

Ideally, wool sheepskin should not be used to repair books, but if thick skins with a firm surface are used and are carefully protected with potassium lactate against acidic atmospheric pollutants, and are then treated with leather dressing, they seem to serve their purpose well enough, especially if the books are not subject to rough handling. The alternative may be to use an unsuitable leather which, because it contrasts with the original skin, is an eyesore.

Hair sheepskin, which comes from the mountainous regions of Africa, India and some other countries, has a tougher, more compact fibre structure and is the better type for bookbinding purposes, but its grain makes it unsuitable for use in rebacking books bound in wool sheepskin. Unfortunately, it is the latter type in which antiquarian books are bound.

It should be noted in passing that some leathers used by bookbinders are supplied unprotected against red decay (red rot) as indicated by the ability to pass the P.I.R.A. test unless the binder specifically requests that they be so protected; therefore it is important that the binder should apply potassium lactate to these leathers both before and after they are put on the book. See also the discussion under *Potassium Lactate* and page 58 for recent advances.

Both thick and thin leathers should be stocked for use on books of various sizes. In general, the larger the book, the thicker the leather should be so as to provide the necessary strength. Where thin leather is called for, as in repairing the joints of small books, it is much better to use leather which is naturally thin, that is, leather from a small skin which was thin to begin with. This is for two reasons. First, it saves one the work of paring; second, and more important, paring tends to weaken leather and to render it less able to withstand the ravages of time and use.

The grain and texture of a variety of bookbinding leathers are shown in figure 12.

Leather Dressing. The recommended mixture, to be used after the application of potassium lactate or citrate solution, consists of 60 percent neat's-foot oil and 40 percent anhydrous lanolin.* It is not claimed that this, or similar preparations, such as the British Museum Leather Dressing, prevent chemical deterioration. All they can do is keep the leather fairly soft and supple and reduce the risk of extensive cracking or powdering. Applied to leather which has already reached an advanced state of deterioration, they can do no more than consolidate the powder and help to improve the appearance of the leather.

The neat's-foot oil and lanolin dressing may be purchased already made, or it may be mixed from ingredients bought from chemical supply houses. See page 58 for revised recommendations.

Lying/Cutting Press (and tub). Almost the oldest piece of equipment used by binders, and certainly the most versatile. This type of press is usually of solid hardwood and is supplied with a track on one side in which a plough can run for trimming book edges or boards. It usually has a screw at each end for tightening or loosening the cheeks, but variant forms are available, including a type with metal cheeks with one central screw, which is often used by professional binders in the United States and France, but to a lesser extent in Great Britain. The longer the press the better, particularly if large folios are likely to be encountered. A

*Carolyn Horton, *Cleaning and Preserving Bindings and Related Materials*, 2nd ed., rev. (Chicago: Library Technology Program, American Library Association, 1969), p. 49.

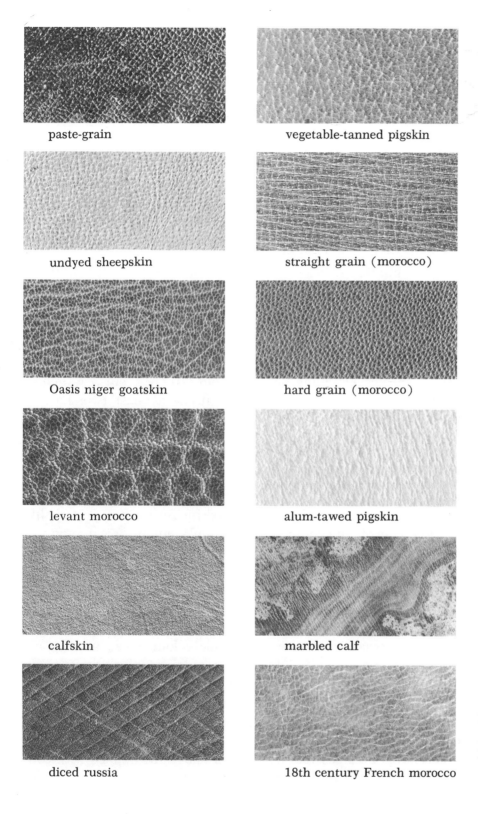

paste-grain

vegetable-tanned pigskin

undyed sheepskin

straight grain (morocco)

Oasis niger goatskin

hard grain (morocco)

levant morocco

alum-tawed pigskin

calfskin

marbled calf

diced russia

18th century French morocco

Fig. 12.

A selection of bookbinding leathers.

press with 24 to 26 inches between the screws is a useful size. When the press is turned over, the other side, which has no runners, can be used for backing and for many other purposes. The "tub" is named after the tub or barrel on which the press rested in early times; today, four-legged stands are more often used.

Methylated Spirit. This has many uses, including the dilution of spirit stains, and a good supply should be kept on hand. It is inflammable, and toxic if swallowed, so must be stored and used with some care.

Nipping Press. This type of press is used when fairly light pressure lasting only a minute or two is required, though it can be used for any length of time. Old copying presses, originally used in offices for letter-copying, are much used by binders. They are usually made of iron. The largest have a platen area of about 24 by 18 inches, but the largest normally available measure about 18 by 12 inches. The maximum clearance between the platen and the base of a nipping press is about 7 inches, but 3½ inches is usual. A man working by himself needs at least two. Larger nipping presses with 22- by 14-inch platens and 15-inch clearances are available.

Paper.
1. Marbled paper. The marbled paper sides or flyleaves of all discarded bindings should be preserved for future use, principally for the repair of inner joints and the replacement or patching up of the damaged sides of books that are not bound in full leather.

The uncombed marbled papers made by the Cockerell Bindery and by Mitchell & Malik in Great Britain look well when used for the re-siding of half bindings of the last quarter of the eighteenth century and the first quarter of the nineteenth. They can be toned down if necessary with a water-soluble colouring agent such as gravy browning or with coffee with a touch of black water-soluble stain in it (or with any one of a number of commercial stains or dyes available on the market), to produce a used or "aged" effect. Spirit stains are more risky, mistakes not being easily corrected, and the use of such stains for this purpose should be avoided whenever possible. The colour should be applied with cotton wool and then immediately rubbed with a wad of dry cotton wool, so that in addition to toning the marbled paper down, some of the marbling colours are rubbed off at the same time, thus reducing their density. A more natural effect is achieved if the colour is rubbed in after the paper has been glued on, because those portions of the paper which overlie edges of the leather will receive more friction and therefore will look more worn than the rest of the sides, and this is more in keeping with genuine old sides.

It should be emphasized that one seldom needs to replace the marbled paper on the outside covers of books. Usually, the only time this is justified is when the book has been stored under damp conditions which have caused the paper to fall off and become lost. Bindings should not be re-sided merely because the original paper is severely rubbed, though the paper corners of quarter bindings or the edges of half or three-quarter bindings where the paper turns in over the boards may sometimes have to be replaced.

Other kinds of decorated papers, such as block-printed papers, paste papers, and sprinkled papers should also be kept on hand.

2. Plain paper. As in the case of marbled paper, nothing should be thrown away, however unlikely its future use may seem. In my experience everything comes in useful sooner or later.

Laid and wove uncoloured paper should be stored separately, and coloured papers should be stored in folders or boxes, one for each colour. This saves much time in the long run. A few suitable high quality hand-made papers designed specially for use with antiquarian books are currently on the market. Among these are Bodleian, Dover and Dover Castle, made by Barcham Green.

3. Repair papers. A good variety of papers used as guarding paper, for the repair of inner joints, for lining backbones, and so forth, should be kept on hand and carefully separated and stored.

In restoration work, one is often confronted with book papers which have deteriorated and have become brittle and discoloured due to the presence of acidic impurities. The restorer is advised to avoid the use of papers of any kind which are highly acidic. Not only are these papers unstable in themselves, but through a phenomenon known as acid migration they may cause damage to adjoining papers or to other bookbinding materials with which they come into contact. If acidic paper must be used for one reason or another, it should first be deacidified.

Paper Cutter. The board cutter will usually serve well enough, but a small paper cutter with a 16- to 18-inch blade and a hand clamp is useful for many small tasks, such as cutting strips of Japanese tissue.

Paring Stone. A large one measuring about 24 by 18 by 2 inches is desirable, and the surface needs to be very smooth. The special stones used for lithographic printing are now much less used by printers than formerly, and they are becoming difficult to obtain. Plate glass and slabs of marble can be used instead, but these are decidedly second-best. Marble, unless it is very thick, has a tendency to crack or split under pressure, and using a hammer or other heavy tools on a glass surface can be risky. If glass must be used, the edges should be ground down to prevent the worker from cutting himself.

Paste. See under *Adhesives*.

Paste Tub. Should have an inside diameter of about 8 inches. The paste can be kept in the container in which it is prepared, but it is better to transfer it to a wooden, ceramic, or stainless steel tub with a wire or cord stretched across the middle against which the paste brush can be scraped before use. The tub should be soaked in water and scraped out before fresh paste is put into it. If a batch of paste has turned mouldy, it is well to wash the tub out with boiling water (or very warm water containing thymol) to kill the mould before using it again.

Petroleum Jelly. A white petroleum jelly, such as Vaseline, can be used for the temporary adhesion of gold leaf to leather or other material before heated tools are impressed. It can be purchased in small tins or jars.

Pliantex. A polyacrylic resin used as a consolidant for powdery leather. Its use facilitates the lifting of decayed leather from the spines of books. It is diluted with 1.1.1. trichloroethane or ethyl acetate, usually in the proportions of one part of Pliantex to two parts of diluent. Pre-diluted Pliantex, together with diluent, is available from Arthur Rich & Partners, Ltd., 42 Mount Pleasant Drive, Belper, Derbyshire, DE5 1AD, England.

Plough (Plow). This is not likely to be much used for the edge-trimming of old books (in fact, the edge-trimming of old books should, in general, be avoided whenever possible because it narrows the margins and creates an uncharacteristic crispness to the edges of the leaves—all of which diminishes the value of the book), but it is useful for trimming boards (other than wooden ones) which are too thick to be cut satisfactorily in the board cutter.

Potassium Lactate. A quantity of a 5 percent solution of potassium lactate in distilled water (with 0.25 percent paranitrophenol added to protect the solution and the leather from mould) or a 5 percent solution of potassium citrate should be kept on hand. Potassium lactate may be purchased as a ready-made solution (usually 50 percent and without the fungicide) or mixed from ingredients bought from chemical supply houses.

It has been found that much old vegetable-tanned leather has absorbed sulphur dioxide from the atmosphere, but has not deteriorated, while more modern leather has perished in similar circumstances.* The reason is that, after leather has been tanned, it contains water-soluble protective salts known as non-tans which are washed out of modern leathers when they are immersed in a drum for dyeing, whereas these salts have remained in old leathers, which were merely wiped over with dye. The non-tans prevent decay of the leather by resisting the deleterious action of sulphuric acid. Potassium lactate sponged on to newly tanned and dyed leather can have the same effect. It is advisable to wipe the leather over again with potassium lactate after it has been applied to the book cover (and after the adhesive has dried) in case some of the earlier application has been washed out by moisture during the binding operations.

Pressing Boards. These used to be made of solid wood, but are now generally made of plywood—usually about ¾ inch thick. They should be stocked in the same quantity and the same sizes as the pressing tins (see below).

Pressing Tins. One needs a range from the largest size which will go into the lying press down to octavo (approximately 6 by 9½ inches)—at least four different sizes with two or more pairs of tins in each size. Many of those supplied to the trade are tinned iron,

---

*Sulphur dioxide in itself may or may not be harmful to leather, but it can form sulphuric acid when combined with atmospheric oxygen and moisture. Sulphuric acid in any appreciable amount can be harmful, not only to leather, but to other bookbinding materials as well.

but these tend to rust after being used for some time, so the use of stainless steel is preferable. The tins commonly supplied in Great Britain are 21 S.W.G. (British Imperial Wire Gauge), or .032 inch thick. This is satisfactory for binding processes, but is too thick for some delicate repair work; slightly thinner tins, 22 S.W.G. (.028 inch), or 23 S.W.G. (.025 inch) are better for the kind of work the restorer is called upon to do.

Rulers. See *Straight-edges*.

Sandpaper. See *Glass Paper*.

Scalpels. These are very useful for delicate cutting and slicing operations. I use Swann-Morton surgical blades, usually No. 10, occasionally No. 11. The No. 10 blade can be used most of the time when one is working very delicately with disintegrating leather on the spine of a book, and it has the advantage of being broad so that it supports crumbling material. The point of No. 11 is useful on some occasions. Care should be exercised when the blades are changed, because they need to be held between two fingers while they are slid into position and it is fairly easy to cut oneself in the process.

Sewing Frame. It is best to have a fairly large one, not less than 24 inches between the uprights.

Shears. Eight-inch shears are the most useful.

Shellac Varnish. Bookbinder's shellac varnish often looks better on old bindings if it is diluted with the addition of 25 percent of methylated spirit.

Spencer Wells Forceps. The handles of this instrument have a self-locking device. Stork-nosed pliers can be used if forceps are not readily obtainable.

Spokeshave. This is a very efficient timesaving tool for the allover paring of leather. It can be obtained with either a curved or a flat sole. Most binders use the latter type and file the back part of the sole so that when the tool rests on the paring stone the blade meets the leather at a less steep angle. The front opening usually needs to be filed so that it is wider and less likely to become clogged with parings, and the front edge may need to be rounded off to give a smoother action. A spokeshave with a double adjustment to control the angle of the blade is preferable.

Spring Dividers. On many occasions these are more convenient to use for making measurements than a ruler.

Stains. As with leathers, the restorer must select his colouring materials with some care. Desirable characteristics are ease of application, colour-fastness, and chemical inertness, that is, they must not have a harmful effect on the materials to which they are applied.

For many centuries bookbinders used various kinds of natural dyes and stains derived from plants and animals. These kinds of dyes and stains are still used, but most restorers find that synthetic dyes and stains are easy to work with and produce satisfactory results.

An assortment of colours and shades of water-soluble stains and spirit stains should be kept on hand.

1.   Spirit stains. These are supplied, in liquid form, in black, dark brown, nut brown, light brown, red, green and navy blue by Carr & Day & Martin Ltd.* The stains can be bought in small (43ml) bottles, but it is far more economical to buy it in 1-litre bottles. 2½-litre containers are available, but these are unwieldy and the quantity is too great for normal purposes. Minimum order, £50. Other manufacturers market similar products, but Carr's Dark Brown has the advantage that it has a colder tone than others and therefore is more useful in matching the tones of old leathers. Unfortunately, it has an odour which many people find objectionable, though others like it. Fiebing's yellow spirit stain for leather is widely available, with other colours, in the United States and is useful as a corrective if one's own staining has produced too warm a tone, but it is not a very strong solution and is therefore most effective when used on pale to medium shades.

Messrs. J. T. Batchelor (9-10 Culford Mews, London N1 4DZ) supply spirit-soluble powders in packs, each of which makes a quarter of a gallon of stain. In June 1983, a pack costs 80p, or £7·20 for ten assorted colours; 26 colours, including yellow, are

---

*Carr & Day & Martin Ltd., Newton Works, Great Dunmow, Essex, England. Sold in small bottles in Great Britain by some hardware shops, shoe shops, and shoe repairers.

available. I have no information about their chemical effect on leather, but they are sold for use on vegetable-tanned russet cowhide and "latigo tanned cowhide." They also stock Fiebing's spirit stains.

2.   Water-soluble aniline leather dyes are supplied in a range of colours (not including yellow) by J. Hewit & Sons Ltd., of London, who use them in the manufacture of their vegetable-tanned leathers. The powders are available in jars containing 50 grammes, but they can be bought in larger quantities as required. The dyes are prepared by mixing the powders into a paste with cold water and then adding boiling water as required for density of colour.

For certain purposes, such as touching up small areas of rubbed or worn leather, restorers will find poster (show card) colours or Dr. Martin's Synchromatic Transparent Water Colors useful.

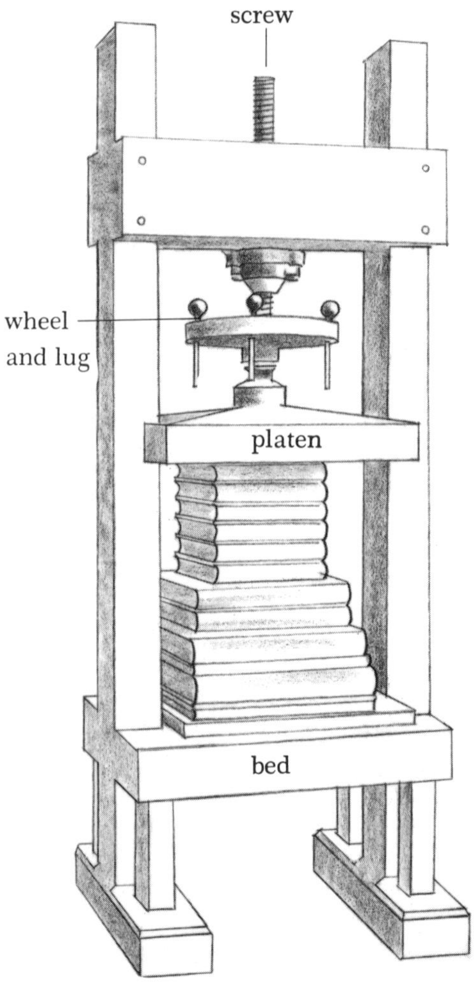

Standing Press. The French type is best for many binders, particularly those housed in domestic premises or with limited working space, because it takes less room to operate and as it does not need to be fixed to the wall or ceiling it imposes no stain on the structure of the building. The platen of the ordinary standing press is raised and lowered by means of a long iron bar, whereas the French type utilizes a wheel-and-lug arrangement requiring much less space to operate (see fig. 13). It must be kept in mind that standing presses are capable of exerting very considerable pressure, and care must be taken not to press books too hard in doing restoration work.

Straight-edges (rulers). Use the 12-, 18-, and 24-inch steel type. The 12-inch straight edges are about 1⅛ inches wide, and nearly ¹⁄₁₆ inch thick, and have many uses in the binding and repairing of books. A bookkeeper's flexible ruler calibrated in both centimeters and inches is also useful.

Strop. A leather strop for sharpening the edge of cutting tools should be mounted, flesh side uppermost, on thick board. A useful size is one measuring about 10 inches long and 1½ inches wide.

Tenon Saw. The kind with a metal reinforcing strip along its top edge has a stiffer blade.

Fig. 13.   French-type standing press.

Thread. Unbleached linen thread, which is extremely strong and durable, is probably the best all-round thread to use in restoration work. It is used primarily for the resewing of the backbones of books, but is also used for such things as overcasting cloth joints to the shoulders of books and sometimes for headbanding.

For resewing, the following thicknesses will suffice: No. 16-3 cord, No. 18-3 cord, No. 25-3 cord, and No. 35-2 cord. The thread is supplied in 15-gramme skeins in 450-gramme boxes. When the skeins are undone, they will be found to be in the form of loops. When these are cut, the ends can be plaited on to a row of nails hammered into the wall or wherever is most convenient. The 35-2 cord thread can be used for overcasting cloth joints. 50-3 cord thread can be used for the same purpose, and this is available in 250-gramme spools.

Thymol. Available in crystalline or lump form. Useful as a preservative for paste and as a fungicidal agent to combat the formation of mould.

Tying-up Boards. Have several pairs of 12- and 18-inch boards.

Vellum. Only a small quantity of thin vellum for the reinforcement of corners, for making headbanding material, and (rarely) for making leather thongs need be stocked.

Vice (Vise). A small one is useful for renewing tool handles, mending clasps, simple tool-cutting, and so forth.

Wood Paste. A variety of commercial products are on the market (under various names), all of which consist essentially of wood flour (or meal), solvents, and some kind of binding agent. They dry quickly, harden upon exposure to air, and when they have dried and hardened, they may be filed, glass-papered, and stained much like ordinary wood. W. H. Langwell has pointed out that some of these products may have a nitrocellulose (cellulose nitrate) base. The use of this material in restoration work is at least questionable. On the whole, therefore, it is probably best that the restorer make his own wood paste by mixing finely ground wood meal with wheat flour paste. Although this dries more slowly than the commercial products, it can be worked and treated in the same way. A little experimentation will allow the restorer to determine the correct proportions of the mixture, depending on the use to which it is to be put. PVA is not useful for making wood paste, as it is not hard enough when dry.

Woodworking Tools. A small range of chisels, planes, gouges, pliers, saws, and the like, for use on bindings with wooden boards and for the repair of old solander cases with wooden frames should be kept on hand.

SOURCES OF SUPPLY

Many firms throughout Great Britain and the United States, as well as in many other parts of the world, manufacture or supply materials, tools, and equipment for hand bookbinding. In addition, many items needed for the restoration work described in this volume can be obtained from craft, art supply, and hardware shops, department stores, and paper and chemical supply houses. Still others, such as plain white wheat flour for making paste, can be obtained at grocers. Many of the chemicals and materials required, such as Klucel G, Industrial Methylated Spirit, thymol and Vulpex soap can be obtained from Frank W. Joel Ltd. (Museum Laboratory and Archaeological Supplies), Oldmedow Road, Hardwick Industrial Estate, King's Lynn, Norfolk PE30 4HH England: *tel.* 0553 60851.

For the convenience of the reader who is not familiar with sources of supply, the following is a list of suppliers who carry a general line of bookbinding and conservation materials and equipment.

Bookmakers
2025 I Street, NW
Washington, D.C. 20006
U.S.A.
Tel. (202) 296-6613

Falkiner Fine Papers Ltd.
117 Long Acre
Covent Garden
London WC2E 9PA
England
Tel. 01-240 2339

Gane Brothers & Lane Inc.
Mail Order Catalog Division
1400 Greenleaf Avenue
Elk Grove Village
Ill. 60007
U.S.A.
Tel. (312) 437-4880

J. Hewit & Sons Ltd.,
97 St. John Street,
London EC1M 4AT
England
Tel. 01-253 6082 & 1431

RELMA
3 rue des Poitevins
75006 Paris
France
Tel. 354 0926

Rougier & Ple
13-15 Boulevard des Filles-du-
 Calvaire
75003 Paris
France
Tel. 872 8290

Russell Bookcrafts
Bancroft
Hitchin,
Herts. SG5 1NF
England
Tel. (0462) 59711

TALAS
213 West 35th Street
New York, N.Y. 10001
U.S.A.
Tel. (212) 736-7744

Wilhelm Leo's Nachf. GmbH
7000 Stuttgart 1
Heinrich-Baumann-Strasse 9
West Germany
Tel. (0711) 43 23 49/28 76

Further information on sources of supply can be obtained from the classified pages of local telephone directories; from the *Abbey Newsletter* (c/o School of Library Service, 516 Butler Library, Columbia University, New York, N.Y. 10027); from the *Directory of Suppliers* (Designer Bookbinders, 6 Queen Square, London WC1N 3AR, England); from the *Guild of Book Workers Newsletter* (Guild of Book Workers, 663 Fifth Avenue, New York, N.Y. 10022); from *Paper Conservation News* (The Institute of Paper Conservation, PO Box 17, London WC1N 2PE); from *Archive Conservationists' News Sheet* (distributed by the Society of Archivists. Editorial address: c/o Portsmouth Record Office, 3 Museum Road, Old Portsmouth, Hampshire, England), and from the *Journal of the American Institute for Conservation* (Klingle Mansion, 3545 Williamsburg Lane, Washington, D.C. 20008).

Leathers of good quality can be obtained in England from J. Hewit & Sons Ltd., listed above; from Harmatan Leather Ltd., Block "J," Penfold Works, Imperial Way, Watford, Herts. WD2 4YY: *tel.* (0923) 38453/4, and from G.A. Roberts & Sons Ltd., 2 White's Grounds, Bermondsey, London SE1 3JY: *tel.* 01-407 2960. Vellum or parchment is available from H. Band & Co. Ltd. Brent Way, High Street, Brentford, Middlesex TW8 8ET: *tel.* 01-560 2025; from William Cowley, Parchment Works, Newport Pagnell,

Bucks MK16 0DB: *tel.* (0908) 610038, and vellum can be obtained from N. Elzas & Zonen Ltd., P.O.B. 1, Celbridge, Co. Kildare, Ireland: *tel.* (01) 28 82 70.

STORAGE OF MATERIALS

Ideally, the materials used in the restoration of book bindings should be stored in an orderly, clean, and carefully controlled environment. Storage rooms should not be subjected to high concentrations of dust or other atmospheric pollution, but in any case, as a safeguard, closed cabinets should be used whenever possible. If possible, the temperature and humidity should be controlled (ideally, the relative humidity should not be above 65 percent and the temperature should be about 60 degrees Fahrenheit—the latter should certainly not exceed 70 degrees). Large map drawers of metal or wood are eminently suitable for the storage of papers, which should be stored flat. The depth of the drawers should not exceed 4 inches, because paper kept in drawers deeper than this may be damaged when it is being removed. Boards should be stored flat under moderate compression, and here open shelves are acceptable because the dust factor is not extremely important. Leather (except for small miscellaneous pieces) should be rolled, not too tightly, with the finished surface (the hair, or grain, side) on the inside. Closed cabinets with horizontal shelves are considered ideal for this purpose. Cloth should also be rolled (again with the obvious exception of small miscellaneous pieces), and stored in a cabinet that has horizontal cubbyholes or compartments. Special racks should be acquired for the storage of finishing tools (fillets, pallets, gouges, etc.). The tools used for preliminary work, such as knives, folders, band nippers, and others, should be kept in shallow drawers attached to the work bench. All tools should be carefully cleaned and put away after use and not left lying around the workshop where they may become lost or damaged. Chemicals that are frequently used should be kept on the work bench (preferably somewhere below the working surface), but others should be stored in closed cabinets. All containers containing chemicals should be carefully labelled. Chemicals and solvents which might be inflammable are best kept in self-closing safety containers. Containers of glue, paste, and the like, should be kept sealed when not in use.

As a logical safeguard, books to be treated, books in process, and completed books should be stored in a vault, safe, or other fireproof type of enclosure if at all possible.

4 Cleaning the Bindings

The first step after one has examined the binding and assessed what repairs are required is to wash the leather covers, including the leather on the edges of the boards and the turn-ins on the inside of the boards. Clearly, if only part of a set of books is to be restored, it is better not to do any washing at all because this will almost certainly create an uneven appearance when the set is returned to the shelves. At any rate, it is highly desirable that one should be given the complete set to clean and furbish. This will not only enormously enhance the appearance of the entire set, but also help to reduce the obtrusiveness of any structural restoration work done on individual volumes in the set. Additionally, there is the thought that if the leather in the bindings of one volume in a set of books is beginning to deteriorate, the remaining volumes may well be similarly affected, so the use of potassium lactate, which is applied during the cleaning process, may be necessary for all the volumes. There is serious doubt about the efficacy of the lactate or citrate once leather has started to deteriorate, but the dressing which is applied afterwards is likely to be beneficial, so for several reasons it is important to have the complete set for treatment.

Washing should be the very first operation for the following reasons.

1. The surface of the leather, and any gold tooling on it, have not yet been disturbed by restoration techniques and are therefore less likely to be washed off.

2. After washing, the tone or shade of the leather may well be found to be different from what it was before, in which case there is a better chance of choosing repair leather which is in sympathy with the original material.

3. If the washing is postponed until the restoration work has been completed, there is a danger that the adhesion of the repairs will be weakened.

The washing of leather is usually best accomplished with a

solution of cold water or, better still, potassium lactate and, either saddle soap or a mild high-quality surgical toilet soap such as is used in hospitals.* When all else fails, Vulpex, a liquid oleate soap will often work wonders in cleaning grimy gold tooling. A 10 percent solution in water may be strong enough to brighten dull gold when ordinary soap achieves nothing. In the case of gold tooling which looks almost like blind tooling a 25 percent or stronger solution may be required, but care should be exercised if the leather is coloured because the soap may shift it. All these can be applied with cotton wool or a sponge. A moderately stiff brush is occasionally helpful in cleaning deeply impressed and very grimy gold tooling, or leather with a deep grain. The amount of water or potassium lactate in the soap solution should be kept to a minimum, and the rubbing should be done as quickly and gently as possible, particularly if a brush is used, so that any gold tooling will not be loosened and lost. Old tooling is much less easily damaged than new tooling, but in any case it is better not to take risks. Powdery leathers are sometimes likely to be severely darkened by washing. An inconspicuous spot should be washed experimentally before the whole binding is tackled. A separate wad of damp cotton wool should be used to remove the residue of the soap, otherwise the leather is likely to dry with a white bloom on it. This is particularly true of leathers which have a pronounced grain, because the soap will tend to settle into the crevices. Any soap remaining after the leather has dried may be removed with a soft brush.

In the case of quarter, half, or three-quarter bindings, the cloth or paper sides may be cleaned with erasers such as the ones recommended in Carolyn Horton's *Cleaning and Preserving Bindings and Related Materials.*†

If a binding has been washed with water and not potassium lactate, a potassium lactate solution should be applied to all leather parts with cotton wool, especially if the leather is in good condition, and the binding should then be thoroughly dried before repairs are started (depending on conditions, this might take from one-half to a full day). Care must be taken during this process not to cause the blackening of any old, powdery leather. If the leather is much decayed there is little to be gained by washing it, especially if there is no gold tooling.

---

*See page 58 for revised recommendations.
†Horton, *Cleaning and Preserving Bindings*, 2nd ed., rev. (Chicago: Library Technology Program, American Library Association, 1969).

5 Removing the Original Spine

The most rapid deterioration of a leather binding usually occurs on the spine as under normal book storage conditions the spine is the area of the cover most exposed to light and to the surrounding atmosphere. Light, both natural and, to a lesser extent, artificial, will eventually cause the fading of colours in leather and may well have other damaging effects; while the surrounding atmosphere, unless artificially controlled, may be subject to more or less severe fluctuations in temperature and humidity, which over a period of time can prove to be harmful to many book materials. The atmosphere may also (and in these days almost certainly will) contain various pollutants, such as sulphur dioxide, which under certain conditions are known to have a deleterious effect on leather. Sulphur dioxide itself is not harmful, but in moist conditions and in the presence of iron, which acts as a catalyst, it forms sulphuric acid which *is* very harmful.

The outer joints of a book, being so close to the spine, are often similarly exposed; in addition, since they are subject to repeated flexing as the book is opened and closed, they are placed under more physical strain than any other part of the cover.

For these reasons, one of the most frequent tasks the conservator, restorer, or binder must undertake is that of reinforcing or replacing the spine and joints of a leather-bound book. The strongest and most effective method of doing this is by putting a layer of new leather over the backbone and joints of the book in an operation known as "rebacking." Before this can be done, the original spine must be removed.

Since the objective of book restoration is to preserve the original binding as much as possible, insofar as this is consistent with a reasonable degree of soundness and durability, it is usually the wisest and most practical course to use the original binding methods and materials whenever possible. The original spine should therefore be salvaged after being removed from the book and later replaced on top of the new leather if at all possible. At any rate, if the book is to be rebacked, the spine must be removed, whether it can be reused or not.

It might be well, therefore, first to describe the procedures for removing the spine. As a logical sequence, we will then describe the series of operations required for preparing leather-bound books for the rebacking operation, and then the rebacking process itself. From there we will move on to discuss some other problems encountered in the restoration of leather bindings, and various methods for solving them.

Removing the spine of a book is one of the processes which can only be learned by actual experience in order that the craftsman can get the "feel" of various leathers, including those which may be badly rotted, and thus be able to anticipate what these leathers will do when attacked with a knife. Very often the removal of the spine is the most difficult operation of all in the restoration of a binding for the following reasons.

1.   As was pointed out earlier, the leather on the spine is usually in a more advanced state of decay than most other parts of the cover.

2.   One is usually working on a curved surface due to the rounded shape of the underlying backbone, unless one is working on a fifteenth- or early sixteenth-century book, the backbones of which were characteristically flat.

3.   One is often working with genuine raised bands which tend to get in the way of the knife. Unless the book is to be resewn, the cords or thongs which make up these bands should not be cut through or removed if they are in sound condition.

The removal of the spine from a book with recessed cords and fake raised bands is not nearly so difficult as removing the spine from a book with genuine raised bands. In the book with fake raised bands, the knife passes readily over the recessed cords, and since the fake bands are merely glued or pasted on, they can be removed with the spine. One can usually (but not always) tell by examining the exterior of a binding whether or not the bands are fake. If the book has a hollow back, it is possible, of course, actually to see that there are no raised cords. If the book has a tight back, it may be possible to see whether there are recessed cords from inside the book if it opens well; if there are recessed cords, any raised bands would be fake. If the cords cannot be seen from inside, it can sometimes be determined whether the book has fake bands by looking for slight bumps at regular intervals along the outer joints. If the raised bands on the spine are not aligned with the bumps caused by the attachment of recessed cords to the boards, the raised bands are fake.

Sometimes, if the leather on the spine is still fairly strong and supple, it may be possible, if one wishes, to lift the leather off the fake raised bands and leave them in place; otherwise they can be sliced through and lifted with the spine (see fig. 14).

There are several things to keep in mind when removing the spine of a book. First, there is the lifting knife. This knife, like the ordinary binder's paring knife, is a piece of flat steel with a cutting edge which runs at an angle across the width of the blade and is bevelled on one side of the blade only. The angle of the cutting edge usually runs in the opposite direction from that of the paring knife, at least for those persons who both pare and lift with the same hand (see fig. 15). The cutting edge of the lifting knife should be fairly short; a long cutting edge can be a nuisance because there is a tendency to use one end of the cutting edge at a time, and while one is closely watching the effect of the end in use, the opposite end may be doing serious damage. This can happen very quickly, perhaps in a second or two. The bevel (about ¾ inch long) on the cutting edge should have as gentle a slope as possible so that the disturbance to the old leather is minimal. A steep bevel may well cause the surface of the old leather to break up and gold tooling, if any, to crack off because of the abrupt increase of pressure as the cutting edge is forced into the material. The breaking up of the surface of old leather, incidentally, while bad enough in itself, may also create difficulties at a later stage because it is likely to cause discoloration when leather dressing is applied during the furbishing process. The dressing will soak in

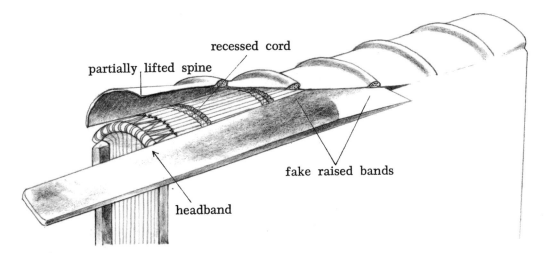

Fig. 14.   Fake raised bands being sliced through and lifted with spine. (This type of binding normally has a hollow tube lining. The tube has been omitted for purposes of illustration.)

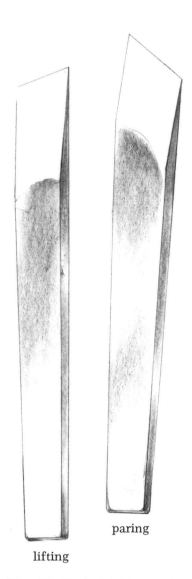

paring

lifting

Fig. 15. Typical lifting and
paring knives.

more freely and will darken the leather where it has been disturbed more than it will in the untouched areas.

The knife should be used flat (unbevelled) side downwards. If much force is necessary to cut through the leather, or some underlying material such as canvas linings or paper linings heavily impregnated with dried glue, there is more control if the knife is held close to the body and is pushed away from one rather than pulled towards one from the far end of the book. Also, if the forearm can be held tightly against the body so that the progress of the knife is governed more by pressure from the body than by the flexing of the arm muscles, a slip of the knife can be more tightly controlled and will probably result in less damage to the spine (see fig. 16). Complete control is often essential because if the knife slips on powdering leather it can cause a great deal of damage, including the loss of any gold tooling that may be present.

Usually, the removal of the spine is a matter of slicing under it and lifting it off the backbone. However, there are occasions, generally when the leather is strong and in sound condition, but its adhesion to the backbone in a tight-backed book is poor, when the easiest way to remove the spine, after the initial cut has been made along the joints, is to use the knife to lever or pry it off. Even in this case, great care must be exercised. If the leather is in poor condition, it is sometimes necessary to slice horizontally through the thickness of the leather, leaving a thin layer of it stuck to the backbone. This layer may be soaked with paste until it has softened and then scraped or peeled carefully off the backbone. If the cutting has been done properly, the top layer can be salvaged and replaced on top of the new leather spine when the book has been rebacked.

For the very delicate removal of small areas of a spine, and for making the initial cut in the leather before the lifting knife is inserted, a scalpel with changeable blades is useful. The removal of an entire spine using only a scalpel is not usually very successful because the small size of the blade makes it difficult to cut through large areas evenly, particularly if the leather is tough. A long, thin spatula with a sharpened edge is found useful by some binders when working with decayed leather spines. One should make the initial incision so that the leather has the longest possible bevel on the edges. If the leather is stuck firmly a long bevel occurs almost automatically, but if it is somewhat loose there may be a temptation to lever the leather off complete with

Fig. 16.   Removal of original spine (in this case, from a book with fake raised bands). Note how the forearms are held closely into the body while the knife is cutting into the leather. Although it may not be apparent from the photograph, the knife is being pushed away from the worker, rather than being pulled towards him.

a thick edge. This can be bevelled at a later stage before it is put back on to the new leather, but it is more easily accomplished on the book before removal.

All too frequently one is confronted with a leather spine so powdery that it is difficult to remove without serious loss. In this case, if the spine is to be saved and used again, the application of leather dressing may help to consolidate the leather and to hold it together while it is being removed. This should be done about two days before the spine is removed because, although the dressing may penetrate well enough into the leather immediately, the surface of the leather will probably still be so sticky that parts of its surface may come off when touched. Not too much dressing should be applied, especially when the leather is very thin and absorbent, because there is a danger that the oily dressing will soak through it and prevent its adhesion at a later stage in the restoration. Water is sometimes used to hold powdery leather together while it is being lifted, but this should be avoided whenever possible, as it permanently blackens some decayed leathers, particularly powdery calf of the eighteenth and nineteenth centuries, and causes embrittlement. Goatskin and sheepskin of the second half of the nineteenth century and later which are suffering from red decay are likely to be similarly affected. (I have experimented with a weak nylon size, but this too has a tendency to blacken these leathers.)

About the time this book was first published in 1972, Pliantex, a material for the impregnation and consolidation of decayed leather came on to the market and was briefly discussed by John W. Waterer in the first edition of his *A Guide to the Conservation and Restoration of Objects Made Wholly or in Part of Leather* (1972) and more fully in the second edition in 1973. Pliantex is a polyacrylic resin diluted with 1.1.1. trichloroethane or ethyl acetate, which makes it highly penetrative. When the diluent has evaporated, which takes just a few minutes, very powdery leather is held together with a strong, colourless film which causes no discoloration, though initially there is considerable darkening. Undue gloss, which is unusual, is easily removed with the diluent. This treatment does not solve all the very considerable problems often encountered when spine leather in an advanced state of decay has to be lifted with minimal damage from a convex spine, but it certainly does help, and the consolidation is likely to be beneficial when the formerly powdery and tender spine is back in position and subject to abrasion.

I have rarely found the need to use Pliantex on the boards, but some may be tempted to apply it locally near the joints, an area which, like the spine, has been exposed to the atmosphere and has therefore deteriorated more than elsewhere. However, local application is not advisable because when leather dressing is eventually put on, the areas not treated with Pliantex will be darkened more than those which have.

My experience with Klucel G (hydroxypropycellulose dissolved in ethanol, isopropanol, or IMS) which has come to notice in recent years, is limited, but it seems to me that its effect on leather is very similar to that of Pliantex. Mr. Anthony Cains, who has much experience of it recommends a 2 percent solution as a consolidant for leather, and a 1 percent solution for the reinforcement of paper.

Robert Muma, an experienced book restorer of Toronto, Canada, has overcome the worst problem associated with lifting and preserving rotted leather spines by applying a PVA latex adhesive (Lewiscraft Leather Cement), which dries on the leather as a thin, transparent and rubbery film and can be removed when the repair is finished without damage to the leather and tooling thereon. Like the Pliantex method this does not make the actual lifting any easier, so skill and care are vital requisites if unsightly damage is to be avoided, but it does hold everything together until the spine is resettled on the new leather.

As a first step he sometimes applies British Museum Leather Dressing (which he finds more suitable than any other for his purpose) to the rotting leather, especially that which is very powdery, because this consolidates the leather and prevents undue penetration of the latex. Next, he applies the PVA with a small varnish brush. The oil and wax in the dressing may resist the PVA too much, in which case a second coat should be applied. When the spine has been lifted Robert Muma advises that it should be bound around a cardboard mailing tube with wax paper, otherwise the drying latex may draw the leather out and cause cracking when it is moulded back into shape on the book.

When the old spine has been pasted back in position and has set for a day or so, the PVA latex can be removed. If the dressing was applied at the start it may be possible to roll or peel the latex off, but if this does not work, Muma recommends that the latex be dabbed with alcohol and then with water to coagulate it. The latex will soon blister and then it can be rolled off with the finger tips. It is advisable not to apply the PVA unless the job can be finished within two or three weeks because after this it is liable to become tougher and more difficult to remove.

Robert Muma's more detailed account of the method was published in the *Guild of Book Workers Journal,* Winter, 1970. Lewiscraft Leather Cement is supplied by Lewiscraft Supplies, 284-6 King Street West, Toronto 2B, Ontario, Canada, but they do not export it.

Sometimes, when a spine has been difficult to remove, the surface remaining on the backbone of an unlined tight-backed book is rough and uneven because parts of the old leather spine are still stuck to it (see fig. 17). Assuming that the book does not have to be pulled and resewn, and assuming that the old spine is to be replaced on the book, this unevenness should be retained and not smoothed down with glass paper or sandpaper because at a later stage, when the new leather backing has been put on and is still soft and pliant, the uneven underside of the old spine can be pressed down on to it for a moment so that the surface of the new leather is moulded to the shape of the backbone underneath. If this procedure is followed, the old leather spine is likely to show fewer bumps when it is eventually stuck down over the new leather—provided, of course, that it is correctly positioned.

When the removal of a spine has been a struggle there is a temptation to lift the label (if any), which is often comparatively easy, and to scrape away its foundation. The result is likely to be that when the old spine is placed back on the new leather the label will look too low and not as it was originally, slightly raised.

The spines of some tight-backed books of the late eighteenth century and the early part of the nineteenth are more easily removed than at first sight seems likely, because the backbones of these books were lined with paper before being covered with leather (see fig. 18). It is usually possible to slice through this paper with comparative ease unless it is too heavily impregnated with old glue. The old paper often splits into two layers when the spine is lifted off, one layer sticking to the spine itself and the other layer to the backbone. The layer on the backbone can be fairly easily removed by spreading paste (not too moist) over it and letting the paste soak in long enough to soften the old glue or paste underneath as well as the paper itself. When the adhesive and paper have softened, the paper can then be peeled or, more often scraped, off the backbone with a bone folder or a dull knife.

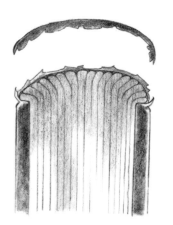

Fig. 17.   Parts of an old spine remaining on the backbone of an unlined tight-backed book.

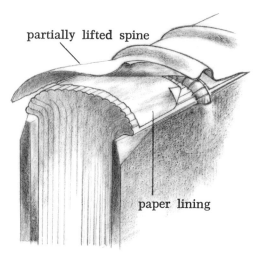

partially lifted spine

paper lining

Fig. 18. A tight-backed book with paper lining.

The paper remaining on the spine may be more difficult to remove because of the danger of damaging the old leather. One must, for example, avoid the use of moisture as much as possible in order not to blacken the leather. Often, however, the paper may be peeled off with the aid of a thin folder without moistening it, or it can be very carefully scraped off with a sharp knife. At any rate, this layer should be removed if at all possible because it may create problems if and when the old spine is replaced on top of the new leather backing. In the first place, it may make the old spine too thick and stiff, and there is also the danger that the paper (often of poor quality) will later disintegrate, thereby precipitating the detachment of the spine.

Much more difficult are books, also tight-backed, of the seventeenth, eighteenth, and nineteenth centuries, the backs of which were lined with a kind of coarse canvas. Often, after the old spine has been removed with a knife, some pieces of the canvas remain on the backbone and the remainder on the lifted spine. This is usually due to the difficulty of removing stiff leather (thick russia, for example) from a curved surface with a flat knife; it is seldom due to deterioration of the canvas. It is usually much safer to leave the areas of canvas where they are and then form a mould on the new leather by pressing the old leather spine down on it when it is still soft, in the manner described previously for the book in which parts of the old spine stick to the backbone of an unlined tight-backed book. If the canvas is in poor condition, it should be removed.

Generally speaking, when one is dealing with old calf it cannot be lifted off raised bands. In such cases, a cut is made on either side of the raised bands so that the panels between them can be raised individually. Sheepskin tends to be more fibrous and becomes less powdery than calf, so there is a greater chance that it can be taken up in one piece. Goatskin, too, provides more opportunities for success, though very often it is impossibly difficult if the book has been in bad condition for many years. If, despite reinforcement with Pliantex, or whatever, the spine comes off in a very fragmentary state, it is a good plan to assemble the pieces and then to stick them to Japanese tissue; otherwise, some may be lost. It is essential to paste the tissue and then lay the pieces down on to it, because the action of pasting the fragments is likely to cause complete loss.

There is, of course, little difficulty in removing the spine of a book which has either a loose hollow back, or a hollow tube back, but in the latter case, some care may be needed to get the upper part of the tube (the part not stuck to the backbone) off the detached spine. There may be a temptation to leave this part of the tube in position on the old spine, but like the paper lining on the spine of a tight-backed book mentioned above, this may create difficulties later on, and should be removed if at all possible. (It should not, however, be removed until the old spine is ready to be put back on the book as it serves to hold the spine together while it is off the book.) In fact, it is best to remove the entire paper tube (the part sticking to the backbone as well), and replace it with a new one. Methods of constructing hollow tubes will be discussed later on.

The old spine should be put away in a drawer for safety until it is time to replace it on the book. If it is in fragments, it should be wrapped in paper or placed in an envelope. The paper wrapping or envelope should be marked to indicate the book to which the spine belongs, and also to indicate which end of the spine is the top, if this is not self-evident.

Only on comparatively rare occasions will the boards still be firmly attached after the removal of the old spine. The cords or thongs of old books in need of rebacking are almost always either broken off at the joints so that the boards have become detached, or they are so unsound that they no longer serve to hold the boards firmly to the book. In the latter case, it is usually best to cut them off flush with the joints and use one of a number of methods to reattach the boards. The cords often look sound and feel firm when lightly tested, but it is important to test their strength with a determined tug to make sure that they will perform adequately in future. Also, if the cords along one joint are broken the cords on the other side of the book must be suspect and unless they are very clearly strong it may be a good plan to cut them so that both joints can be reinforced similarly. When the original spine and any linings have been removed, the condition of the backbone should be carefully inspected to see whether it must be repaired or resewn. Techniques for repairing the backbone as well as for forming new slips for reattaching boards will be discussed in the next section. The condition of the original headbands should also now be inspected to see whether they need to be repaired or replaced.

6   Alternatives to Resewing

One of the most difficult problems a restorer must face is the book in which the sewing is weak or defective and some of the leaves or sections have become loose or detached. In many such cases, the book must be resewn.

Before this is done, every possible alternative method of securing the leaves or sections and strengthening or reinforcing the backbone should be considered. The reasons for this are two-fold. First, the edges, especially the fore edges of resewn books are seldom as smooth as they were originally. Although this may often be of trifling importance, it can in some cases spoil the appearance of the book, particularly if the edges are gauffered, marbled, or gilded, or there is a fore edge painting. Second, and more important, the resewing of a book often involves an enormous amount of time and labour, and should therefore be avoided whenever possible.

When only one or two sections of a tight-backed book are loose, it is sometimes possible to secure the loose sections with the aid of thread and a semi-circular needle without removing the old leather spine if the backbone is not too tight and has not been too heavily glued up. In this kind of book, if the spine is still strong along the joints but is no longer stuck down to the backbone, thread can be worked from inside the sections with a semi-circular needle to encircle the cords or thongs. The sections can then be pulled into place and secured to the cords or thongs with the thread. Because of the thickness and curvature of the semi-circular needle, it may be necessary to pass the thread through the folds some distance from the cords or thongs on both sides instead of immediately alongside them as is usually done. If necessary, Spencer Wells forceps or stork-nosed pliers can be used to press the needle out through the backbone and to pull it back through again. When the sewing has been completed, the loose ends of the thread can be stuck down along the inner folds, or, better still, they can be poked out through the folds to the backbone, where they will be perfectly secure when the loose spine is once more stuck down to the backbone. (It should be noted that in a book with raised bands, this technique cannot be used if the cords or thongs are too heavy and thick to allow the semi-circular needle to reach around them.) In this operation, the final sticking down of the loose spine can be accomplished by running adhesive down the back between the leather spine and the backbone.

This same method can, of course, be used to secure loose sections in the backbone of a book after the old spine has been removed, but in this case it is easier to secure the sections with a straight needle rather than a semi-circular one.

If there is just a little weakness in the backbone here or there, or a general looseness, it may be possible to reinforce it, once the spine and any linings have been removed, by making shallow sawcuts between the head and tail ends of the book and the kettle-stitches with a tenon saw, and inserting cord to which glue or PVA has been applied into the grooves (see fig. 19). When the glue or PVA has dried, the ends of the new cords (these ends are called "slips") can be used to strengthen the attachment of the boards, if necessary, by fraying them out and sticking them down on to the boards (or lacing them into the boards) after the leather on the sides has been partially lifted. If this is not necessary, the ends of the cords can be cut off flush with the joints. The use of recessed glued-in cords is not advocated for small books printed on thick paper because the backbones of these books are usually somewhat stiff and they tend to be difficult to open properly. The presence of the glued-in cords will make the backbones stiffer, and the books consequently will be even more dif-

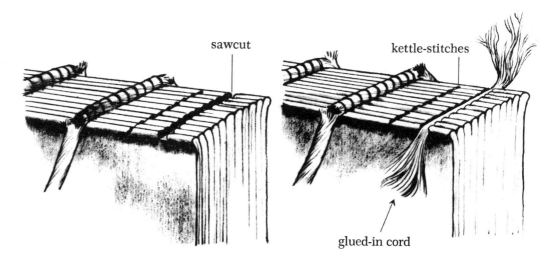

sawcut   kettle-stitches

glued-in cord

Fig. 19.   Reinforcing backbone with glued-in recessed cords.

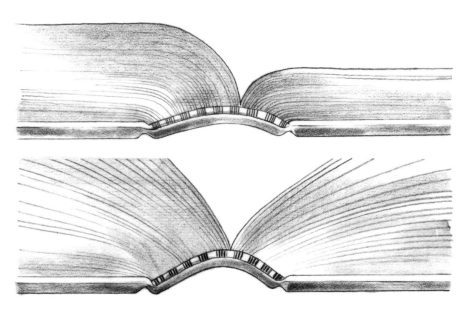

Fig. 20. Books with thin paper (*top*) and with thick paper (*bottom*).
Note the difference in the arching or "throwing up."

ficult to open. In general, much more can be done in the way of reinforcing the backbone of a book if the paper is thin and tends not to throw up (arch) much when the book is opened than if the paper is thick and the backbone has a tendency to throw up heavily (see fig. 20).

Sometimes a backbone which is loose but not broken can be tightened up sufficiently by gluing it up and lining it with a layer of jaconet or some other thin, strong material. Again, this should not be done if the book is small and printed on thick paper, because it might tend to make the backbone so stiff that it will not open well.

Finally, it may be useful to point out that although the sewing of some tight-backed books may appear to be somewhat shaky, the rebacking operation itself may firm the book so that it will prove in the end to be perfectly sound. Whether or not this will be sufficient must be a matter of judgment on the part of the re-storer, based largely upon his past experience.

The operations described above can, if necessary, be carried out without detaching the boards, but, as was stated in the previous section, the cords or thongs will usually be broken at the joints, or will have been cut off at the joints by the restorer, so that the boards have already become detached.

Even when the backbone is still basically sound, some binders will resew books merely for the sake of removing these broken cords or thongs* and replacing them with new ones with which to reattach the boards. However, since there are effective alternative methods of reattaching boards, this is not necessary and is wasteful of the restorer's time.

Large numbers of books, some with hollow backs, have been rebacked without reinforcement of the attachment of the boards, so there has been nothing to hold the boards on to the book when the leather has deteriorated. Many others have been given a mull lining on the spine, the ends of the lining being stuck down under the pastedowns. This is useful as a means of relieving strain on possibly shaky cords, but is not very effective if there is no lacing in because the covers can be pulled away from the book.

One alternative to resewing which is widely employed is to sew new cords over the old ones, and then to use the new slips to reattach the boards. In this method, the new cords are first pasted down over the old (which may be either single or double), and then the new cord is sewn on to the old, usually from the outside as shown in figure 21 (second band from the left). If the backbone is not too tight and the book opens well, the new and the old cords can be sewn together from the inside. This is seldom easily accomplished, however, particularly when the book has been heavily backed. Heavy backing bends the end sections on each side of the book sharply over to form prominent shoulders, and in books like these, the first and last sections are extremely difficult to sew through from the inside. At any rate, the place where the sewing on of the new cords must be the strongest is near the joints, since that is where the greatest strain on them will inevitably take place. Semi-circular surgical needles and Spencer Wells forceps or stork-nosed pliers are useful for this kind of sewing. The ends of the new cords are then frayed out to form slips, and after the leather on the old sides has been lifted to expose the boards, these slips can be either pasted on to the outer surface of the boards, or laced in to them, as will be described in section 11.

*In the books discussed in this volume, the sewing usually will have been done on cords, rather than leather thongs, so that, unless otherwise stated, the assumption will be that the book has been sewn on cords. At any rate, leather thongs will more often than not be found to be in such poor condition that they must be replaced entirely. As will be pointed out in the next section, in this case it is usually best to replace them with cords.

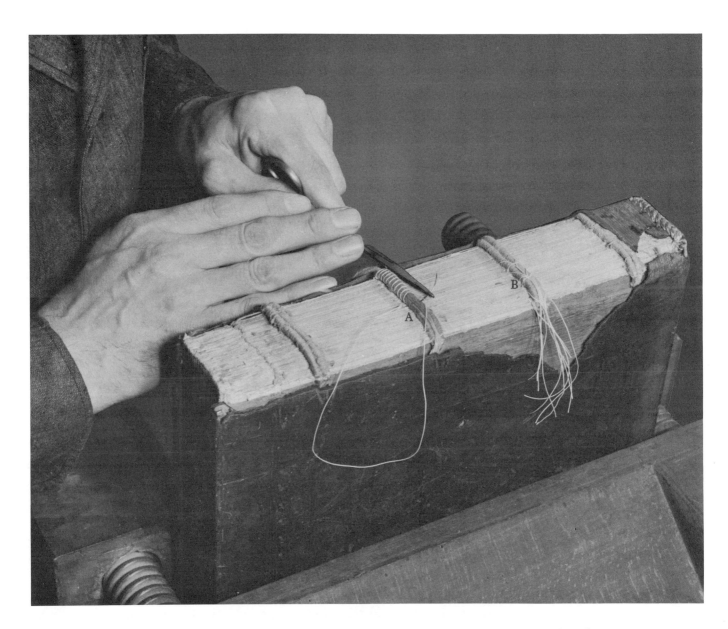

Fig. 21.   Two methods of forming new slips for reattaching boards.

A. New cord pasted over old, then the old and new cords
     are sewn together.
B. Linen threads are secured around old cords.

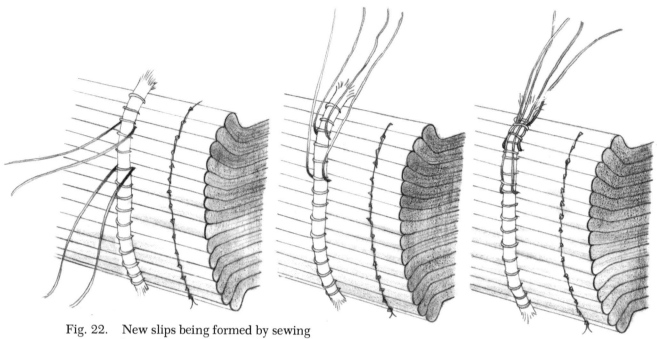

Fig. 22.   New slips being formed by sewing
linen thread around old (single) cords.

Two alternative methods for reattaching boards are described by Sydney Cockerell.* In one of these methods, linen threads are passed out on either side of original raised cords at every third section (more frequently if the book is large), so that the ends of the threads come to the outside of the backbone from inside the sections (see fig. 22, and fig. 21 [second band from the right]). When this is done the loose ends of the threads can be gathered together and taken over the shoulders to form new slips and either pasted down on the boards or laced in. The original cords and the new threads should be encircled with thread at various points so that the strands cannot be pulled away from the back of the book. Here again, the most critical point that needs to be reinforced is that near the joints. If it is felt that having the new thread behind only one thong or cord creates too localized a strain, one can span pairs of thongs or cords, as illustrated in figure 23.

The other method described by Sydney Cockerell is intended for books sewn on recessed cords. In this method, tapes are

*Sydney Cockerell, *The Repairing of Books* (London: Sheppard Press, 1958), p. 48.

Fig. 23.   New slips being formed by sewing linen threads
around pairs of cords.

placed between the existing cords and sewn on through the centres of the sections at intervals throughout the book (see fig.
24). The free ends of the tapes are then used as new slips to reattach the boards by pasting them down on the inside of the
boards and covering them with the pastedown; by splitting the
boards horizontally, inserting the slips, and gluing them into
position inside the boards, which is useful if there is no pastedown, or lacing them in by using a chisel instead of a bodkin.
The second technique can only be used on those kinds of boards
that split well and are at the same time firm and strong.

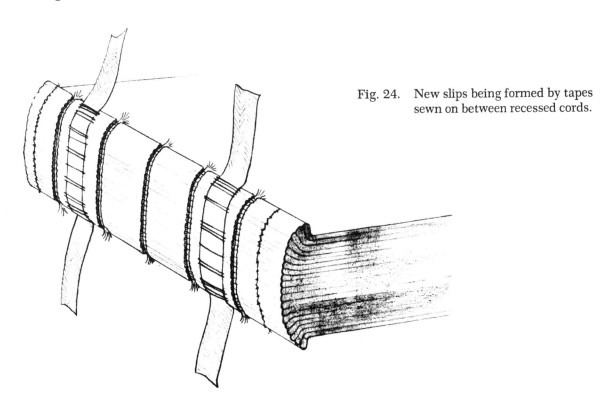

Fig. 24.   New slips being formed by tapes
sewn on between recessed cords.

The technique I frequently employ to reattach boards, which I believe to be the easiest and strongest of those here described, and which has the further advantage of being applicable to almost all books, involves pasting one side of a strip of jaconet or similar material on to the inside of each shoulder and then overcasting it on to the book with thin thread to make a cloth joint, the other side of which will be stuck down on to the board at a later stage when the new leather has been stuck on. In this case, unlike cords or thongs, the cloth will be pasted down on the inside of the board instead of the outside. This serves to strengthen the inner joints of the book. If jaconet is not used, the material should be one which does not readily allow adhesive to penetrate through the material to the opposite side, and which does not immediately lose its stability.

Before the overcast joints are applied, any necessary repairs should be made to the original headbands. If the threads used to tie down sewn-on headbands are more or less intact but loose, the tying down can be reinforced with thin, strong thread anchored to the backbone through every third or fourth section of the book, or by loops passed around the headband and stuck to the spine. If the thread is fine and of matching colour the reinforcement is inconspicuous. If the headbands are too badly deteriorated, or are missing, new headbands must be made (see section 9). If stuck-on headbands were used originally and are in a state of disrepair, the easiest course is to remove them, cut new headbands which more or less match the old to the proper length, and stick them down into position with an adhesive. Cane ones tend to be rather springy and are perhaps best avoided, but if they are used it is usually best to use an adhesive that sets fairly quickly, such as glue or PVA. If, after the attachment of cloth joints, it is going to be necessary to put the book under a lot of pressure in the lying-press in order to re-form the shoulders, it is better to defer the repair and reattachment of the headbands until after this has been done because the compression may buckle and weaken the headbands.

In overcasting the cloth joints, a long, sturdy needle is fixed into a wooden finishing tool handle, and this tool is then used to pierce a series of holes about ¾ inch apart at the base of the shoulder through the cloth joint and down through the backbone at an angle of about 45 degrees. If the needle meets strong resistance, it should be rubbed with soap or wax in order to make it penetrate more easily. After the piercing has been done, the overcasting can be completed without difficulty. (See figs. 25 and 26A-B.) The sewing illustrated in figure 26B is recommended because threads which run parallel with the joints on the spine are likely to be less noticeable than those which are oblique.

If the raised bands are of normal height they can be ignored when the cloth joints are sewn on. However, if they are abnormally prominent there is a danger that when thread which straddles them is pressed down on either side the increased tension may cause breakage of the thread. In this case, the holes should be pierced on each side of the bands as shown in figure 26C.

Sometimes, the shoulders of a book have more or less disap-

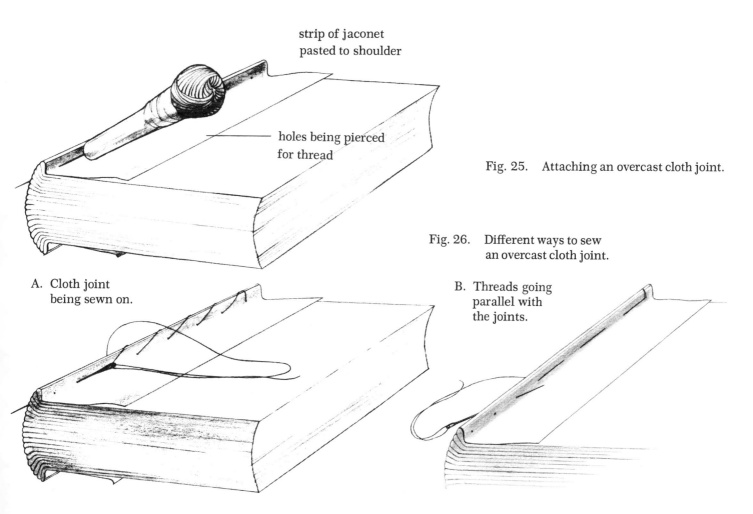

strip of jaconet
pasted to shoulder

holes being pierced
for thread

Fig. 25.   Attaching an overcast cloth joint.

Fig. 26.   Different ways to sew
an overcast cloth joint.

A. Cloth joint
being sewn on.

B. Threads going
parallel with
the joints.

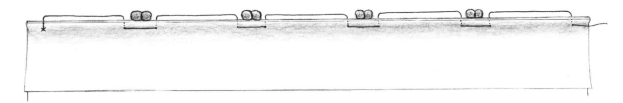

C. Passing the thread along the foot of the shoulder instead
of over the raised cords.

Fig. 26.   (continued)

peared so that the boards no longer have support. Clearly, it is
desirable that the shoulders be restored, though not with the precision found in modern bindings. After the backbone of the book
has been glued up (see section 8) and before the glue is completely dry, the book should be put between backing boards in
the lying press. A hammer can then be used to sharpen up the
shoulders and to embed the threads used to sew on the cloth
joints well down into the backbone so that they will not form
bumps on the spine. This must, of course, be done very carefully so as not to damage either the thread or the underlying
paper so for this reason the edges of the backing boards should
be slightly rounded rather than sharp as is usual for modern
work. It may well be that the shoulders are already adequate so
that all one needs to do is folder the spine to flatten the threads
and the holes where the piercer emerged.

At a later stage in the repair, after the new leather backing has
been put on, the pastedowns are lifted and the loose sides of the
cloth joints are pasted down on to the boards underneath them
(see fig. 64).

This method of reattaching boards provides a strong and continuous bond between the book and the boards from the head to
the tail of the book, and has the additional advantage that the
overcasting (which may pass through three or four sections) se-
curely fastens the weakly attached leaves often found at the beginning and end of old books. However, I am fully prepared to
concede that it is not suitable for all books. Some conservators
feel that it should never be employed because, they say, the
leaves will break off along the line of the sewing. This may well
happen if the paper is too thick and very brittle, but where the
paper flops open as it does in most antiquarian books there is
little danger even if the paper is weak because the leaves bend

back well away from the point of sewing. There is the argument that the movement of the leaves is impeded, but an examination of a number of books will show that the impediment is very little greater than that already caused by the formation of the shoulders. Some object because this method of attaching the boards does not follow the original form of construction. However, very often there is no satisfactory alternative, as in the case of a book which opens in a manner which allows no access to the backbone from the inside and which has negligible raised bands, or no raised bands at all, so that nothing can be attached to them as a reinforcement. It is sometimes possible to open up recessed sewing with a bodkin, push cord down into the hole with adhesive, and then paste the ends of the cords on to the outer surface of the board, but as the cord has to be fairly thin this has limited value for substantial books. Resewing, if the original sewing is sound, involves more loss than gain, economically, aesthetically and bibliographically.

If the book is tight-backed, and it is thought that the overcasting thread will show on the spine in spite of the use of the hammer to embed it into the paper, the backbone of the book can be lined with paper. When the lining has dried, it can be rubbed down with glass paper to make it as smooth as possible. Linings are less likely to be needed on the backbones of large books with heavy leather covers because on these books the thread will not normally show through. In any case, if the spine is tooled the distribution of the tooling may be such that any slight bumps from the threads will be camouflaged.

It should be pointed out that, as a general rule, all overcast cloth joints should be hidden when employed on books bound before about 1840, as cloth joints (almost invariably stuck in) are not found in books before that date.

If there are no pastedowns or other linings and the bare boards are showing so that the ends of the cloth joints which lie over the inside of the boards cannot be hidden, the restorer may or may not be able to use the overcast cloth joint to reattach the boards. There are three courses open to him.

1. He can abandon the use of the overcast cloth joint and adopt one of the other methods described above for reattaching the boards.

2. He can use the overcast cloth joint and then cover the part showing on the board with a new pastedown or lining

(which some may consider to be a bibliographically dubious practice since it alters the character of the original binding).

3.   He can use the cloth joint, but paste down the first flyleaf of the book just far enough to cover the cloth joint so that most of the flyleaf is left free (see fig. 27). Partial pasting down was not uncommon in cheap bindings of the sixteenth and seventeenth centuries, so if the book is very old, this technique surmounts the difficulty without being out of character with the rest of the binding.

There is one other occasion on which the restorer may not be able to use the overcast cloth joint. Books dating up through the early years of the sixteenth century were not rounded or backed in the manner characteristic of the vast majority of later books (see fig. 28). If the boards of these books are detached it may be necessary to reattach them by the other means described above and not with overcast cloth joints, because there may be little or no shoulder on which to sew the cloth.

It should be pointed out as a final word of caution that the insertion of overcast cloth joints imposes something of a strain on the outer joints of the book. This strain will be increased if, as is often necessary, the cloth joint is covered over with addi-

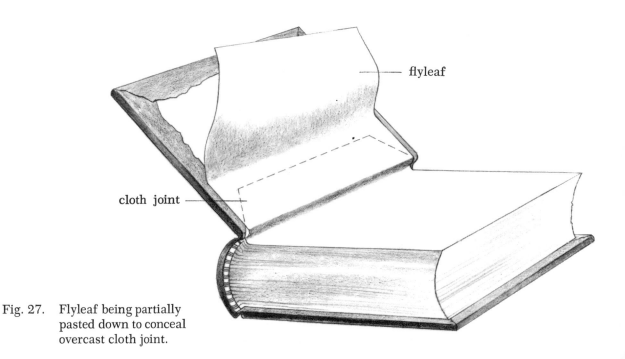

flyleaf

cloth joint

Fig. 27.   Flyleaf being partially pasted down to conceal overcast cloth joint.

tional paper along the inner joints of the book. The strain arises from the fact that extra thicknesses of material are being added into an already tight-fitting area (see fig. 29), so that if the boards are to close properly there has to be a strong compression of the materials along the inner joints of the book. However, if the boards are closed before the inner joints have become bone dry and if the book is put under a weight for several hours to settle down all should be well. Those who have doubts about this can put a strip of thin card with a bent edge into each inner joint at the time the new leather is pasted on and leave it there until the leather is dry and thus create a little space for inserted material. The larger the book, the less reason there is to do this.

If the backbone has a bad shape and is, perhaps, concave, it may sometimes be rectified by soaking it with paste for fifteen or twenty minutes, fingering it into a good shape, and then leaving it under a weight overnight to set. The paste should, of course, be scraped off.

If the methods described in this chapter will not suffice to restore the backbone to a sound condition, there is no alternative but to resew the book. This operation, and those of gluing up, rounding, and backing, which must follow before the rebacking of the book can be completed, are described in the next two sections. If resewing is not necessary, and any necessary repairs have been made to the headbands, the next step is the lining up operation described in section 10.

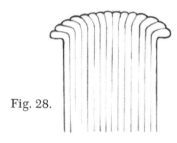

flat back and small shoulders characteristic of books up through to the early years of sixteenth century

Fig. 28.

well-rounded back and prominent shoulders characteristic of the majority of later bindings

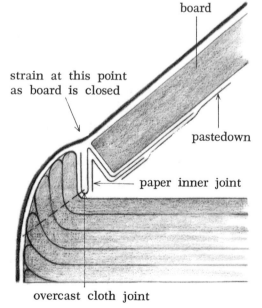

Fig. 29.   Profile of book fastened into its binding with an overcast cloth joint covered over with paper inner joint.

7 Resewing

If none of the alternatives described in the preceding section are satisfactory, and the book must be resewn, it should now be "pulled," that is, the entire cover, the cords, the linings, the headbands, and the old sewing thread must all be removed so that the book is reduced to its pre-bound state.

Before being pulled, the book should always be collated to ensure that it is not incomplete and does not contain misbound sections or leaves. This should actually have been done by the librarian, collector, or other owner of the book before it is turned over to the restorer, but it is well for the restorer to do it again on his own. If any parts are missing, and the owner has not noted this fact, the restorer may have difficulty in proving that he has not lost them once the book has been pulled. A careful record of missing leaves, misbound sections, or any other binding flaws (such as out-of-sequence plates or maps, for example), should be kept, and the restorer should check with the owner of the book to see what, if anything, should be done about them before he proceeds with his work. It is seldom wise for the restorer to make these decisions himself, particularly if the book is considered rare or valuable.

If the book contains unnumbered plates which must be removed from the book for mending or other treatment, they must be marked in such a way that there can be no doubt where they belong; the tendency to rely on one's memory should be resisted.

Some early books are neither foliated nor paginated, so if the book in hand is to be reduced to single leaves or folios (for the bleaching and resizing of the paper for example), a soft pencil should be used to foliate it throughout, including the endpapers and any blank leaves. The pencil marks should be placed on the inner margins deep into the backbone of the book where they will not be seen when the work is finished; pencil marks are not removed by bleaching, and they may be permanently fixed by the size. If the book is to be pulled and resewn only, and the sections are not reduced to single leaves or folios, so that there is little or no chance of these loose leaves or folios becoming lost or getting out of sequence, it is usually unnecessary to foliate it, because the restorer, already having collated the book to ensure that everything is present and in correct order, can make subsequent checks by reference to the signature marks; or to the catch-words at the beginning or end of each section which are almost always present in books up to the end of the eighteenth century. If these are not present, he can draw a pencil line obliquely across the backbone of the book before it is pulled so that any inadvertent transposition of the sections when they are reassembled will be made apparent by interruptions or zigzags in the line. Of course this method is useless if the outside folds of some sections are likely to need repair.

Pulling a book for resewing consists of a number of steps. First, the spine of the cover, any linings, and the headbands must be removed. Next, the boards must be detached. If the boards are still attached to the book by cords, these must be cut through at the joints so that the boards can be removed from the book. Then, if the cords are raised, they should be cut off right across the backbone by severing the sewing threads that encircle them. Next, if there is glue on the backbone and it needs to be removed, this can be done by applying a layer of paste over it and letting the paste soak in until the glue has softened. Then the softened glue can be scraped off with a folder or some other blunt-edged tool. This should be done as carefully as possible, so as to minimize the damage to the back folds of the sections. The use of too much moisture in the paste must be avoided. If the book can be pulled without removing the glue, so much the better, as this is sometimes a risky operation. If the book is sewn on recessed cords, each section in turn must be opened in the middle, the threads cut on the inside, and the section pulled carefully away from its neighbour. If the book is sewn on raised cords and these have been cut away by the restorer, it is usually possible to separate the sections without cutting the threads on the inside, and the loose threads merely need to be pulled out or brushed away with the hand. It is important that all old thread be removed from the book before any resewing begins, mainly because its retention would cause extra and possibly unmanageable swelling. Finally, if the book has been rounded and backed, the shoulders must be flattened out. This can be done by placing the end sections on a hard working surface and carefully hammering the bent-over back folds with a backing hammer, and by manipulating them with the fingers. This also often helps to remove unwanted flakes of old glue from the folds.

If, as is commonly the case after pulling a book, it is found that the outside folds of a few sections are broken so that the outer leaves are torn or detached, they can be mended with medium-thickness Japanese tissue or some other thin, strong mending paper. This is a strong method and is particularly advisable if the text paper is thick and there is likely to be much leverage on the back folds when the book is opened. The mending paper should be somewhat longer than the sections (the excess length to be trimmed later), and torn into strips wide enough so that, when they are placed over the broken ends of the sections, they will overlap about ³⁄₁₆ inch on each side. These strips are known as *guards*. If machine-made paper is used for mending, its machine-direction (or grain) should be parallel with the back folds of the sections so that any contraction along the fold will be minimal and also so that the guard will fold more easily. When the guard has been pasted with medium-thick paste and laid on clean waste paper, the section should be laid almost halfway across the guard, after which the waste paper can be used to bring the guard over evenly and to rub it down so that no direct contact with the finger is necessary (see fig. 30). It is better to use paste for this purpose than PVA, because paste dries more slowly, and one has more time to work and to manipulate the guards into position, apart from which, paste is more easily reversed. If the fingers are used without the waste paper it is more difficult to bring the guard over evenly and to rub it down to make firm contact with the leaves; also, the work is more likely to be made dirty. As far as possible, the guarding tissue or paper should blend in with the paper of the book.

When many of the outside folds are broken, and the paper is thin, the outer leaves can be narrowly tipped back on to the sections with paste along the inner edge of each leaf; this will avoid the excessive swelling in the backbone which would result from many added thicknesses of guarding paper. (It should be noted that the bibliographical integrity of the book may be disturbed by this method in that the evidence of conjugate leaves will be obscured.)

In tipping on the leaves, a strip of adhesive (see fig. 31) ⅛ inch wide is sufficient for most books, and as little as ¹⁄₁₆ inch wide enough for very small books. Once the strip of adhesive has been applied, the loose leaf must be positioned and secured to the surface of the adjoining leaf in exactly the same position it was in originally. (This method can, of course, also be used to reat-

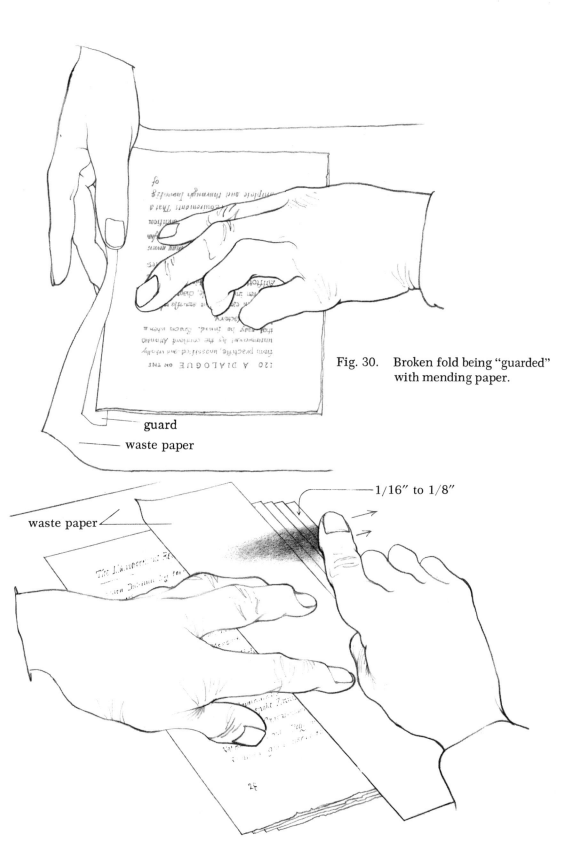

guard

waste paper

Fig. 30.   Broken fold being "guarded" with mending paper.

waste paper

1/16" to 1/8"

Fig. 32.   A book being oversewn by hand on a sewing frame.

tach occasional leaves throughout the book, not just those on the outsides of the sections.)

A method which may be used for consolidating a large number of single leaves or badly damaged folds, particularly if the book is to be sewn on raised cords and all-along or two-sections-on sewing would cause excessive swelling in the backbone, is to oversew the book on the sewing frame. This method is similar to overcasting, but differs in that the sewing of each group of leaves catches up the previously sewn part of the book and simultaneously fastens it to the cords (see fig. 32). It is a great deal faster and more satisfactory than overcasting the leaves into "sections" or groups and then sewing all-along, because the book is held together more firmly and evenly throughout. Books sewn in this way never have excessive and unmanageable swelling, and although when the book is removed from the sewing frame its backbone is frequently somewhat lopsided (see fig. 33), this defect is easily remedied with a few taps of the hammer before the book is glued up, and the subsequent rounding and backing is straightforward. It should be pointed out that oversewn books are difficult to pull should this ever be necessary, but provided that the paper is not too thick, so that the book will open without too much strain, and good, strong thread is used, the sewing is likely to be very strong and durable. When the rest of the binding in an oversewn book eventually wears out, it can usually be replaced without resewing. It should also be noted that in overcasting leaves into groups for all-along or two-sections-on sewing it is necessary to pierce the leaves at close intervals so that the thread is held firmly at the band positions. In oversewing, the leaves need be stabbed only at the band positions, thus eliminating a large number of possibly damaging perforations. If, however, the inner margins of the leaves are very narrow or the paper is too thick in relation to the leaf area, so that the leaves will not lie down without persuasion, oversewing may well be an unwise technique to adopt, and if the paper is thick there may be no practical objection to guarding throughout so that the sections can be sewn through the folds.

Whenever possible, the book should be resewn in the original style and in the same holes, but there is one important qualification to this generalization. Two-sections-on sewing (see fig. 34) has been very widely practised, certainly in England, since the early years of the seventeenth century, sometimes as a means of

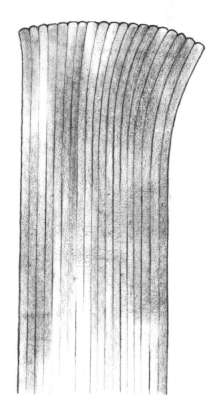

Fig. 33.   One-sided swelling which may result from oversewing.

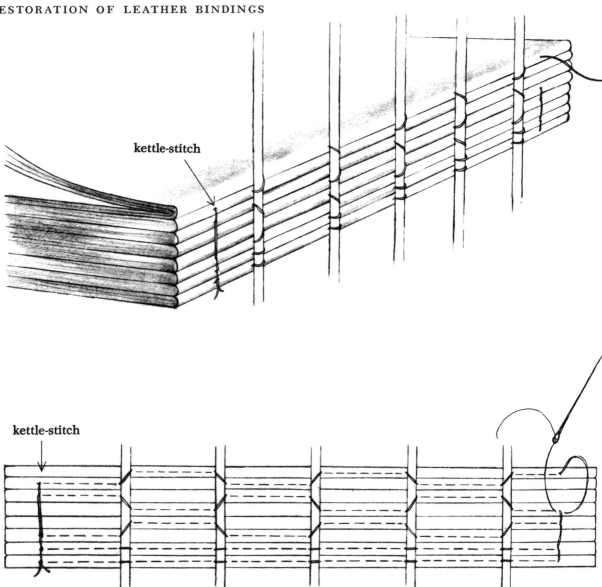

kettle-stitch

kettle-stitch

Fig. 34.   Two views of the backbone of a book being sewn two-sections-on
(the first one or two sections are usually sewn all along for
added strength).

keeping to a minimum what would otherwise be unmanageable
swelling in the backbone, but more often simply for the purpose
of reducing sewing time and therefore labour costs. If two-sec
tions-on sewing provides no structural advantages, as in the case,
say, of a small book with either raised or recessed cords and six
or eight sections of thick paper, the restorer may well feel that he
should sew all-along (see fig. 35) even though this does not follow the original method. In this kind of book there is bound to
be considerable leverage on the back folds, and if the book is

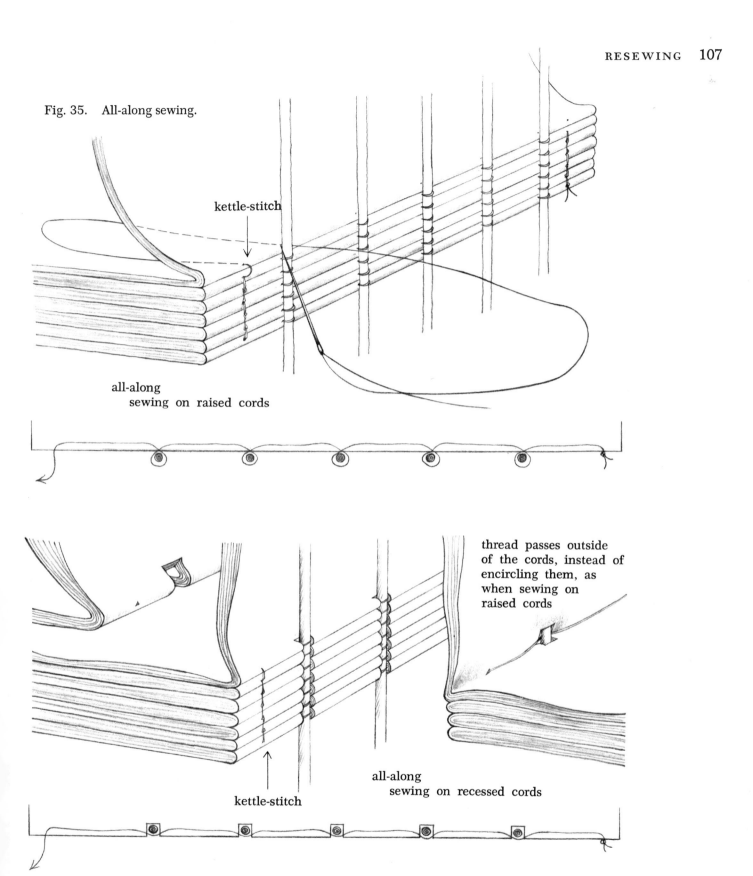

Fig. 35.   All-along sewing.

kettle-stitch

all-along
sewing on raised cords

thread passes outside
of the cords, instead of
encircling them, as
when sewing on
raised cords

kettle-stitch

all-along
sewing on recessed cords

Fig. 36. Folded-back section
sometimes resulting
from two-sections-on
sewing.
Note: headband has
been eliminated for
purposes of illustration.

sewn two-sections-on, the loose ends of the sections which have not been sewn are likely to come out of alignment and be folded back on themselves when the book is closed (see fig. 36), thus setting up various strains and perhaps causing a structural breakdown. (This particular defect is found in many books bound in the seventeenth century.) The loose ends were sometimes held by a stitch stabbed through the side, but this device does not always work very well with too thick paper because strain may cause the thread to break, and then the structure is likely to disintegrate.

There is another exception to following the original style of sewing. It is advisable to resew books on cords even though leather thongs were originally used, because the leather thongs break easily when they lose their flexibility. (If a book must be resewn on thongs for some reason, the new thongs should be made up of alum-tawed leather, perhaps with a strip of thin vellum laminated between two layers of the leather.) Jap paper guards are sometimes placed around the backs of the sections to act as a barrier against the destructive effect of glue and to facilitate pulling for resewing when the book is eventually rebound, more especially in the case of vellum-leaved books. This procedure also enables the book to open more freely, but if there are many sections the thickening of the spine may cause difficulties with the preservation of the original spine leather.

The sewing on of the endpapers sometimes creates special problems. For example, the majority of endpapers were sewn through the centre opening fold until the early years of the nineteenth century. These endpapers usually consisted of a double folio (four leaves), as the thread would have quickly pulled out of a single folio. The outermost leaf was usually cut short and pasted down to the board, while the second leaf was left intact and pasted down over the first to become the visible pastedown (see fig. 37). (There were many regional variations on this general technique.) In most modern bindings the sewing thread is placed under the flyleaf, so that the thread is not seen when the board is open. The flyleaves in these modern bindings are usually "made" flyleaves, that is, they are made up of two layers of paper, one marbled or otherwise decorated, the other plain. The two layers are then laminated together with paste to make the flyleaf thicker and stronger—and also to cover the marks made during the marbling (see fig. 38).

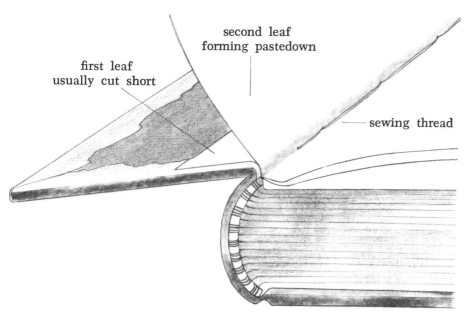

first leaf
usually cut short

second leaf
forming pastedown

sewing thread

Fig. 37.   Endpaper sewn through centre fold, with
outermost leaf cut short and second leaf
pasted down over it.

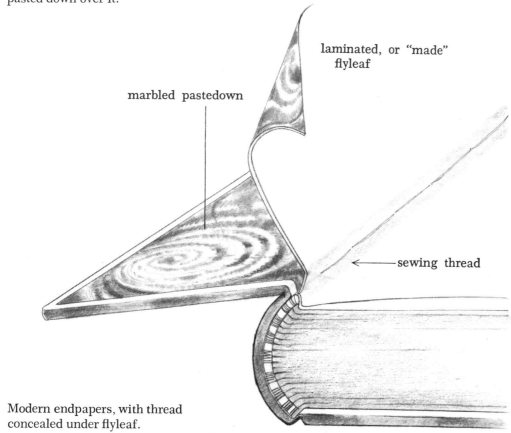

marbled pastedown

laminated, or "made"
flyleaf

sewing thread

Fig. 38.   Modern endpapers, with thread
concealed under flyleaf.

Ideally, the original endpapers or, if these are missing or too damaged to be saved, other paper of appropriate character, should be sewn on in the same way as the originals. It should be added that until the early years of the nineteenth century all endpapers,

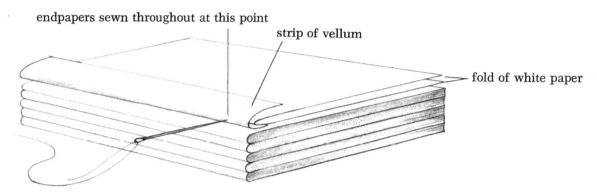

In use in England late fifteenth, early sixteenth century. Very often these endpapers were not pasted down to the board.

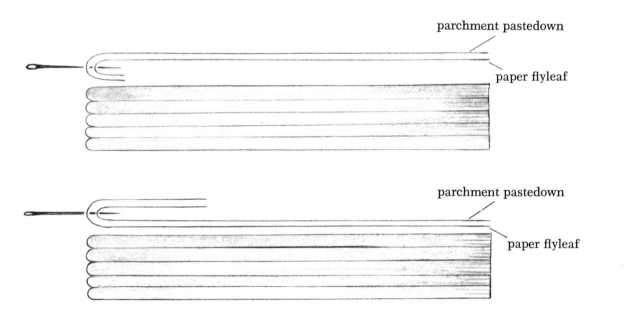

The above two endpapers were used during the greater part of the sixteenth century, mostly at Oxford and Cambridge, and in decorated bindings rather than undecorated ones.

Fig. 39.   Various forms of endpapers.

at least in books bound in Great Britain, were sewn on, never merely tipped on with paste as they sometimes are today. For the interested reader, a variety of endpaper constructions is shown in figure 39.

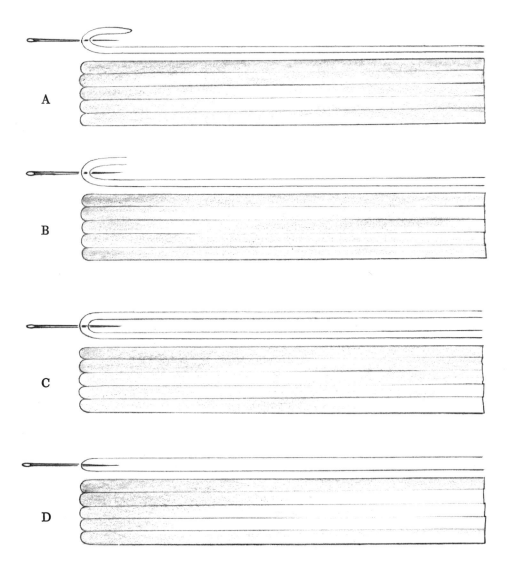

These four endpapers were much used in cheap bindings from the sixteenth century to the early part of the nineteenth. Sometimes they were not pasted down, thus leaving the board exposed. Occasionally endpapers A and B were used in conjunction with separate pastedowns.

Fig. 39.   (continued)

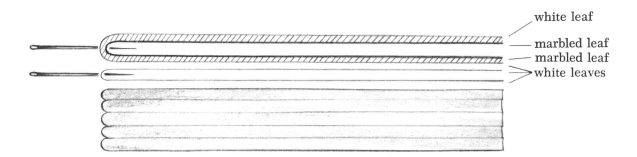

These endpapers were much used in England in the second half of the seventeenth century and the greater part of the eighteenth. They were made by folding one marbled paper and two whites, placing the marbled paper inside one of the whites and sewing on as two sections. The pasting together of the marbled and white leaves was probably done after the endpapers were sewn on. (Note: hatching indicates paste.)

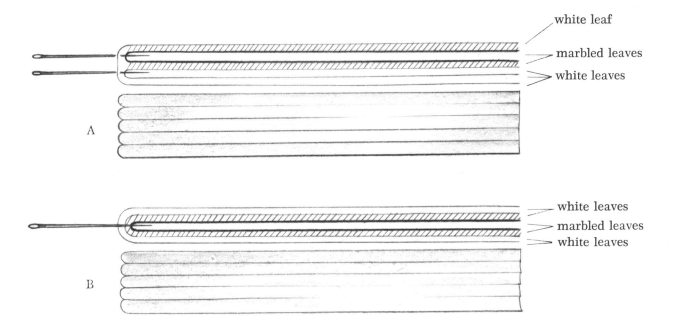

The above two endpapers were used in the better class of bindings in the second half of the eighteenth and the early decades of the nineteenth. In endpaper B the sewing thread is hidden under the marbled paper because the marbled paper was stuck in after the white leaves were sewn on the book.

Fig. 39.   (continued)

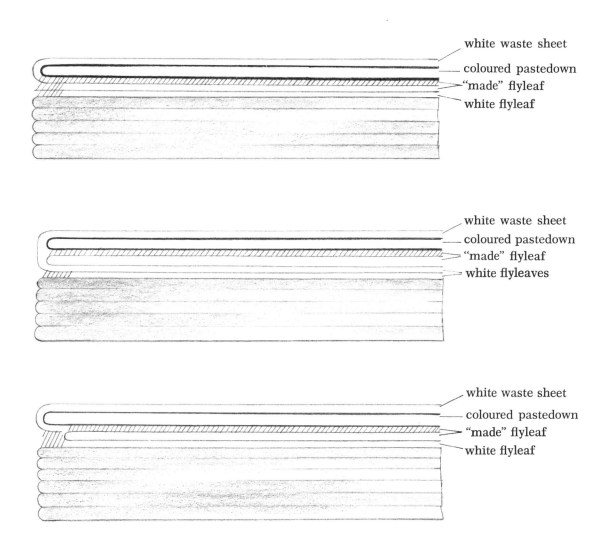

Three tipped-on endpapers commonly used in the nineteenth century. The waste sheets were removed before the endpapers were pasted down to the boards.

Fig. 39.   (continued)

8 Gluing Up, Rounding, and Backing

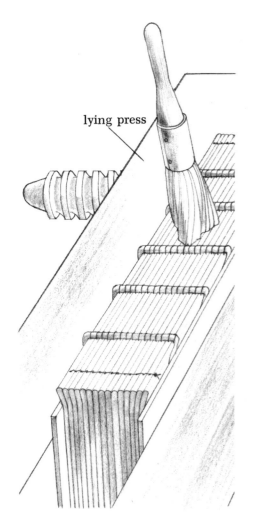

lying press

Fig. 40.   Gluing up.

If the book has been resewn, the next operations to be considered are gluing up, rounding, and backing.

The procedures are as follows. The backbone and the head edges of the book are knocked up on a flat surface until the sections are well aligned. The book is then placed in a lying press with boards on each side to keep the ends of the cords on which the book has been sewn out of the way. Next, fairly thin glue is applied to the backbone with a brush (see fig. 40) and is rubbed well down between the sections with one's fingers. A thin coat of CMC or starch paste rubbed in and allowed to dry before the application of glue provides a barrier against the penetration of the glue into the paper and makes what has been termed a "release layer," which facilitates pulling. This is not necessary if guards have been incorporated to protect the folds.

When the glue is almost dry, but before it has set hard, the book is removed from the press and the backbone is rounded. The rounding is accomplished partly by tapping the back folds of the sections gently with a hammer (see fig. 41), and partly by finger manipulation. Rounding a book so that its shape is just right and the sections do not form "steps" at the fore edge is an operation that takes a fair amount of practice and skill. When using the hammer, care must be taken not to damage the cords.

Once the rounding is completed, the book is put back in the press with a backing board on each side for the backing operation. The backing boards are positioned so that their top edges are slightly below the back folds of the end sections of the book —the exact distance is determined by the size of the shoulders which one wishes to form when the operation is completed. The size of the shoulders, in turn, is determined by the thickness of the boards to be used on the sides of the book; the shoulders should project beyond the sides of the book just enough to accommodate the thickness of these boards. If there is excessive swelling in the backbone, the backing boards will probably slip down when the book is placed in the press, in which case 3-inch strips of plain white blotting paper should be placed at regular intervals between the leaves close to the folds to increase the thickness of the body of the book until the boards no longer slip down. The backs of the sections should now be drawn gently over to form the shoulders by glancing blows with the claw of the backing hammer, the hammer being used alternately on either side of the book (see fig. 42). When the shoulders have been formed, their

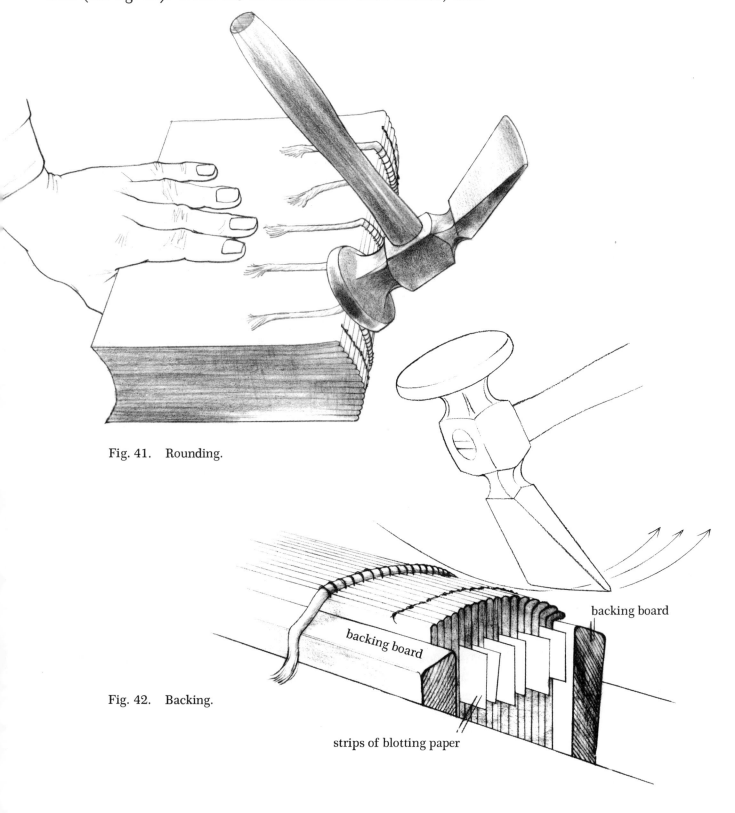

Fig. 41.   Rounding.

Fig. 42.   Backing.

backing board

backing board

strips of blotting paper

edges can be smoothed and the backbone can be consolidated with the face of the hammer. Care must be taken during backing not to damage any raised cords and to keep them correctly aligned and spaced. Minor adjustments to these cords can be made before the glue has set hard; once the glue has finally set, even these adjustments are impossible to make. Band nippers can be used for the final shaping of the raised bands when the hammering is finished.

Gluing up the backbone was not generally practised until late in the sixteenth century. Each restorer must decide for himself whether to glue up the backbone of earlier books. I favour doing it because I feel that by so doing one can better mould and set the backbone the way one wants it. This advantage, however, must be weighed against the damage that may be caused to the back folds of the sections if and when the book is eventually pulled for rebinding, though this is not likely to be serious if the backbone has been "primed" with paste. Some binders glue up with PVA, but I prefer to use animal glue, because after rounding and backing, glue can be softened with paste in order to help set the final shape of the backbone, whereas most PVAs cannot easily be softened and as a result spines glued up with this adhesive tend to become flat over a period. If PVA is used to glue up the backbone of a tight-backed book there should be a paper or fabric lining between the backbone and the leather spine because the paste used to stick down the spine may not readily adhere to a dried coating of PVA.

When rounding and backing a book, it should be kept in mind that the shape of the backbone should be appropriate to the period of the binding. Books of the late eighteenth and early nineteenth centuries call for a semi-ellipse with heavy shoulders (see fig. 43) but a very early book, say of the late fifteenth or early sixteenth century, should have a rather flat backbone without appreciable shoulders (fig. 43A). In the 1820s there was a reversion to the flat backbone, but this was followed a few decades later by a return to the very rounded shape. The binder must decide whether to back books which were bound before backing came into popular use shortly after the beginning of the sixteenth century. My own policy is to retain the characteristic flat backbone of these early books, but to knock the end sections over to form small, unobtrusive shoulders which will provide some measure of support for the boards (see fig. 44). This support is important, given the

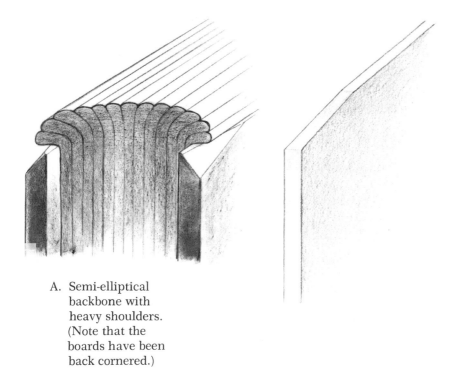

A. Semi-elliptical backbone with heavy shoulders. (Note that the boards have been back cornered.)

Fig. 43.   Back cornering.

B. The back cornering style that preceded that shown in figure 43A.

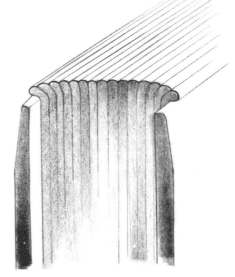

Fig. 44.   Flat-backed book with small shoulders.

large size and weight of most books of this period. The operation is fairly easy, since most books of the time were printed on rather thick paper.

The next step is "cleaning off"; that is, the backbone is soaked with medium-thickness paste for a few minutes so that the glue on the backs of the sections, though not that which is between them, can be scraped off. Afterwards, the backbone can be cleaned with a damp rag or cotton wool. The cleaned surface provides a better foundation for the adhesion of the leather or hollow back and sets the backbone in the shape which has been formed. This is a very important operation and one which is now often omitted.

After these operations are complete, the next step is head-banding.

9   Headbanding

Basically, there are two kinds of headbands: those which are sewn on the book and which thus become an integral part of the binding; and those which are merely stuck on with adhesive and serve almost entirely a decorative purpose, having little or no functional value. The former must, of course, be sewn by hand directly on the backbone of the book, while the latter are made separately, either by hand or by machine, and are then cut to size and stuck down to the backbone with an adhesive.

Sewn-on headbands have been and are made in a great variety of ways. Mediaeval headbands (on vellum-leaved books which had been cut to size before sewing) were sometimes sewn at the same time as the backbone, with the same thread. This was a very strong method, particularly for large books with heavy sections, as the thread ran continuously from one end of the sections to the other, circling all cords on the backbone, and the headbands were "tied down," or sewn into, every section. The ends of the leather thongs or strips of cord which formed the cores of many early headbands were nailed or stuck down or laced into the boards to reinforce the attachment of the boards to the book.

Headbands of later date are formed separately from the sewing on the backbone, with different thread, and the ends of the headband cores are cut off flush with the joints, though up to the seventeenth century they were also sometimes laced in or stuck to the boards.

Headbanding is not too difficult once one has learned the fundamentals and has had some practice, but describing the process is not easy. For one thing, there are many different ways of making a sewn-on headband, depending on the preferences of the individual binder, on the style of headband he wishes to create, and on the kind and condition of the book on which it is to be sewn. Headbands may be sewn on only one cord or thong (these are called single headbands), or on two cords or thongs (called double headbands); they may be sewn with only one colour of thread, or with several different colours to make a decorative pattern. The details of construction, such as the position of the "bead" (see below), may vary. The restorer, of course, must usually attempt to duplicate the original headband as closely as possible in all details. The following description is of one method which has been and still is commonly used for the formation of a single, two-colour headband. While deliberately oversimplified, and while the reader should remember that there are many other methods, it will perhaps give the reader some idea of how headbands are made. It might help if the reader were to refer occasionally to figure 45.

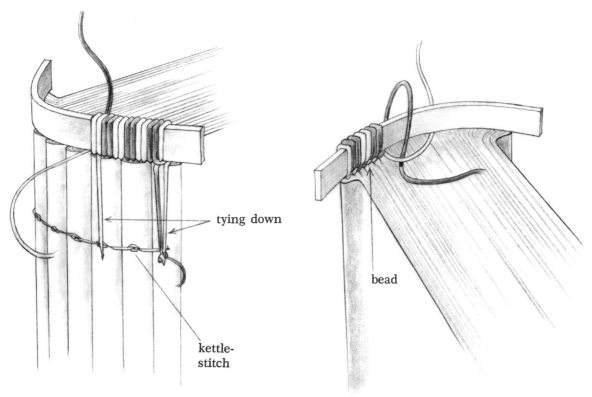

tying down

bead

kettle-
stitch

Fig. 45.   Sewing a single headband with two threads.

First, a length of cord or thong slightly longer than the width
of the backbone is cut. This will serve as the core on which the
headband is sewn, and is laid across the top of the leaves of the
book at the head of the backbone. Next, a needle threaded with
a length of (let us say, green) thread is stabbed through the
centre fold of the first section near the head of the book from the
inside (usually just below the kettle-stitch) and is pulled out
through the backbone. The needle is removed and the second
length of (let us say, white) thread is tied to the first on the outside of the backbone. The knot is pulled tight to the backbone
from the inside and serves as the basic anchorage point.* The
needle is now fixed to the loose end of the second (white) thread,
which is then passed along the outside of the backbone to the

*This knot may prove to be troublesome if the spine is eventually to consist of a single
layer of thin leather, in which case the knot may form a small but unsightly bump under
the leather. In this case, a different method of sewing on the headband, with the knot
placed on the *inside* of the section, will have to be used.

head of the same section, around the cord or thong which forms the core of the headband, and back down through the inside of the section, forming a loop of thread around the core. It is then stabbed through the same hole below the kettle-stitch to the outside of the backbone, passed back to the head of the section, and wound around the core again one or more times (the number of times depending on the pattern of colours one wishes to make). The first (green) thread is now brought up from where it was hanging loose on the inside of the section, crossed over in front of the white thread, and itself wound around the core one or more times (again depending on the pattern desired). The two threads are then wound around the core, the white thread alternating with the green, across the entire width of the backbone. After each of the coloured threads has been wound around the core the number of times desired, the thread of the other colour is passed over in front of it underneath the core before being itself taken around the core. This passing of one coloured thread over the other forms a small lump called a "bead," which should lie evenly and neatly at the base of the headband against the top edges of the leaves of the book. As the threads are wound alternately around the core across the width of the backbone, the second (white) thread is taken back down through the inside of a section from time to time (perhaps every third or fourth section), stabbed out through the backbone below the kettle-stitch with the needle, and back around the core to "tie down" the headband to the backbone of the book. In the early days of headbanding (up to the beginning of the sixteenth century), headbands were often tied down through every section, and invariably through the centres of the sections. Since then, the tying down has usually been done only every few sections, and not necessarily through their centres.

When the headband has been completed, it is tied down through the last section and the two lengths of thread are tied together, with the knot on the outside of the section or, alternatively, the ends of the thread may simply be pasted down to the backbone without being knotted. Any excess length of core is then cut off so that both of its ends are flush with the shoulders of the backbone. If the book is to be tight-backed, the threads on the backbone may be effectively concealed by the back linings, if any, or if there are none, a layer of thin leather can be pasted over the threads and then be glass-papered or sanded down until the surface is smooth. If the book is to have a hollow back, this is, of course, not necessary. It may also not be necessary if the old spine is to be replaced on the book, as the extra thickness of leather will help to conceal the threads.

If there is any weakness of the paper or in the kettle-stitch at the head and tail of the backbone of the book, before beginning to sew the headband it is a good idea to paste or glue a lining of thin jaconet or some similar material over the entire backbone if there are no raised bands, or at least over the end panels at the head and tail of the book if there are raised bands. If this is done, the thread used to tie down the headbands through the sections will have a firm anchorage.

As was indicated above, new headbands should be made in the style of the original ones as far as possible. Even when the original band at the head of the book has disappeared, the band at the tail, or part of it, often remains as a guide. If nothing remains, the restorer should try to find a binding of the same geographical origin, style, and date for reference. Failing this, he should bear in mind the general principle that flat headbands (those sewn on flat strips of leather lined with vellum—see fig. 46B) are incorrect for bindings dating before about 1780, that run-of-the-mill bindings of the sixteenth to the late eighteenth century, both English and Continental, usually had two-colour single headbands sewn on cord (the cores of many were made of rolled paper, and some of cane, but these do not last well as they are brittle or become brittle in time, and tend to break), and were sewn with coloured linen thread. Another interesting point to note is that in most of these headbands, two strands of each colour were used alternately, each pair of strands being used as if it were one. In these bands, therefore, each bead consists of two strands instead of the normal one strand (see fig. 46C).

Double headbands (those having two cores) are rare in English bindings of the sixteenth century, but were commonly used in fine English bindings of the seventeenth and eighteenth centuries. These bindings usually had two- or three-colour double headbands sewn with silk thread on one thin and one thick cord with the thinner one uppermost (see fig. 46D).

Headbands are one of the features of a restored book that are not noticed unless they are wrong. For example, a three-colour double headband of silk would be hopelessly inappropriate and irritating if sewn on a "common sheep" retail binding of the sev-

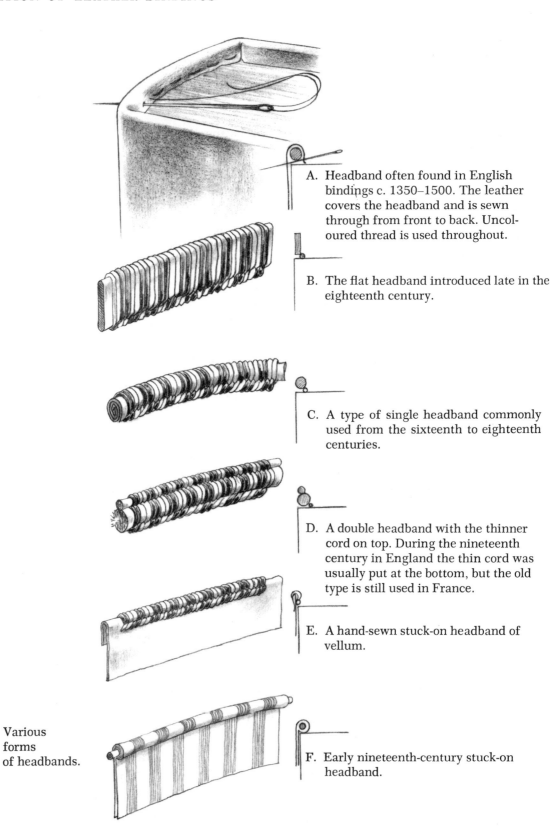

A. Headband often found in English bindings c. 1350–1500. The leather covers the headband and is sewn through from front to back. Uncoloured thread is used throughout.

B. The flat headband introduced late in the eighteenth century.

C. A type of single headband commonly used from the sixteenth to eighteenth centuries.

D. A double headband with the thinner cord on top. During the nineteenth century in England the thin cord was usually put at the bottom, but the old type is still used in France.

E. A hand-sewn stuck-on headband of vellum.

Fig. 46.   Various forms of headbands.

F. Early nineteenth-century stuck-on headband.

enteenth century, as would a two-colour single headband sewn with linen thread on an elaborate russia or morocco binding of the late eighteenth century. Appropriate styles for these bindings are, respectively, two-colour single headbands sewn with linen thread, and three-colour double headbands of silk. Admittedly, one does occasionally come across genuine examples of simple headbands on elaborate bindings, but never the reverse.

An interesting form of headbanding is often found in English bindings from the middle of the fourteenth to the end of the fifteenth century. In these bindings, the leather headcap covers the headband and is sewn through from front to back, with uncoloured thread being used throughout (see fig. 46A).

A minority of German bindings of the late fifteenth and early sixteenth centuries (though simple examples of the fourteenth century are known) have plaited thongs covering primary thread headbands and passing through the leather on the spine. A headband of this type can just be seen in figure 21.

Contrary to the general belief that stuck-on headbands were not introduced until some time in the nineteenth century, handsewn stuck-on headbands with cores made of strips of vellum (see fig. 46E) are found in German bindings dating from the last years of the sixteenth century, and were used up to the beginning of the nineteenth century. They were also used in England to a very small extent in the seventeenth century, but rarely in the eighteenth. They appear on the Continent fairly regularly, however, throughout the eighteenth century. In later times, cloth strips were sometimes used for the core instead of vellum.

Stuck-on headbands of a simpler type became popular in England during the early decades of the nineteenth century. These consisted of a strip of pasted linen or calico (sometimes striped, often monochrome) folded around a core made of a piece of string (see fig. 46F). Similar headbands with a cane core are still available. Machine-made stuck-on headbands have been in use since the 1850s and have been widely employed on all but the finest leather bindings ever since.

New headbands will look much too fresh, so they need to be aged, unless, of course, this is contrary to the policy of the owner of the book. This can be done very slightly so that the starkly clean headbands are merely somewhat mellowed, while still being obviously modern, or they can be stained down to a greater degree, depending on the condition of the binding, even, perhaps, to the extent of ageing the headband more than the tailband. The ageing is best done with spirit stains, especially if waxed thread has been used because water stains "take" less readily. Usually, dark brown spirit stain, with a touch of black to make a dingy tone, and then diluted with methylated spirit according to requirements, will impart the desired effect. The stain should be applied with a pointed paint brush, the spine of the book being parallel with the floor, or tipped down, so that there is a minimal danger of stain from an overcharged brush running into the book. As the stain has a tendency to spread, it is best to apply the stain just short of the beads so that it will spread on to them; if the stain is applied directly on to the beads, perhaps too liberally, there is a possibility that it will run on to the book and down the tie-downs.

After the book has been glued up, rounded and backed, and headbanded, the next step is the lining up operation described in the next section, after which the book is rebacked. It should be pointed out that whenever a book is being rebacked, or new joints and headcaps are being applied, and one is required to use stuck-on headbands, it is better to do the subsequent lining up of the rest of the backbone of the book with PVA rather than with glue, because most PVAs soften less quickly than glue when moisture strikes through from the paste used to perform these operations, and the stuck-on headbands are therefore less likely to become loose, detached, or skewed out of position.

10   Back Lining

Before the boards are prepared for the application of the new leather spine and joints, and are reattached to the book (if this is necessary), the next operation that may be necessary is the lining of the backbone.

A number of factors must be considered in deciding whether to line the backbone of a tight-backed book. First of all, a lining will help to prevent the threads used in sewing the backbone from forming bumps on the spine. This is particularly important if overcast cloth joints have been used on the book. However, note that if the original spine is to be preserved, its replacement on top of the new leather may effectively hide thread bumps, so that in this case lining may be unnecessary, and that if the new spine is to be elaborately tooled instead of having the old spine preserved, this too provides effective camouflage. Apart from this, the lining material would destroy the possibility of using the "mould" technique described in section 5. Second, there is no question but that a strong lining will help to reinforce the backbone of a book, and in a heavy volume this may very well be desirable. However, one must always balance these advantages against the fact that linings also tend to stiffen up the backbone, and if the text paper is thick and the inner margins are narrow, the book will be difficult to open and the parts of the text near the inner margins difficult to read. One or two thin linings which have been rubbed down are not likely to affect the opening of a large, heavy volume, but if, in order to give the backbone effective support, several layers of fairly heavy linings are glued on, the functioning of the book may well be adversely affected.

Another thing to keep in mind is that if the backbone is to be lined, the lining material should be strong and chemically sound; if it deteriorates the whole structure will be weakened. It must also be a material which can be easily glass-papered to form a smooth surface. Good-quality cartridge paper or brown, unglazed, acid-free kraft paper of medium thickness are suitable.

In lining a backbone, the first thing to do is to dampen the lining paper with water (being certain that the grain of the paper runs parallel to the length of the backbone) so that the fibres swell and the paper stretches and becomes limp. If this is not done, the paper may stretch with the gluing and become less manageable, and may also "bubble up" on the backbone.

If the book is to have a tight back, the backbone is now covered with glue (or PVA) of medium consistency, one edge of the paper is lined up evenly with a shoulder of the book, and the paper is laid across the glued backbone to the opposite shoulder. Another layer of adhesive is then applied, the paper is folded back again to the other shoulder, another layer of adhesive is applied, and the paper is now alternately folded and glued back and forth across the backbone. When enough layers have been applied, the end of the paper is then trimmed off evenly with a shoulder of the book. The number of layers to be applied depends upon the size of the book and the degree of strength and—more important —rigidity, desired. The top layer should now be moistened with water and the linings rubbed down with a folder, especially along the edges of the shoulders. If the backbone has deep ruts between the sections, it may be a good idea to fill them in with frayed-out sewing cord glued into position before the lining is put on.

In making a hollow tube back, a layer of adhesive is liberally applied to the backbone which has previously been lined with a soft fabric of some kind, such as mull or jaconet, especially if the sewing is weak. A piece of paper a little longer than the backbone, and a little more than three times its width, is laid down across the backbone with one edge of the long side of the paper lined up evenly with the edge of one of the shoulders of the book. The paper should then be folded back across the backbone once more. It is then slid (not lifted) off the backbone so that the adhesive is well distributed over the under-surface of the paper. The paper is then folded once more and the glued surface is stuck down to the final folded layer of paper to form a three-layered hollow tube (see fig. 47). Finally, any excess paper is trimmed off along the shoulder and at the head (or tail) of the backbone. (This is a little more difficult, perhaps, than making the entire tube away from the book and then putting it on, but since the backbones of old books are seldom perfectly straight from one end to the other, it will result in a better fit.) If the single thickness of a three-layered tube is attached to the backbone, the tube will form a "one on and two off" hollow back. If the double thickness of the same tube is attached to the backbone, the tube will form a "two on and one off" hollow back. By making an extra fold it is also possible to make a "two on and two off" hollow back, in which case there will be two thicknesses of paper on each side of the tube. A "one on and one off" hollow tube is made by cutting a strip of paper twice the width of the backbone and then folding it over in such a way that the two edges form a butt joint. This tube is often reinforced with a cloth strip, the ends of which can be folded over the backbone and stuck down over the tube (see the hollow tube shown in fig. 48). The number of layers in the hollow tube depends on the size and weight of the book—"a two on and two off" hollow tube being, of course, a stronger construction than the three-layered tube or the "one on and one off" tube. As some backbones are wider at one end than the other, due to faulty sewing or construction techniques, it is rather important that if the tube is made off the book, it should not be reversed from head to tail when it is put on the backbone. The restorer can

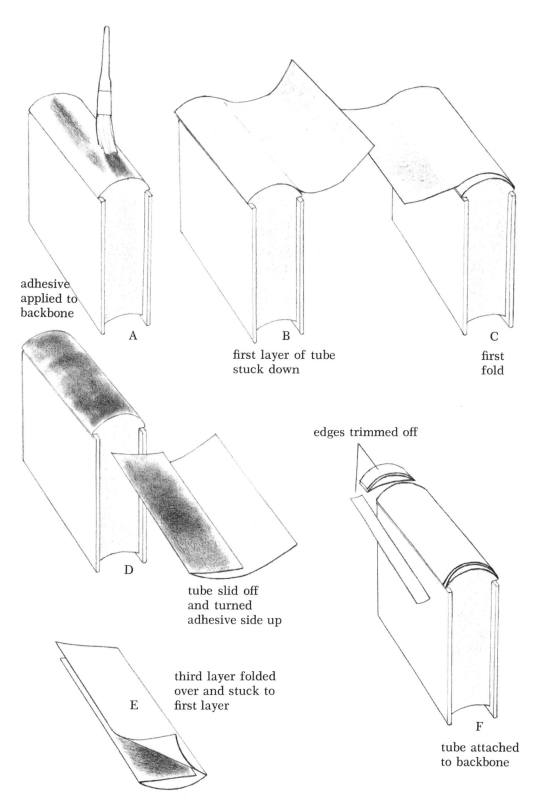

adhesive
applied to
backbone

A

first layer of tube
stuck down

B

first
fold

C

tube slid off
and turned
adhesive side up

D

edges trimmed off

third layer folded
over and stuck to
first layer

E

tube attached
to backbone

F

Fig. 47.   Forming a three-layer hollow tube, in this case a "one on and
two off."

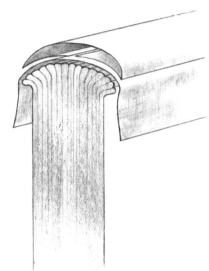

Fig. 48.   A "one on and one off" hollow tube overlying a cloth strip, the end of which can be folded back over the tube to reinforce it.

ensure that this will not happen by making a small mark on the edge of the paper, say at the tail end, and then putting the hollow tube on so that the mark remains at the tail end. Once the hollow tube has been made and is thoroughly dry, the top or outer layer may need to be glass-papered to ensure a smooth surface on which to stick down the leather spine.

Extra linings can be put down on the backbone before the hollow tube is constructed if the book needs extra support, and more linings can be stuck down to the outer layer of the tube if the thinning of the paper caused by subsequent glass-papering is likely to make this necessary.

11   Preparation of Boards for Rebacking

After the old spine has been removed, any necessary repairs have been made to the sewing of the backbone, new slips have been formed to attach the boards if necessary, the headbands have been repaired or replaced, and the book has been glued up, rounded, backed, and lined, the next step is to prepare the boards for the rebacking operation. If the boards have been detached from the book, they can be prepared away from the book. If the boards are still attached, the work must be done with the boards still on the book, and since this is somewhat more difficult we shall describe the procedure as though this were the case. Either way, the basic techniques will be very much the same.

It is advisable to raise, or "lift," the old leather turn-ins on the inside of the head and tail ends of the boards (and, of course, the pastedowns which cover them) far enough to insert the new leather backing before the old leather on the outer sides parallel to the joints is lifted. If the leather on the outer sides is lifted first and the boards are still attached to the book, there is a strong possibility that the leather will be damaged along the edges by rubbing against the backbone when the boards are opened to lift the turn-ins and pastedowns (see fig. 49).

In the case of books which are being reinforced with overcast cloth joints, the pastedowns must also be lifted along the inner joints on the inside of the boards to a depth of at least 1 inch, so that the side of the cloth joint which comes over on to the board can be placed underneath.

All of this work can be done by cutting with a sharp knife; it is seldom necessary, as is often thought, to lift the turn-ins or pastedowns by moistening them with water. The use of water in lifting small areas of leather or paper takes longer, is often dangerous, and is usually less effective than cutting. (In the case of wooden boards, however, it may be necessary to moisten, or even soak, paper pastedowns before they can be lifted. It is also usually necessary to use water if *large* areas of paper are being lifted, no matter what kind of board has been used.) If the paper in the pastedown is fragile or worn, the restorer should not hesitate to cut into the board and lift a thin layer of it along with the pastedown so that the minimum of strain will be placed on the paper. This cannot be done, of course, if the boards are of wood.

Next, the leather on the sides along the outer joints should be lifted. The initial cut should be made at a shallow angle and parallel with the joints, taking care not to cut through the slips if they are sound and the boards are still attached. This first cut is most successfully made with the point of the knife drawn towards

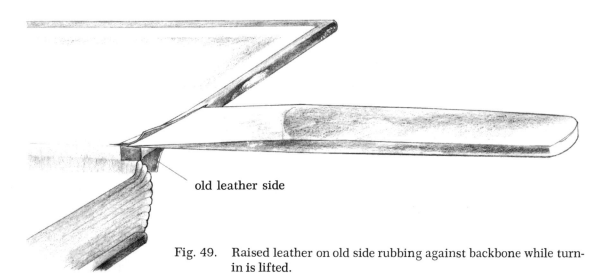

old leather side

Fig. 49.   Raised leather on old side rubbing against backbone while turn-in is lifted.

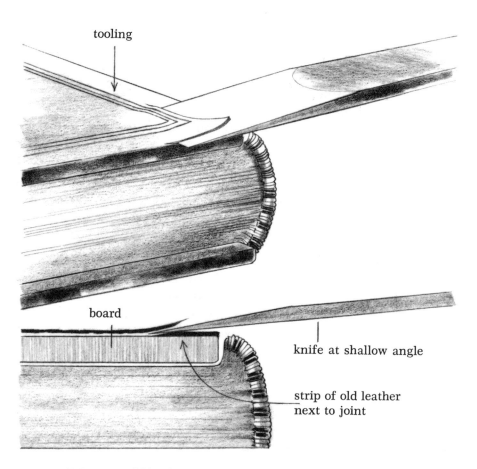

tooling

board

knife at shallow angle

strip of old leather
next to joint

Fig. 50.   Lifting an old leather side along a tooled line.

one so that it can follow the wanderings (if any) of the gold or blind lines, but the actual lifting can be done with most of the cutting edge. Some lines meander so much that it would be impossible to make the initial cut with the full length of the cutting edge. If there are gold or blind tooled lines near the edges of the boards, the cut is usually made alongside the line nearest the joint, because the tooling will help to disguise the joint where the old and new leather will come together (see fig. 50). If there is no tooling, the cut should be made fairly close to the joint. If the cut is made too close to the joint, however, and the new leather is thick, when the repair is finished and the board is thrown back to open the book, the edge of the old leather may be forced up into an unsightly ridge instead of lying flush with the new leather. It is usually the best practice, therefore, to make the cut a small distance from the joint whether there is tooling or not. The strip of old leather next to the joint should be left in place. The reason for leaving this strip will be explained a little later on.

Occasionally, even when there is tooling near the joints, it may be necessary to cut closer to the joint than would normally be desirable, because the colour, texture, or grain of the original leather is difficult or impossible to match (this is particularly likely when the original leather has deteriorated to an advanced stage or when it has been embossed with a design from engraved plates), and one wants as little as possible of the new leather to show as a contrast to the old (see fig. 51).

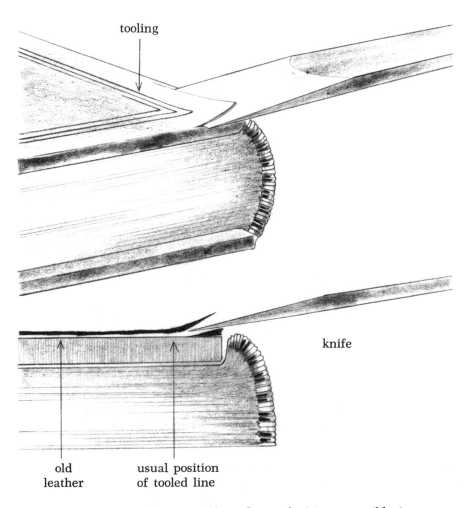

Fig. 51.   Lifting an old leather side as close to the joint as possible, ignoring tooled lines, so that a minimum amount of new leather will show.

In many cases it is not feasible to lift the old leather that covers the head and tail edges of the boards near the joints because it is too worn or powdery, in which case when the book is rebacked, the new leather will be laid over the old. However, if these edges are decorated with a tooled pattern which cannot be matched reasonably well, and the leather is still at least somewhat flexible, it is worthwhile to try to lift it so that the new leather can be put underneath. (This can be done on many morocco bindings, but seldom on those covered with calf or russia, which have a greater tendency to powder.)

As was pointed out earlier, the knife used for lifting leather should have the shallowest possible bevel because a steep bevel tends to crack the surface of badly deteriorated leather when the knife slices in and may also mean the loss of any gold tooling that may be present. The lifting is done with a sweeping motion of the knife, which is a combination of strong pushing and slicing. If the pushing is stronger than the slicing there is a greater likelihood of bumps being formed under the leather. It is much better to start lifting at the far end of the board so that one is pushing towards an already lifted area rather than starting at the near end so that one is faced with the harder task of advancing on completely solid parts. With correct technique and a knife of suitable shape a side can be lifted for rebacking in three or four minutes. Attempts at lifting with scalpels, spatulas and folders are almost certainly doomed to failure; the leather is likely to be damaged and the work will take far too long. The steel in many lifting knives is comparatively soft with the result that when tough leather pasted to rope-fibre board is being lifted the blade may quickly develop a large burr. This is worse than using a rather blunt knife because the edge is much thicker and can easily cause ridges to form under the leather, so it is advisable to stop work immediately and put the knife on an oil stone or strop it strongly.

The lifting of the original leather sides may be especially difficult when they are stuck to certain types of rope-fibre board of the eighteenth century. As the knife is pushed in, it tends to push loosened fibres together and thus form bumps. In books with boards like these, once the initial cut has been made it is better to pull the leather up with the fingers or to use the knife as a lever to pry it up. Obviously, this is possible only when the leather is strong and its surface will not be affected by the strain placed on it in using this technique; for this and other reasons it is unwise for the inexperienced worker to attempt it.

When the leather sides along the outer joints have been lifted (a strip of leather from 1 to 1¾ inches deep is sufficient for most books, but one should err on the generous side because the more leather one lifts the less it will have to be bent and disturbed as the pasted leather is put on), it is nearly always advisable to rub the boards with a folder through paper to flatten any disturbed fibres. A little thin paste applied to the exposed boards may occasionally be needed to consolidate their surfaces, and obstinate bumps may need to be tapped with a hammer, but this is best done through the old leather because the action of bending it back to get at the board may well cause serious damage.

When the old leather on the sides is brittle or powdery, some binders stick tissue on to its surface before it is lifted, with the object of holding it together, but the paste used for this purpose often blackens the leather. An additional hazard is that one cannot see whether damage is being done by the knife since the surface of the leather is hidden by the tissue. It is therefore usually best to avoid this technique.

The strip of original leather left at the inner edge of the board along the joint should be lifted and restuck to the board if, as is very often the case, it is insecure; or if this strip is in very poor condition, it can be replaced by a strip of new leather or thin card, suitably bevelled. Many binders discard this strip and do not replace it with anything else, but this is an extremely serious error and usually results in the old leather forming a ridge where it joins the new when the new leather is put on. Many binders who make this mistake compound the error by making a vertical cut into the old leather side instead of cutting at an angle to make a bevelled edge, and this makes an even more unsightly join (see fig. 52). Other binders replace the old leather strip with thinner material, but this results in the new leather being lower than the old where they join. If the old strip is retained intact (or a new strip of leather or card of the same thickness is put on), and the edge of the new leather is properly pared and bevelled, the join will be level (see fig. 53).

Finally, after the boards have been prepared to receive the new leather backing, they can be reattached if necessary. If new slips have been formed on the old cords by one of the methods described in section 6, including the Sydney Cockerell method as il-

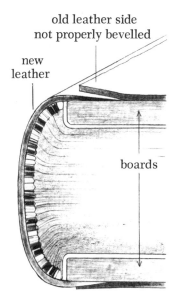

Fig. 52. Rebacked book, showing ridge caused by removal of strip of old leather near the joint.

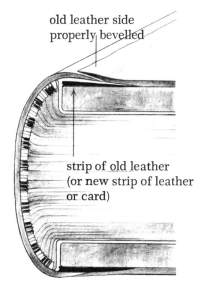

Fig. 53. Rebacked book with strip of old leather near the joint retained (or replaced by a new strip of leather or card), so that the join will be level.

lustrated in figure 22, they can now be laced into the boards or frayed out and pasted on to their outer surfaces, either under the strip of old leather remaining along the joints or over it (see fig. 54). If Sydney Cockerell's other method of forming slips by attaching strips of tape between recessed cords has been used (see fig. 24), the boards should now be split and the ends of the tapes glued in.

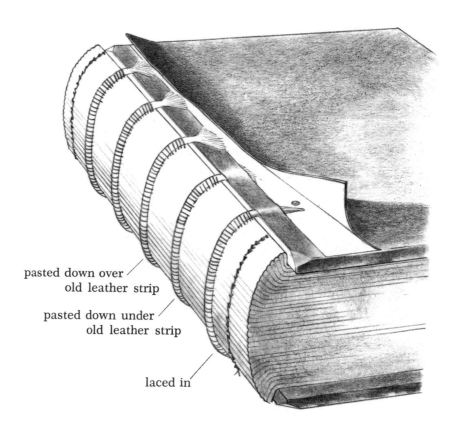

pasted down over
 old leather strip

pasted down under
 old leather strip

laced in

Fig. 54.   Slips laced in or frayed out and pasted down to boards
under and over old strip of leather.

12   Rebacking

The book is now ready to receive the new leather backing. The new piece of leather should be long enough from head to tail to provide sufficient leather for the new headcaps and turn-ins. It should also be wide enough to overlap the backbone of the book about 1 inch on each side. This is sufficient for an octavo, but about 2 inches is needed for a large folio. The edges of the new leather should be pared on a long bevel on all four sides so that the extra thickness under the original leather sides and turn-ins and under (or over, as the case may be) the leather on the head and tail edges of the boards will be imperceptible, or at least not unsightly. It is a good idea to pare away the corners of the new leather because when it is turned in the corners tend to turn back on themselves and make a lump under the pastedowns, especially if the area is rather inaccessible.

Knives of various designs are used to pare the edges of leather. The ordinary binder's paring knife (sometimes called an edging knife) shown in figure 15 is often used, but some binders prefer the French paring knife, which has a handle and a broader blade. For the allover paring or thinning of leather, many binders today use a spokeshave, reserving the paring knife for bevelling the edges. (A spokeshave is seen in use in fig. 55.) Paring leather properly requires some practice, and actually doing it is really the only way to learn. When using a paring knife, which must have a sharp edge, one must take care to keep the fingers well away from the blade.

After being pared, the new leather should be stained to the approximate tone and shade required (see section 22 for a discussion of staining techniques). It should then be moistened on the hair side with water or, better, with a solution of potassium lactate, to make it more pliable and easier to work. Potassium lactate or citrate should certainly be used if there is any doubt that the leather has been protected by the manufacturer against red rot as indicated by the ability to pass the P.I.R.A. test. Even if the leather has been so protected, the use of the potassium lactate safeguards against the possibility of the original protective non-tans being washed out while the leather is being worked. If unprotected or inadequately protected leather is used, the use of potassium lactate or some other effective agent is imperative,

Fig. 55.   Leather being spokeshaved.

though these may not be as effective as was once thought. Ideally, it should be applied to all new leather before the leather is put on the book and again after the leather has been put on and the adhesive has had a chance to dry. If both of these steps cannot be taken, it is more important to apply the potassium lactate before the leather is put on rather than afterwards, because once it is put on, some areas of the leather will be inaccessible. Lactate should not be applied to chrome or semi-chrome leather.*

If the book has a hollow tube back, the tube may now be split along its folds far enough back to accommodate the turn-ins of the leather at the head and tail of the book which form the headcaps. The splitting may result in some weakening of the tube, however, so that it may have a tendency to come apart in later years. This can be avoided by not splitting the tube and simply turning the leather in over the top of it. However, it should be noted that this may make the concealment of the turn-in more difficult.

The underside of the new leather should now be coated with medium-thick paste, folded over with the pasted surfaces together, and set aside. When the paste has soaked in for about five minutes, the leather should be opened up and repasted. It should then be stretched down the middle if it has to go over prominent raised bands. This is best accomplished by folding the leather lengthways so that the pasted surfaces are together. The leather is then gripped with both hands on either side of the fold and stretched by twisting the hands in opposite directions. The fold itself should not be squeezed because this may show on the spine if it is not covered with the original spine or with tooling. If it is not stretched, the leather may not adhere properly on each side of the bands and in fact may fail to stick at all in some panels. In a tight-backed book, the backbone should also be pasted to assist the adhesion of the leather, but it is better not to apply paste to the boards because the old leather on the sides may well be damaged by the moisture in the paste before the new backing is put on. If the restorer is a slow worker, he should give the new leather a more than usual liberal pasting so that the paste will not "set" before he has had time to manipulate the new leather into its proper position.

The new leather may now be "drawn on," that is, moulded on to the back of the book so that it settles comfortably between the bands and lies flat along the outer sides. The ends should then

*See page 58 for revised recommendations.

be turned in at the head and tail and smoothed over with a folder along the head and tail edges of the boards so that the new leather merges well with the old. (The process for books without raised bands would be much the same, except that it would not be necessary to stretch the leather down the middle.)

While the leather is being turned in at the head and tail, assuming that the boards are still attached by the cords, the body of the book should be held fore edge up with its back down on the working surface (which should be as smooth as possible), with the boards lying open and extending at head or tail about 2 inches beyond the edge of the working surface. Unless the book is very large, it should be held in this position under one arm, or should be supported by one's body, so that both hands are left free for the sometimes awkward operation of turning the new leather over the top and bottom edges of the boards and then under the pastedown. If in order to accomplish this it is necessary to exert considerable pressure on the boards, the damp new leather spine should be protected by laying a wad of cotton wool or several layers of soft cloth under it. If the book is unmanageably large, an assistant should hold it in position while the leather is being turned in (or it may be possible to prop up the book between two padded bricks). If the boards are not still attached by the cords the book can be taken away from the "case" after the leather has been drawn on, then the leather can be turned in. After this the book can be put back into its case. When turning in one is well advised never to squeeze the air out of the folds at the head and tail because this enables them to be knocked over into a good shape for the caps. A creased fold is likely to make a bad cap.

When a binding has no pastedowns and must be kept in the same state, and when the old leather turn-ins are very narrow, the turn-ins of the new leather either must be made equally narrow, so that they will line up evenly with the old turn-ins, or, preferably, a cut should be made into the board so that while the new leather turn-ins can be made wider for a better grip, they may be hidden inside the board (see fig. 56).

After the leather has been turned in at the head and tail, if the book is pre-nineteenth century and has raised bands, it should be "tied up" with cord passing around the book and over the new spine on both sides of the raised bands in a manner similar to that shown in figure 57, using, of course, tying-up boards in the process. In a great many cases this is really not necessary to

old leather turn-in

Fig. 56.   Unlined board being opened to receive new leather turn-ins.

make the leather stick, but as virtually all pre-nineteenth-century bindings with raised bands were tied up to emphasize the bands instead of using band nippers, the indentations made by the cords on the sides of the cover help to impart the right characteristics to the binding. The operation needs to be carried out in such a way that the cord used to tie up the book is wound fairly tight and has a fair degree of tension. In fact, if the volume is a large one, and the leather tends to lift on either side of the bands, the tension needs to be considerable. The thickness of the cord to be used will depend on the size of the book, a thick cord being used for heavier volumes, but this is for appearance rather than strength. It is usually not desirable to tie up books bound in the nineteenth century or later because they were probably not tied up to begin with and therefore lack the indentations on the covers near the joints made by the tying-up cords. In these books, band nippers can be used to mould the leather over the bands. However, if the bands are large and prominent, the band nippers may not be adequate. In this case, the book should be tied up with sheets of card placed on either side of the book to prevent the cord from making indentations in the leather on the sides. Alternatively, the book can be tied up as shown in figure 59, or it can be placed in a finishing-press with tacks on the sides for the attachment of cord, a German arrangement often employed in the United States.

If the new leather spine is sticking without difficulty and the leather on the old sides is powdery, it is a good plan to remove

Fig. 57.   A book being tied up with cord on both sides of raised
bands. Note tying up boards protecting the fore
edges of the binding.

the tying-up cord after a few minutes, so that the old leather can be pulled away from the damp new leather; otherwise, the old leather may become permanently blackened.

The new leather should now be smoothed over and moulded with the flat side of a folder along the joints and down over the outer sides so that it will be smooth and level (see fig. 58). When working on a light-coloured binding (especially if it is calf), it is

Fig. 58.   New leather backing being moulded and smoothed down with a folder. The book shown here has been tied up with cord. Note the tying-up boards.

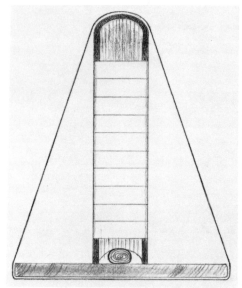

Fig. 59.   The book has been bound with tape to stabilize it and a roll has been placed under the fore edge to help prevent collapse of the spine when the cord is tightened.

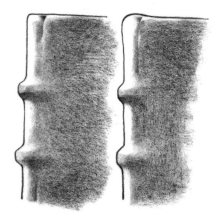

A   B

Fig. 60.   Side view, showing profile of spine (A) with a cap which is too square on top. Rounded shape (B) is typical of caps up until about 1780.

wise not to rub directly on the damp new leather because of the danger of bruising its surface, but in no other case should one hesitate to use the folder directly on the leather. If rubbing is necessary, but bruising is possible and must be avoided (sometimes it is desirable to bruise the new leather somewhat so that it will match the old leather more closely), a layer of waste paper should be placed between the leather and the folder.

On these occasions when the old leather on the sides has become pitted and the smooth new leather makes a jarring contrast with it (as often happens in the case of calf), the wet new leather can be tapped with a stiff, coarse brush, like a Hush Puppy brush, or a whisk broom until the texture of the new leather matches the old. This can be done after the leather has dried, but more force may then be needed, thus increasing the risk of damaging the old leather.

The time has now arrived for the headcaps to be set into their final shape. This can be done immediately after the new leather has been turned in at the head and tail, but it is more conveniently done after the tying up (if any), because the book is then firmly held together and there is less risk of the wet new leather shifting out of position as one is working. Many restorers set the caps on old bindings as they would on modern ones, which is unfortunate. Although it is difficult to generalize, and any date given must be arbitrary, I suggest that caps for bindings which date from before 1780 should be formed so that they are rounded (see fig. 60), and the ends should not be pinched in at the joints (see fig. 61). Post-1780 caps can be tapped gently with a straight-ended folder and be squared up. They should then be tied around with thread to pinch them at the joints as is usually done in modern fine binding (see fig. 62), unless one has evidence that this was not done to the binding originally.

When small books are rebacked or recapped the new leather must be pared so thin, especially at the caps, that only the weakest part of the skin remains. On these occasions I sometimes line the flesh side of the pasted leather with nylon gossamer at the turn-in areas and add a little PVA to aid adhesion. The nylon has insufficient bulk to affect the repair, but it appreciably strengthens the leather. Whether or not the migration of acid from air-polluted leather will, in the long term, weaken the nylon is a moot point.

After the new leather has been put on, whether or not the book has been tied up, it should now be left to dry overnight (twenty-four hours may be necessary if the leather is very thick). In conducting many workshops in the United States, Great Britain and on the Continent, I have noticed that many of the participants have laid the books down to dry with the underside completely against a lithographic stone or some other surface. However absorbent the surface may be this is a dangerous thing to do because trapped moisture is very likely to discolour the old leather. When the book is ready to be put aside for drying one should ease the old leather away from the wet new leather and then lay the book on a bench or pressing board with the wet part of the book overhanging the edge so that the moisture can evaporate. A weight (covered if made of metal) should be put on the upper cover, but not over the wet part, of course. When the leather is dry the boards should be opened to inspect the condition of the new leather joints. They must be opened carefully so as not to cause

Fig. 61.   Typical shape of cap of book dating from before about 1780. Note lack of "pinching" at joints.

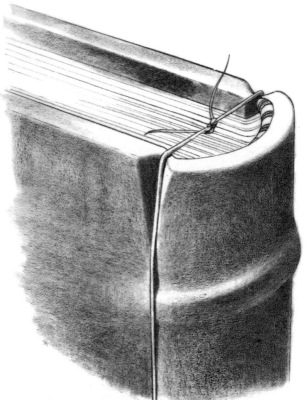

Fig. 62.   The square cap of a book dating from after about 1780 being pinched at the joints with thread. Note that the boards have been back cornered.

the raised leather on the old sides to be damaged by rubbing against the backbone. At this stage some moisture remains in the leather and the boards can be opened without strain, but if too much time elapses (more than twenty-four hours), it is a good plan to moisten the new leather at the joints, especially at the turn-ins, with water or potassium lactate before the boards are opened. If this is not done, the strain of opening the boards for the first time may cause the new leather to split along the inner joints where the leather is turned in. Sometimes when the boards are first opened the flyleaves stick to the boards along the inner joints. Damage to these flyleaves can be avoided or minimized if a straight-edge or some similar straight, smooth object is laid on top of them as close to the joint as possible and is held down firmly while the board is eased gently into the open position.

We now have to consider the sticking down of the old leather sides, where they were lifted to allow the new leather to pass underneath. This sticking down is frequently accomplished without difficulty, but the outcome can sometimes be disastrous if great care is not exercised. The most likely casualties are some eighteenth- or, more particularly, nineteenth-century, tan-coloured calf bindings which are in a fairly advanced state of decay. The danger is that if too much paste is used and if the pressure applied is too great and too prolonged the old leather will be blackened. Once this has happened nothing can be done to alleviate the situation. When this kind of binding is being handled, extra care must be taken, but there is a potential danger of blackening with all leather, particularly when it is old, so that the amount of paste used should always be minimal and not too thin (it takes very little to make a firm bond).

Many restorers, especially the less experienced, apply the paste with a brush, but I feel that greater control can be exercised, lumps in the paste are more easily felt, and less damage may be done if the fingers are used instead. If the leather is very brittle and cannot be lifted sufficiently for the insertion of pasted fingers or a brush, a slip of pasted paper can be slid underneath. The old leather can be pressed down on to it briefly before the paper is slid out. Usually, not a lot of paste is transferred, but weak leather needs little persuasion to stick, and as it is easily darkened it is important to minimize moisture.

Once the paste has been applied, and a check has been made to ensure that the new leather has not been inadvertently turned back on itself, thus making a ridge, and that there are no other bumps which need to be cleared or pared away, the book is ready to put in the nipping press. If the leather is exceedingly delicate and absorbent it may be better not to press it at this stage but just lightly folder it down through paper and then, when thoroughly dry, crush one board at a time (see page 146). The pressure exerted on the book in the press should be fairly light and of short duration. Thirty seconds to one minute is sufficient for most bindings, but some awkward ones with thick, springy leather may need two or three minutes of greater pressure for firm adhesion. For this kind of pressing, one should use fairly soft binding boards on the sides of the book rather than the usual wooden pressing boards or tins, because the soft boards absorb moisture and lessen the danger of blackening the leather. Also, if the soft boards should inadvertently become stuck to the sides they are more easily removed than wood or tin, and with less danger of damaging the old leather. The boards should be placed level with the edges of the old leather, partly because in most cases this helps to bind them in, and it also reduces the danger of crinkling the new leather on the spine.

Another method of reducing or avoiding the blackening of the leather is to use PVA adhesives, which have a low water content, but I prefer to use paste whenever possible, because its greater penetration provides a better grip. (PVA tends to peel off smooth surfaces, but if the surfaces are rough, or can be roughened, PVA will hold very well.)

Some books are very awkwardly shaped, so that when the old sides are stuck down and pressure is applied in the nipping press, no pressure is exerted where the old leather overlaps the new near the joints because the book is thinner at that point than at the fore edge of the book. Dutch and German books of the sixteenth and seventeenth centuries are often wedge-shaped. Dirk de Bray, a Haarlem bookbinding apprentice, writing in 1658 said, "But I would point out that a book which is given clasps must be beaten thinner at the spine than at the fore-edge; to this you must pay particular attention."* Apparently, this was done to create tension on the clasps. The remedy for this difficulty in normal pressing is to put wedge-shaped backing boards on each side of the book with their thick edges level with the join, and then to place the whole in a lying press for a few minutes (see fig. 63). Not more than moderate pressure should be applied, because of

*Dirk de Bray, *A Short Instruction in the Binding of Books,* with an Introduction and a Paraphrase by K. van der Horst and C. de Wolf (Amsterdam: Nico Israel, 1977).

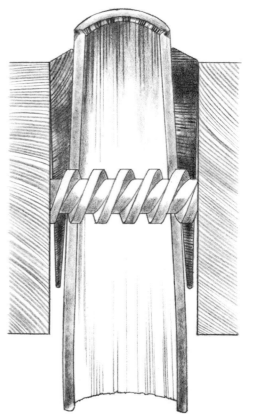

Fig. 63.   Wedge-shaped book in lying press with backing boards on either side of the book.

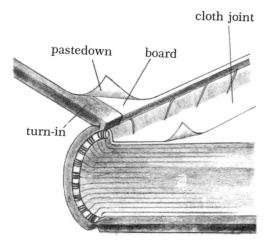

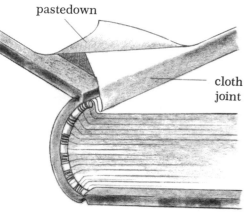

Fig. 64.　Overcast cloth joint being stuck down under pastedown.

the danger of creasing the leather on the new spine. If the book is sewn on raised cords, and the ends of these cords are very prominent on the outside of the boards, the leather on the outer sides between them often gets no pressure while in the press. These areas must then be rubbed down with a folder (over a layer of waste paper) in order to make the leather stick.

If there are no overcast cloth joints to be inserted under the original pastedowns, the turn-ins on the inside of the head and tail of the boards can be stuck down by applying paste or PVA to them and nipping them at the same time as the sides. If cloth joints have been sewn on, it would be better to hold off sticking them down until after the sides have been nipped and have thoroughly dried. Then, the cloth joints should be stuck down with PVA while the boards are open (see fig. 64). After 10 or 15 minutes the joints will have set so that they do not crinkle up too much and the boards can be closed. PVA or paste can now be applied to the under surface of the lifted areas of the pastedowns, tins should be placed right up to the joints inside the boards, pressing boards should be placed up to the outer joints and then the whole should be given moderate pressure for about 3 minutes, though if PVA has been used about 2 minutes will suffice. This adhesive is less likely than paste to come through the pastedowns and cause staining.

After the book has been removed from the nipping or lying press, and the adhesive has completely dried out (this would ordinarily take about twelve hours), each board can be pressed separately in the standing press (as illustrated in fig. 65), using fairly considerable pressure for fifteen minutes or so in order to crush down the join where the leather on the old sides overlaps the new. This can be remarkably effective in improving the finish of the repair. Polished plates (chromium-plated, or made of stainless steel) with rounded edges are often used for this pressing, but ordinary pressing tins can be employed. It is important, however, that if ordinary pressing tins are used, they be in good condition, because any flaws in their surfaces are likely to be reproduced on the covers. In order to avoid having ridges indented into the leather at the joints, the pressing plate (or tin) should be set right up to the joints and pressing boards placed on top of it, but ⅛ inch or more farther back, so that pressure on the inner edges of the plate is reduced (see fig. 66). Pressing of this short duration should not cause undue glazing of the old leather where

Fig. 65.   The boards of a rebacked book being pressed one at a time in a
French-type standing press.

it lies over the new, but one can make certain of this by placing paper with a slightly rough texture between the pressing plates and the old leather.

It is of the greatest importance that no moisture be present when the boards are pressed, because the slightest dampness is likely to cause the leather to stick to the pressing plate. Even dry powdery leather may occasionally stick, so it is usually a good idea to place a piece of silicon release paper between the leather and the plate to prevent the surface of the leather being removed.

Care must be taken when pressing the covers if there is important blind tooling at the point of greatest pressure, because otherwise the tooling may be flattened out and obliterated. In such cases five minutes or less of moderate pressure in the press may be enough.

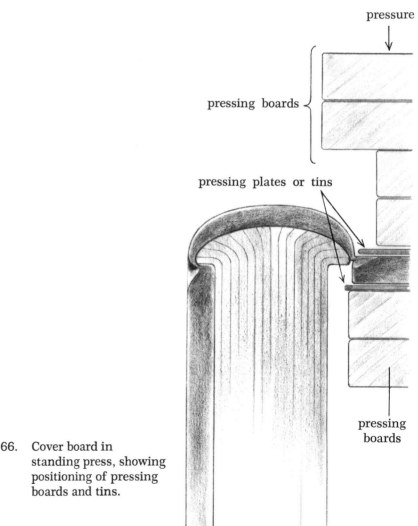

Fig. 66.   Cover board in
standing press, showing
positioning of pressing
boards and tins.

13   Repairing Inner Joints

If the original spine is to be replaced over the new leather it is a good plan to make any necessary repairs to the inner joints first; otherwise, when the boards are closed the added thickness of the material used to repair these inner joints may exert such pressure on the outer joints that this may force up the edges of the stuck-on old spine and cause these edges to become detached from the new leather backing. Although this situation can be improved by rubbing down the edges with a folder, this may not always be completely effective, and they may eventually have to be pasted down again.

Paper used for repairing the inner joints is best stuck on with PVA adhesive, which has the merits of great tenacity and quick drying. If Japanese tissue, which tends to be quite porous, is used, however, one is well advised to employ paste instead of PVA, because PVA sometimes squeezes through and causes the tissue to stick to itself when the board is closed, even when the joints are quite dry.

If the right adhesive is used, and the paper for repairing the inner joints is not too thick for the purpose, there is no need to do more than paste a strip of paper from the head to the tail of the inner joint wide enough to reach from the edge of the pastedown to the flyleaf, on to which it should overlap for a short distance, about 1/32 inch. It is not necessary to put the edge of the strip up on the board and underneath the pastedown; however, if the pastedown has been lifted to accommodate an overcast cloth joint, the new strip of paper can be inserted under the pastedown on top of the cloth joint (see fig. 67). One of the more substantial Japanese tissues is recommended because it sticks easily to small surfaces and blends in very well with many different kinds of plain paper. Very often, however, in order to match marbled or coloured endpapers it is necessary to cut up old "made" flyleaves to make the strips. Since these flyleaves are lined with an extra layer of white paper, they are too stiff and thick for the purpose, so the white lining leaf should be soaked off in hot water, and the old adhesive carefully cleaned off the marbled paper. As long as the colours match reasonably well the pattern is not always terribly important and it is surprising how well unpromising marbles merge in when they are fitted into the joints. How-

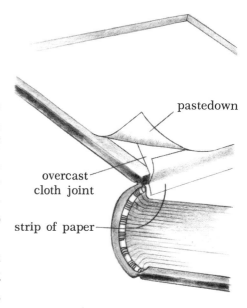

pastedown

overcast cloth joint

strip of paper

Fig. 67.   Repairing the inner joint.

ever, if nothing is acceptable the joints can be painted with water colours, but a painstaking copy is not normally necessary. This is best done on top of Jap tissue because this camouflages the sewing of the joints and helps to merge the joins.

Leather inner joints can be repaired in the same manner as paper ones. Leather used in this particular way has no structural advantage, however, especially since it must be pared extremely thin. There is therefore no virtue in using leather if another material will serve just as well or better, unless one is forced to use it in the interest of preserving absolute fidelity to the original binding; otherwise original leather inner joints are best replaced with strong paper or heavy tissue stained and possibly treated with wax or grease of some kind to resemble the old leather.

The new inner joints must be applied, of course, with the boards in an open position. If Japanese tissue has been used, the boards should not be closed until the adhesive has thoroughly dried, because even if paste, as opposed to PVA, has been used, the joints are likely to stick. If other paper has been used, the boards should be closed before the adhesive has completely dried, otherwise it may be difficult to get the boards to lie flat and a hard ridge may form along the outer joint.

14   Replacing the Original Spine

After the book has been rebacked and the inner joints repaired, and after everything has thoroughly dried (at least one full day should be allowed for this), if the original spine was salvageable, it should now be replaced on the book. Too often these old spines are discarded, regardless of their condition. The retention of this important part of the original binding whenever possible seems to me to be much more in line with the objectives of restoration work, as opposed to mere repairing or mending.

First, the edges of the old spine should be pared on as long a bevel as possible. If the leather is brittle and powdery, it probably will not be possible to do this in the way leather is usually pared. This is particularly true when the spine is stiffly rounded and cannot be flattened without damage—a difficulty most often found in nineteenth-century bindings with well-rounded backs.

An effective way of overcoming this problem is to place the spine on a piece of cover board with its outer surface uppermost and then to work a sharp knife from underneath the edges of the spine on each side, from the outer edge in towards the centre (see fig. 68). Even though this may seem more awkward than the usual method of paring, the fact is that the inward pressure on the old leather prevents pieces being broken off, which would be the likely result of the usual outward movement. The knife should have a very shallow bevel in order to produce the proper corresponding bevel on the edges of the spine so that it will adhere well to the new leather underneath and will lie flat along the edges of the shoulders. It should be noted that usually the act of cutting a spine away from the backbone of a tight-backed book automatically produces a good bevel at the edges, so that in this case no further paring is necessary.

The old spine is now pasted with medium-to-thick paste and placed in position on the new leather. The new leather should be scraped or glass-papered first if it is very smooth and hard so as to ensure firm adhesion of the old spine. In many cases, scraping or glass-papering is not required unless the leather has been "doped"* or has partial chrome tannage. The old leather spine is often very thin (either because it was thin originally or because the lifting and paring has made it so), and only the minimum of paste is necessary to make it stick. In fact anything more may cause serious discoloration.

The original spine often has a tendency to spring up again immediately after being pasted down, in which case the book should be wound with wide cloth tape or webbing (preferably with a fairly smooth surface) as soon as the spine has been placed in position (see fig. 69), and the tape should be left on for about ten minutes. It is best not to leave it on much longer than this because:

1. The spine may have shifted out of position during the taping and have to be slid back before the adhesive sets. (It cannot always be determined that the spine has shifted before the tape is removed.)

2. The tape may make marks on the old leather which cannot be removed once the paste has dried.

*"Doped" leather is leather which has been given a pigmented resin and/or nitrocellulose surface finish. This kind of leather is difficult to deal with in restoration work as it is hard to stain, at least with water-soluble stains, and resists other restoration or preservative treatments which require the penetration of the surface of the leather.

Fig. 68.   Paring the edges of an old leather spine.

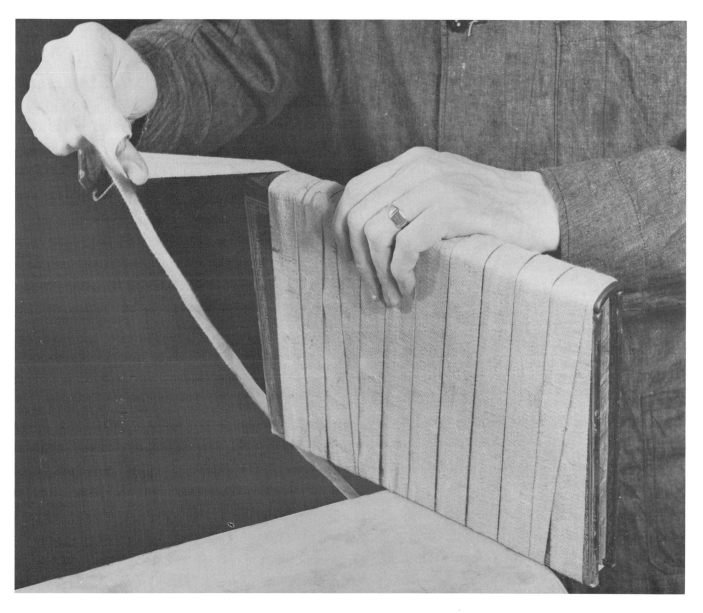

Fig. 69.   A book being bound with wide tape after replacing the original
spine.

3. Given more time, the wet paste may be forced through the old leather and cause it to blacken.

If the old spine has shifted out of position and the tape is removed within ten minutes it may be possible to reposition it by pressing the palm of the hand down hard and giving a sideways movement. Pulling with the fingers is a risky proceeding because of the danger of disintegration.

Many binders in the United States use elastic bandage for the purpose of binding the old spine but I have found it to be less precise and manageable than firm tape.

Just before the adhesive used to stick it down has dried (and after the tape, if any, has been removed), the spine should be gone over with a folder or a bandstick to make sure that it is not lifting anywhere, particularly on each side of raised bands near the joints. Straight downward pressure with the folder is safer than rubbing at this stage (unless the rubbing is done through fairly thick waste paper) because some old leather, particularly calf or sheep, is easily damaged or even destroyed by friction if much moisture is present. If the book has been bound with tape, any undesirable marks made by the tape should be smoothed out with a folder through a layer of waste paper.

If the spine still lifts a little at the edges, it can be rewound once more with tape. If the leather is lifting alongside raised bands, local pressure can be exerted more effectively by tying up with cord as described in section 12.

When separate panels have been lifted the leather is sometimes extremely delicate and cannot be pasted for replacement on the spine because of the danger of disintegration. If the weak panels were not reinforced with Jap tissue (see page 85) at the time of lifting it can be done at this stage, or the new leather on the spine can be pasted so that the panels can be laid down. If the panels are so fragile as to require this treatment it probably will not be necessary to do more than folder them down through paper. Whatever the method the result is likely to be unsatisfactory in that the colour of the new and old leather will not match, the edges of the replaced panels will be very evident and some tooling is likely to be missing, especially on the raised bands and around the edges of the panels. Much of this can be satisfactorily rectified. The first step can be taken when the old leather has been drying for something like two hours. At this stage a lightly greased folder can usually be used to rub and press down the edges, not only along the joints but also on either side of the raised bands. The whole should be directly foldered, if possible, so that it all feels smooth and natural. Further steps are described on page 192.

The replacement of the original spine completes the rebacking operation. The next step, unless the book needs other repairs such as the repairing of corners, etc., is to complete the staining, tooling, and furbishing of the book as described in section 22. If the original spine cannot be replaced on the book for some reason, the final staining and tooling must, of course, be done on the new spine.

15 Repairing Caps and Outer Joints without Rebacking

The operations of removing the original spine and completely rebacking the book as previously described will automatically provide the book with new caps and outer joints. There are some occasions, however, when the original spine of a binding which has broken caps, or outer joints, or both, must be preserved and yet cannot be removed and replaced on top of a new leather backing. This difficulty arises most frequently when the book is sewn on raised bands, because the cords or thongs get in the way of the knife and create many awkward right angles in the leather. Sometimes, however, the difficulty is due to the fact that the original binder may have burnt some of the gold or blind tooling through a thin leather (usually calf) spine in a tight-backed book. When this has happened, the tooled areas stick stubbornly to the backbone of the book and also make the surrounding leather very hard and brittle. When, in addition to these hazards, the rest of the old spine is in an advanced state of decay, the difficulties involved in removing it are often insurmountable.

In these cases, the only practical solution is to insert new leather joints and caps without attempting to remove the entire original spine.

The first thing to be done is to lift the old pastedowns near the head and tail of the book, the underlying turn-ins, and the outer sides of the cover (the latter along tooled lines if possible, as suggested previously) as for rebacking. As much as possible of the head and tail ends of the spine should also be lifted. If the leather on the spine is in very bad condition it may only be possible to lift it as far back from the ends as the turn-ins of the original caps—the double thickness of leather in these areas is a great help. Once these ends of the spine have been lifted up, the turn-ins of the old caps should be cut or peeled away and removed so that the old spine will now have only a single thickness at each end. This is done so that the new caps will not be too thick.

Once the ends of the spine have been lifted, and the turn-ins of the old caps have been cut away, the old headbands should be repaired or replaced if necessary. This may be difficult if the old spine cannot be lifted very far back from the head and tail ends of the book, in which case it may be better to cut away and put aside the lifted portions (to be replaced later) rather than to leave them in position and run the risk of having pieces knocked off and lost during the headbanding operation, particularly if the old leather is in bad condition.

The edges of the spine all along the joints should then be lifted. The farther across the width of the backbone the spine can be lifted, the better, so that when the new leather joints are pasted down underneath they will have the maximum grip. If the book is sewn on raised bands, and the leather lying over the cords can be lifted, so much the better; otherwise, cuts must be made on both sides of the bands (taking care not to cut through the threads sewn around the cords) so that the new outer joints can go over the old leather on the bands and under the panels between them (see fig. 70). When the old spine is made of a strong leather such as goatskin, it is often possible to lift it off the cords, but if it is, say, a thin, powdery calf, made even thinner by abrasion, any attempt to lift it off the cords to put the new leather underneath is a waste of time and energy. (In any case not much of the new leather will be showing, and it can therefore be fairly easily blended in with the old leather on the rest of the spine if it is put on properly.)

Occasionally, the original leather on the spine cannot be lifted up from the backbone along the joints at all, perhaps because it is too much decayed. In this case it must be scraped completely away from the backbone near the joints so that the new leather joints will be firmly based instead of being stuck to powdery

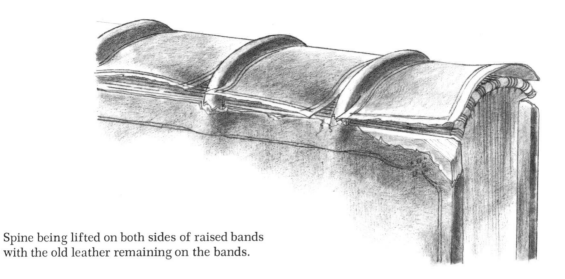

Fig. 70.　Spine being lifted on both sides of raised bands with the old leather remaining on the bands.

leather that may later disintegrate. If this is done, however, the new leather joints will be completely exposed where they lie over the backbone, and are likely to contrast to some degree with the remaining leather on the old spine, no matter how much trouble one takes to obtain matching leather and to blend it in—though they may be at least partly camouflaged by gold tooling if the area covered was already tooled. This method should therefore only be used as a very last resort. For the purposes of this volume, we will assume that enough of the old spine can be lifted off the backbone to get the new leather joints underneath.

The next step is the insertion of the new caps. First, the leather for the new caps should be cut to size, pared, and treated with a potassium lactate solution. The entire piece of leather must be pared thinner than one would normally wish, particularly where it will go under the head and tail ends of the old spine (at these points the new caps will eventually have three thicknesses instead of the usual two—one thickness formed by the leather on the old spine, and two thicknesses by the new leather), and also where it will go over the head and tail edges of the boards near the joints. All four edges of the leather for the new caps must be pared on a long bevel so that when the caps are pasted down the edges will taper off to a thin point and not form conspicuous ridges under the old leather.

When the new caps are being inserted, especially when only small areas of leather at the ends of the spine have been lifted, it is usually a good plan to attach the leather to the inside of the boards first to form the turn-ins, and then fold the remainder back over itself and work it under the raised spine and the leather on the outer sides of the boards. (This is, of course, the reverse of the method usually employed in forming the cap in a new binding or in rebacking. In a new binding or in rebacking, the leather is first attached to the outer sides and to the backbone and *then* turned over the boards to form the turn-ins.) Therefore, after the new leather for the cap has been cut and pared, the next step is to apply paste to that part of its flesh side where it will form the turn-ins on the inside edges of the boards (either under or over the old turn-ins, depending upon their condition), and at the same time to that part of its hair side where it will be stuck down to the backbone. (It is of no consequence at this stage if the paste goes beyond these points on either side.) To ensure firm adhesion, the end of the underlying backbone should also be pasted. The leather is now inserted (one side at a time) between the inside of the board and the raised edges of the pastedowns (which must be lifted far enough back to get the leather underneath) and over the backbone (see fig. 71). During this process the book is stood on end and is supported between the body and the forearm while the upper part of each board in turn is held away from the book by pressure from the thumb, and the lower part of the board is held firmly to the book with the four fingers (see fig. 72). This will prevent the straining or breaking of the cords. It is necessary to move the book from one side of the body to the other when the second turn-in is inserted. If the book is very large, or is unmanageable because both boards are detached, it can be laid on its side with the end of the book extending beyond the working surface while the new cap is inserted.

Many large books of the eighteenth and nineteenth centuries have over-large shoulders and very rigid rope-fibre boards which cannot be bent far enough to clear the shoulders so that the leather can be taken around them and inside the boards. With these books, the only way to get the new leather into position is to open each board in turn to an angle of about 90 degrees so that an opening is formed for the insertion of the turn-ins.

When the leather on the turn-ins and over the backbone is holding firmly, the remainder of the new leather cap can be dampened on its hair side and pasted on the flesh side. Now, while two fingers hold the old raised leather on the sides away from the

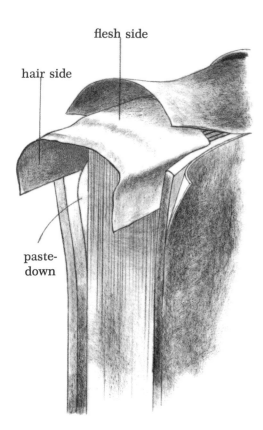

flesh side

hair side

paste-
down

Fig. 71.   Inserting leather for new cap.

Fig. 72.   Holding board away from book while inserting leather for new
cap.

boards, the new leather cap is turned back over on itself underneath the old spine (which usually can be bent up away from
the backbone of the book so that it does not get in the way) and
under the sides (see figs. 73 and 74). A folder is then used to
smooth everything down, to mould the leather over the edges of
the boards, and to shape the end of the cap. When this has been
done at each end and the new caps are firmly set and dried, the
book is ready for the new outer joints.

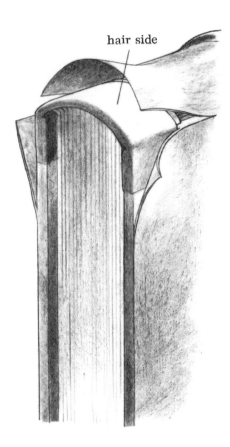

hair side

Fig. 73.   New leather cap being folded over backbone and under old spine and sides.

The two strips of new leather for the outer joints should be the length of the book and about ¾ inch wide, the exact width depending on the size of the book and how far the strips are to extend underneath the old spine and sides. (In general, the larger the volume, the wider the strips should be.) They should be pared fairly thin, with a long bevel on all four sides, and the edges should be feathered. While it is obviously not good to thin the leather unnecessarily, it is equally unwise to leave it very thick along the line of the joint because if it is too thick it will tend to lever itself off the backbone of the book each time a board is thrown back to open the book. This is an example of strength being a source of ultimate weakness. The restorer must judge the proper thickness of the leather according to the size of the book and the extent to which the new joint will overlap on to the backbone.

After the strips for the new joints have been cut to size, pared, and treated with a potassium lactate solution on the hair side, they should be pasted on the flesh side. When they have soaked for about five minutes, they should be repasted with fairly thick paste, and each in turn should be slipped under the old leather on the sides and then under the spine. If the book has raised bands and the old leather on the bands has not been lifted, the leather must be slipped under the raised panels, one panel at a time, and over the cords (see fig. 75).

If the leather on the old spine is very powdery and breaks off at the slightest touch, the insertion of the new joints can be a very delicate operation. Damage can be minimized by lifting or bending the leather on this kind of spine only as far as is absolutely necessary to get the new strip of leather underneath. It should be lifted as gently as possible; any sudden movement can cause serious flaking and loss of tooling, or even cause the old leather to break off completely. Once the new leather strip is underneath, it can be worked slowly up across the backbone without lifting or bending the spine any farther.

The amount of paste to be used on the new joints will depend on circumstances, such as the absorbency of the leather and the boards, but on the whole the pasting should be liberal, because in most cases the backbone cannot be pasted as it would be for rebacking, and the thinness of the leather shortens the drying—and therefore the working—time. If the craftsman is a slow worker and the leather begins to dry too soon, it can be remoistened on the outside.

Fig. 74.   Folding leather cap over backbone and under spine. Note how the
old leather sides are being held away from the boards.

Fig. 75.   A new leather joint being inserted under
the raised panels of an old spine.

If the book is pre-nineteenth-century and has raised cords, it should now be "tied up" with cord. This operation will be the same as that previously described in section 12.

When the new joints have dried and the tying-up cord (if any) has been removed, the old leather sides and the lifted parts of the pastedowns and the old turn-ins under which the new leather has been placed can be pasted and stuck down. It is then the turn of the old spine. Often, as was pointed out previously, the old spine is very thin and therefore only the minimum of paste should be used. As was also previously pointed out, if the old spine has a tendency to spring back up, the book should be bound with tape, but for no more than about ten minutes.

The temptation to paste down the edges of the old spine immediately after the new outer joints have been inserted and before the paste used to stick them down has dried should be resisted, because the moisture from the leather in the new joints, plus that in the paste used to stick down the spine may be enough to discolour the old leather, and also because the moist leather of the new joints is very soft and may be badly marked and distorted if the book has to be bound with tape.

No binding should be recapped and rejointed as described above if it can be completely rebacked (either with or without the replacement of the original spine) because this is not a strong method, though it is tolerable if it is done well and if the boards were still firmly attached. The lack of strength is due to the fact that the new leather joints are not in one continuous piece across the backbone of the book as they would be in rebacking. Also, the area of adhesion on the backbone is small and the leather of the new joints must be fairly thin (and consequently weak) if the repair is to be reasonably neat and the boards are to open properly without pulling the new leather off the backbone. There is the additional limitation that this method does not allow one to reinforce the attachment of the boards by means of overcast cloth joints, or in any other really satisfactory manner. Even the mending of the inner joints of a book (particularly a small one) with the thick paper that it may be necessary to use to match the existing endpapers may, if the outer joints have been repaired in this way, cause the new joints to pull off the backbone when the boards are closed. If medium-weight Japanese tissue is used, however, this is not usually a problem. This particular problem can also be overcome by mending the inner joints before the outer ones are repaired (but after the recapping has been completed), thus eliminating the strain on the new leather.

Sometimes it is not necessary to replace the entire outer joints of a book. The leather joints of many bindings are sound except at the ends near the head and tail of the book. In this event, the best course is to insert new caps as described above, and this will automatically take care of the ends of the joints. This is the strongest possible local repair because the new leather goes completely over the backbone and is therefore one continuous piece from one board to the other. However, if the volume is part of a set, and not all volumes in the set are to be recapped, it may be desirable to mend the ends of the joints of one or more of the volumes without recapping. This can be done by lifting the old sides and the edges of the spine along the joints just far enough back from the ends of the book to get new strips of leather in.

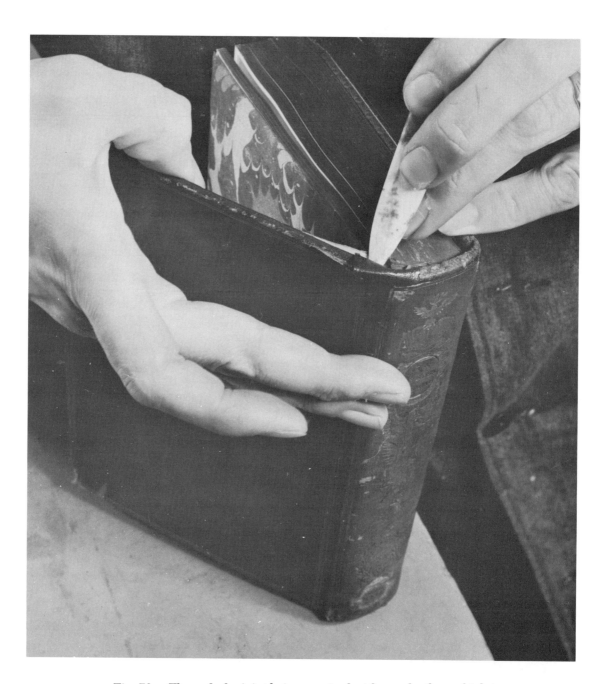

Fig. 76.   The end of a joint being repaired with new leather, which is
shown being turned in over the boards.

The new leather can then be inserted and turned in over the boards after the pastedowns and the old turn-ins have been lifted (see fig. 76); less satisfactorily, the new leather can end at the edge of the board without making the turn-in. When the book has raised bands it is often best to repair the joints all the way down to the top band (or up to the bottom band, as the case may be), because this tends to make the repair less conspicuous than finishing it somewhere between the band and the end of the book.

If, in addition to the ends, one or more additional parts of the joint are badly broken, it may be better to renew the whole joint as previously described than to attempt to patch it locally.

One further observation. Sometimes there are no tooled lines on the covers alongside which cuts can be made for lifting, and the old leather may be so hard that the cut edges show very distinctly when stuck down. In these cases, an overlay of extremely thin new leather, with feathered edges, covering the edges of the repair, although having no functional value, will much improve the appearance of the book. This type of overlay can also be used, if necessary, when completely rebacking a book if the edges of the old spine and lifted sides are too much in evidence.

16   Repairing Caoutchouc Bindings

Not infrequently the restorer is called upon to fasten in the loose leaves of caoutchouc bindings the backbones of which have disintegrated. This nineteenth-century binding process, a forerunner of the modern "perfect," or "adhesive" binding process, involved reducing the book to single leaves by trimming off the back folds and then securing the back edges of the leaves by means of a coating of liquid rubber. No thread was used to consolidate the backbone. The process was patented by William Hancock in England in 1836, the first commercial example was produced in 1839, and the technique was used rather extensively in England, and to a lesser extent elsewhere, throughout the nineteenth century. Many large colour-plate books which have now become valuable are bound in this manner, so it is important that effective remedial action be taken to preserve them.

In many cases the rubber has disintegrated so badly that the leaves have separated throughout the book, but in others only part of the backbone has broken down and the remainder can be taken apart only with the greatest difficulty. On these occasions one can understand the Victorians' faith in the efficacy of rubber, which was just coming into widespread use in their time.

These books were case-bound with either hollow tube backs or loose hollow backs, and the backbones were generally lined with canvas, the ends of which were stuck down under the pastedowns on the inside of the boards to reinforce the joints and to strengthen the attachment of the boards.

In order to expose the backbone of these books for repairs, the endpapers (which were always tipped in rather than sewn on in these books), the hollow tube (if any), and the canvas lining should be removed intact along with the cover if possible. The book should then be put between backing boards in the lying press, and the hard, sandy rubber scraped off the backbone with a rasp.

Some of these books were rounded and backed, and some had flat backs. It is usually best to try to retain the original rounding and backing, if any, because some of the backbones were formed in a special concave mould before the rubber was applied. As this usually produced a more pronounced rounded shape than can be obtained by the usual method of rounding a collection of loose leaves, that is, with a hammer, the backbone thus shaped by the restorer will not always fit snugly into the original covers of these books, especially when the spines are stiff and set in their shape. (This particular difficulty arises more often in the case of leather bindings than cloth ones, because cloth spines can be adapted more easily to the new shape of the backbone.)

Therefore, if the book was originally rounded and backed, the next step is to manipulate the backbone, if necessary, so that it is set as nearly as possible into its original shape. This should be done before a new coating of adhesive is applied. The new adhesive should then be well rubbed into the backbone so that it penetrates down in between the back edges of the leaves, thus providing them with a better anchorage.

The adhesive now generally used on unsewn bindings, both for the binding of new ones and the repair of old ones, is PVA, which has the requisite tenacity and flexibility.

If the book had a flat back, that is, was not rounded and backed, the next step after the removal of the old adhesive is simply to knock up the book by tapping the head and fore edges of the leaves on a flat surface until all the edges are even. Once this is done, the book should be put into the lying press (not too low, otherwise pressure will prevent the slight penetration of the adhesive), and the PVA can be applied to the backbone as described above.

Sometimes, particularly if the book is a large and heavy one, the foregoing method of applying the adhesive to the backbone will not suffice to hold the leaves together. In this case, a stronger method must be adopted.

First, the old adhesive must be removed as before and the book reduced to single leaves. Then, if the book was rounded and backed, the shoulders must be removed by bending, tapping, or pressing them flat. Next, the leaves should be fanned out while they are lying flat on the table or other working surface, in a manner similar to that shown in figure 31, and PVA applied so that the back edge of each leaf has a narrow strip of adhesive. The amount of fanning out depends on the width of the strip of PVA to be applied to the back edges of the leaves, and this in turn depends on the thickness of the paper. For thick, stiff leaves, a strip of adhesive no more than $1/32$ inch should be applied because the leaves will be levered apart when the book is opened if the area of adhesion is any greater. On the other hand, $1/16$ inch is not excessive for thin, soft papers because, since they are more flexible, there will be little, if any, leverage on the inner margins of these leaves when the book is opened.

As soon as PVA has been applied to the leaves, they should be knocked up so that they are all even. This should be done immediately because PVA sets quickly.

If the paper is sufficiently flexible, the fanning out can be done in a different and rather more convenient way if the book is placed in a lying press as shown in figure 77. The book can now be bent over to the left and right while the adhesive is applied. Before the book is put into the press, it should be carefully knocked up to align the edges of the leaves, and thin board should be put on either side of the book to prevent the outer leaves from bending too far over and coming away from the rest. (Board which is too thick will not allow the leaves to be bent over.)

At this point, if the book is large and printed on heavy paper, it is sometimes a good idea to recess cords into the backbone of the book to strengthen it, making sure that the cords are well

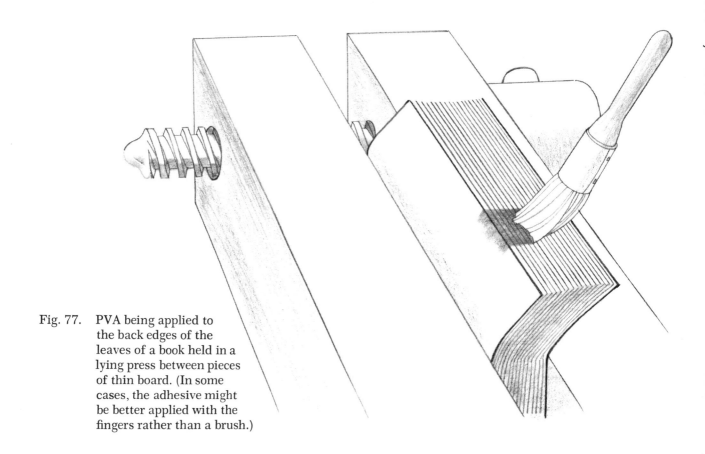

Fig. 77. PVA being applied to
          the back edges of the
          leaves of a book held in a
          lying press between pieces
          of thin board. (In some
          cases, the adhesive might
          be better applied with the
          fingers rather than a brush.)

set into the sawcuts with glue or PVA. If the book was originally
rounded and backed, it should now be manipulated as nearly as
possible into its original shape, using the original spine of the
cover as a guide. If necessary, the book should be put into the
lying press with backing boards on either side so that the shoulders can be consolidated. (As was pointed out earlier, getting the
backbone back into its original shape may be very difficult for
those books in which a special concave mould was used to form
the backbone, and for this kind of book taking the leaves apart
and fanning them out should be avoided whenever possible.) If
glued-in cords are used, they should now be trimmed off at the
joints.

In unsewn bindings, the first and last leaves of the book are
often easily detached, but, at least in books which have been
rounded and backed, this can be overcome if a cloth lining is
stuck down over the backbone and overcast on to the book with
a needle and thread, with the thread passing through both the

cloth lining and the shoulders of the book. If this is done, the overcast leaves cannot be pulled out of the book in a block as may otherwise happen. The cloth lining should be wide enough to extend down the sides of the book on the insides of the boards under the pastedown to reinforce the attachment of the boards (see fig. 78).

If the paper is fairly thin, so that the book will not be too difficult to open afterwards, the backbone can be oversewn throughout instead of simply sticking the back edges together with an adhesive or merely overcasting the shoulders. This can be done by making up groups of leaves into sections by overcasting them together and then sewing the entire book either all-along or two-sections-on on recessed cords. It should be pointed out that this may sometimes prevent the book from fitting back into the spine of its original cover due to the swelling caused by the added bulk of the threads, unless a great deal of work is done in paring the back edges of the leaves, but, generally speaking, the cased bindings are sufficiently loose-fitting to take the extra thickness.

Finally, after the backbone has been properly consolidated, and the leaves are holding firmly together, if the book had a hollow tube back and the tube and the canvas lining of the book are still attached to the cover and are in sound condition, the book can now be reinserted into its cover with another coating of PVA. (If a cloth joint has been added, however, it is wise to trim off the old canvas lining at the joints.) If the hollow tube and the canvas are not in good condition, they must be removed entirely, and the book should be provided with a new lining of cloth (if this hasn't been done already, as described above) and a new hollow tube. This should be reinforced with cloth (see fig. 48) if the attachment of the case has not been strengthened with overcast cloth joints (see fig. 78). If neither of these methods is adopted only the adhesion of the spine of the case to the top of the paper hollow tube and the tipping on of the endpapers will hold the case on to the text block, and this is certainly not adequate for large, heavy books. New endpapers may also have to be provided if the old ones are in bad condition; but this should be done only as a last resort.

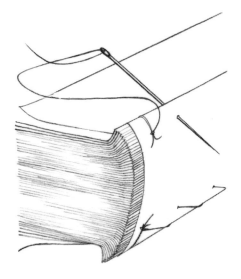

Fig. 78. Overcasting a cloth lining on a caoutchouc binding. The lining extends completely across the backbone, and its loose ends are pasted down on the inside of the boards under the pastedown.

17 Repairing Corners

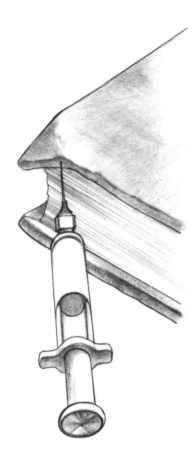

Fig. 79. Paste being forced into board with hypodermic needle and syringe.

The corners of a binding, like the spine and joints, are among its most vulnerable areas. In old books that have been subjected to much use, the corners are frequently badly worn, cracked, or broken. Sometimes parts of them, large or small, may be broken off entirely.

Occasionally the original leather on a corner may still be usable even though the board underneath is damaged and needs repair. In some cases, if the corner of the board is not too badly damaged, a hypodermic needle and syringe can be used to force paste into it without the necessity to lift the covering leather (see fig. 79). However, in many instances, this may not be sufficient. In such a case, after raising the pastedown where it lies over the turn-ins, the leather should be lifted all around the edges of the corner including the turn-ins, the board repaired as will be described later, and the leather should be stuck back down with paste and smoothed over with a bone folder and perhaps bent over a little with the fingers, particularly if the binding is an old one. For more recent bindings it may be appropriate, when the paste has dried, to nip the repaired corner in a press to flatten it, but it should be borne in mind that it should match the shape of the unrepaired corners, if any. Extreme care must be taken to avoid damaging the leather while the board is being repaired.

More often than not, however, the leather on the corners is missing, or so worn and damaged that it is beyond repair and must be removed and discarded. The restorer may or may not want to replace this leather with new leather depending, among other things, on the wishes of the owner of the book, and the kind and condition of the remaining old leather on the sides (including the difficulty of matching it with new leather) and of the board underneath. It is clearly cheaper not to attempt to replace the missing leather, but simply to colour the exposed board so that it matches the remaining leather as nearly as possible, and then to repair the board if necessary. This kind of treatment may be perfectly adequate if the board is basically sound, particularly if it is millboard made from rope fibre (identifiable from its long, mid-brown fibre), if the book is not destined to have heavy and continuous use, and finally, of course, if one is content to stop short of a complete restoration of the book.

If the missing leather is not to be replaced, the first step is to colour the exposed board with water-soluble or spirit stain, or some other suitable toning agent. This should be done before any repairs are made to the board, because after the adhesives used to make the repair have been applied, especially after they have dried and hardened, the stain will not be fully absorbed.

If the missing leather is to be replaced with new leather, once the board has been repaired and has dried and hardened, the remaining old leather on the sides adjacent to the corners must be lifted for some distance back, all along the edges of the repair, including the leather on the outside of the board, over the edges of the board, and on the turn-ins on the inside of the board. If the new leather does not already match the old, it should be at least partly stained before being pasted and moulded on. This initial staining should be done before the pasting and drying because stain may not be fully effective afterwards owing to the seepage of paste up through the new leather which would prevent the penetration of the stain.

The new leather for the corner should now be cut to size and pared to the requisite thickness with long bevels on all sides ending in feathered or ragged edges so that adhesion to the board will be good, and so that where the old leather will overlap these edges there will be no ridge and the join will be as inconspicuous as possible. (The feathered or ragged effect will occur naturally when leather such as goatskin is pared away at the edges.) The edges of the old leather on the sides adjacent to the damaged or missing corner are usually very thin and do not need additional thinning. Occasionally, however, it may be found that these edges, too, need to be pared. This should be done by the method described on page 151; otherwise, damage may result. It should be remembered that the slightest extra thickness where the old and new leather overlap will show up as a ridge.

The new leather should then be treated with potassium lactate, pasted, and applied to the corner of the board, and the raised old leather on the sides adjacent to the corner should be pasted down so that its edges overlap on to the new leather. The old leather should not be pasted down over the new until the latter is dry, otherwise when it is pasted down and the repaired corner is nipped in the press, the corner may be crushed and distorted. The nipping, if the old leather is springy, should be done before the old leather is dry, and should be of short duration in most cases—not more than half a minute—because otherwise the paste on the old leather (the paste used should be minimal) may be forced through to the surface of the leather and cause it to blacken; or the pressing boards used in the nipping press may stick to the old leather and pull off its surface when the press is released. Very often it is not necessary to nip the repaired corner. If this is the case the old leather can be merely foldered flat through paper and then be nipped or pressed when it is thoroughly dry.

In some cases, especially when the old leather on the sides is very brittle or powdery, the repair will show less if the edge of the new leather is pasted over the edge of the old leather, instead of the other way around. If this is done, careful paring of the new leather with a long bevel and an extremely thin edge is even more important. One may also want to lay the new leather over the old if, for the sake of strength, it is necessary to use a large area of new leather even though only a little of the old leather is missing. Even in such a case, however, it might be better to put the new leather underneath the old as usual and then, if the join shows too much, overlay it with a small area of extremely thin new leather so that the join will be hidden.

Once the leather on the corner has been replaced and the repair is complete, it may be necessary to restore any missing or defective blind or gold tooling, and to complete the staining and finishing of the new leather so that it more exactly matches the rest of the cover. (The techniques for accomplishing this will be discussed in section 22.)

Something should be said here about the turning in or formation of the corners on the inside of the boards. When the corner of a book is being restored, the form of the existing inside corners, should, of course, be duplicated as closely as possible. Corners have been, and are, formed in many different ways, whether the covering material is leather, paper, vellum, or cloth. Some examples are shown in figure 80.

The method used to repair the corners of boards depends upon the nature of the board and upon the extent and kind of damage it has sustained.

In some old boards the fibres in the corner are separated and spread out, making that part of the board thicker than the rest (see fig. 81). In this case, the board should be opened up as much as possible and fairly thick paste pressed in and distributed among the fibres. In those cases where the board is broken or cracked some distance in from the corners, it may be necessary to inject

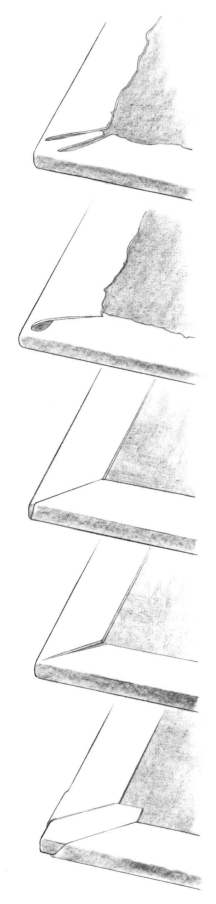

A. A method of cornering in which the leather is cut to form a tongue. This was much used in England from Saxon times until well into the sixteenth century.

B. A method of cornering employed on all classes of work from the second half of the sixteenth century to the end of the eighteenth or early part of the nineteenth century.

C. A corner commonly used from the seventeenth century to the present day. In this case, the edges of the two layers of leather must be bevelled to avoid a ridge where they overlap.

D. A corner frequently used up to the middle of the sixteenth century.

E. The so-called library corner. Not used for leather corners, but occasionally used on quarter bindings with paper or cloth sides. In this method of cornering, none of the covering material is trimmed off.

Fig. 80. Various methods of forming corners.

fibres separated
in corner of board

Fig. 81.   Type of damage often
found in corners of old
bindings.

Fig. 82.   Corner of damaged
board built up with wood
paste. The extra thickness
of wood paste allows for
contraction as it dries.
Note that the wood paste
overlaps the board for
strength.

paste with a hypodermic needle and syringe. The corners of the board should then be hammered down (or pressed flat with a bone folder), the extruded excess paste should be wiped away, and the corners finally moulded to shape with the fingers or a bone folder. If the boards are thick and a lot of paste has been used, two or three days may be needed for drying. Adhesives other than paste can be used, but paste has the advantage over most other adhesives in that it penetrates into the fibres of the board better. If the repair is to be covered over with leather it may, on rare occasions, be a good plan, if the corner of the board still lacks solidity and stability, to reinforce it by pasting down over it a layer of thin, strong material such as mull or, better, vellum. If vellum is used, it should be pared thin at the edges so that when it has been pasted on to the corner the edges will not show as a bump under the leather covering. A second piece of mull or vellum stuck down on the inside of the board after the pastedown has been lifted, will counterbalance a tendency for the mull or vellum on the outside to pull the cover outwards and cause it to warp and will appreciably increase the stability and strength of the weak corner.

Sometimes, if a small piece of the corner of a board has been knocked off or, more commonly, if it is still attached but has become too worn and thin as a result of prolonged abuse, it may be possible to replace or restore it with wood paste. In this case, the repaired corner must be re-covered with leather (or cloth or paper); otherwise it is practically impossible to conceal the repair with any degree of success, and also because this will strengthen the repair. Needless to say, whenever the repaired board is to be covered over it is pointless to colour the board.

In making this kind of repair, the best method is to harden the board close to the corner by the injection of paste with a hypodermic needle and syringe, as already described, and then to mould the wood paste on to the corners with the fingers, leaving extra bulk on all sides to allow for the contraction of the wood paste when it dries, and spreading it ½ inch or so over the edge of the existing board so that the possibility of breakage at the junction of the board and the wood paste is minimized (see fig. 82). It is also best to bevel the edge of the old board, and perhaps rough it up somewhat with glass paper or a file, so that the wood paste will have a better grip. A thin, strong material such as mull or thin vellum can be laid down to reinforce the join between the wood paste and the board, if this seems necessary; but there are

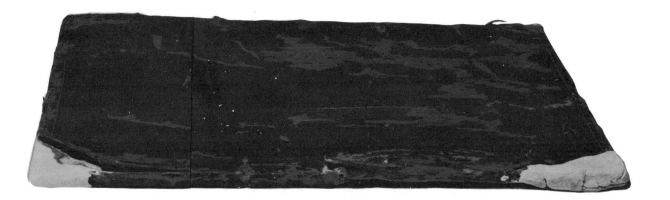

few occasions when this is required. If a considerable quantity of wood paste has been used, two or three days may be required for drying and contraction in addition to the drying time for the paste used to stiffen the edge of the original board. When hard, the wood paste can be glass-papered, sandpapered, or filed to the proper size and shape, taking into consideration the thickness of the leather which is to be put down over it (see fig. 83).

When a large piece of the corner of a board is missing and it is not possible to build up the missing area with wood paste, a new piece of board can be attached to make up the deficiency. In this case also, the repair must be covered with leather if the repair is to have maximum strength and is not to be too obvious or unsightly. In addition to being the same thickness as the original board (if a piece the same thickness cannot be found, a piece slightly thicker can be used and sanded or glass-papered down to size), the new piece of board should be the same kind as the original so that the strain on the join is kept to a minimum (rope-fibre board attached to pasteboard, for example, may prove to be an unsuccessful partnership because the former is so much stronger and more stable than the latter). Both the original board and the new piece should be bevelled with as long a bevel as possible to provide the maximum area of adhesion where they are joined together with paste. The attachment of the new piece of board can be reinforced if necessary by means of one or two non-corrosive metal dowels of the size of fairly large needles (see fig. 84). The dowels can be glued in (I recommend an epoxy adhesive, or a hard-setting fish glue, but the type of adhesive used is not important, because the purpose of the dowels is to prevent breakage from downward pressure rather than from sideways pulling).

Fig. 83.
An old board with both corners built up with wood paste. The corner on the left has been glass-papered down to its correct size and shape.

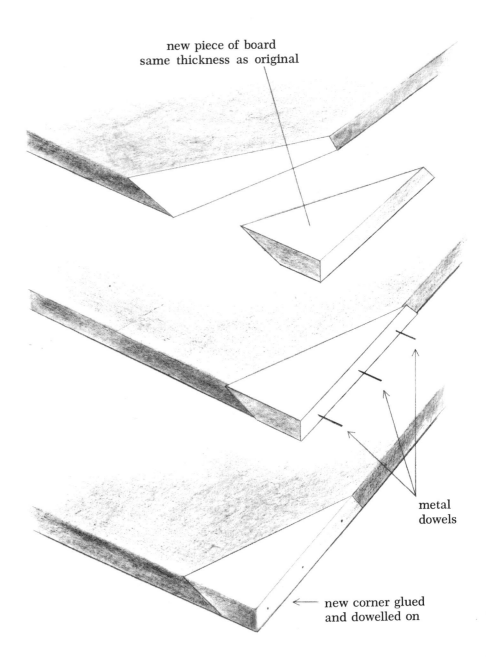

new piece of board
same thickness as original

metal
dowels

← new corner glued
and dowelled on

Fig. 84. Attaching a new piece of board to corner.

If the original board is of wood, the method of repair is the same as for other types of board, that is, if only a small piece has been knocked off the corner, or the corner has simply been rounded off or worn down, it can be built up with wood paste, but if a large area is missing a new piece of wood may need to be glued and possibly dowelled on.

It should be emphasized that in all cases, particularly when new material has been used to build up or replace a corner and this material has to be filed or glass-papered down to match the thickness of the old board, extreme care must be taken to avoid, as much as possible, any damage to the remaining old leather adjacent to the repair while the work is being done. For this reason it is sometimes better to build up and glass-paper the corners before the old leather is lifted.

If the damaged corners were originally covered with cloth, vellum, or paper in a quarter-bound book, material sympathetic to the original covering material is then chosen to complete the repair. In the case of paper sides, any matching old paper can be used on the corners, perhaps reinforced underneath with silk gauze which, while lending strength, will not appreciably increase the bulk of the paper. In the case of cloth-covered corners, if matching cloth cannot be found the repair can be made with any good, thin fabric which can be stained to match the original covering material.

It remains to be said that in old bindings a little rounding of the corners is extremely common, and if this is all that is wrong, and if the board and cover are basically sound, repairs to the corners may be unnecessary and inappropriate.

18   Blending In New Endpapers

If the original endpapers of a book are present and in good condition, or are repairable, there is seldom any need to replace them with different paper. Far too many books are automatically re-endpapered and, to make matters worse, bright modern paper is used that is wholly out of character with the book. Undoubtedly it costs time and money to find the right paper, but if this cannot be afforded it should at least be possible to use cream- or

Fig. 85.   Pastedown and flyleaf with wrinkles
or corrugations.

buff-toned laid paper on dark-coloured old books instead of the brilliantly white wove paper so often employed.

If new endpapers must be inserted in the book, it may be found that, even if more or less matching paper has been chosen, the new endpapers do not blend in with the rest of the book and present a starkly new and unnatural appearance. The reasons for this are several.

Many old original pastedowns and flyleaves have wrinkles or corrugations in the same positions as those in the text of the book (see fig. 85). This, incidentally, is complete proof that the boards were pressed down on the newly pasted endpapers with the book closed, as opposed to the modern practice (in tight-jointed bindings) of laying the pasted leaf down with the board in the thrown-back, or open, position, in which case these kinds of corrugations do not appear. Not all old pastedowns have these corrugations—possibly because they were rubbed down to smooth out the wrinkles before the paste dried—so it is not always necessary for the restorer to reproduce them, unless perhaps it is desirable to match a remaining pastedown at the other end of the book. If corrugations must be reproduced, the restorer should

Fig. 86.   End section
of book with dragging
flyleaves.

paste the leaf, leave it for a minute or two to expand from the
moisture in the paste, close the board on it, and then put the
book into the nipping press for two or three minutes. If one
partly opens the board before nipping, and it seems likely that the
action of fully opening the board will pull the flyleaf up badly
(see fig. 86), or if it seems that the board cannot be fully opened
without difficulty, the freshly pasted pastedown can be slid back
a little from the fore edge of the board towards the inner joint
with the flat of the hand to provide greater freedom in the inner
joint, after which the book can be nipped. Before doing this, however, one should bear in mind that, originally, the boards of old
bindings seldom opened as freely as they open, or are supposed
to open, in modern bindings. Pasting down "open," that is, with
the board in the thrown-back position, gives this freedom more
easily, but then there would be no corrugations picked up from
the body of the book, and these corrugations are difficult to simulate convincingly.

More pronounced corrugations result if the paper is not allowed
to expand very much from the moisture in the paste before the
board is closed on it and the book is nipped in the press, but
usually some expansion is needed so that the subsequent con-

traction of the paper as it dries will provide greater pulling power on the board.

If the book is pressed with the board closed, the few minutes in the nipping press will also cause moisture to pass to the new flyleaf (assuming there is one) and press it into the undulations of the body of the book so that it will also appear, like the pastedown, to "belong" instead of merely lying loosely on top when the book is opened. Only a little pressure is needed, though heavy pressure for a minute or so will do no harm. Protracted heavy pressure when moisture is present, however, imparts an unnatural appearance to the flyleaf.

When the book is taken out of the press, each board should be opened in turn to ensure that the flyleaf is free. The book should then be stood up with the boards open for between one-half and one hour so that most of the moisture escapes. Finally, the book should be placed under a moderate weight overnight.

Books pasted down in the "open" position should be closed and put under a weight when most, but not quite all, of the moisture has evaporated. This will enable the boards and flyleaves to settle down to the shape of the book.

The corners of the leaves of old books are usually slightly rounded as a result of wear and tear, so it looks better if the corners of inserted flyleaves are similarly rounded. On the other hand, the points can be retained as proof of the leaves' status.

Even when old paper has been used for the re-endpapering of an old book, its margins and newly cut edges may look unnatural and need treatment. If a new flyleaf has been inserted to match an existing pastedown, for example, it may be necessary to wipe its outer margins and edges with gravy browning or some similar liquid colouring agent, so that it matches any discolorations on the pastedown. These discolorations are often present, and are caused by stains from the underlying leather turn-ins. Gravy browning by itself looks too fresh, however, so it is usually best to add a touch of a mixture of brown and black water-soluble stain until a suitably dingy tone is obtained. This stain can be kept in a bottle and a little can be taken out and modified as required. Never use spirit stain for this purpose because it will go through the flyleaf and into the book. In any case it gives the wrong result.

A satisfactory method of applying the stain to the margins and edges of a flyleaf is to wipe the paper with cotton wool charged with the colouring matter, while following as closely as possible with the eye the shape of the discoloration on the pastedown. Immediately afterwards, the palm of the free hand should be rubbed over the stain once or twice (outwards towards the edges to avoid smearing the stain on to the rest of the leaf, and also to avoid wrinkling the paper), thus removing some of the stain and at the same time softening its edge and making it look more natural. The other side, or verso, of the flyleaf may also need to be similarly treated, though possibly more faintly, in order to match the end pages of the main body of the book if they are also discoloured.

Usually, the best effect is obtained if the cotton wool is first well rubbed on waste paper so that the wool is damp rather than wet.

It should also be pointed out that, if the end pages of the main body of the book are discoloured and a new pastedown and flyleaf have been inserted, it is advisable to stain the margins and edges of the pastedown as well as both sides of the flyleaf. The reason is that this kind of natural discoloration normally starts with the staining of the margins of the pastedown by the underlying leather turn-ins and is passed on from there to the adjacent flyleaf, and from that leaf to the next, and so on; so that it would appear unnatural to have discolorations on the end pages of the text and not on both the flyleaves and the pastedown.

If the edges of inserted flyleaves look unnaturally "hard" and sharp they can be lightly scraped while damp with a knife, a piece of board having been placed underneath and level with the edge of the paper. This method can be intensified for the purpose of simulating deckle edges, but generally speaking the results are not very convincing. The edges can also be "softened" if they are rubbed with fine glass paper while dry.

It may be necessary to "age" the staining after it has dried. This can be done by charging a wad of cotton wool with white petroleum jelly and ordinary household dust (the sootier the better) and rubbing the cotton lightly over the margins and edges of the leaves. Other areas of the leaves may have to be treated by "dirtying them up," particularly the lower left-hand corner of the new pastedown and the lower right-hand corner of the new flyleaf, because these areas receive the most handling when the book is being used. Dust rubbed into cotton wool which has been previously used for applying leather dressing is also useful for this purpose. Dust by itself has little effect because it will not stick to the paper, and the use of dust or dirt on cotton wool dampened with water is inadvisable because the combination of rubbing and moisture spoils the surface of many papers and also because it simply does not produce the desired result. A partly finished flyleaf, aged to match an existing pastedown, is shown in figure 87.

The use of these techniques is not a matter of faking or attempting to deceive anyone, but of creating harmony between the pastedown, the flyleaf, and the body of the book by softening the unnatural starkness of the new leaves. It should be stated here that some conservators are opposed to this procedure on the grounds that the dirt may be acidic and therefore harmful to the paper.

Fig. 87.   A new flyleaf with only the lower half "aged."

If the restorer is concerned that the inserted endpapers are likely to give rise to confusion as to their originality, especially if old paper is used, I suggest that the simulated staining from the turn-ins be made to deviate somewhat from the edges of the leather. This provides the bibliographer with proof that the endpapers are not original and will not give offence because the average owner will not notice the slight discrepancy.

19   Straightening Warped Boards

It is not unusual to find that cheap calf or sheep bindings of the sixteenth and seventeenth centuries, and also, though possibly to a lesser extent, of the eighteenth century, have yawning boards; that is, they gape outwards (see fig. 88). This may be due to flood or fire-damage or, more likely, to the fact that the end sheets were not pasted down when the book was bound—this last factor being a not uncommon feature of English trade bindings of these periods.

This kind of warping has been the cause of much damage to the joints of books due to the leverage exerted on them by pressure on the fore edge of the book when the boards are forced into a flat position (by being placed on a tightly packed shelf, for example). In time, this warping, if not corrected, is very likely eventually to cause the breakdown of the joints.

If the book has recently been in an excessively hot and dry atmosphere, the mere action of putting it into normal atmospheric conditions for a few hours, so that the covers can absorb moisture, and then leaving the book under a heavy weight overnight may be sufficient to flatten the boards. In most cases, much more radical action needs to be taken, such as temporarily removing the pastedowns (if any), lining the boards underneath with thin, strong paper, and then replacing the pastedowns. When pasted down on the boards, the new lining paper will tend to pull the boards inwards and thus to straighten them out. In some cases it is possible to pull the pastedowns off the boards in a dry state, but usually it is necessary when lifting such a large area of paper to moisten it until it can be peeled off without difficulty. The pastedowns can also be sliced off the boards with a knife, but when

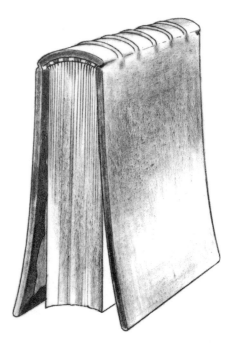

Fig. 88.   Warped boards pulling outwards. Pressure on the fore edge may damage the joints of the book.

lifting large areas of paper, this tends to produce bumps and a general unevenness.

If a machine-made paper lining is used to pull the boards inwards, the machine-direction, or grain, of the paper should run parallel with the joints in books in which the boards are warped as shown in figure 88. If the boards are warped in the other direction, that is, along the length of the boards instead of across the width, the grain of the lining paper should run at right angles to the joints. If the boards are warped in more than one direction, it is best to use hand-made paper which has a better all-direction pull. In any case, the paper should be pared at the edges with a paring knife so that the edges do not form ridges under the pastedown.

In bindings which have never had their end sheets pasted down, and in which the boards are warped, the obvious action is to paste the outer leaf of the endpapers down now, though the bibliographical purist may object. If, however, as is often the case, the outer flyleaf which would normally be pasted down to the board has an inscription on it which must be preserved, or for some other reason cannot be pasted down, the conjugate leaf in certain types of endpapers can be taken out and used instead. If this is not possible or desirable, another sheet of paper sympathetic in colour and texture can be used. If the pasting down of an end sheet is not sufficient to straighten out the boards of these books, it may also be necessary to paste down extra linings as described above.

Sometimes the warping of the board is caused by the leather cover being too tight over and around the boards due to shrinkage. If this is the case, and the leather covers are not too firmly stuck down, the best course may be to lift the leather covers off and then, if the squares are sufficiently large to allow it, trim a narrow strip off the fore edge (or the head or tail edge, depending on the direction in which the board is warped) of each board. If paste is used to put the leather back on the boards, the leather is very likely to stretch from the moisture and then contract as it dries, resulting in again warping the boards, even if a paper lining is applied to their inner surfaces. Therefore, *glue* should be applied to the outer surfaces of the boards, and the leather should be laid down on them and lightly nipped. Finally, the turn-ins of the cover can be pasted, turned in, and rubbed down.

In all cases, when the pasting (or gluing) down is nearly dry (this normally takes from one-half to one hour), the book should be left under a heavy weight at least overnight to settle down.

20   Rebonding Old Pasteboards

On rare occasions, pasteboards which have lost their rigidity are found in old bindings. Usually, this is because dampness has caused the laminated sheets of waste paper of which the boards are formed, as well as the leather on the outside of the boards and the turn-ins and pastedowns on the inside of the boards, to become unstuck. When this has happened, it is often fairly easy to remove the leather covers and the pastedowns from the boards. It is not essential, however, to remove the pastedowns if they are still adhering fairly well to the boards, in which case they only need to be lifted where they cover the turn-ins of the leather cover, so that the leather can be removed.

After the leather covering has been removed, the loose sheets of paper which make up the old pasteboards should be pasted together again by applying paste in between the layers and then nipping the boards in the press. They should not be heavily pressed, because this will impart greater rigidity to the boards than they had originally, and will also make them too thin and smooth. If the boards are still firmly attached to the book by cords, it may well be possible to repaste the boards without detaching them from the book; in this case, pressing tins should be placed between the body of the book and the board so that moisture is prevented from soaking into the pages of the book. A board which has been heavily repasted may take several days to dry out. If the cords are broken at the joints, the boards should be detached and repasted, and the cords should then be repaired by one of the methods previously described, or the boards reattached by means of overcast cloth joints. Once the boards have been repaired, the old leather cover (and the pastedowns, if they were removed) can be replaced.

21   Salvaging Old Sides

Sometimes the entire cover of a leather-bound book is in very bad condition, having a decayed spine, broken joints, and large parts of the edges and corners of the boards, and the leather covering these edges and corners, missing or unrepairable. The centre portions of the leather on the sides of the covers are often in sound condition, however, and it is frequently desired to save as much of this old leather as possible. The most effective and economical course of action, usually, is to rebind the book, using new boards and new leather, and then to inlay the salvageable areas of the original leather sides into the new cover. Because rebinding a book is a major operation, and is also likely to ruin the binding in the eyes of many collectors, even if the work is done very skilfully, it should be regarded as a last resort.

First, the old cover must be removed from the book. The backbone should then be repaired or resewn if necessary, using the techniques described earlier in this volume. Next, new cover boards should be selected.

The new boards should have about the same weight and flexibility as the old ones (otherwise the completed binding will not have the right "feel" for the period) and the back corners should be trimmed as shown in figure 43 (if the original boards were so trimmed). The new leather should be about the same thickness as the original so that the surfaces of the old and the new leather will be level after the inlaying process has been completed. The textures of the old and new leathers, too, should be matched as closely as possible, and the new leather (at least the part of it that will be showing) should be stained to match the colour of the old as nearly as possible before it is put on. Localized staining to match variations of colour of the old leather can be done later.

After the new cover has been put on the book and is dry, each of the two old leather panels (which have, of course, been carefully removed from the sides of the original boards, the cuts being made alongside gold or blind lines if they are conveniently positioned), should in turn be laid over the new leather sides and a line drawn around their edges with a sharp bone folder. Then the old leather panels should be set aside, and a knife—held at a fairly shallow angle so as to form a shallow bevel on the edges of the new leather—should be used to cut all around the line. The areas of new leather inside the line should then be lifted out. Next, the old leather panels should be bevelled around the edges at the same angle (but with the bevel in the opposite direction), pasted, and inserted into position (see fig. 89). The cover should then be lightly pressed for two or three minutes to set the old leather

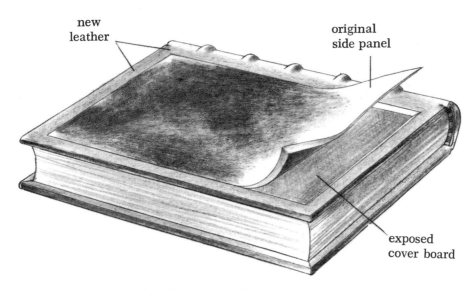

new
leather

original
side panel

exposed
cover board

Fig. 89.   Original leather panel being pasted into position.

panels firmly into position. Protracted hard pressure is both unnecessary and unwise because it may blacken the old leather due
to moisture from the paste soaking up through it, and it will almost certainly cause the impression of any tooling to be flattened
out and possibly obliterated, thereby creating an unnatural appearance.

If the old leather sides are very thin, perfectly satisfactory results may be achieved by giving them as long a bevel as possible
and then pasting them over the surface of the new leather instead of inlaying them, though care must be taken not to press
out any tooling that may be present.

If thin old sides are inlaid, the rest of the book must be bound
in equally thin new leather, or, preferably, thicker leather, but
with the cutout areas built up with thin card so that the surfaces
of the old and new leather will be level.

Once the binding of the book has been completed, if the old
spine can be used, it should be placed over the new leather as
described earlier. The final staining, texturing, tooling, and so
forth, can be carried out the next day to finish off the binding
and to blend the old and new leather together as closely as possible. If the original pastedowns and flyleaves are sound, they
should, of course, be saved and used again.

On older bindings it is a good plan to bend the corners of the

Fig. 90.   Corners of new
boards bent over
to simulate age.

new cover inwards somewhat (see fig. 90), because this looks and feels right on old bindings, the corners of which are invariably bent over. This is a small point, but it is the small points which in the aggregate have a considerable effect on the success of the work.

22   Staining, Aging, Tooling, and Furbishing

A very important step in the restoration of leather bindings is the final staining, texturing, tooling, and furbishing of the cover. Great care and skill are required in these operations, plus some knowledge and appreciation of the bookbinding techniques and styles of design of the past. Mistakes due to carelessness or ignorance will mar the success of the restoration, no matter how skilfully and carefully the rest of the work has been done.

First, about staining. It should be repeated here once more for emphasis that it is better and safer to do most of the staining of leather before it is pasted on to the book, leaving only minor staining (or restaining) to be done for local variation when the repair is being finished off. When the staining is done after the leather has been pasted on to the book and has already dried, there is often some difficulty in getting the stain to penetrate, especially on the edges of the boards, where the leather is thin and the paste may have soaked through to the surface. On the other hand, if stain is used *before* the paste has dried and while the leather is still wet, when the leather finally dries out the colour may turn out to be quite different from what was expected. Therefore, on all counts, it is better to do as much of the staining as possible before the leather is put on the book.

Generally speaking, it is better to do one's own staining than to try to find a piece of tannery leather of exactly the right tone and shade. An exact match is seldom found, and even if a piece which more or less matches *is* found, it will almost certainly be too evenly coloured and new-looking. (If only a small area of it is going to be exposed, however, its surface can sometimes be broken up satisfactorily by means of brisk rubbing with a bone folder which will bruise and darken the surface on any bumps in the leather.)

Spirit stains and water-soluble stains are most commonly used in restoration work for the staining of leather. Spirit stain used on calf sometimes hardens the surface, and this hardening increases the difficulty of moulding the calf over prominent raised bands, but I have noticed no appreciable effect of this kind in the case of goatskin or sheepskin. More than usually protracted soaking of calfskin with paste (say fifteen minutes) after staining and before the calfskin is put on the book can help to mitigate this disadvantage, and in any case the hardening is not serious unless immoderate quantities of the stain are used.

In my experience it is wise to buy leather already dyed or stained to a fairly light shade of the final colour which is desired, since this provides a satisfactory base for any of the darker shades one is likely to need. It is a mistake to buy leather which is too dark, as it is far easier to darken leather to the final desired shade than it is to lighten the original tanner's colours. The extra staining which will usually be necessary to darken the colour also helps to eliminate the evenness and freshness of the surface of new leather that can often make repairs obvious. The use of leather which has already been partially stained is particularly important if water-soluble stains are to be used, because they tend to look rather thin and anaemic when applied to unstained, flesh-coloured leather, especially goatskin.

My own preference in recent years has been for spirit stains, and I find I can get most of the brown shades I need with various combinations of Carr & Day & Martin Ltd.'s Black, Dark Brown, and Light Brown, with the occasional application of a yellow water-soluble stain to the leather for colder tones after the spirit stain has dried out. "Fancy" colours in spirit stain, such as red, blue, or green sometimes tend to fade badly, but mixtures of dark brown and black, which are the ones mostly used, are more stable, though not to the extent one would like. The aroma of leather stained with Carr's Dark Brown is much disliked by some people, though there are others who like it.

The advantages of spirit stains are that they dry out more quickly than water-soluble stains, the colour seems to have more "body," and if the leather must be stained (or restained) after having been pasted on, there is less risk of weakening its adhesion than there is with water-soluble stains, though even with water-soluble stains the risk is not great unless the leather is very thin.

Spirit or water-soluble stains can be mixed to the requisite tone and shade in a dish or saucer, remembering always to keep them well away from books in case of spills—especially in the case of spirit stain since it is difficult to bleach out of paper. When the stain has been mixed, the leather should be laid down over a layer of waste paper, a large wad of cotton wool should be charged with the stain and then rubbed over the leather with quick circular movements. Rubber gloves should be worn for this operation; otherwise, if one's fingers have picked up any stain, one may inadvertently mark the pages of books as much as several hours later.

The stain should be allowed to dry out for ten or fifteen minutes before the leather is pasted and put on to the book. This is especially necessary in the case of spirit stain because, if it is not thoroughly dry, it may well strike through the pastedowns which overlie the turn-ins of the new leather in most books. This does not happen very often, but it is a possibility if the stain is applied very liberally and the overlying pastedowns are very thin.

Salts of tartar (potassium carbonate) was much used for staining in the past, but it is not easy to match particular tones with this chemical, and it is disastrous when used in too strong a solution because it will then stain unevenly and severely harden the surface of the leather.* I understand that in the nineteenth century, when it was much used for the hand-staining of calf, one weak coat was applied each day for many days until the requisite warm shade was achieved and there was no streaking of the surface; but in these less leisurely days there is a temptation to try to get the desired shade with only one or two applications. Since much the same effects as those resulting from the use of salts of tartar can be achieved by the use of the proper mixtures of spirit or water stains, it is seldom, if ever, necessary to use it.

Copperas (ferrous sulphate) produces a slate-grey colour or, if applied after a coat of salts of tartar, a dull black. Copperas may have a deleterious effect on leather (in time, it may cause pitting), so its use cannot be recommended, but there are occasions when the greyish tones which were produced by the sprinkling of cop-

---

*For staining leather the usual method is to make a solution consisting of 4 ounces of salts of tartar dissolved in a quart of boiling water; this solution is then diluted before use at the rate of 2 ounces to about ½ pint of cold water.

peras on calf bindings during the nineteenth century (when this chemical was very widely employed) can be matched by nothing else. These occasions are infrequent, however, and I find I can almost always use a black water-soluble stain to get a fairly close match, especially as the area of new leather to be sprinkled is usually small. (There is one disadvantage in using water-soluble stains for this purpose, however, in that the sprinkling may be smeared if and when the binding is washed with aqueous solutions at some later date.)

Anatto is a dye produced from the seeds of a tropical shrub, and is mainly imported from Central and South America. It is useful on some occasions when a certain warm shade of light brown is required to match existing leather, but although it does not chemically harm the leather if used properly, it will streak, darken the leather too much, and cause hardening if used in too concentrated a solution.* The colour obtained from anatto tends to be fugitive. When anatto is used in combination with spirit stain, the leather sometimes has a white bloom on it when it has dried, but this disappears when leather dressing or shellac varnish is applied and, to the best of my knowledge, does not reappear. All things considered, however, the use of this material should be avoided whenever possible. Again, water- and spirit-soluble stains can be used to achieve approximately the same shades.

Bindings in which the leather is coloured red, blue, green, or other "fancy" colours, and which are rubbed and chafed so that underlying areas of unstained leather show, are sometimes effectively coloured with opaque poster (show card) colours, These colours get lighter as they dry, but revert to their proper tone when leather dressing and shellac varnish are applied. A better practice might be to use Dr. Martin's Synchromatic Transparent Water Colors.

The surfaces of some old leathers tend to resist water-soluble colours, in which case faded leather may be stained with spirit stains, especially if the required colour is dark blue or black, the easiest to match. However, there are certain dangers. One, in the case of light colours, is that the stain may seep under the edges of the leather surface and cause that area to darken when rubbed, cut and de-surfaced parts are recoloured. Another is that

*Generally, a solution consisting of 2 parts anatto and 1 part water, or sometimes equal parts of water and anatto, is used, but the correct solution depends on a number of factors, including the concentration of the anatto one is using, the kind of leather being stained, and the colour one is trying to match.

if cracked, broken or crumbly joints are too liberally coloured with spirit stain it may well spread to the inner joints thereby staining the endpapers and even the text paper, which is disastrous because the stain cannot be entirely removed. There are many occasions when the leather of an elaborately gold-tooled binding has badly faded and the owner insists on having the colour restored. This usually involves tedious labour with a fine brush and painting around the gold. Normally, spirit stain is used because it takes easily and there is the advantage that if the leather is fairly absorbent, one can often dab the colour in the interstices of the decoration and it will spread up to the gold and thus eliminate the need to follow the contours of the design. An additional advantage is that the colour cannot be washed off when the binding is furbished in years to come. When leather dressing is applied the colour is enhanced and the results can be very gratifying.

In addition to the colour, the texture of the new leather must also blend in with the rest of the binding. Once the leather has been put on the book it is quite often found that the texture of new leather is simply too smooth to match the surface of the old. It has been mentioned previously that this can to some extent be got over by tapping the wet new leather with a coarse, stiff-bristled brush. Another technique which produces a different effect involves mixing thick paste with water-soluble stains, smearing the mixture on to the new leather, and then patting it with the palm of the hand to make a rough texture. Alternatively, paste can be put on and ordinary household dust sprinkled over its surface while it is still wet. When this has dried, the surface can still be restained, tooled, and so forth, if necessary.

Another method I have employed with considerable success when it has been necessary to match the texture of old leather in an advanced stage of decay involves scraping the surface of the new leather, pasting it and then covering it immediately with fairly fine leather scrapings from old, discarded covers (see fig. 91), only a small portion of which are suitable for the purpose. When this is dry and firm, loose particles are brushed off with the fingers and then a second coat of paste is applied and smoothed out, again with the fingers. The next day, when all this is thoroughly dry, the textured area can be rubbed with a folder, if necessary, stained, glaired and gold tooled, and it can be treated with leather dressing with the rest of the covers. This texturing process must not be employed after the application of leather dressing because its greasy nature will cause the texturing to flake off.

Although the above two surface techniques produce a good hard surface which appears to wear well, I do not advocate them for much-used books; but for important books which are little used, and perhaps only shown in display cases, these techniques can very successfully disguise otherwise disfiguring repairs. The paste does not seem to crack off along the joints of the book, probably because the layer is extremely thin when it has dried. The leather scrapings do not crack off either, unless they are plastered on very thickly, but even when they do crack along the joints the effect can be quite natural looking. Only old calf and russia covers are potentially suitable for scraping, and only a small proportion of even these can be scraped successfully. It cannot be emphasized too strongly that these surface treatments can only be effectively applied to leathers with absorbent surfaces, and should not be attempted on "doped" or other moisture-resistant leather surfaces.

This camouflaging technique is regarded with disapproval by many conservators because they fear that the application of degraded material to the surface of good may prove to be deleterious, and because the principle itself is offensive. If the first point is

Fig. 91. Scraping leather from an old cover. The book on the right has been patched with two pieces of new leather, one of which (see arrows) has been covered over with scrapings.

valid and the argument is taken to its logical conclusion, original spines should not be laid down on the new.

Sometimes when new joints have been inserted in a book, and the new leather is too smooth, this may often be remedied if a pallet with a straight-grain pattern engraved on it (see fig. 92) is heated and impressed with its lines running in a parallel direction along the joints so that a natural wrinkling or creasing effect is obtained in the leather. The same tool can be used on other parts of new leather surfaces that require a straight-grain pattern.

Assuming that no texturing is necessary, once the new leather has been put on the book, exposed areas should, if necessary, now

Fig. 92.   A pallet with a straight-grain pattern.

be restained or sprinkled, or both, so as to match the old leather more exactly.

Until the middle of the nineteenth century, sprinkling was done by drawing a folder or finger across a short, square-cut brush of hog's bristle charged with copperas, or by knocking a longer brush against an iron rod or bar. The more modern method involves rubbing a stiff-bristled brush charged with black water-soluble stain or other colouring matter (depending on the effect desired) over a sieve, which should be moved about so that the sprinkling is evenly distributed. Needless to say, the more fully charged the brush, the larger the spots. The brush should be scraped only in one direction, otherwise the liquid will fly in all directions. Waste paper can be used to protect the part of the cover that is not to be sprinkled (see fig. 93).

The techniques of blind and gold tooling must now be considered. In blind tooling a modern binding, a tool which is quite hot is usually used on damp leather to get a dark impression, but this is seldom necessary or wise in the field of restoration, Usually, a tool which is only moderately hot (one which gives only a slight hiss when moistened) on dry leather will achieve the desired effect, though it may need to be used considerably hotter if the calf being tooled is partially chrome tanned. When a greater darkness of impression is necessary, the hot tool can be dabbed on to black carbon paper and then applied to the binding; or, if this produces too dense a black, the tool can be impressed on to the carbon and then lightly on to waste leather first before being pressed into the binding.

There is also a danger involved in tooling on damp leather in blind tooling old bindings in that if old powdery leather is dampened for the purpose, say, of running a two-line fillet along it, a hot or even merely warm tool is likely to char it and make too deep an impression.

In gold tooling, glaire must first be applied to the surface of the leather. If only very small areas need to be tooled with gold, the glaire can be applied locally, but if the tooling is to be extensive, the glaire should be put on over the whole area to be tooled. If the leather is to be sprinkled with a water-soluble colour, the glaire should be applied before sprinkling. If the glaire is not applied first, the sprinkling may be smeared when the glaire is put on, though it may be possible to avoid this by gently applying the

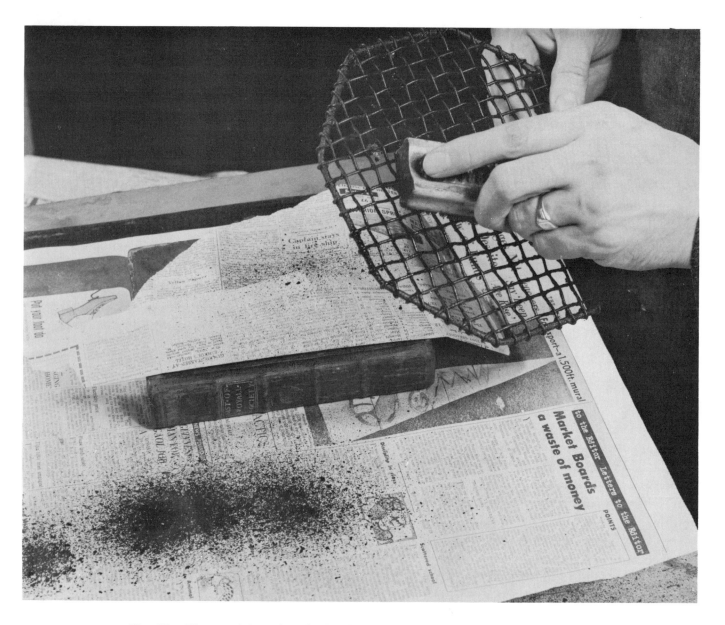

Fig. 93.   The new joints of a rebacked book (with original spine preserved)
being sprinkled to match the rest of the cover.

glaire with a quick dabbing motion. Alternatively, it is possible to use waterproof inks for sprinkling, though this is more expensive than water-soluble aniline.

The two principal kinds of glaire in use are the traditional white of egg and the solution of shellac which is now gaining popularity. Egg glaire works best when the leather is somewhat moist; if the leather is very dry, the gold tends not to stick when the hot tool is impressed, whereas leather prepared with shellac glaire can be tooled many hours after it has dried, and this makes it by far the more convenient of the two.

I find that one coating of glaire, applied with a fine brush to the areas of leather to be decorated, is sufficient for "antique" tooling, but some craftsmen like to apply a second coating after the first has dried. For sharp definition, when shellac glaire is used, the gold tooling should be done after the glaire has thoroughly dried out (particularly if the tooling overlaps on to decayed old leather). This may take from one-half hour to one or two hours depending on the state of the leather and the temperature and humidity in the work area. In the case of egg glaire, it is advisable that a little moisture be present; otherwise, parts of the gold tooling may not "take," and therefore one must use egg glaire with great caution on decayed leather so as not to cause charring when the hot tool is applied.

Next, the leather should be lightly greased with petroleum jelly applied with cotton wool (to hold the gold down while it is being tooled) and gold leaf should be laid on, after which the tooling can commence.

After the desired amount of gold leaf has been cut from the 3¼-inch sheets in which it is supplied, the leaf can be picked up by forming a compact wad of cotton wool and then brushing this over the hair or face to create static electricity or to pick up a slight film of oil or grease before pressing the cotton wool down on the gold. If the wad is given a fairly straight edge on one side, and the gold leaf is allowed to overlap it slightly, one can press the gold on to the leather with greater accuracy.

The heat of the tools for an egg glaire should be such that when the tools are brought into contact with water they hiss, but for shellac glaire the tools should be below hissing heat. Large tools often need to be rocked in all directions when applied to the leather so that every part of the design is properly impressed—they may therefore have to be in contact with the leather for several seconds—but most tools need only be applied for one or two seconds.

Some early gold tooling has a crude and fuzzy appearance. This can be imitated by using somewhat hotter tools than usual while the glaire is still damp.

When modern bindings are gold tooled it is important that the gold should be bright, to which end the finishing tools are frequently cleaned by being rubbed on a piece of leather which has a fine abrasive powder on it. However, this is not necessary for "antique" gold tooling, which is an advantage because the tools wear out less quickly, and in any case dull gold is more easily aged than brilliantly polished tooling.

When the tooling has been completed, the surplus gold should be removed with the aid of a gold rubber and the excess petroleum jelly taken off with cotton wool charged with benzine or similar grease solvents. If the old leather is in a fragile state, however, it may be safer to use only the solvent, and not the rubber.

It not infrequently happens that the gold has come out of original tooled impressions, in which case small areas can be painted in with genuine shell gold. This gold has a granular finish which is good for many old bindings, though not so satisfactory for the restoration of more modern and brilliant tooling. It is useful to remember that if there is a small gap in a rolled border or some other area of tooling, the retooling of the area will often be overlooked if the massing and the texture of the new gold are more or less similar to that of the original gold tooling surrounding it, even though the pattern is different. What shows badly is either a greater or lesser amount of gold or too brilliant a gold in relation to the surrounding area.

New gold tooling will in most cases need to be dulled or stained so that it does not contrast too strongly with the original tooling. How this is done must depend on the appearance of the old gold and the amount and distribution of the new. If a new spine has been tooled to match original sides, for example, it is often best (if the binding is a brown one) to leave the final staining of the new leather until after it has been gold tooled; cotton wool charged with brown spirit stain can then be rubbed over both the leather and the gold. If the gold is too solid, a little extra pressure on the cotton wool while rubbing in the stain will give the gold a "thin" look. If this simultaneous staining of the leather and the gold cannot be done, perhaps because the stain used is to be red, blue, green, or some other colour which would give the gold the wrong hue, or because the area of new leather and tooling is too small to be treated in this way without overlapping on to the original leather, one may have to paint a mixture of dark brown and black spirit stain on to the gold with a fine brush after shellac varnish has been applied and has dried. Stain merely painted over the gold rather than rubbed on it does not readily penetrate and ordinarily tends to run off the gold like water on grease, but the shellac varnish will hold it. If new gold tooling needs to be only slightly dulled, a little paste wiped over it will do this effectively.

A final word about tooling. When a book has been rebacked, and the original spine has not been put back over the new leather, the new spine may have to be lettered. Something should be said here, therefore, about the lettering of spines. The lettering is normally done with glaire and gold leaf, but occasionally it is blind tooled.

As a rule, books were not lettered on the spine before about 1670, and were lettered even more rarely before 1600, most of the exceptions being Italian or French. However, many collectors and librarians wish to have the spines of books from this period lettered because of the confusion caused when large numbers of books stand on shelves anonymously. In these cases, the restorer must make the lettering as appropriate as possible to the period in which the book was originally bound.

A cardinal rule is that no binding dating from before about 1670 should be lettered on a "lettering piece," or label, but should be tooled directly on the spine. Bindings of the sixteenth century or earlier look particularly out of place with labels. The most common colour of labels in the seventeenth and eighteenth centuries was red. In making new ones for rebacked books, or when replacing labels missing from original spines, I find that brick-red native-dyed niger provides a much better effect than do the dark reds produced by English tanners because the latter contain too much blue. The less grain the leather has the better.

Another point to note is that most early lettering is large and brief (notable exceptions to this rule are the titles on some fanfare bindings), the words being contracted at the whim of the binder and allowed to end at any point when space runs out. This kind of lettering might look something like this:

Lettering on books of the late seventeenth century and those of the eighteenth century tends to be smaller and more regularized with formal contractions such as:

HEAWOOD
ON THE
HIST͟Y OF
PARLIAM͟T.

Very often the author's name is in the genitive form:

HEAWOOD'S
HIST͟Y OF
PARLIAM͟T.

The lettering on virtually all pre-nineteenth-century bindings is in only one size of letter. Also, the earlier the binding and the poorer its quality, the more uneven the lettering tends to be, so the restorer must exercise some skill and judgment when titling books. When striving for the proper amount of unevenness on older books, experience will show that quick, careless lettering probably produces a better effect than a deliberate, calculated effort.

It seems that pallets (typeholders) were not in use in England before the last quarter of the eighteenth century; but they were certainly employed in Germany in the first quarter of that century. On the whole, unless a large set of books is being lettered, it is better to use handle letters. (A pallet is shown being used to tool lines around a label in fig. 94, which also shows some handle letters in the background.)

A common mistake is to put a short rule between the author's name and the title when lettering the spines of early books. This was not usually done until well into the nineteenth century.

When all of the staining and tooling is completed, leather dressing should be applied to the cover, making sure not to neg-

Fig. 94.   The edges of a new leather label being tooled with a pallet
in a finishing press.
In the background, a gas-heated finishing stove can be seen with
a fillet (*left*) and several handle letters (*right*).

lect the leather on the edges of the boards and on the turn-ins,
caps, and joints. A dressing consisting of the proper mixture
of neat's-foot oil and lanolin (see page 62) will help to prevent the leather from drying out and cracking or powdering. The
dressing is best applied in the first instance with a small amount
on a wad of cotton wool passed lightly and rapidly over the covers. This minimizes uneven penetration. Once this has been done,

a greater amount of dressing can be used and the covers can be gone over more thoroughly. The danger of getting too much dressing in one place is reduced if the charged wad of cotton wool is rubbed or dabbed on clean paper before it is passed over the binding. The dressing should be applied to all accessible parts of the leather covers.

The application of dressing to the new leather is particularly important not only for the maintenance of suppleness, but also, I believe, for its effectiveness as a barrier against absorption of sulphur dioxide.*

Some old leather covers are so badly rubbed and chafed that they almost look like rough calf. These are sometimes given a wash of thin paste to consolidate the fibres before leather dressing is applied, and are unlikely to turn black and look charred as powdery calf would if so treated. The dressing improves the appearance of the covers, but it probably does not penetrate the leather and do any good. Paste should not be used *over* the dressing because it is very likely to peel off the oily surface. If patches of the leather are sticking up here and there, they must be pasted down; otherwise I think leather dressing and a light coat of thin shellac varnish is sufficient treatment for this kind of leather, and the paste wash should not be used.

After a day or so, when the dressing has dried out and the covers have been polished with a soft rag, an extremely light coat of thin shellac varnish applied with cotton wool eliminates tackiness (which tends to gather dust and promotes the formation of mould) and also helps to improve the colour of the leather. As with the leather dressing, the shellac varnish on the cotton wool should first be evened out by rubbing or dabbing the cotton wool on clean paper. The binding should then be gone over with quick circular movements. This is important because shellac varnish dries quickly, and streakiness and sticking tufts of cotton wool will result if the application is made too slowly and the cotton wool is taken back over shellac varnish which has already partly dried.

The use of shellac varnish or similar substances on leather bindings is a matter of some controversy. One school of thought believes that the application of these substances may cause the leather eventually to lose its flexibility and to crack along the joints, and, further, that it prevents the later treatment of the

*See page 58 for important new recommendations.

leather with potassium lactate and leather dressings. The other school, of which I am, currently at least, a member, believes that a thin coat of shellac varnish applied over leather dressing helps to protect the leather, and certainly, in some cases, to enhance its appearance and eliminate tackiness. Penetration of the varnish into the leather is minimal because it is applied over dressing, and if further treatment of the leather seems desirable at some later date the shellac varnish is easily removed with methylated spirit or some other suitable solvent. At any rate, if the neat's-foot oil and lanolin dressing recommended in this volume is used,* the need for shellac varnish is less evident than when some other dressings, such as the one used by the British Library, are used because it leaves a less tacky surface. On the other hand, neat's-foot oil and lanolin leaves a rather dull surface which is not aesthetically desirable in every case. Finally, the use of shellac varnish is probably a matter of personal choice on the part of the individual restorer.

When the leather dressing has dried out, it is not unusual to find that the colour of the new leather no longer matches the old, so this will have to be adjusted by the use of stain either before or after varnishing—preferably before. If there is a tendency for the stain to be removed by the shellac varnish, the latter must be dabbed on rather than rubbed or wiped on. Spirit stain is much more effective than water-soluble colours after the application of leather dressing, because the oil content of the dressing repels water. (The oil content of the dressing also reduces the penetrating power of spirit stain to some extent, but not seriously.)

As we have previously indicated, if marbled papers are used for re-siding quarter, half, or three-quarter bindings, they can be aged and stained with water-soluble colours, such as gravy browning, or with any one of the stains already described, with the exception of spirit stain, which is somewhat hazardous to use on paper because any mistakes are very difficult to correct. The plain papers and most of the cloths used on the sides of these bindings can, of course, be aged and stained in the same way.

I have often found that the application of leather dressing and a light coat of shellac varnish to old marbled paper sides improves their surface and helps to prevent chafing and further loss of the patterns, but at least one conservator feels that this is harmful to the paper.

*See page 58 for new information on this subject.

The colouring and matching of leather, paper, and cloth, the restoration of blind or gold tooling, and the final furbishing of the leather all involve a good deal of time and trouble, but they make a vital difference in the appearance of the restoration and must be done with great care and attention to detail.

23   Record of Repairs

When the restoration of a book has been completed, a note describing the work done should be made. This will serve as an historical record for the collector, librarian, bookseller, or bibliographer, and should also include a description of the condition of the book when it was received by the restorer. This record is particularly desirable if the book is thought to be rare or valuable, or is likely to become so (I leave the question of how one decides this to others), and anyone interested in the history of the particular book involved, or in bookbinding techniques in general, may well be thankful for this information at some future date.

The note should be written or typed on a piece of good, strong, acid-free paper which can then be tipped in somewhere in the back of the book. The note might read something like the following:

THE THEATRE OF THE EMPIRE OF GREAT BRITAINE
By John Speed, London, 1676

Bound in contemporary panelled calf.

When received, the outer joints of this book were broken, the boards were detached, the corners of the boards were badly damaged, and the final eleven plates were detached from their guards. The book had been re-endpapered with marbled paper over the original plain ones, apparently early in the nineteenth century. The sewing structure was sound, but the headbands were missing.

Treatment

The loose plates were replaced on their guards. The book was reheadbanded, rebacked, and the corners were stiffened with paste, built up with wood paste, and repaired with new leather. The marbled paper covering the old pastedowns was removed. The flyleaves were replaced with matching seventeenth-century paper. Attachment of the boards was reinforced with overcast cloth joints which have been concealed under the original paste-downs. The original spine was replaced over the new.

PVA was used to stick down the cloth joints; otherwise, boiled wheat flour paste containing thymol was employed throughout.

The binding has been treated with a 7 percent solution of potassium lactate in distilled water with 0.25 percent paranitro-phenol added to protect against mould, and with a leather dressing consisting of 60 percent neat's-foot oil and 40 percent anhydrous lanolin.*

signed and dated

If for some reason a tooled spine or side cannot be saved, it is a good plan to take a rubbing of it with a soft pencil on thin paper and attach it with the note. Any interesting features which are going to be lost or covered by the restoration should also be noted and, ideally, photographed. The finished work should also be photographed.

For a particularly important book, much more extensive documentation may be desirable. A monograph describing the work might, for example, be published, or an article prepared for a trade or scholarly journal.

24 The Rebinding of Antiquarian Books

During recent decades the rebinding of antiquarian books has become a very contentious matter; it is viewed subjectively by dealers and collectors, but more objectively by some of those who do not own the books—librarians and conservators. For a disturbingly large number of binders, principally those in trade binderies, it is a matter of complete indifference. Until about fifty years ago it was usual to rebind books of earlier periods in much the same way as newly published books would be rebound in conventional "extra" styles for sale at, say, Hatchard's bookshop in London or Brentano's in New York. Some antiquarian books

*See page 58.

were put into up-dated "antique" bindings; that is to say, early cover designs were used, but the technique had modern precision and certain "improvements." One of the most popular of the "Victorianized" designs was Cambridge-style calf of the second half of the seventeenth century and early years of the eighteenth, at which period it was usually blind-tooled (fig. 95); in the nineteenth century it was often wholly or in part immaculately gold-tooled (fig. 96). Very often, too, the leaves of early books were re-sized and heavily pressed while still slightly moist so that they became brick-like and functioned like modern books, type impression and corrugation of the text-block having been eliminated and making each leaf look like a bad facsimile. Hundreds of thousands of old books were so treated and bound in polished levant complete with trimmed and gilt edges by Riviere and many others in England and other countries, including the United States, at the behest of collectors such as Thomas J. Wise whose collection, the Ashley Library, is in the British Library. Nearly all of his pre-1800 volumes were rebound in smart morocco. It is clear that vast numbers of contemporary bindings which could have been preserved by Wise and others were destroyed, as they continue to be, and there is little record or remaining evidence of what has been lost. The bibliographical loss is immense, even though the majority of the destroyed bindings were probably of the seventeenth- and eighteenth-century "common calf" or limp vellum variety in which the books were originally issued, but many bindings of the sixteenth century were not spared. There are still those who regard such humble bindings as worthless and uninteresting because they are plain and are not sumptuous examples of fine craftsmanship, but this attitude is unjustified and the loss is serious for several reasons. For a start, the book has lost "atmosphere" in its new, precise and shiny garb, and cannot be enjoyed fully as it could have been in its original period covering, and one is deprived of the tactile and aesthetic dimensions as well as any sentiment which may attach to a binding which has been through many hands down the centuries. More seriously, rebinding involves destruction of bibliographical details such as which leaves are cancels—this can often be determined in the original state, but is less easy when the book is tightly rebound and perhaps even oversewn. Often lost with the original covers and endpapers are owners' signatures which, collectively, provide evidence of the extent of a man's library and a guide to his tastes. Rebinding also makes it more difficult to determine, for instance, the relative popularity of calf, sheep and vellum for retail binding at various periods, and which styles of sewing and types of endpaper construction were most favoured. These and many similar points seem trivial individually, but in the aggregate they have significance. Needless rebinding means that we have less evidence than formerly about the early use of marbled paper in the seventeenth century, and such a policy can lead to our picture of the past being distorted. For instance, if as is probably the case, the majority of discarded bindings are of the humble common calf or common sheep type, and signatures and bookplates have been destroyed, one could falsely gain the impression from the finer remains of his library that a particular collector, perhaps a well-known man of letters, was in the habit of having all his books finely rebound, whereas, in fact, his sole interest was in the contents.

The needless destruction of finer, more elaborate period bindings, is more serious than is readily apparent and is nothing less than vandalism. If the restoration of an old binding is going to cost more than rebinding there is a temptation for the collector or custodian to opt for the cheaper course and to persuade himself into thinking that the loss of one binding will not make much difference. If that attitude were widespread, the loss of potential research material and period interest mentioned previously would be significant. There is also a temptation for the binder to sidetrack a possibly difficult task of repair and to talk the owner into rebinding instead. If the binding really is in such a poor state that it no longer protects the book, and if its repair is going to be hopelessly uneconomic, the least one can do is to preserve the covers and endpapers with details of the book and sewing, and so on, or take photographs or rubbings with details of both book and binding noted thereon. All concerned must appreciate that what appears mundane and unimportant to the layman may be of vital interest to the bookbinding historian. One can cite the case of school books published during the last third of the eighteenth century, many of which were side-stabbed and covered with canvas—few now remain as tangible evidence of what such bindings looked like and which books were issued in this state. In the 1950s and 1960s great numbers of modest houses of the early decades of the nineteenth century were demolished because, individually, they were not of great interest or strikingly

Fig. 95.   *The History of the Life and Adventures of Mr. Duncan Campbell*
(London, 1720). Contemporary Cambridge calf.

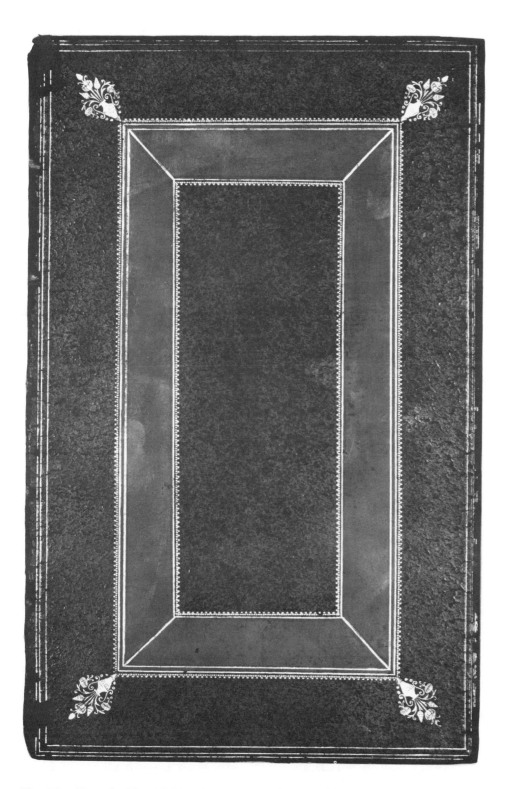

Fig. 96.   Detached board from binding, c. 1860. Cambridge calf, gold-tooled.
The board has a Dutch marbled paper pastedown and the wide turn-
ins are gold-tooled.

beautiful. Then, fortunately, there developed an appreciation of the charm of terraces or groups of such houses and a programme of rehabilitation was officially encouraged. It is to be hoped that a similar appreciation of period bindings of all grades will flourish.

The preservation of all old bindings is a matter for serious concern, but when we consider those which pre-date the sixteenth century that concern is far greater because, apart from general cultural considerations the study of binding structures of these very early periods is still in its infancy and every example is important for the study of the development of the codex. Christopher Clarkson's brilliant article "The Conservation of Early Books in Codex Form" in *The Paper Conservator* (vol. 3, 1978), is essential reading for anyone who seeks enlightenment in this field, and few who read it can thereafter fail to have a conscience when dealing with early books.

Not surprisingly, Douglas Cockerell was one of the first binders to display an enlightened approach to old books. In his *Bookbinding and the Care of Books* (1901), page 76, he says: "Sheets of very old books are best left with the stains upon them, excepting, perhaps, such as can be removed with hot water or size. Nearly all stains *can* be removed, but in the process old paper is apt to lose more in character than it gains in appearance." And on page 306: "It is far more pleasant to see an old book in a patched contemporary binding, than snug and tidy in the most immaculate modern cover." Today, having been conditioned by a welter of information and argument along these lines, Cockerell's remarks seem obvious to most of us, but at the time they must have seemed a trifle cranky to the majority of book people, and there are still those who take the same view.

BINDING STYLES

When there is no alternative to rebinding there are three principal approaches. The first, rebinding in modern style (fig. 97) without regard to the age or physical characteristics of the book has been mentioned already. The second policy is to rebind and to employ the most durable and most satisfactory structural techniques for that particular book in a style which is no more than vaguely evocative of earlier styles. One of the best-known examples of this is Douglas Cockerell's bindings (fig. 98) for the fourth-century *Codex Sinaiticus* which are sewn on raised cords, have exposed wooden boards and white, alum-tawed goatskin spines

Fig. 97. *Valuable Secrets in Arts and Trades* (London, c. 1780). Half royal-
blue morocco, gilt top, c. 1880.

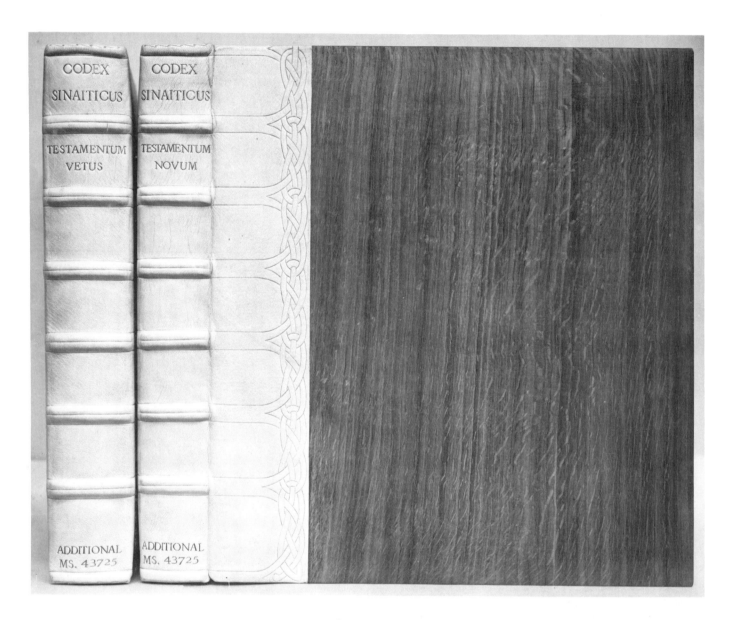

Fig. 98.   *Codex Sinaiticus*. Manuscript on vellum, probably written in Egypt or Palestine in the fourth century. The sections are thrown out on meeting-guards which are sewn on to raised cords. Oak boards with alum-tawed goatskin spines. Bound in 1935 by Douglas Cockerell with the assistance of his son, Sydney.

(a northern European style of the mediaeval period which is far more robust than Coptic binding styles) blind-tooled in a manner reminiscent of some early Coptic bindings. In order to obviate excessive, unmanageable swelling resulting from the reinforcement of the back folds and also to avoid contact between glue and the vellum leaves, the sections were thrown out on meeting-guards. Although the bindings are clearly of recent date they are not modern in style, and as already described they incorporate modern techniques designed to overcome particular technical problems. A development of this approach can be seen in Roger Powell's bindings (fig. 99) for the *Book of Kells* and other early manuscripts. These, again, are evocative of earlier periods, but in their structure they involve much that would be unfamiliar to a mediaeval binder. This elegant suggestiveness is perhaps more easily achieved with early manuscripts and incunabula than with books of later periods because the early ones have distinctive features such as the exposed wooden boards and clasps which, even without decoration, are reminiscent of the fifteenth century and earlier. It is much more difficult to bind an early eighteenth-century book in a manner which subtly suggests, say, a Harleian binding—it would either have to be a fairly close copy, which would be expensive and would in any case be unacceptable to many, or it could be tooled simply so that the style is merely hinted at, but then run the risk of looking very "thin" and weak by comparison with the elaborate original. It can be done, but not inexpensively. It is interesting to compare two efforts in this direction: Jean Gunner's evocation of an English Restoration binding and Ivor Robinson's of a cottage-style binding of the same period, both reproduced in *The Tradition of Fine Bookbinding in the Twentieth Century* (Pittsburgh: Hunt Institute, 1979), pages 66 and 96, respectively.

The third approach, which I practise, is to rebind in period styles (see figs. 100 and 101) which more closely resemble the originals, though ideally incorporating better structural techniques than the originals would sometimes have had. This policy is very popular with many book owners, but there are those, mostly conservators, who denigrate it on the grounds of possible falsification, and also because it is felt that the rebinding should be regarded as just one more phase in the book's history and that it should therefore very clearly proclaim its modernity. It is held that there is no justification, moral or aesthetic, for attempting

Fig. 99.   *The Book of Kells* (one of four volumes). Manuscript on vellum, eighth century. No adhesive used on the spine. Primary headbands tied down in the middle of the sections. Secondary headbands formed round gut (cello strings) in front and behind the inner fold of pads. Sewn herring-bone style on double cords. Alum-tawed pigskin spine and pads. Stainless steel pillar screws with 18 carat gold washers. Bound in 1953 by Roger Powell.

Fig. 100.   A recent Cambridge calf binding on an English book of the late
seventeenth century. Bound by the author.

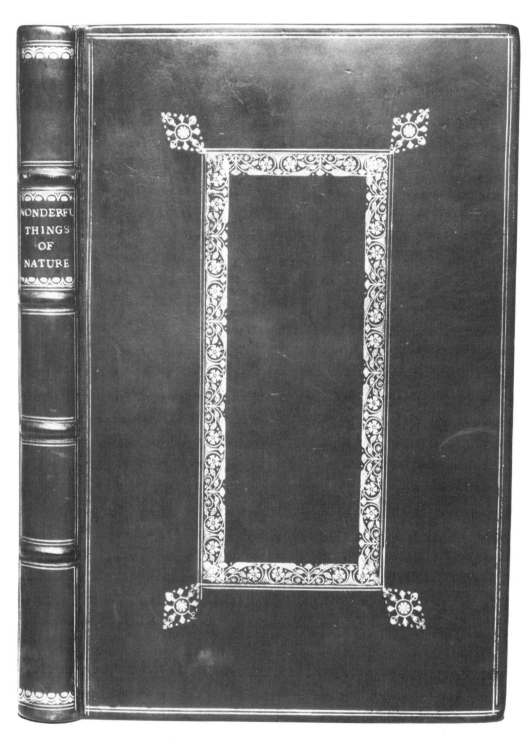

Fig. 101. *An History of the Wonderful Things of Nature* (London, 1657).
Bound by the author in calf and gold-tooled in a style of the period
of the book.

to make a binding appear to be a close approximation of what it is not, even if deception is not intended or likely. I can see that this argument has much force but my feeling is that a well-made "antique" binding should merge with genuine period bindings as happily as the new leather of a sympathetically rebacked book merges with the leather on the boards. For instance, a binding produced according to the principles of the second policy would have clean endpapers even though the book inside is very grubby and discoloured, whereas the "antique" binding would have endpapers stained down and aged around the edges to make an easy lead-in to the book. I believe that this can be done without risk of confusion as to authenticity (see page 183) and to the satisfaction of both the fastidious collector and the critical bibliographer. Furthermore, it can be done without reliance on an inserted binder's note, which is easily removed by the unscrupulous. I think it fair to say that only a small minority of collectors would want a book rebound in such a manner that it could be taken as an original period binding even after close examination by the well-informed, and then it would probably be for financial gain. However, I also think that the majority of collectors and dealers prefer rebinding to be a close approximation to the tactile quality and atmosphere of a period binding, though without necessarily having every minor detail considered. What they do not want is a stark contrast between book and binding, a visual shock. I suggest that those who prefer, say, seventeenth- and eighteenth-century books to be rebound in a clearly modern style can more easily accept an old-style binding than those who favour the old style can tolerate a modern binding on an old book, a combination which many find quite distressing. If this is true, it follows that even if a dealer prefers a modern-style binding he is unlikely to commission it because of market considerations. Old-style binding seems to me a harmless indulgence provided that there is no risk of deception (and there rarely is because such a standard of verisimilitude is excedingly difficult to achieve) and the materials are not degraded, physically, in the process.

REASONS FOR NOT RESEWING

When antiquarian books are rebound it is, I believe, unwise to resew them as a matter of course and without due thought. As pointed out earlier in this volume (page 87) the alignment of the leaves is rarely perfect after such a disturbance, the process can involve a great deal of time which the value and importance of the volume may not justify, damage may be done to the back folds during the pulling, and sometimes the book does not feel quite the same again. However, every book is different and, indeed, every copy of the same book presents different problems because of the treatment it has received and the conditions in which it has existed, so discretion must be exercised. Very early books (i.e., up to the first few decades of the sixteenth century) and some much later ones of the seventeenth and eighteenth centuries, more especially those bound in limp vellum, or Italian books in limp paper covers, were not glued on the spine and can be pulled easily and without damage; in such cases there are fewer objections to resewing, but it does not necessarily follow that they should be resewn. There again, it seems quite pointless to resew a perfectly sound copy of, say, Johnson's folio *Dictionary* of 1755 which consists of a great number of single-fold sections and would almost certainly involve a great deal of guarding, and hours of sewing, just for the benefit of lacing in the boards. The paper is so thin that the volumes lie open easily with minimum strain on the backbones which, therefore, seldom break down, and the combination of a tight back and a good reinforcement for the joints provides considerable strength for the attachment of the new binding. When the leather eventually deteriorates, the binding can be renewed in the same way and with no damage to the text-block.

In the case of a fairly thin octavo there would be little point in not resewing for rebinding because damage to the folds could be mended inexpensively, and misalignment of the edges of the leaves probably would not be critical or even noticeable. If such a book were not resewn it probably would have to be cased in because overcast cloth joints would have only small shoulders to which they could be sewn, and if the overcasting were taken further into the text-block the opening of the book would be impaired, especially if the paper were too thick, and this could not be justified.

RE-COVERING

It sometimes happens that a binding is quite sound apart from the loss or almost complete loss of the leather and possible looseness of the pastedowns. Having ensured that the cords are still sound, the best policy is to slice under the edges of the pastedowns and remove the leather turn-ins if they are still present, which in many cases they are not because dampness has loosened both the leather and the pastedowns. At this stage thick paste can be worked well into the fibres of the board corners so that they can be consolidated with a tap of the hammer, and new leather can be pared and stained. If the leather is pasted all over, the likelihood is that when dry the covers will warp outwards because there is insufficient counter-pull from the already stuck down endpapers, so the best policy is to paste only the backbone and turn-in areas of the leather and the backbone of the book. Next, the upper board of the binding is glued and placed down on the leather; the other board is then glued and the leather is drawn over tightly and pressed down on to the board with the palms of the hands. The corners can be mitred, the leather can be turned in as usual, and the backbone can be tied up with cord on either side of the raised bands, if any. The next day the edges of the pastedowns can be stuck down on to the new leather. The damp conditions which caused the loss of the leather often make it possible to pull the endpapers up without damage, in which case the leather can be pasted all over so that the covering operation can be carried out in the conventional manner, and counterpulling linings can be pasted on to the boards before the endpapers are pasted back into position. If the pastedowns are tight it is better to avoid the disturbance.

It may well be that dampness has caused mould growth. This is likely to stain and weaken materials and spread to other books, so the affected volume should be sterilized, preferably before being restored or re-covered.

BACKBONE CHARACTERISTICS

If, after all, the book is to be resewn and rebound one should bear in mind the backbone shape which is typical of the period of the book and arrange for the amount of swelling accordingly. Very early books of the fifteenth century and earlier usually had fairly flat shapes. The reasons for this, in the case of vellum-leaved books, were that very often the gatherings were thick and comparatively few in number, also that the natural cockling of the material cancelled out whatever swelling was created by the sewing. Similarly, the gatherings of most paper-leaved books and the paper itself were thick and corrugated, so the few sewing threads were embedded in it and the swelling which is so necessary for rounding was not created. Furthermore, and no less importantly, the binders of the day saw no reason to round the spines of their books, which they could have done by adopting different sewing techniques, because books were not stood on end for storage purposes and were therefore less subject to concavity of the spine.

Books pre-dating about 1500 were not backed, but, as stated on page 116, I do form small shoulders on volumes of this period for the boards to rest against, bearing in mind that most books are now stored vertically and therefore need the support thus provided. In the sixteenth century, books became smaller and had thinner paper and more gatherings, both of which factors created greater swelling which in turn induced a natural rounding of the backbone and the formation of rudimentary shoulders or joints. The majority of seventeenth-century backbones are similarly rounded, but I have seen many quite flat ones dating from about 1660 to the early years of the next century, helped, no doubt, by the prevalence of two-on sewing in even gold-tooled goatskin bindings. Well-rounded backbones were usual throughout the eighteenth century, but during the last two or three decades the semi-elliptical shape with heavy shoulders (fig. 43) was favoured by many fine binders including the German immigrants working in London. About 1820, very flat backs became fashionable and were much used in conjunction with hollow backs and wide, flat bands. This weak, unsatisfactory style flourished for about twenty years and then gave way to well-rounded, sometimes over-rounded backs. In the 1880s Cobden-Sanderson adopted the flat back as part of his mediaeval revivalism and because the book opened more easily with this shape. Of course, in rebinding in period style one can often achieve the authentic effect without incorporating the worst structural characteristics of the original bindings. For example, the flat, hollow-backed bindings of the 1820s were often further weakened by being sewn on only three or four thin cords, headbands were tied down infrequently and hollow backs were made with poor paper merely folded along its length on one side, the edge on the open side being tipped down with adhesive. Sometimes there was just a strip of canvas on the back of the book with a strip of paper edged on to it down both sides. The result of this is that many bindings of the period have come away like cases. However, there is no reason why one's own bindings should not be sewn on five (or more, depending on size) substantial cords, have strongly tied-down headbands and have a tight back if the physical nature of the book allows it, as most books of the period do, especially as the flat backbone allows a fair degree of access to the back margins. If a hollow back is necessary it can be made with strong, durable paper and perhaps have the folds reinforced with jaconette or other material. Outwardly, the more strongly structured book will blend with genuine bindings of the period without having the weaknesses which have brought the genuine bindings into disrepute.

Sixteenth- and seventeenth-century books usually have rather small shoulders, so this has some bearing on the amount of swelling one intends to create during the sewing. The shoulders are not sharp and precisely formed and probably never were, so in backing books of this period it is a good plan to remove the sharp edges of the backing boards so that the resulting right angles of the shoulders are somewhat rounded (fig. 102) rather than sharp (fig. 103). This is not only more in character but also, and more importantly, less injurious to the possibly tender old paper. Instead of hammering the back of a sixteenth-century book in a lying-press one may prefer to create shoulders naturally by lacing the boards on very tightly and then shutting them so that the sections are drawn over towards the boards, and then finishing off with the aid of a folder. Mr. Roger Powell was the first to suggest that this was the original method. In this case it is important to have the correct amount of swelling, otherwise a great deal of coaxing will be required and the gatherings will not readily spread towards the joints sufficiently to support the back and retain its shape.

The smallness of the shoulders does not necessitate the use of thin boards, or, to put it another way, the use of substantial boards does not necessitate the formation of large joints. Suitably substantial ones can be employed on an early book and then be glass-papered down on the outside until the back edges match the depth of the shoulders in the same way that the back edges of some early pasteboards seem to have been beaten to the requisite thinness. The inner edges of the pasteboards were also often sloped off on the lower side to fit the shoulders, so it is a good plan to round off the inner edges of one's own boards and thus eliminate the hard right-angled look which is not at all characteristic of old bindings (fig. 104).

TREATMENT OF BOOK EDGES

It is very important that the already trimmed edges of antiquarian books be left intact and not further reduced unless there are

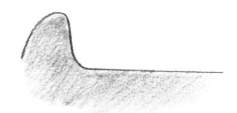

Fig. 102. Rounded shoulders, old style.

Fig. 103. Right-angled shoulders, modern style.

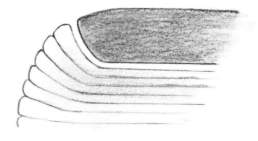

Fig. 104. Back edge of board sloped off to fit shoulders in the manner of early bindings.

exceptional circumstances such as irreparable damage caused by damp, but, unfortunately, it is not so very uncommon for antiquarian books to be needlessly and thoughtlessly cut down. This seems to happen most often when they are entrusted to a binder who normally handles only new books. Trimming not only reduces the margins but also ruins the atmosphere of the book by removing the often almost imperceptible ageing of the paper which frequently and pleasingly frames the leaves. Trimming gives the leaves "hard" edges and destroys the slight rounding of their corners which is characteristic of old books, and of course the mellow colour of the edges is lost.

A great many antiquarian books dating before about 1830 were issued uncut and many have come down to us in this state, sometimes with extremely rough and tatty edges. If the book is to be rebound in an original retail style such as white paper spine and blue sides, the edges should be left as they are, untrimmed, but if the owner wants conventional half- or full-calf or goat the book would normally be trimmed as it would have been if bound in that style in earlier times. Obviously, only the minimum amount should be removed, preferably leaving a few short leaves as "proof."

Newly trimmed edges which have not been decorated look much too fresh, but in treating them one needs to be careful that the decoration is appropriate to the date of the book or to the nationality and period of the new old-style binding, if, for some reason, this is to be of later style than the book. The binding does not necessarily have to reflect the nationality of the book (large numbers of books were bound for the first time in countries other than those in which they were printed), but as a general rule it is desirable that a French book be bound in French style, and so on. Incorrect decoration, such as gauffering on the edges of a book bound in English mid-eighteenth century style, is irritating.

One would hope that no fifteenth-century book would ever be trimmed, but if for some very good reason it were necessary one would certainly not gild the edges of an Italian book pre-dating around 1470, which is the time edge-gilding is first found on Venetian books. The technique reached England about sixty years later, so one would be guided by this in the case of English books. Having said that, I think it is very unwise to gild the edges of early books because the effect will almost certainly look vulgar and lack the mellow charm of old edge-gilding, though some ageing can be done with brown aniline stain.

However, I do think that one can have some success with seventeenth- and eighteenth-century books if they are not very large or thick. It is better not to burnish the gold directly (or at least, very little) on books of earlier date than the eighteenth century, and it may be necessary to wipe the gold very carefully, when finished, with a mixture of brown and black water-soluble aniline stain to improve the colour and to "thin" the gold a little. No edge-gilding should ever be done on a book which is to be bound in simple calf or sheep style or in the popular "Cambridge calf" style of the second half of the seventeenth century, but gilt edges are not inappropriate on elaborately gold-tooled calf bindings of all periods or, of course, on goat bindings.

Many English book edges were stained pale yellow during the latter part of the fifteenth century and throughout the sixteenth. The problem with solid colouring, especially if it is rather dark, is that if in trimming a previously untrimmed book (or a badly imperfect book which has been made up with many short leaves or sections from another imperfect copy) and some of the short leaves have been left untrimmed in order to minimize reduction of the margins, it may be difficult to achieve solid coverage without getting colour on the sides of some leaves. It looks bad to have white paper appearing as streaks along the edges, so sprinkling is often more effective than solid colouring. German alum-tawed pigskin bindings of the sixteenth to the eighteenth centuries almost invariably have stained edges, usually blue or green.

Sprinkling with red ochre (preferably with a drop of black aniline in it to make a dingy tone for the earlier books) is an easy and inoffensive way of decorating the edges of most retrimmed antiquarian books of the sixteenth, seventeenth and eighteenth centuries bound in calf or sheep, but it should be done fairly finely and not crudely with large drops as one finds it on much modern cheap stationery.

Trimmed English books of the second half of the eighteenth century bound in half- or full-calf look well with acid-yellow edges, and Irish books of the same period can be appropriately stained green or blue. If no decoration is applied I think it better, whatever the period, but more especially in the case of books over a hundred years old, to give the edges a wipe over with very dilute brown or brown-black water colour so that they will have a more or less naturally aged appearance and not be starkly clean and fresh.

Transparent water colours (anilines are suitable) should be

used unless red ochre is employed for solid colouring or sprinkling, and *not* spirit stains which are highly penetrative. A little paste mixed with the ochre will prevent the colour coming off on the fingers or smearing. Some old papers are very absorbent, so it is advisable to place the book under some pressure (especially if there are folded maps or short leaves which make gaps in the edges) between cutting or backing boards in the lying-press while the edges are wiped over with a pad of cotton wool which has been sparingly charged with stain.

The gilding of the top edges only, the other edges being left plain, is a style which seems not to have become popular until the 1870s and was little employed much before that date, so I think it better not to do this on books published before about 1850.

Notwithstanding all the foregoing, it needs to be stressed yet again that antiquarian books very rarely need to be or should be trimmed or retrimmed.

ATTACHMENT OF BOARDS

When books of the sixteenth century and earlier are rebound, the cords can be thicker than would be normal for later books, assuming that they are raised. When they are laced in I think they should be recessed, but not to the extent that no bumps appear on the sides because this would detract from the antiquarian character of the binding; indeed, the absence of evidence of lacing in is not desirable at any time. On the other hand, the full thickness of the cords on the surface of the boards would look crude and clumsy. Partial sinking of the cords is much preferable to reduction of their thickness because the former method involves no loss of strength. Grooves were sometimes cut on the outer surfaces of wooden boards of bindings as early as the thirteenth century, but they were not cut in the pasteboards which came into use early in the sixteenth century because the thongs and cords became embedded into them to some extent, and they were not cut into the rope-fibre millboards which came into use in England early in the eighteenth century. It follows, therefore, that the lacing in of most bindings of the seventeenth and eighteenth centuries shows quite clearly and should be a feature of old-style bindings.

On the whole, French bindings of the seventeenth and eighteenth centuries have survived in much better condition than English ones of the same period. To some extent this has been due to the use by the French of thin parchment linings on the spine, the ends of which crossed the joints and were secured under the pastedowns, thus reducing strain on the laced-in cords. It was usual, whatever the cost of the binding, to put the reinforcement on the end panels of the spine; other volumes had them on only the middle panels, but the best quality bindings had them along the whole length of the spine. Such reinforcements were used in England to a very limited extent and then they often did not cross and strengthen the joints, which was the most important factor. It would seem that there is something to be said for the adoption of this technique on old-style bindings, depending on size, and so on, even if they are not French because it does not significantly affect the character of the pastedowns and scarcely shows at all if they are marbled, not that this matters.

HEADBANDS

Few non-binders are acutely conscious of headbands and their shapes and colours, but on the basis that many small details are important to the overall effect one should try to sew headbands which are reasonably appropriate to the age of the book and the quality of the binding, and in most cases this can be done with little difficulty (see pages 121–23).

BACK LININGS

Until about 1770 in France and about 1800 in England all leather-covered books (with certain exceptions such as almanacs, which were cased) had tight backs, so if one wishes to be strictly correct one follows this rule. However, there are books which are physically unsuitable for this treatment because they either have narrow back margins or too thick paper, so in such cases it may well be felt that function should take precedence over pedantry and that a hollow should be fitted. More often, one may feel that the hollow back almost automatically used from about 1820 is often unjustified on functional grounds and that the books will open very well and be stronger with tight backs.

I have noticed that some English seventeenth-century books have a canvas lining on the backbone, but the vast majority, even the largest, have the leather stuck directly to the backs of the sections, with the result that many of the backbones sag. Most large, heavy tomes of the period have wide back margins and relatively thin paper which means that they can flop open and be read without difficulty even though the spines do not move, so it is possible to improve on the earlier binders' work and line up the back, with non-acidic paper, sufficiently to obviate or at least delay the onset of sagging and consequent extra strain on the whole structure. Clearly, books must be very carefully selected for this treatment.

COVERING

A few easily remembered points need to be borne in mind if the new binding is to sit comfortably on the shelves with genuine period bindings. The first of these is that the slight unevenness of one's own staining looks far better than the "flat" uniformity of ready-coloured leather supplied by the tanner, though it may help if one merely darkens the supplied colour which gives "body" to one's own. Brick-red (or red ochre), native-dyed niger stained down with dark brown spirit stain, possibly containing a touch of black and somewhat diluted according to circumstances, makes a very good colour for old-style bindings on books pre-dating the Restoration, when brighter colours came into fashion. Second, tying up with cord on either side of the bands was usual on all books (except those which were bandless, of course) until the end of the eighteenth century when band nippers were used instead, so for the sake of appearance, if not for practical reasons, it is advisable to tie up books printed before about 1800. Nipped up bands on early books, particularly, give the back quite the wrong character. Third, back cornering and tying round with thread was unusual in English bindings before the 1780s, but I think the French started rather earlier (see page 142). On many occasions I have seen smart, precise caps with a back-cornered setting on sixteenth- and seventeenth-century books which have been rebacked or rebound with much detriment to the general effect. The French, in the seventeenth century, used double headbands much more than English binders, and they not uncommonly pressed the leather on the spine into the cavity found at the back of the headbands between the larger roll at the bottom and the smaller roll above it (fig. 105). Characteristics such as these are very useful as a means of imparting period and nationality flavour.

One advantage of old-style bindings is that the leather can be left thicker in all parts than would be acceptable in normal bindings which are expected to have a modern finish and complete freedom of movement in the joints. In general, the earlier the book the less easily did the boards throw back, so it is not appropriate to make the boards of old-style bindings swing back very freely, though of course it is not suggested that the boards should

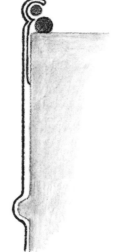

Fig. 105.   Indentation in covering leather at end of spine behind the headband.

function like a rat trap. I do suggest that the leather can have sufficient substance to impart a feeling of strength in the joint movement without impairing sound functioning.

When books dating from about 1770 to about 1840 are bound, the use of straight-grained goatskin is useful as a means of imparting period flavour even though the plated grain on present-day skins is more pronounced than the hand-boarded grain of the eighteenth century and later. Although straight-grain has remained in use since 1840 it has been much less employed in elaborately gold-tooled bindings. In the early years, red and green skins were popular, and early in the nineteenth century dark blue was much used also.

SIDING AND PASTING DOWN

Half-calf bindings were much in evidence in England during the second half of the eighteenth century. Half-goat bindings seem to date from the last decade or two of that century, but if books printed as early as about 1750 are bound in this style they do not look incongruous, provided that they are done in period style with appropriate proportions. Half-bound books invariably had a narrow spine and small corners until about halfway through the nineteenth century. Typically, a small octavo would have a spine width of ½ to ¾ inch and the corners would be the same or smaller, measuring at 45 degrees from the corners of the boards, so if modern proportions (perhaps one and a quarter inches for the same book) are used, as indeed they often are, the effect will be spoilt. It is also quite wrong to run gold or blind lines or other ornamentation along the edges of the paper sides on books dating before about 1830. The proportion of leather to board area started to become more generous about the middle of the nineteenth century, and about twenty years later binders started to trim the leather before siding, and the turn-ins before pasting down the endpapers, so that bumps under these areas were eliminated. During this period Britain had become the "workshop of the world" and there was a concomitant expansion of the lower middle classes with pretensions to higher status, and it may be that the increased quality and output of half-calf and half-morocco bindings reflected these social pretensions while at the same time there was an inability to afford the more expensive full-bindings which, in any case, looked no more impressive on the bookshelves.

The pastedowns of half-bindings were not normally trimmed to provide wider margins until about 1830, and I think this is true of French work also, although I have seen examples of earlier date. The pastedowns of full-bindings were trimmed at about the same time, though only to a modest extent at first and then more so as time passed to provide greater scope for richly tooled borders.

I think it is stylistically inappropriate to use cloth as a siding material for half-bindings on books printed earlier than the late 1830s, though books were being published in cloth more than a decade before this. Needless to say, it is important not to use marbled paper on books which predate its introduction, if one is trying to be stylistically correct, and it may be advisable to use the right patterns for books of various dates and countries. Marbled paper was in use in Holland by the end of the sixteenth century, appeared in England fifty years later and was in common use by the 1670s. In England the Dutch pattern, with variations, was employed virtually exclusively until the last quarter of the eighteenth century, so it would be out of keeping to employ, say, the Spanish pattern on an English book of the early years of that century. After the virtual demise of the combed Dutch pattern there was a reaction which manifested itself in the great popularity of the uncombed Shell, Stormont and Antique Spot patterns, which lasted until the 1840s.

It is not vital that exact copies of old marbles be used, but it is desirable that an appropriate type or pattern with more or less sympathetic colours be employed so that the atmosphere of the binding is not ruined. The paper always looks too fresh, especially when it is used for siding, so rubbing down with cotton wool charged with brown water colour of some kind is advisable, not only to tone the paper but also, sometimes, to remove some of the colour and to make it less dense. Greater care is needed with some papers than others because the colours may tend to spread, especially, perhaps, the reds and blacks. When dry, the surface of the papers can be improved with a light application of wax. For the best effect all this should be done while the paper is on the book.

FINISHING

One of the fortunate aspects of binding in period style is that it can be done comparatively expeditiously and thus economically. The tooling and lettering part of the work is no exception because until the last decades of the eighteenth century much of it was done rather inaccurately, though on the whole the impressions of the tools were sharp. Filleted lines were not mitred until about 1820, but merely crossed; sometimes, early in the nineteenth century, a rosette was used to cover the overlapping lines at the corners.

Gold tooling was practised in England from about 1530, and much earlier in Italy, but blind tooling was more common and this is the best thing to do on most old-style bindings certainly of the sixteenth century, because it is cheap, appropriate and is likely to be more acceptable aesthetically. The leather does not need to be moistened for "antique" blind tooling—tools heated to the point when they make a fairly fierce fizz when moistened will make a dark enough impression on most leathers when they are in a dry condition. However, there is no reason why one should not use moisture, provided that the tooling does not become too dark as a result. The use of carbon paper gives impressions which are too dark and uniform, apart from which it needs to be fixed with varnish if it is not to smear and come off on the hands, and in general this produces an unconvincing effect. Lines around the edges of the surfaces of the boards can be done entirely by eye. If there are several panels within each other on the covers it is often a good idea to make guide lines for the outer tooled lines (unless they are close to the edges of the boards) and then to work inwards by eye; otherwise, if everything is marked out, there is likely to be too much precision. It is seldom necessary to work through a tooling pattern. The blind tooling of Cambridge-style bindings can easily be done entirely by eye once the covers have been sprinkled and the mask has been removed.

A useful form of decoration for sixteenth-century books is a large device of suitable design blind-blocked in the centre of each cover. This can be done by moistening the leather and laying on it, cold, a deep-gauge binder's line-block; the board and block are then placed under the screw of a large nipping-press or standing-press (with the rest of the book hanging out) and pressure is applied for about two minutes. The block has a tendency to stick to some damp leathers, so the block should be greased before it is placed in position. There is no point in going to the trouble of setting up a heated blocking-press for this simple operation, which in any case does not call for great accuracy or finesse. Even gold blocking can be done this way on early books, in which case one can either make a blind impression, glaire it, lay on the gold and then set the heated block into the blind impression, or the whole cover can be glaired, gold leaf can be laid on the general area, and then the block can be laid in position to marks made on the gold. It is not a good idea to glaire the central area of the board without having a blind impression because at a later stage when dressing is applied the glaired area around the block will remain lighter than the remainder of the leather.

It is inadvisable to use film gold on old-style bindings because there is loss of detail and sharpness; the gold is too bright, it does not "age" well, and the whole effect is wrong. Lemon gold can be used appropriately on French books of the seventeenth and eighteenth centuries.

The choice of alphabets for titling (fig. 106) is very important because even those who know nothing about typography can sense that something is amiss if, say, a Bodoni alphabet has been used on a seventeenth-century book. Unfortunately, none of the styles of handle letters at present being cut is very suitable for the lettering of sixteenth-century books and those of the early seventeenth, but sometimes it is possible to find worn old sets which are somewhat better. The current alphabets are not a great deal more suitable for the later books of the seventeenth and eighteenth centuries, but after that one can use lead type and there is a wide variety of faces from which to choose. The examination of many old bindings is essential if stylistic errors are to be avoided, though in the choice of alphabets and in laying out the title one is seeking compatibility rather than complete fidelity.

BINDING STYLES AND DECORATION

This is a very difficult subject and one in which many mistakes are made either because of inexperience or because the binder has no interest in or feeling for binding design and its evolution over the centuries. The inexperienced will do well to study well-illustrated catalogues issued by dealers such as Maggs Bros. in London, and Martin Breslauer in New York who handle many fine bindings of all periods, and provide useful information in addition to the period and nationality of the binding. Christie's and Sotheby's auction catalogues can also be very informative in this respect, especially catalogues of major collections. Most of the reproductions are of bindings which are much more elaborate and sumptuous than one would normally be required to produce, but they do at least give the binder some idea of trends and of the

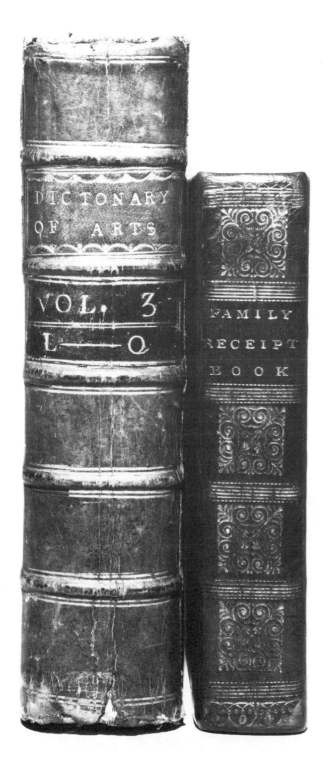

Fig. 106.   *Dictionary of Arts and Sciences.* 4 vols. (London, 1763). Contemporary sprinkled calf.

Family Receipt Book (London, 1824). Contemporary half-calf. These two volumes illustrate styles of lettering which are characteristic of their periods and which would look very odd if interchanged.

varieties of decorative tools in use during the last five hundred years. After a time it is possible to devise simple schemes with a few tools which, although perhaps not very authentic, will at least not be offensively incongruous.

When many books have been handled, certain national and period characteristics become apparent. For instance, the gilt two-line panels on the spines of many French eighteenth-century bindings are positioned a long way in from the joints and from the raised bands. This style is never found on bindings from other countries, so even though only a minority of French panelled bindings have it, it is a useful thing to do on French books as a means of imparting a French atmosphere to the new binding, especially if it is combined with the use of lemon gold.

The inexperienced are also advised to look at and handle the greatest possible number of antiquarian books for the purpose not only of absorbing trends in decoration but also to note the subtle characteristics of binding structures and their evolution in various countries and successive periods, and this is useful experience for getting to know the "feel" of old books. This process has its limitations as a solitary activity because many books were rebound fifty or more years after they were printed and bound for the first time, and perhaps not in the same country, so reference to the title page can be misleading as, I note, it has been for many television and film set designers. This being the case, the examination of a collection is best conducted in the company of a well-informed person.

Certain structures and materials are very evocative of particular countries and periods. In the case of German books of the sixteenth century to the eighteenth one immediately thinks of blind-tooled tawed pigskin and wooden boards which have a sharp bevel on the inner edges sloping towards the book edges, and sometimes a bevel in the middle of each edge on the upper surface (fig. 107), though a great many gold-tooled bindings in other leathers were also produced in Germany. It is appropriate to bind Italian and Spanish sixteenth-century books in brown goatskin, but not in tawed pigskin, and vellum is very appropriate for Dutch books, though of course the Dutch did also use leather extensively.

A quite reliable rule (with just a few exceptions) which should be noted is that clasps were put on the upper covers of English and French books, with the catches on the lower boards, and that

Fig. 107. A typical blind-tooled German binding of the late sixteenth century. Its bevelled wooden boards are covered with alum-tawed leather and the book has a characteristically well-rounded spine with prominent raised bands. The edges are green-blue.

they were fitted the other way round with the catches on the upper covers of German and Dutch books. Italian (and occasionally French) bindings often had clasps or ties at the head and tail in addition to those on the fore edge, so that there were four instead of two, but for practical reasons it is better not to incorporate the extra ones unless the book is boxed, and even then it is not a very good idea. Many Italian bindings of the sixteenth century had half-bands between the double bands and in the end panels, and many French bindings of that period had half-bands only in the end panels. The use of these and other features can be helpful in creating the right atmosphere.

REMBOÎTAGE

Remboîtage is the practice of transferring a book into a different binding, usually because that binding is more elaborate, more nearly contemporary or in better condition than the book's original cover. It is not a very common practice because it is extremely difficult to bring together a book and a suitable binding which matches it for thickness and page area. Even when the area is right the actual shape often varies because antiquarian books were frequently trimmed out of square. The book can be trimmed and regilded, but this immediately creates problems as the purpose of the exercise is usually deception. A more common practice is to reback the book into boards taken from another book.

CLASPS

Most restorers and binders concerned with early books are at some time required to fit clasps, usually on vellum-leaved books in order to keep them compact, and some incunabula call for them. Two types are suitable for use on books with boards and they are fairly simple to attach. The first is shown in figure 108. The catch is a brass knob attached to a thin plate which is fastened into a "made" board. It is a good idea to make a three-ply board with the shapes of the plates cut out of the middle one. The boards are stuck together with the two plates in position and the knobs protruding not less than ⅛ inch. When the book is covered two holes must be made in the turn-in so that the leather can be fitted around the knobs. Catching on to each knob is a brass ring which can be either completely circular or partly flattened to take three thongs. The thongs are passed through the ring, the ends are pasted together and then they are plaited. When

Fig. 108.   One type of clasp.

A. An antique-style binding in blind-tooled goatskin on an early sixteenth-century book printed in Lyon. A catch, similar to those embedded in the board, is shown lying on the cover. Bound by the author.

B. Showing the attachment of the plaited thongs with an overlying brass plate, a feature commonly found on bindings of the sixteenth century and earlier.

the book has been covered, the ends of the plaited thongs can be passed through a slit made in the leather and then stuck in a depression cut in the outer surface of the board before the leather was pasted on. When it is certain that the clasp fits well when the book is lightly compressed tacks should be passed through the ends of the thongs and through the board (this is accomplished more easily if fine holes are made first), afterwards being hammered over and covered with the pastedown. Lining the leather with thin jaconette or other stable material before it is cut into strips strengthens it and reduces stretch. The plait also tends to stretch, so it should be well pulled before being fastened into the board.

The second type of clasp is rather more elaborate (fig. 109). As before, the first part to be fitted is the catch which is rivetted on, after the book has been covered, so that the ends of the rivets can be turned over on the inner surface of the board. When this has been done, the clasp, which has been rivetted to a leather strap, can be precisely fitted. The strap consists of a strip of vellum sandwiched between fairly thin leather which matches the cover. When the covering leather is dry, a slit is made on the edge of the board and the strap is slotted in with adhesive so that it can lie in a previously made depression in the outer surface of the board. When it is certain that the clasp fits well, rivets can be driven through the end of the strap and through the board to the inner surface where they are turned over (fig. 109B).

Many early clasps had a plate (fig. 108B) to cover the attachment of the strap to the board, but this is not necessary if the work has been done neatly and it merely provides one more hazard to adjacent books unless, as is to be hoped, the book has been boxed.

Clasps can be made individually, of course, but it is more economical to design a type which will be suitable for a wide range of binding styles and then have two or three dozen sets made in two sizes.

Very often the straps of old clasps are defective, in which case it is usually advisable to renew rather than repair them. This can be done by cutting a strip of strong vellum and then covering it on both sides with old-looking leather. New rivets are likely to be needed for the attachment of the metalwork. The strap can be blind-tooled with initials and date, on the side nearer the book and close to the board so that confusion as to authenticity is avoided, and the metal, too, can be marked inconspicuously.

Fig. 109. A more elaborate clasp.

A. An antique-style binding in blind-tooled goatskin on a mid-sixteenth century book printed in Basle. The catch has been placed on the back board because the book is printed in Hebrew. Bound by the author.

Fig. 109.   (continued)

B.   Showing the attachment of the strap with three rivets.

The brass fittings look better on antique-style bindings if they are aged, or at least have their brilliance diminished, and of course this is particularly desirable if new fittings are used on genuine period bindings. W. Canning Materials Ltd., of Birmingham, England, supply a Brown Bronze Powder (P22649) which I have found to be very effective for this purpose and easy to use. Canning's handbook says, "For immersion treatment 6g of *Brown Bronze Powder* is mixed with 6ml of ammonia liquor and the whole added to 1 litre of boiling water; this boiling solution give a rich iridescent brown coloration to small brass articles." In practice, I have found that 2 or 3g of powder mixed with 10ml of ammonia and 25ml of cold water produces the desired result (without iridescence) when the brass has been immersed for two or three hours, or longer, depending on the degree of aging required, but the quantities are not critical. If the metal is immersed in a boiling solution of the same strength, aging is achieved in about three minutes, but I prefer the effect produced by longer immersion in a cold solution. The powder is obtainable from Canning's London agent, T. A. Hutchinson Ltd., 16 St. John's Lane, Clerkenwell, ECl; unfortunately, the minimum order is 4 kilograms, which in April, 1983, costs about £36.

Brass is an alloy of copper and zinc, so many of the methods advocated in restoration manuals for the aging of copper can be applied equally well to brass objects.

THE RESTORATION OF VELLUM BINDINGS

Cleaning. Minor cleaning of vellum covers can be done by dry means, but if the cleaning is to be really effective it is necessary to use aqueous solutions; in general, these are not recommended and should be employed only by experienced restorers. Saddle soap or other high-quality soaps can be used, but a cardinal rule, if the stability of gold tooling and ink inscriptions is not to be adversely affected, is to keep pressure and moisture to a minimum, so soapy swabs should be damp rather than wet, and rinsing with damp cotton wool should follow quickly. Milk is sometimes used for the cleaning of vellum because the fat content helps to obviate roughening of its surface, but there is some objection to this on the grounds that in an unsatisfactory environment it may give rise to microbiological problems. Ink inscriptions are best avoided altogether and certainly any rubbing should be very light and brief because many are easily marred or even completely removed.

Vellum-covered Boards. Technically, vellum bindings are treated in much the same way as leather-covered ones, but a few points are worth mentioning in relation to rebacking. One is that if, as is often the case, the old vellum is lined with paper which is loose, the new vellum should underlie both the old vellum and its paper lining on the sides, otherwise the new vellum is likely to show through darkly when the old vellum is stuck down on to it. It is easy inadvertently to position the new vellum between the two layers.

Much modern vellum has little stretch, so it is often quite difficult to form it over prominent raised bands and to make it stick between them, so tying-up cords may need to have considerable tension. The cord may also need to be kept in position for several hours, and there is no problem about this because there is no danger that the old vellum on the sides will be discoloured by contact with the wet new vellum, which is certainly a hazard in the case of leather-covered bindings. If the raised bands are very large, as they tend to be on old Dutch books, and the new vellum is intractable even after much soaking with paste, some creasing of the vellum on the sides may result, but if these cause unsightly ridges they can be sliced off when dry without detriment to the strength of the work. The surface of the new vellum should be scratched and scraped where it underlies the old vellum on the sides and the spine, if any, so that firm adhesion with paste or PVA is aided. Pressure can be protracted unless there is a danger that blind tooling will be obliterated, in which case the book can be put between backing boards in the lying-press after the first few minutes so that pressure is then localized at the edge of the old vellum.

Colouring of the new vellum can be done very satisfactorily with spirit stains, the technique being to apply the stain with a swab of cotton wool and then to rub it almost immediately in a circular motion with clean cotton wool as the stain dries, which it does fairly quickly. If this is done too soon the stain may be removed, and if it is too long delayed streaking may result. Staining is best done on the book so that local variations of tone and density can be made to match the ageing of the original vellum. At one time much green vellum was used, especially on blank books used for estate accounts, and the like. If matching vellum is not available one's own green staining should be done before the vellum is pasted on so that inaccessible parts do not show white, and then local colouring can be done at a later stage.

The headcaps on many antiquarian vellum bindings were made by tying cord around the fore edge of the book and the back of the headband, and then bending the vellum back against the cord so that the vellum is at right angles to the line of the backbone instead of knocking the vellum over on to the headband to form a conventional cap. This better suits the nature of the material.

If the boards are warping outwards very badly it is likely that the only satisfactory remedy will be to remove the vellum from the book, trim a small amount from the edges of the boards and then replace the vellum as described on page 184 for leather-covered bindings.

Limp Vellum. Many limp covers (i.e., without boards) have become detached from their text-blocks because the vellum slips which hold them on at the joints have broken. In such cases all one needs to do is resew and reheadband the book and then lace the ends through the joints in the original manner. Very often only the bridges (which are very small) between the slits have broken so that the vellum slips are no longer able to hold the cover on to the book, in which case they will need to be mended with thinly pared vellum patches on the inner surface of the cover, and then be recut in two places at each station for lacing through the joints as they were originally. If it is not possible or desirable to resew the book in order to replace broken slips it may be possible to re-attach the cover to the text-block by sewing on cloth joints as shown in fig. 26B and then sticking these down under the paste-downs, but as, usually, there are no well-formed shoulders on books bound in this style, this procedure may not work very well. The only alternative is to try to attach new slips without resewing the book, but this needs to be well done because if the vellum is thick there is quite a lot of leverage at the joints when the cover is thrown back.

Occasionally, the actual covers are broken at the joints. Many can be repaired off the book by lining the damaged areas with new vellum and then fitting them back on to the book with the original slips laced through new slits in the joints. This method has the advantage that the repairs can be dried under considerable pressure. Sometimes it is better to reback the case while it is on the book so that it can be more closely moulded to the shape of the book. Assuming that the sewing is intact, the first step is to attach a hollow tube to the backbone with the ends slit to facilitate turning in of the new vellum which should overlap the book by about ¾ inch at each end and on the sides and have all edges pared. If the vellum is thin and flexible it may be possible to paste it, allow it to soften, draw it on and turn it in straight away, but very often it is easier to do this in two stages; apply PVA to the hollow tube, put the vellum in position and allow it to set for at least half an hour, after which the turn-ins can be pasted, softened and turned in. When this has dried, the edges of the old covers should be pared along the joints in order to eliminate unsightly ridges, and then the covers can be stuck down on to the overhanging new vellum with PVA or thick paste, or a mixture of both, the old turn-ins being fitted around the turn-ins of the new vellum. This should dry under pressure, so it may be necessary to pack the book a little to avoid slippage. The next day the slips on which the book was sewn can be slotted through new slits in the joints, likewise the ends of the headbands, if any. Now, the new spine should be scraped to aid adhesion and the edges of the old spine should be pared. When the old spine has been pasted and allowed to soak for a few minutes it should be bound on to the new vellum spine with tape to ensure a firm bond. If the old turn-ins are still intact it is best to retain them and turn them in over the new vellum because this looks better and is more secure. The tape should be removed after about ten minutes so that the position of the old spine can be checked and parts rubbed down, if necessary. Set aside until the next day.

If, as is commonly the case, the endpapers were not originally pasted down, the new vellum will show on the inside of the covers, so if this is unsightly the pastedowns can be stuck sufficiently to cover the new vellum, leaving the turn-ins and attachment of the ties in view. If the first and last flyleaves were not originally pasted down it is better to follow this style, but if for some reason they must be put down it is better to drum them (i.e., paste only the edges of the leaves) rather than paste them all over because this avoids stiffening and warping of the covers and accentuation of the turn-ins on the outside of the covers.

A final very light application of leather dressing imparts a pleasant appearance to the surface of the vellum if it has been cleaned, but as this material is not very absorbent the effect is almost wholly cosmetic. If spirit stain has been used the dressing should be applied with slight pressure, otherwise much of the stain is likely to be removed, though if this does happen it can be replaced.

Selected Reading

The literature on the conservation of books and other library materials is large and constantly growing, reflecting the current lively interest in the subject. Published material directly relevant to the subject matter of this book is relatively scarce and scattered, however. There are a great number of books, for example, on the basic techniques of bookbinding, some very good, some certainly not so good, but—good, bad or indifferent—very few deal specifically with the problems peculiar to the restoration of leather bindings. The literature on the history of bookbindings is even more extensive, although much of it deals more with the changing styles of decoration or "finishing" and with the identification of binders, than with historical developments in the basic structures of the book, though publication of this kind of information has been increasing in recent years, principally in periodicals. The following list contains the titles of selected references which we think the reader will find most useful and relevant to the subject matter of this volume and will provide him with a good starting point for further study. As an aid to this study, the reader will find the following publications very helpful: *Library and Information Science Abstracts* (Library Association, London); *Library Literature* (H. W. Wilson Company, New York); and *Art and Archaeology Technical Abstracts* (published in New York at the Institute of Fine Arts, New York University). There are useful references in: "Appendix 5: Selective List of Useful Periodicals," *Preserving Library Materials*, by Susan G. Swartzburg (Metuchen, N.J.: Scarecrow Press, 1980), pages 176–82.

243

1. BANKS, PAUL N.
    A Selective Bibliography on the Conservation of Research Library Materials
    Chicago, Newberry Library, 1981
    The many hundreds of entries covering every aspect of conservation are very well organised by subject with many subheadings. There is a good author index.

2. BAYNES-COPE, A. D.
    Caring for Books and Documents
    London, British Museum Publications Ltd., 1981
    This booklet outlines the ideal conditions under which books and documents should be kept, explains the principal causes of damage and offers straightforward, practical advice on how to avoid them.

3. BELAYA, I. K.
    "Methods of Strengthening the Damaged Leather of Old Bindings"
    Restaurator, vol. 1, no. 2 (1969), 93–104
    Discusses methods of strengthening and preserving the damaged leather bindings of old books in the State V.I. Lenin Library of the USSR. *Restaurator*, which began publication in Copenhagen in 1969 as "the first international periodical covering the fields of restoration and preventive care of library and archival material," covers a wide range of conservation activities and has been a valuable addition to the field.

4. BUCK, MITCHELL S.
    Book Repair and Restoration: A Manual of Practical Suggestions for Bibliophiles
    Philadelphia, Nicholas L. Brown, 1918
    The book has some interesting discussions, most of which are of only historical interest, on the techniques of general restoration, removing stains, rebacking, repairing old bindings, and rebinding. Many of the recommendations made by the author must now be viewed with considerable reservation. Included are some translated selections from *Essai sur l'art de Restaurer les Estampes et les Livres*, by A. Bonnardot, Paris, 1858.

5. BURDETT, ERIC
    The Craft of Bookbinding: A Practical Handbook
    Newton Abbot, David & Charles, 1975
    One of the best and the most comprehensive of the more recent manuals, and packed with information and "wrinkles."

6. CAINS, ANTHONY
    "New Attitudes to Conservation"
    In *New Directions in Bookbinding*, by Philip Smith
    London, Studio Vista, 1974

This spells out the basic, honest approach to conservation with a brief evaluation of methods and materials, and deals principally with the operations preceding binding.

7. CAINS, ANTHONY
"Techniques of Preservation Based on Early Binding Methods and Materials"
The Paper Conservator, vol. 1 (1976), 2–8
The author outlines the soundest methods and most durable materials for conservation binding.

8. CAINS, ANTHONY
"Book Conservation Workshop Manual; Part One: Preparation of the Book for Conservation and Repair"
The New Bookbinder, vol. 1 (1981), 11–25
This is the first part of a manual based on the methods the author helped to develop when he was in charge of conservation at the Biblioteca Nazionale Centrale di Firenze and has since amended while serving as Technical Director of the Conservation Workshop at Trinity College, Dublin.

9. CLARKSON, CHRISTOPHER
"The Conservation of Early Books in Codex Form"
The Paper Conservator, vol. 3 (1978), 33–50
An important, scholarly consideration of the principles and ethics of conservation.

10. CLEMENTS, JEFF
Bookbinding
London, Arco Publications, 1963
An excellent book on the fundamentals of hand bookbinding, clearly and simply written, and well illustrated. Includes a useful chapter on the history of bookbinding.

11. CLYDESDALE, AMANDA
Chemicals in Conservation: A Guide to Possible Hazards and Safe Use
Edinburgh, Conservation Bureau, Scottish Development Agency, Scottish Society for Conservation and Restoration, 1982
Hundreds of chemicals are listed with their associated hazards, if any. First aid measures are detailed where the dangers are significant. Issued in loose-leaf form so that revision sheets, possibly to be issued annually, can be incorporated.

12. COCKERELL, DOUGLAS
Bookbinding and the Care of Books (with an Appendix by Sydney M. Cockerell)
London, Pitman, 5th ed., 1953 (rev. 1978)
This is the classic work on hand bookbinding. Part 2 discusses the injurious influences to which books are subject, proper shelv-

ing, insect pests, how to preserve old bindings, the paring of leather, headbanding, and the rebacking of books. The chapter on leather quotes generously from the Report of the Committee on Leather Bookbindings published for the Royal Society of Arts (see below). The Appendix covers many important points not dealt with in the original text of 1901.

13. COCKERELL, DOUGLAS
Some Notes on Bookbinding
London, Oxford University Press, 1929

Discusses the deterioration of the quality of materials used in bindings and gives interesting historical and sociological reasons for its occurrence.

14. COCKERELL, SYDNEY M.
The Repairing of Books
London, Sheppard Press, 1958

Librarians and collectors will find this an interesting summary of some of the possible ways in which books can be repaired. To quote the author: "It contains some 'first aid' operations that can be carried out by careful labour, but it is not a technical work on binding procedure, nor is it intended to give the impression that anyone can repair a valuable book without practical instruction and experience; and it is hoped that this experience will not be obtained at the expense of fine books." Readers will find the chapter entitled "Repairing Leather Bindings and Re-Binding" especially useful.

15. CUNHA, GEORGE MARTIN AND CUNHA, DOROTHY GRANT
Conservation of Library Materials: A Manual and Bibliography on the Care, Repair and Restoration of Library Materials
Metuchen, N.J., Scarecrow Press, 2nd ed., 1971–72, 2 vols.

The authors discuss the nature, general care, repair, and restoration of library materials, and provide an extensive bibliography.

16. CUNHA, GEORGE MARTIN AND CUNHA, DOROTHY GRANT, assisted by SUZANNE ELIZABETH HENDERSON
Library and Archives Conservation: 1980s and Beyond
Metuchen, N.J., Scarecrow Press, 1983, 2 vols.

This book is designed to be used in conjunction with the preceding item and provides a survey of developments during the past fifteen years in addition to general guidance in techniques and discussion on training and education. The bibliography, which contains more than 5,800 new citations, supplements the one in the authors' earlier book, and together they constitute the most comprehensive bibliography covering conservation literature in English.

17. DIEHL, EDITH
   Bookbinding: Its Background and Technique
   New York, Rinehart and Co., 1946, 2 vols. Reprinted by Hacker
   Art Books, New York, 1979
       The first volume of this work is on the history of the production, binding and distribution of books; the second volume is on bookbinding methods and materials. Although the work is questionable in part, it contains useful information.

18. DÜHMERT, ANNELIESE
   Buchpflege; ein bibliographie
   Stuttgart, Max Hettler, 1963
       A comprehensive, multilingual bibliography of the literature on the treatment and repair of books.

19. GARDNER, ANTHONY
   "The Ethics of Book Repair"
   The Library, vol. 9, no. 3 (1954), 194–98
       In this article the author discusses such matters as the difference between attempting to achieve an aesthetically satisfactory restoration and "conscious faking," and whether the ultimate structural soundness of the restored book should be sacrificed in the interest of preserving the original binding materials and techniques.

20. HORTON, CAROLYN
   Cleaning and Preserving Bindings and Related Materials
   Conservation of Library Materials, Pamphlet 1
   Chicago, Library Technology Program, American Library Association, 2nd rev. ed., 1969
       The author discusses the cleaning and minor repair of books and other library materials, and the care and preservation of leather bindings. The work contains a list of supplies and equipment, sources of supply, and a selected bibliography.

21. INNES, R. F.
   "The Preservation of Vegetable-tanned Leather against Deterioration"
   Chapter 18 in *Progress in Leather Science*
   London, British Leather Manufacturers' Research Association, 1948
       A pioneering work in the explanation of the causes of the decay of leather and its prevention. The author discusses preferred tannages—considering pyrogallol-tanned better than catechol-tanned hides—and confirms that salts added to leather increase its durability. He also concludes that potassium citrate or lactate as well as neutralized syntans protect the leather, and that alum retannage and an impermeable finish improve durability.

22. JOHNSON, ARTHUR W.
    The Thames and Hudson Manual of Bookbinding
    London, Thames and Hudson, 1978
    A very sound manual written by a teacher and binder of long experience. Well illustrated by the author.

23. KUHN, HILDE
    Wörterbuch der Handbuchbinderei und Einbandrestaurierung
    Hannover, Schlütersche, 2nd ed., 1979
    1033 terms in German, English, French and Italian. These cover "bookbinding and restoration of papyri, manuscripts, engravings, autographs, documents, bindings and globes."

24. LANGWELL, W. H.
    The Conservation of Books and Documents
    London, Pitman, 1957; Westport, Conn., Greenwood Press, 1974
    Advances have been rapid, so the text of this book, written by a pioneer, is somewhat dated. However, it contains much useful information on sewing materials, adhesives, and other bookbinding materials, as well as on binding techniques.

25. LEHMANN-HAUPT, HELLMUT
    "On the Rebinding of Old Books"
    In *Bookbinding in America: Three Essays*
    (H. Lehmann-Haupt, ed.)
    New York, R. R. Bowker Co., rev. ed., 1967
    A sound, thoughtful, and very useful discussion of the ethics and esthetics of the repairing or rebinding of books of value.

26. McCANN, MICHAEL
    Artist Beware
    New York, Watson-Guptill Publications, 1979
    In addition to specifying the hazards associated with hundreds of chemicals, the author has provided wide-ranging chapters covering every aspect of safety in the workshop, including ventilation, storage of chemicals, personal protective equipment, first aid.

27. MEJER, WOLFGANG
    Bibliographie der Buchbinderei-literatur
    Leipzig, Karl W. Hiersemann, 1925
    Though much dated, and far from complete at the time it was published, this bibliography, together with its supplement, *Bibliographie der Buchbinderei-literatur, 1924–1932*, by Herman Herbst, contains many valuable references to books and articles in several languages on the history and techniques of bookbinding, the care of books, and bookbinding materials.

28. MIDDLETON, BERNARD C.
    A History of English Craft Bookbinding Technique
    London and New York, Hafner Publishing Co., 1963; Holland Press, 2nd ed. (supplemented), 1978

In this volume, Mr. Middleton discusses in great detail the history of the techniques of bookbinding; tracing the various methods that have been used for sewing books, attaching boards, headbanding, forming endpapers, and so forth. An indispensable companion to the present volume for anyone interested in restora-ation work.

29. NIXON, HOWARD M.
Five Centuries of English Bookbinding
London, Scolar Press, 1978

One hundred reproductions of bindings covering the period c. 1483 to c. 1928, with a short article accompanying each. Very useful as a guide to period styles. The extensive bibliography, which embraces both books and articles on the history of English bookbinding, is divided into subjects and periods.

30. PETHERBRIDGE, GUY AND HARRINGTON, MALCOLM J. (eds.)
"Safety and Health in the Paper Conservation Laboratory"
The Paper Conservator, vols. 5 & 6 (1980–81)

This provides exhaustive coverage of the subject in the com-bined volumes, which amounts to 184 pages.

31. PLENDERLEITH, H. J. AND WERNER, A. E. A.
The Conservation of Antiquities and Works of Art: Treatment, Repair, and Restoration
London, Oxford University Press, 2nd ed., 1971

This is the second edition of a basic reference work which has been widely used by conservators in the museum as well as the library field. There are useful chapters on the tanning, causes of decay, and treatment of animal skins, as well as on papyrus, parchment, and paper.

32. POLLARD, GRAHAM
"Changes in the Style of Bookbinding, 1550–1830"
The Library, vol. 2, no. 2 (1956), 71–94

This important paper deals with the introduction of many tech-niques and materials and should be helpful to those who wish to restore bindings in a manner appropriate to their period.

33. POLLARD, GRAHAM
"Some Anglo-Saxon Bookbindings"
The Book Collector, Spring, 1975, 130–59

A pioneering paper on the techniques of Anglo-Saxon bindings.

34. POLLARD, GRAHAM
"On the Repair of Mediaeval Bindings"
The Paper Conservator, vol. 1 (1976), 35–36

The guidance provided here is intended for librarians who have early books in their care, but it is also useful for conservators and others concerned with books of later periods. The paper discusses what should and should not be done, the importance of photographing books before and during repair, the recording of work carried out, and so on.

35. POWELL, ROGER
"Case History of repair and rebinding of an eighth-century vellum manuscript"
Chapter 22 in *New Directions in Bookbinding,* by Philip Smith
London, Studio Vista; New York, Van Nostrand Reinhold Company, 1974

The binder's account of how he approached the rebinding of the Lichfield *Gospels of St. Chad,* a national treasure, and the manner in which he recorded the volume's makeup. The techniques and qualities of materials are specified in detail. Essential reading for everyone concerned with early, vellum-leaved books.

36. REED, R.
Ancient Skins, Parchments and Leathers
London and New York, Seminar Press, 1972

A very detailed and scientifically based account of early methods of manufacturing parchment and leather.

37. ROBERTS, MATT T. AND ETHERINGTON, DON
Bookbinding and the Conservation of Books: A Dictionary of Descriptive Terminology
Washington, D.C., Library of Congress, 1982

An extensive compilation which contains much historical and technical information about materials, in addition to binding and conservation techniques, definitions of scientific terms and biographies of well-known binders.

38. ROGERS, J. S. AND BEEBE, C. W.
Leather Bookbindings: How to Preserve Them
Leaflet no. 398, United States Department of Agriculture
Washington, D.C., May 1956

The standard United States government bulletin about the preservation of leather bindings. Eight formulas for leather dressings are given.

39. ROYAL SOCIETY OF ARTS, LONDON
Report of the Committee on Leather for Bookbinding
Edited for the Royal Society of Arts and the Company of Leathersellers by the Rt. Hon. Viscount Cobham and Sir Henry Trueman Wood. London, published for the Society of Arts by George Bell & Sons, 1905

Amplification of the 1901 report which is quoted in Cockerell's *Bookbinding and the Care of Books.* Although this report is now badly dated, it was highly influential in its time, and still makes interesting and useful reading.

40. SMITH, PHILIP
   New Directions in Bookbinding
   London, Studio Vista; New York, Van Nostrand Reinhold Company, 1974
   An important book by a highly creative binder. Although much concerned with the philosophy of design in fine binding and recent developments in design and technique, the book has, in addition to the Cains and Powell chapters listed above, much information about materials, chemicals, and techniques that is useful to the conservator and to the less creative binder.

41. STORM, COLTON
   "Care, Maintenance and Restoration"
   In *Rare Book Collections* (H. Richard Archer, ed.)
   Chicago, ACRL Monograph no. 27, American Library Association, 1965
   A statement of principles of the conservation of rare materials.

42. TRIBOLET, HAROLD W.
   "Trends in Preservation"
   Library Trends, vol. 13, no. 2 (1964), 208–14
   Mr. Tribolet, former manager of the Graphic Conservation Department of R. R. Donnelley & Sons Co. in Chicago, discusses developments in the treatment of rare books and manuscripts.

43. THE USSR STATE LIBRARY IM. V. I. LENIN
   Department for Book Preservation and Restoration
   Collection of Materials on the Preservation of Library Resources
   Jerusalem, Israel Program for Scientific Translations, 1964
   No. 2, L. Petrova, ed.; No. 3, L. Belyakova and O. V. Kozulina, eds.
   This work included chapters on inspecting books, collections, dusting and cleaning books, and softening leather bindings.

44. WATERER, JOHN W.
   A Guide to the Conservation and Restoration of Objects Made Wholly or in Part of Leather
   London, G. Bell & Sons, 2nd ed., 1973
   Although this book does not deal with the structural restoration of bindings and only briefly with the application of potassium lactate and leather dressings, it will be found useful for its information about the nature and properties of various kinds of leather. Also valuable are the appendices which include details of some of the products used in conservation and the addresses of the suppliers.

45. YUSUPOVA, M. V.
   "Conservation and Softening of Leather in Book Bindings"
   Restaurator, vol. 3, no. 3 (1979), 91–100

To quote the summary: "The author gives short information on structure, tanning and greasing of leather, analyses the causes of leather ageing in book bindings, as well as features of materials used for their conservation. The author proposes new preservation lubricants made on the basis of mineral substances; shows its advantage in comparison with earlier known materials. He gives the methods of softening old dry leather using water, inert abrasive, and hard oxidized oils."

Index

by Marianne Tidcombe

Page numbers for definitions are in *italics*.

Bernard C. Middleton received his early training in the Central School of Arts and Crafts in London and served his apprenticeship in the British Museum Bindery. He is a Fellow of the Society of Antiquaries of London, a member of the Art Workers Guild, and a past president and Fellow of Designer Bookbinders. Prominent among his many published works is *A History of English Craft Bookbinding Technique*.